# WILDE'S END

## THE WILDE MEN
### BOOK 1

## SAXON JAMES

# BLURB

**Hudson**

Give me the smallest reason to make a shitty decision, and I'll jump in with both feet. It's not that I enjoy the chaos, it's that I literally never see it coming, and after drunkenly buying an abandoned town with my brothers, it's clear I'll never learn.

As builders, we plan to renovate and flip the town, maybe turn it into something worth seeing, but the longer we're here, the more things feel … off.

It's not until a bearded mountain man breaks into my room in the middle of the night and threatens for us to get out of his town that I realize Wilde's End isn't as abandoned as we were told.

But there's nothing waiting for me in the life I left behind, and in making his demands, Wilde has accidentally tapped into my competitive side.

Shitty decisions? Me?

Wilde can bring it on.

**Wilde**

I escaped to Wilde's End twenty years ago, and I've maintained a level of forced peace since. My life is dedicated to the town and people who live here, because if I focus on others, I can't focus on everything I left behind.

The Bellamy brothers coming to town is like three horsemen of the goddamn apocalypse. They leave destruction in their wake, and when the eldest, Hudson, ignores my *very kind* request to leave, it's time to take things into my own hands. Protecting this town is all I know how to do.

But I've never faced someone like Hudson.

His stubbornness matches mine, and his attitude has an irritating way of worming under my skin. The more I push him, the harder he pushes back, until we're locked in a game neither of us will walk away from.

With his smart mouth, bullheaded recklessness and those *fucking eyelashes* I'm starting to question whether I can win this one.

But if I lose, this town isn't the only thing on the line.

# THANK YOU

I want to spare a second to thank everyone who picked up Wilde's End. There's nothing like a bit of enemies to lovers to kick off a series and these guys made it too easy to write.

If you're someone who needs a visual for the characters, you can check out my Pinterest board here:
**https://pin.it/7J2KRkEG6**

If music is more your vibe, you can find the Wilde's End playlist here:
**https://open.spotify.com/playlist/0elHTrpPYqVYqxDjFILoc7? si=9c0ab6a6b7a347f3**

(While every effort has been made during the editing process, if you're someone who likes to spot and report ninja typos, you can send them to: admin@saxonjamesauthor.com)

*To anyone who's ever wanted to leave this shitshow behind and run away to live in the woods.*

*Welcome to Wilde's End.*

# TRIGGER WARNINGS

*Reference to past substance abuse*
*Reference to parental neglect*
*Reference to death of a family member*
*Dark humor surrounding death/suicide*

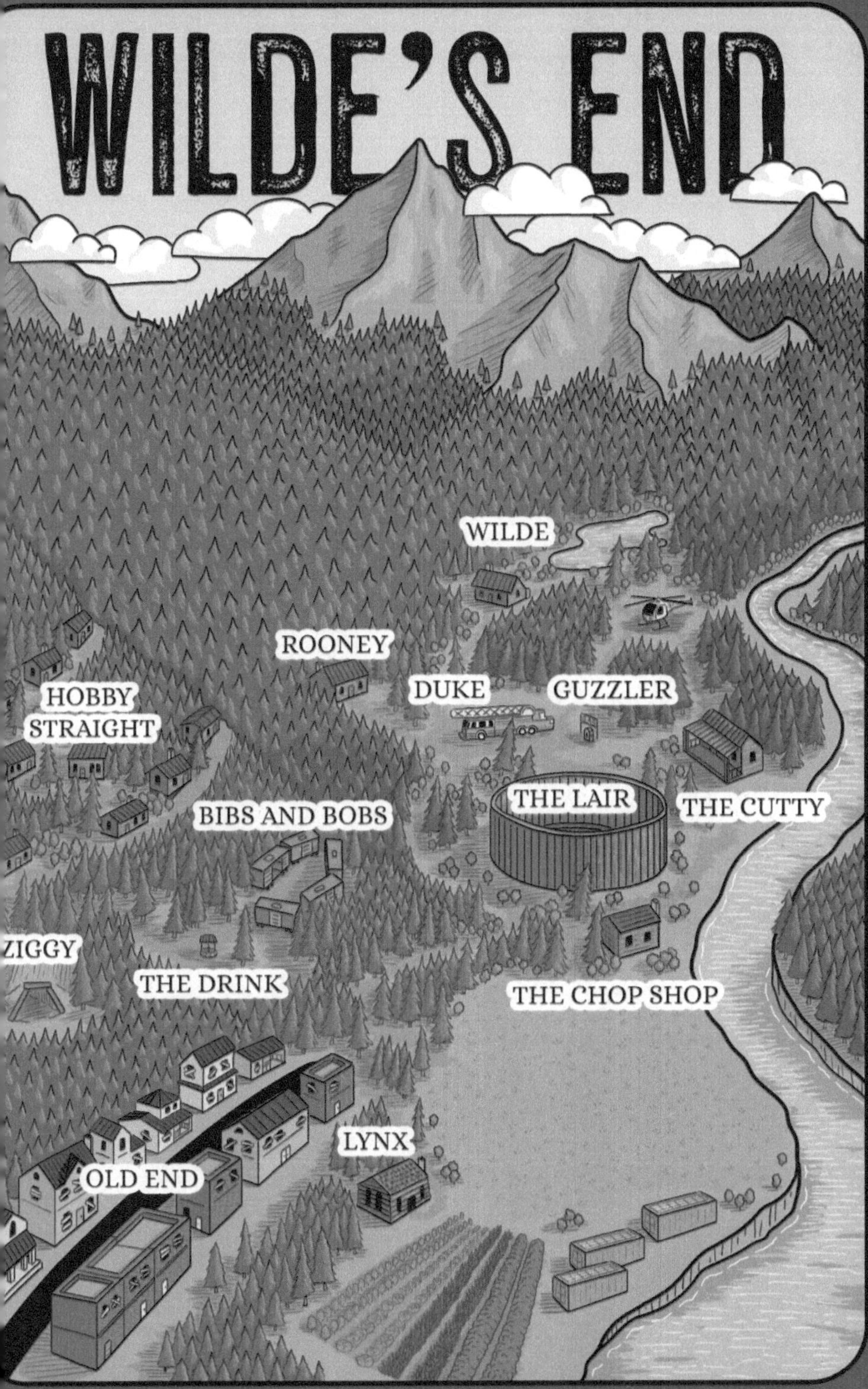
WILDE'S END
WILDE
ROONEY
HOBBY
STRAIGHT
DUKE
GUZZLER
THE LAIR
THE CUTTY
BIBS AND BOBS
ZIGGY
THE DRINK
THE CHOP SHOP
LYNX
OLD END

# PROLOGUE

## HUDSON

There are only so many times the sky can fall before I get tired of hearing about it.

My head is light and wobbly as I force the key into my front door and give it a hard jiggle until the lock springs free. I've gotten good at tuning out my brothers' voices, but with my mindset lately, everything is irritating as fuck.

"Yeah, yeah, yeah," I drunkenly mutter as my twin brothers and I stumble into my apartment after a night out. It's getting to be a regular thing with us, and while I love that we're close, it's starting to feel … repetitive. Boring. Bland.

Work all week, write ourselves off on the weekend in an attempt to forget about everything.

"I'm *just* saying," Hartwell slurs over one of his usual rants, kicking out of his shoes and almost flinging himself through the drywall for his efforts. "What's the point of living? The more money we make, the more expensive everything gets. The capitalist rat wheel keeps spinning faster, and we're running as hard as we can to try to keep up." He stumbles a few steps as he fishes in his pocket for a joint. It's all bent out of shape, but he tugs it out, clamps it between his lips, and lights up.

I don't like the way the smell creates a longing tug in my gut.

"Told you not to do that in here," I grumble, but considering I'm seeing two of him—and not because he's a twin for once—I'm not in a position to make him stop.

Kennedy goes to my fridge and pulls out the pitcher of margarita he made before we left. "Any takers?"

I wave him off while Hart falls backward onto my couch without an answer and blows smoke at my ceiling. His long, lean form is the complete opposite of how thick Kennedy has gotten, and for identical twins, they're as opposite as it comes.

Where Hart is a heavy, low-lying storm cloud, Kennedy is sunshine.

"Why is everything so shit?" Hart asks, sounding more like he's talking to the smoke unfurling above him than either of us. "Life is all gray, and when I look forward … more gray. Gray, gray, gray. And shitty people getting shittier."

I lift my eyebrows at Kennedy, who shoves Hart's legs off the couch and takes the spot they were in.

"You're fucked," Kennedy says lightly. "If you're unhappy, fix it."

The look Hart gives Kennedy could cut glass. "When we retire with absolutely nothing to our names after a lifetime of working our asses off, I'm going to tell you to be happy. Just be *happy*, Kenny." He snorts and stubs his joint out on my coffee table.

"Do that again and you'll be lucky to reach retirement age."

Hart's bored voice answers me. The one that would suck the happiness from the room if it had the energy to bother. "Threatening to kill me doesn't have the effect you want it to have."

My hands itch to close over his shoulders and shake him. If it wasn't for Kennedy, I probably would have. He's the mediator between Hart being so fucking bitter about everything and my extremely short fuse toward it all. There's only so much I can do for him though. We started Bell Building—named after our last name, Bellamy—with Hart in mind, as a way to motivate him and stop with the cynical talk, and it's doing better than we predicted. We're pulling in good money, but of course, it's not enough. Nothing ever makes that shithead happy.

Lately, I worry he's rubbing off on me. I'm in a toxic on-again, off-again relationship that I can't find my way out of, I drink to numb the negative thoughts, and I worry if I keep down this path, I'll end up in the same dead end that I finished high school with.

Still, I shove my attitude aside and try to force positivity for both of our sakes. "When you have your own place, you'll think differently."

He lets out a hollow laugh and tosses his phone my way. It clatters to the floor, but when I turn it over, it thankfully hasn't broken. "I'm signed up for every real estate alert within an hour's driving distance. Tell me when I'll be able to afford even a piece of shit at those prices. I'm still not convinced the one I was sent this morning wasn't a cardboard box."

I unlock his phone and scroll through the email alerts he's been getting. Each listing I glimpse only proves his point because shit on a stick, these prices can't be real. If only one of us owned Bell, we'd be able to buy something livable, but between the three of us?

California is fucking crippling.

I scroll back up to the cardboard box he was complaining about, trying to figure out how it justifies a high-six-figure price tag. At first, I think I'm so fucking drunk that I'm reading it wrong, but I shove down the vodka haze and force myself to focus. The numbers don't change, and I'm positive that's one of the most run-down houses in existence.

"Wilde's End," I read aloud, tapping on the link and opening the whole listing.

I skim through the details and pull up short. Then I reread it. Then I forcefully shake my head and shove down more of the vodka haze before I try again.

*Wilde's End is the perfect project for an investor who wants to be able to say they own their own town!*

"Town ..." I squeeze my eyes closed and open them again. The words haven't changed. "Kennedy, read this. I'm drunk."

He grins over the pitcher of margarita, liquid dripping from his dark blond moustache—the only facial feature that differentiates him from Hart—and barely catches the phone I peg at his head. "Jesus, you almost killed me with this thing." He squints one eye closed to try and focus on the screen. "Okay, I'm drunk too. Something about a town?"

Hart snatches his phone back and skims the listing. "It's a town for sale. And?"

"And?" A spark of excitement hits. "Holy shit, we could afford that!"

I only get a blank expression back.

"Listen, if we buy a whole fucking town, we can do up those shit boxes and sell them off one by one. It's like a gold mine."

Hart's pale green gaze flicks back to the listing. "It's far away."

"We don't have to live there forever. We'll leave Sonny to manage our Bell contracts, move to that place while we work, do it up, then sell it on."

"What's it called?" Kennedy asks, pulling out his phone.

"Wilde's End."

He spends a few minutes looking it up, and I'm not sure if it's the alcohol or this incredible spike of excitement that's making me all head spinny, but this could actually be it. The thing that pulls us out of this rut and gives Hart some goddamn purpose in his life.

I crawl across the floor to steal the phone back. The listing shows a few ugly houses down one side of the street and a few ugly shopfronts down the other. When they say small town, they obviously mean it, but the land size is enormous. We could build whatever the fuck we wanted, wherever the fuck we wanted … right? I don't actually know any of the logistics, but if we own the town, that sounds pretty fucking cool.

Before I stop to think it through, I send an email with my details, almost going cross-eyed with how close I bring the phone to my face to make sure I've typed my shit out right.

"I'm not finding anything on it," Kennedy says. "Think it's a scam?"

"The real estate is legit." I think. It looks familiar. I need my brain to brain better.

Hart chuckles darkly and folds his arms over his face. "Wake me when you two are done with this."

I thump him on the thigh, but he ignores me. "For that, I'm not renaming the street Hartwell after you."

"Oh no …" he monotones.

"And you're getting the smallest of the houses."

"The houses we won't ever have."

A flicker of bullheadedness hits me. "You don't think we'll do this."

"I think you get excited over things and they fizzle out."

"What about our building company, dick?"

"That was all Kenny."

"Fuck you."

He flips me off and doesn't look up.

"I'm going to buy this stupid place, and you're going to be sorry."

He peels one arm back and pins me in a stare. "It's an abandoned piece of shit in the middle of nowhere. Why would you even want to?"

Abandoned? Okay, I definitely missed that part. This would be the perfect time to pretend to pass out or play it off as a joke, or … or …

Hart's lips twist in a humorless smirk. "Exactly. All action, no thoughts."

I shove to my feet and almost launch over the coffee table but catch myself in time. "We're doing this."

"Uh-huh."

"We are."

Kennedy thrusts the pitcher into the air, margarita sloshing down his arm. "Hell yes, Hudson."

"Let's buy a town!"

"Let's buy a *town*!"

Hart only sighs and covers his face again.

I help Kennedy finish the pitcher as we toast to our newest business venture.

A whole town all for us. This is exactly what we need.

# CHAPTER
# ONE

## HUDSON

"Holy shit," Kennedy murmurs from the passenger seat, smile in his voice as he cracks the car door open. "This is *ours*? Wow …" He climbs out slowly, eyes wide like they'll take in more of the creepiness that way.

The boarded-up, dilapidated houses cast shadows from one side of the road, and the busted-glass, paintwork-peeling shopfronts taunt us on the other. When I'd drunkenly declared we buy Wilde's End, all it had taken was half a bottle of vodka, an unexpected call from the Realtor while I was hungover, and Hart giving me *that* look. The one daring me to prove him wrong. Apparently, I'm more bullheaded than even *I* thought because here we are.

My situationship, Sutton, laughed in my face when I told him about our plans, called me an idiot, then fucked me over the dining table and left before he even made me come. Between his disdain and Hart's doubt, it made me dig my heels in more than ever.

Obviously the only mature and reasonable response.

I sit here for a moment, staring out the windshield at a towering view of *what the fuck have I done?* It's not often my mistakes loom over me in physical form, so it's hard not to feel like I'm being sac-whacked with it.

We're parked on the edge of a dusty sealed road, and up ahead where the buildings end, the road turns to gravel and disappears into the trees. It's very green all around, and at least where the buildings are, the grass has been cut somewhat recently. The old guys who sold the place to us couldn't keep up with maintaining it, and I'm confident that decision came about twenty years too late.

Where the clean lawns end, the forest begins, looking like it's trying to press forward and swallow the small town whole. And when I say small, I mean it. It's one street and nothing but acres of wilderness surrounding it.

The panic creeps its way back up my throat, and I tilt the rearview mirror to see Hart. His sandy-blond hair hides most of his face from me as he looks down at his phone.

"You wanna come look around?" I ask.

"Nope."

"You're not the tiniest bit curious?" Considering how vocally he was against this, the fact that he signed right away made me hope that deep beneath his disdain for the entire world, he secretly had ideas for this place.

Hart drags his focus from his phone and meets my gaze in the mirror with hooded eyes. "I'm curious how many knocks to the head it takes for this to seem like a good idea, but I'm guessing that's not the curious you mean."

"Keep it up and we'll find out that number on you."

Hart chews back whatever he desperately wants to say, then pops the door and climbs out too.

I watch his slow gait as he moves toward the houses, and no matter how much this panic of completely fucking up makes me want to puke, I push it down. For them. And also mostly because there's nothing else I can do. I follow my little brothers out of the car, determined to fake positivity until it sinks in.

"Looks promising."

Maybe Hart can see through the shit because he shakes his head at me like he's never been more disappointed. I ignore him as he drifts away.

Meanwhile, Kennedy all but *bounces* out of the nearest shop. "I think this one is salvageable," he says, crossing to look in the window of the next one. The wooden deck creaks concerningly under his weight, but he either doesn't notice or doesn't think it sounds as close to death as I do. "This one's a bit more dramatic inside, but maybe."

"It fucking stinks," Hart calls back over to us from where he's circling one of the houses. "Everything smells like death here."

"You'll fit right in, then," I send back. The last thing my panic needs is for him to keep throwing negatives at me. I'm not sure if it's the buildings or the forest, but it smells like damp earth and decay. As a builder by trade, I'm no stranger to getting filthy, but this is something else. A dense blanket of dirt sits in the air and clings to my skin. It's cooler than it should be, every sound amplified while the silence somehow rings louder, and there's a mist clinging to the trees like it's waiting to creep out and strangle us.

Kennedy's smiling broadly as he comes back our way. "Listen to you two. You sound like a pair of city boys. This is probably the coolest thing we've ever done in our lives, and you're complaining about the smell?" He fills his lungs with a deep inhale. "All I smell is grass and sunshine and fresh air."

"And delusion," Hartwell throws at his twin.

"Better than self-loathing and cynicism," I point out.

Kennedy isn't deterred by either of us. He takes off along the street, excited and overinterested in everything. Sometimes I wish I could see the world the way he does, like he's incapable of a bad thought.

Hart shoves his hands into the pockets of his jeans. "He's going to love this place until you tell him it's shit. You know that, right?"

"Lucky I don't think it's shit, then."

"I saw your face in the car. You're already freaking out."

"I'm excited."

"And freaking out."

I turn my glare on him. "Shockingly, the world doesn't revolve around you, so can you at least *try* and pretend for him?"

Hart stares at me, same speckled green eyes we all share studying my face. "No."

"You're an asshole."

"Well, that's news to me," he says flatly.

"Which house do you want?"

Hart turns his gaze back to the narrow, shiplap two-story structures, lips pulling into a sneer. Before he answers, he stoops down, picks up a rock, then covers his eyes. He throws it as hard as he can, and it bounces off the third house down before clattering back onto the road. "That one."

"The roof looks a light breeze away from caving in."

"Hope I'm under it when it happens."

I don't let his morbid comments get to me. "It'd be a fast way to shut up the whining."

Hartwell doesn't bother answering, just paces closer to the house he chose. He reaches it as Kennedy does, and before Kennedy can get a word out, Hart says, "Mine," and takes the stairs two at a time ahead of him. He needs to slam his shoulder against the front door three times for it to unstick, and then he disappears inside.

Kennedy turns to me with hope lighting up his expression. "You know, I didn't want to get ahead of myself, but I've got a good feeling that we're onto something."

*Sepsis and gangrene?* I bite back that response.

"If only we knew what that something was." I scan the street again. I'm not an easy guy to rattle, but I now know why it's called a ghost town. There's something so deeply haunting about buildings that have been abandoned and now stand as markers of time. Apparently, this place had a hard and fast mining boom before a tragedy hit that caused the mines to collapse and people to move away. This was all left behind and forgotten about by everyone except the previous owners. And now us.

The oppressive silence weighs on me as discomfort creeps up my spine, like a primitive throwback to survival instincts I had at one point in my life.

"That something is money," Kennedy says, bringing his hands together. "You're right that we could turn this place into a rich-people haven. It's going to take a lot to make the town sing, but I can see the vision." He turns and points into the trees behind the storefronts. "There's a river down that way. Clear out the trees, and there'll be so much waterside property space. It doesn't look like much now, but the possibilities are there. Can't you see it?"

Through the panic trying to blind me, I can. He's only repeating my words back to me, but when they come from Kennedy, it's so much easier to buy into. He believes in what he's saying, and we might be two hours' drive from the nearest town, but that's easy enough to make into a selling point. It's secluded. Private. Exclusive.

And thank fuck we'll be able to do most of it ourselves because it's also going to be very, very expensive. Buying this through the business and taking out loans was risky after everything we've built, but we still have contracts bringing in guaranteed income, and if we can pull this off, we'll be able to take the foot off the gas for a minute. Living just to work isn't how it should be.

We need this. All three of us.

It's an overcast day, and while there's enough light to see with, it's a whole other experience when I enter the closest house. Dark and still. No sound except birds outside and the breeze that finds its way past cracks in the building and whistles ahead of us down the hallways. None of the cars or shouts or random sirens of LA, none of the slow, background construction work from the town we live in. It makes every creak in the floor or groan of a door sound so much louder.

I'm locked with tension as we pass from one barren room into another that consists only of a bed frame and a mattress half hanging off it. The walls are stained with age, and dirt and dry leaves have stolen their way inside to crunch under our feet.

"I keep expecting someone to jump out at me," Kennedy whispers as he creeps deeper into the house. "Do you feel it?"

I lie. "Nah. It's just a house." But I'm whispering too, like I'm worried speaking too loudly will disrupt it. "Besides, Hart's alone. Surely a murderer would go for easy prey first."

Kennedy stops suddenly. "Should we check on him?"

"He's *fine*," I insist, but now that I've said that, my subconscious is getting paranoid. Logically, I know there's a slim chance some random killer would be hanging out in the middle of nowhere waiting for us to show up, but … "If you want to go and check on him, I promise not to laugh too much." Because I'd sort of like to go and check on him myself.

"Promise not to laugh *at all*?"

I take a moment so it looks like I'm thinking about it. "That's a big ask. But maybe this once, I'll let it slide."

Kennedy leads the way outside again, and leaving the stuffy house behind doesn't help to dissolve the way the hairs on my arms are prickling to attention. I cast my gaze around, from window to window, one side of the street to the next, and then finally, up the tree-covered hill that rises slowly behind the houses.

It's as abandoned as we were told it was. The last guys were looking after this place for thirty years and never saw a soul.

We're fine here.

It's the perfect place for us to leave the funk we were in behind, and if Hart can't gain some life perspective here, it's never going to happen.

At least I can say I tried.

# CHAPTER
## TWO



'm sweaty, shoulders burning, and I take a swing with my post again. My heavy wooden stick collides with the fence, and I swear it shifts under my blow. Every month, I prepare for the town's Peril match like it's my day job, and in a way, it is.

It's the only way to make money around here.

Our fight nights draw a crowd, and I'm determined to be the best.

Chest heaving with exertion, I pass the heavy post to my left hand to practice with my less dominant grip. Most people go with a lighter stick since they're easier to land a hit with, but the heavier posts hurt the most.

I lunge into a side swipe, when the crunch of tires cutting through gravel pulls my attention from the fence. The old, blue Jeep pulls to a stop a few feet away, and Ziggy climbs out from behind the wheel, worry written all over his usually relaxed face.

I'm immediately on alert.

"Did someone go off Hobby Straight again?" That winding

mountain road has travelers skim the edge of Wilde's End without knowing we're here. A few times a year, someone takes the bend too wide, so I have to head up there and haul their car back up out of the trees.

Ziggy shakes his head, lips tightening and eyes getting darker, which doesn't fill me with confidence. Whatever the hell has shaken him up isn't going to be something I like.

My thoughts immediately jump to Foley, mayor of the township closest to us. He's an asshole who's suggested once or twice that the Dale absorbs Wilde's End, but we've never seen eye to eye on that. Both towns are completely off the grid, but his is larger, and they don't have the same values as we do.

Values, like, you know, respect. We're radical like that.

I hold up my hand, and Ziggy tosses the keys to me. The snap of metal as I catch them in the air sets my teeth prematurely on edge. Maybe I'm reading too far into the vibes Ziggy is throwing off … but I doubt it. Not much rattles him.

"Do we need to grab the doc?" I ask, passing the front of my house to reach his car.

Ziggy again rejects the question and takes the passenger seat. I'm a bit of a control freak, and riding shotgun isn't something I do, which people in Wilde's End picked up on fast. Our rule out here is "don't ask," and I've thankfully never had to explain myself, just like Ziggy's never had to explain why he hates to talk. We all have pasts, but the only thing that matters is who we are after we get here.

Which is why I'm set on keeping Foley's ideas out of my town.

We climb into Ziggy's Jeep, and I get the engine going before pulling out again. Whenever we need to turn, he taps the dashboard and points, but otherwise, I keep going straight until I realize where he's taking me. My gaze swings to where he's worrying his thumbnail between his teeth.

"Old End?"

Ziggy's messy black hair is held back by a wire headband, but tufts have pulled free to block the expression in his brown eyes. Slowly, he nods, and his unease has my muscles wound tight as I switch gears.

I've always felt a protectiveness toward Ziggy, so anything that gets to him gets to me.

When we're close to the road that will take us into the original town, Ziggy taps the dashboard again.

"Right here?" I check.

He gestures right again.

Considering turning right means going off road through the trees, I'm skeptical, but I do it. Roads are an optional route anyway, but he said we were going to Old End, and this will take us to a squat lookout above the town instead. It's not until we're at the lookout that Ziggy holds up his hand to stop.

I put the car in park and cut the engine, but he's looking toward the town like he's seen a ghost. Ziggy will talk when he absolutely has to, but this doesn't seem to be one of those times, so I get out, leaving the door open behind me, and cross the knee-high grass to the overhang.

The first thing I spot is a car.

It's a large white SUV. The overly shiny exterior is throttled with dirt, and the front driver's door is propped open.

The fuck?

I drop into a crouch, heart pounding, as my gaze sweeps the main road, looking for its owner.

Ziggy approaches and crouches silently beside me.

"No chance Bert got a new car?" I ask. Bert has owned Wilde's End since before I got here, and other than the one conversation we've had, we keep our distance. He knows we live out here, but he doesn't come into our space, and we stay out of Old End out of respect for him.

Ziggy's lips pinch in the corners. I'll take that for a no.

As much as the need to panic creeps over me, I push it down again. Change and surprises aren't things I'm good at taking in my stride, not when the last twenty years of my life have been spent learning everything there is to know about this town. We have plans and contingencies in place for everything.

Including strangers.

Occasionally, people will show up to explore the abandoned town and take videos walking through it. Judging by the fancy car, I'd bet money that's what they're doing now. It's the logical option.

So why the fuck am I so uneasy?

"We'll keep an eye on them," I tell Ziggy. "They'll move on quickly." No one hangs out in Old End after dark.

I go to stand when he tugs me down again; for a wispy guy, he's stronger than he looks. Ziggy jabs his finger back toward the buildings, and I follow his gaze to where three blond men have walked out of one of the houses.

At first thought, they remind me of the three bears. One is as wiry as Ziggy, the next is a little smaller than me, and the third is larger, but I can't tell from here whether he's muscular or chubby. They're talking about something as they approach the car I'm expecting them to climb back into, but the middle-sized one heads around for the trunk instead. It lifts open for him, and then he pulls out—

"Is that a suitcase?"

Ziggy sighs, folding his arms over his knees before propping his chin on them. His bottom lip is pierced twice underneath and juts out like he's upset.

My worry inches higher as I watch as all three men unload the trunk. I count five suitcases between them, plus a large backpack each, and then armfuls of shopping bags.

"What the hell are they doing?"

I'm not looking for an answer, and Ziggy doesn't bother giving me one. We both watch; me, with my jaw dangling and a sickening feeling setting in as these guys carry their shit into the house.

Like they're preparing for a long stay.

"Maybe they're lost," I suggest weakly.

Ziggy taps his mouth three times with his index finger, his way of suggesting I get Rooney up here. Rooney is as close to a right-hand man as it gets and can talk to anyone about anything. He's the whole reason the town is kept well supplied and probably the only one of us who doesn't have a severe dislike and distrust of strangers.

It's a good idea, but I'm hesitant.

"They've only just shown up. Bert and his brothers are due soon for their usual maintenance, so they'll send these squatters on their way." The thought of people hanging around for an unknown amount of time unsettles me. "We'll keep watch, but I think Rooney is a last resort. We don't want outsiders knowing we're here if we can help it."

My decision must satisfy him because Ziggy pushes to his feet and leads the way back to the car. I can't exactly place why those men are prickling that panic center of my brain, but I'm not going to let on that I'm worried. We've dealt with strangers before, and we will again. It's not a big deal. Once the custodians find out someone is squatting in their town, they'll handle the problem for us. We just have to be on our guard until then.

All week, we wait for Bert to show up, and he never does. Instead, the three men in town get hard to work, and the moment I see them pull the first house apart, it hits me with sickening certainty that they're not leaving in a hurry.

I need to get to the bottom of this.

The three men have all turned in for the night, and the fire outside is snuffed out, so as much as I don't want to do this, I remind myself that there's no time like now. I leave the lookout, make my way through the trees, and into Old End.

I hate being here. Not only for the memories but for how everything feels so different. The car parked by the furthest two-story house, the piles of debris littering the road, and the camp chairs set around a gas burner all bring the town … alive. It has no right to feel that way when I've buried so many demons in its walls.

It's been almost two decades since I last stepped foot in Old End. Back then, I was tired to my bone, emotionally wrung out, running from a life that only wanted to use me and spit me out, just like with—

I cut those thoughts off before I can go back down a path I keep barricaded. This is why I avoid Old End. It's the town I'd stumbled across, squatted in, and then used to wallow in memories for longer than I want to admit. If it wasn't for Bert finding me and giving me the push I'd needed to keep going, I don't know what would have happened.

My footsteps slow as I reach the house I watched them enter. The old two-story shiplap dwelling is the only one in the line of them that has been left untouched. The way they're gutting buildings that have existed longer than they have proves they're the exact type of out-of-towners I don't want anywhere near my home.

Now, I need to figure out exactly why they're here.

A fresh lock has been placed on the front and back doors, but the old windows slide right open. They're tacky from years of swelling wood and expanding joints, but I get the one closest to the back door wide enough to hoist up and pull myself through. The smell of dust and mildew coats my nostrils as soon as I straighten and look around. This wasn't the building I took refuge in, but the layout is almost identical, and I'm thrown back to my seventeen-year-old self, too scared and powerless to keep running.

I'm not that person anymore.

The city rots and corrupts. Creates monsters and strips souls bare. I've created a new life for myself out here, and I'll protect Wilde's End with everything that I have.

I creep through the living area that has a distinct feeling of loneliness broken only by the fresh color pops of shopping bags and condiments cluttering the kitchen counter. A thick layer of dust muffles my footsteps as I enter the short hall and pause by what should be a bedroom door. I have no idea if any or all of them are in here, but I set my hand on the door handle and turn it slowly before sliding the door inward. It skims the carpet with a soft *chhhh* that makes me catch my breath as I peer into the room.

All that's here is an inflatable mattress and a man snoring softly through my intrusion.

I step inside, glaring down at the sleeping form as I make my way across the room. Out of the three men, I think this guy is the middle-sized one, and settling my eyes on his relaxed features stirs up the type of feelings I only let myself indulge in occasionally.

This man is gorgeous. His dark blond hair is growing out of a stylish haircut, and his eyebrows are relaxed over closed eyes with eyelashes so long they throw shadows over his cheeks. His nose is small, his jaw is wide, and the bare arm he has flung over his head shows off his bicep even in the dark.

A deep exhale leaves me slowly.

He's shirtless, the deep dip between his pecs disappearing under the blankets. It shouldn't be so tempting to glimpse more, but I don't think I've ever seen a man like this. At least not for a very, very long time.

I set my jaw and force myself to walk away. He's attractive, but I'm on a goddamn mission.

I comb the house for signs of what they're doing. Has Bert hired them? Do they assume this place doesn't belong to anyone? The other two are sleeping upstairs, in bedrooms as empty as the first. Their wallets give away nothing except their names—I'm assuming with their surname, Bellamy, they're related—and I'm not game to touch their phones. I leave things where I found them, but I'm not careful, and I don't plan to be.

Let them think a ghost has visited them in the night.

I search through everything I can find until I spy a set of keys sitting on the kitchen counter. I creep closer, eyeing the tag, and when I pick them up and read it, my gut sinks.

*For: sale of Wilde's End, California.*

Sale? *Sale?*

The keys crunch in my fist.

Bert … what the fuck have you done?

# CHAPTER
# THREE



t's been a long time since I've felt this kind of ache in my muscles, and I don't hate it. Hart, Kennedy, and I have hit the ground running, and with nothing else to do around here, our only focus has been work.

Because if I'm focused on work, I can't be focused on the random shit going on. Like how my keys got from where I left them on the kitchen counter to the table when Kennedy and Hart swear they didn't touch them.

Though it would be just like Hartwell to mess with me.

Thankfully, he has his uses too.

He's drawn up plans for extending the houses, and hopefully, today is the day he gets the plans back from his engineer friend. Of the three of us, he's always been the smartest, and while I wanted him to stay at college and get his architecture degree, he'd scoffed at the idea and told me to fuck off. Mom and Dad gave up on us all forever ago, so I'd had no one in my corner to help convince him.

I walk along the street, hoping today will be the day I get used to the place. It's still creepy, but with each day that passes, the early fog and thick trees in every direction don't play with my mind as much.

Kennedy is loudly bashing away at something inside, the constant *thunk* echoing through the deep silence. As someone who's always surrounded by people, this complete isolation is new. The cell service is spotty at best, which is something we'll need to fix, and I keep bouncing between being completely at ease in what could be a hidden paradise and close to panic over us doing something so fucking stupid.

I stoop down to pick up a rock and send it sailing down the street. It bounces off the road with a *chink ... chink* before hitting dirt, and when I pull my eyes up from where it's landed—

*Holy fuck.*

My heart jumps out of my fucking chest as I throw myself against the nearest house. My pulse is racing like I've launched myself off a goddamn cliff, and it takes me a second to process what the hell just happened.

A man.

I think I saw a man.

I lean forward, easing off the wall to look back up into the trees. I'm not confident on exactly where I saw him, and with each passing second, I'm wondering if it happened at all. My brain is swimming in *what the fuck* as I try to get myself to calm down.

"Hudson?" I jump at my name before I recognize Kennedy's voice. He's paused on the stairs from the house we're working on, rolled-up carpet slung over his broad shoulder. "What are you doing?"

"I dunno, fucking turtles? I'm panicking, what does it look like I'm doing?" I start toward him, not able to stop from flicking looks back toward the trees. Was it a ghost? An axe murderer? My imagination well and truly losing it? "I think … I saw someone."

His eyebrows hit his hairline. "What? Where?"

I'm still not confident on exactly where, but I point in the general direction. "Up there. It was a guy. I think he was watching me."

Kennedy tilts his head, but the trees rising above us on that side stay empty. With a *hmm*, he heaves the carpet over the short metal railing and into the junk pile we've started on the street. "Someone hiking past?"

I turn the suggestion over as he joins me, admitting that probably makes sense. There's a main-ish road further up the hill, so the guy probably parked there and took a walk down.

My heart rate calms into something normal. "Probably." I crack a smile. "Freaked me the fuck out."

"I bet. We've been here … almost a week? Haven't seen anyone. I probably would have pissed my pants."

"Yeah, but you did wet the bed until you were ten, so …"

He gives me a friendly shove. "It was seven, you dick, and that's a totally average age."

"Is it though?"

Kennedy brushes off his gloves. "Should we go for a walk and check it out? Make sure the guy isn't lost?"

Lost? That hadn't even occurred to me, which only goes to show that my brother is a million times better than I am. I'd seen the guy and thought serial killer. Which means I'm not at all interested in going searching for him, but Kennedy has already headed that way.

"You sure about this?" I check, falling into step with him. "What if he's waiting to skin us alive?"

"Well, there're two of us and one of him, so I think he's shit out of luck. Come on, getting an answer will make you less dramatic."

"There you go, underestimating me."

I'd leave a note behind for Hart to save himself, but knowing my brother, possible death will be an incentive for him to follow us.

My hands burrow into my pockets and I follow a step behind Kennedy. I never claimed to be the brave one. "So what's your plan?"

"Head in that direction and see what we find? We've been talking about exploring anyway."

"Yeah, toward the river. There's nothing else to explore."

"Where's your adventurous spirit?" he asks.

"Hiding behind my self-preservation."

"I'm telling you, this will be fine."

I don't bother to point out that's what everyone tells themselves before they end up in a situation that's very much not fine. "If I am right and you're wrong, can you at least promise me you'll die first so I have a chance to get away?"

"Deal." The fact that he can agree so confidently helps settle that off feeling. "Anything else?"

I think for a second and come up empty. "I'm doing this under duress."

"Noted."

We leave the small town behind. There's plenty of room to walk between the trees, and it's easy to keep track of which way we're going. This close to the town, the forest looks more complicated than it is, and even though I have a rough direction for us, we don't find anyone. I keep my ears strained as we search, but it's only trees and more trees, even the birds that were calling earlier have disappeared.

"Weird," Kennedy mutters on our way back.

"What is?"

He stares at the wide path we're walking along. "Those sort of look like tire tracks."

I follow his gaze to the leaf-covered ground, trying to see what he sees. The way the dirt and grass have been compacted could be tires for sure.

"Someone *was* out here."

Kennedy doesn't answer. Which is probably a good thing because a tire means a car, and a car means a person, and if they didn't drive through town … where the hell did they come from?

"Right," Kennedy says suddenly. "Well, at least we know to listen out. If someone is driving around, we'll hear them first."

I don't point out that we didn't hear them this time, but I'm still not sure *this time* even happened. These tracks could be from a while ago.

We leave the forest behind, and it's a relief to be back on familiar ground, even if my back won't stop prickling with awareness.

Nothing we can do about it now.

Except maybe send Hart out to buy some hunting guns tomorrow.

Hart's only reaction was a disinterested "cool" when we told him what I saw, but as the days pass with nothing else weird, I have to grudgingly accept that Hart has the right idea.

With no available electricity, we have to rely on the small generator we brought with us, so we make dinner on a gas hot plate outside most nights. Which would be fun. If I could shake the feeling of someone watching me.

Instead of creeping me out further, it's only making me more pissed off. I want to shake the paranoia and enjoy this time with my brothers, but my senses won't quit thrumming. I don't believe in ghost stories, but Wilde's End almost makes me think that I do. Between that man and my keys, I can't shake the feeling something is up. The town itself is a yawning bridge between the past and now, and that kind of history isn't easy to ignore.

For me.

The twins seem to have no issue with it.

"I'd sort of like to keep one for myself," Kennedy says from his camping chair.

Hart wrinkles his nose. "Why? What will you do with it?"

"Live in it? What else do you do with a house?"

There's a beat while Hart processes that. "Wait. You'd *move* here? Like, permanently?"

"I think so. It's peaceful."

"It's dirty. And smells. And there's some guy out there who wants to murder Hudson."

I slump. "Well, now I won't have any issues sleeping tonight."

"We're in the middle of nowhere, doing up houses that no one will ever buy, digging ourselves into a financial grave, and acting like this isn't all because Hudson thought he had something to prove."

"Don't drag me into this because you're worried you'll lose Kennedy."

"Oh, fuck you," Hart says, forcing that bored drag back into his words. "I give it a month before we move back home. Tops."

Hartwell should know better than to taunt me. He says I'll give up after a month? That only makes me more determined. We've made great progress with the demolition, but unfortunately, that's usually the easy part. Getting supplies up here, services hooked up, tradespeople we need for work is going to be the part that fucks up our plans. We have some good contacts, but convincing them to drive the four hours here is going to cost us, and we need a place for them to stay once they're here.

Not everyone is interested in slumming it like we are.

My head already aches over the logistics, and I shake it off as I push to my feet. "I'm going to bed. I'm going to need cell service tomorrow, so I'll take the car out early."

"Sweet dreams," Kennedy says, stretching his arms back.

Hart flicks me a disinterested wave as I pass, and as I'm walking back to the house, my gaze immediately seeks the same spot it has over the last few days. It's always empty.

Until now.

I stagger to a halt, squinting into the dark that the moonlight isn't strong enough to shift. The forest is patchy blacks and grays right now, but I could have sworn I saw something. Something that looked like the shadowy figure of a man.

"You okay?" Kennedy calls out, snapping my attention back to him. The figure is gone, and from this angle, it could have easily been a tree.

Is my brain messing with me?

I suck down a breath and keep walking. "Yep," I call back, bounding up the front steps. "Just a trick of the light."

I'm not so sure I believe that. I grab the flashlight resting by the front door and make my way into the only ground-floor bedroom. We're leaving this house until last so we have somewhere to sleep, and with my clothes hung in the closet and my inflatable mattress set up on the floor, it's almost cozy.

But I ignore those things and cross to the window, flicking the flashlight on and pointing it back toward the forest. The circle of light bounces dimly from one tree to the next, and I hold my breath, convinced it's about to glint off a pair of eyes.

It takes a few minutes of searching before I'm satisfied.

I *am* seeing things.

I click off the flashlight and turn to sink down against the wall. This town is getting to me.

# CHAPTER
# FOUR



All weekend, I've been twisted in knots over what the hell to do, and I'm still not convinced I'm making the right choice.

But here I am, forced back into this town I hate, creeping through an eerily familiar house, and pushing the bedroom door open on a man whose presence sets my teeth on edge.

These men have been here for far too long, and it's time to let them know they're not welcome.

I'm not a bad guy. I'm not even a mean one. But when it comes to this town, I'll do anything I need to in order to keep it safe. For me and for all the people who have landed here. Wilde's End is a safe haven from the harsh realities of the outside world, and that will never change for as long as I have the power to protect it.

It's the same man sleeping in the downstairs bedroom as last time—Hudson, according to his ID—and I creep closer, curious if he's still as attractive as I remember or if I've built him up in my head. Unfortunately, even watching him from a distance all week isn't enough to prepare me for seeing him again.

He's unnaturally fucking hot.

I hate him for it.

Thankfully, it won't be a problem for much longer.

On a night out, he's exactly the type of man I'd pick out of a crowd. Here, in my town, he's exactly the type of man I never want to see again.

So I cross to the bedroom window and shove it open so hard the glass shudders in the frame.

The man's jolt upright takes a few seconds too long to be useful under attack. He grunts, then mumbles something unintelligible as he sets an unsteady hand to his forehead. At first, I worry he's going to roll right over and fall back asleep, but slowly, his eyes blink open. Once. Twice.

Then they drift to me.

He watches me for one sleepy moment before he jumps so hard his back hits the wall. "Who the fuck are you?"

"Wilde," I forcefully admit, folding my arms across my chest to stop the way my hands keep folding into fists.

Hudson's jaw is working madly like he's trying to choose how to respond, and his gaze keeps darting to the door. The last thing I want is to have to deal with all three of them when I can have him pass on my message, so I get my warning in before he can call for help.

"*Leave.*"

"Excuse me?"

"I want you gone."

His fists curl into the bedding as the shock melts away and a panicked sort of anger takes over. "What the *fuck* do you mean by that?"

"Keep your voice down," I force out through my teeth.

He chokes on his response. "You're not going to break in here and tell me what to do."

"I can and I am."

"*Fuck* you."

"I said to keep your damn voice down."

"Make me."

"It would be too fucking easy." The way he's bringing my blood to boiling has me desperate for a fight. He's supposed to be scared. Supposed to cower and promise to leave.

I underestimated him.

Hudson meets my eyes. "My brothers will get here before you have a chance to lay a hand on me."

A bitter smile tries and fails to cross my face. "I have no interest in touching you. I'm here to talk."

"Talk?" The way he spits the word makes it clear he doesn't believe me. "You broke into my house to *talk*?"

"Yes."

"Get out." He isn't bothering to keep quiet, and it's rattling me.

"I *told* you to shut up."

"And I told *you* to fuck off."

I move closer to his mattress, standing at full height, and look down at him. He's coiled for a fight and watching me like a caged animal. "Don't test me," I warn.

The blond man snorts, the wariness slipping from his face as a spark of defiance takes over. "*You* broke in *here*. You don't get to make the calls."

This conversation proves, yet again, why I hate people. All he had to do was keep his mouth closed and let me talk so I could be on my way, and instead, he threw self-preservation out the window. I could kill him out here, and no one would ever know.

He's lucky that while I might be many things, I'm not a murderer.

But I am low on patience.

I cross to his bed in two strides, crouch down, then grab hold of his calf. The inflatable mattress makes it too easy to haul him close enough for me to get in his face.

"I'm only going to say this once," I warn. "Get your people, and get out of my fucking town."

Instead of looking intimidated, he leans closer. "Or what?"

"You don't want the answer to that question." Just thinking of Lynx has tension tugging at my muscles.

"I'm a pretty curious guy, actually."

"There are people out here …" My grip on him tightens. "That you don't want to test."

His gaze, silvery in the darkness, moves from one of my eyes to the next. "You're lying. This town is abandoned."

"Then what the hell am I doing here?"

Suddenly, his expression changes. "You're the man who was watching me the other day."

"And every day since."

"That's creepy."

"No, you being here is creepy." I'm trying so hard to keep my cool. "I've been keeping an eye on you and what you're doing here."

"Why?" he asks. "You into me?"

Before I can dispute it, he shoves forward so suddenly it forces me back onto my heels. He tries to get in my face, but my hand shoots out and catches him around the throat. All I want is to put him on his ass, scare him enough to leave, but instead of shriveling up and giving in, the asshole fights back. He elbows me away and throws a fist at my head. I duck it, push to my feet, and he follows with all his weight. Hudson throws me into the wall but only manages to pin me for a second before I shove him so hard he loses his footing and lands back on the mattress.

I follow without thinking. My weight lands on top of him, his back flat against the bed as I pin him at the wrists and try to hold down his struggling. "Don't be stupid!"

"Get off me!"

I catch both wrists in one hand and use my other to cover his mouth. "I *told* you to keep your fucking voice down."

He thrashes under me, and I strain to keep him pinned, but I'm determined to win this one. I *will* protect my town from people like him, and if that means scaring him off, then so fucking be it.

"I will only give you this one warning, so keep that smart mouth closed and listen. Pack up your car. Pack up your shit. Get the fuck out. We don't take kindly to strangers, and if Lynx finds out you're here, even I won't be able to stop him from skinning you alive." I'm exaggerating. Mostly. Where I hate people, Lynx completely loathes them. I tolerate him in town because he keeps the wild animals managed, but I don't trust him, and he seems to revel in people being scared of him. I'd use it to our advantage here, but he's beyond control, and as much as I want these guys gone, I don't actually want them hurt. I don't think.

The man tries to say something, but it's muffled under my hand. We're both panting slightly, chests separated by less than a foot of distance as my knees drive into his legs.

Fuck me, he is really, really pretty. I hate it.

"Just nod that you understand me," I demand.

He glares, but his head moves up and down.

"If I let you go, will you keep your mouth shut? If you make me fight all three of you, you'll regret it."

His glare deepens, and he tries to say something again before he nods.

I keep his wrists pinned as I slowly release his mouth.

"You have two seconds to get off me before we test out that theory." He bucks his hips, and they brush up against mine.

The sudden contact makes me release him and back up. When he sits, his glare is still deep, but at least he doesn't look like he's going to start screaming for help.

"I want you gone by tomorrow," I warn, standing and turning toward the window.

I'm not expecting his humorless laugh to follow me. "Prepare to be disappointed."

It takes all my willpower not to walk over there and manhandle him again.

"You don't want to play that game with me," I whisper.

"Why? Because you're some big, bad mountain man? If you were going to kill me, you would have done it already."

I hate the tiny flicker of respect his words create, and I shove it down hard. He's not being brave; he's being a city boy with a big mouth. He's not in the land of law and order anymore, and he clearly hasn't worked out that the rules don't apply. "Where you're from, if something happens to you, if someone breaks into your home, who do you call?"

His glare lessens at the sudden topic change. "The police."

"And who do you think we call around here?" He doesn't answer, and the sneer I give him is mean. "*I'm* the police. *I'm* the judge. I'm the fucking jury. My word is law. And when I tell you to leave, you leave."

"That's a lot of power … Careful. You wouldn't want it to go to your head."

"I hope you're this funny when you're being run out of my town."

I'm not expecting him to smile, and I'm definitely not expecting him to push to his feet and approach me. He's a breath away, and his low voice is a gentle hum that steels his confidence and puts a dent in my own. "*Your* town?" he echoes. "Try again. My brothers and I just bought this place. And we're not going anywhere."

# CHAPTER
# FIVE

## HUDSON

The second the enormous stranger is out of my window, I slam it closed, jam a pole into the frame to stop it opening again, and jog up the stairs to wake the twins. I'm fucking rattled, still not totally convinced that wasn't a dream, and worried if I fall back asleep now, I'll forget it even happened.

My heart rate is sickening as I barge into Kennedy's room and kick the mattress he's sleeping on. "Hey, get up!"

He doesn't move, so I kick the mattress again, harder.

"Huddy?" he grumbles, voice thick with sleep.

"We've got a problem. Get up now."

He sits, movements jerky and tired, and when I'm sure he's conscious enough that he won't drop off again, I leave him and head for Hartwell's room.

Hart took the one furthest from the stairs, and when I push open the door, I can't see a damn thing because of the tarp he's pinned up over the window. I stumble blindly forward, hands searching at knee height, until I make contact with something.

There's a grunt, and then Hart kicks out, sending pain shooting through my shin.

"*Ah, fuck!*"

"The hell you grabbing my ass for?"

"I can't see anything! Did you have to kick me so fucking hard?"

"You try being snuck up on while you're sleeping and see how you react."

If he only knew. "Well, I can tell you I didn't kick the man. Now, get your ass up. That's exactly what I need to tell you."

A confused "*wha*'" leaves him, but his blanket rustles like he's thrown it back. I stumble toward the door and out into the hallway, where it's fractionally less dark. We're trying to save the generator we brought with us, but I could really use some light to shake off the lingering creepy feelings of my visitor.

Kennedy is hovering outside his room, and I motion for him to follow me. We thunder down the stairs, the loud, quick thuds matching my heartbeat, and it's not until we reach the moonlit living area that Hart's slow footsteps sound behind us.

"What's going on?" Kennedy asks around a yawn, arms crossed over his bare chest as he leans back into the kitchen counter.

"Someone was in our house."

Hart jerks to a stop in the doorway. "*This* house?"

I nod quickly. "He said his name is Wilde and claimed it's his town. It also sounded like he's not the only one who lives here."

Kennedy, mouth gaping, points at the floor. "Like *here* here?"

"Bullshit," Hartwell spits. "We've been all through these houses, and there's nothing in any of them."

That's a good point. "I'm only repeating what he said. He also threatened us to leave."

Somehow, Kennedy's mouth drops further, but Hart's expression doesn't change.

"I'll grab my stuff, then."

"Hart—" Kennedy looks lost. "We can't go."

"He sort of implied he'd kill us if we didn't," I add.

"*Kill* us?"

Through the hurried and confusing visit, I remember his muttered *I'm not a murderer.* "Actually, maybe not him." With how sudden and unexpected it all was, my memory is hazy. "He mentioned there was someone or something called Lynx that would."

"Like the big cat?"

"I don't *know*." Through my confusion, frustration bleeds out. "I woke up, there was some mountain man in my room, and he started making demands at me. Sorry if I didn't catch all the details."

"It sounds simple to me," Hart says. "Let's pack our shit and go."

"But … but …" Kennedy looks from his twin to me and back again. "We *can't*."

"Oh, we definitely can," Hart points out.

"*Hudson*?"

I can't meet Kennedy's eyes. I'm too tired and worked up to make a decision I'll trust. I don't want Wilde to know his threats worked, but I'm not all that eager to be a sitting duck. On the flip side, without this town, we're fucked. Our business is tied up in this place, and I'm not sure that my willpower can handle returning home a failure. It's only been a week. If I can't do this, I can't do anything, so what's the point of continuing to try? I might as well—

"Sure." Hart leans against the doorframe and studies us. "This is definitely the kind of decision that needs thinking about. Take your time."

I ignore the snide tone and pace to the other side of the room, muscles agitated and restless. "It didn't sound like something we have to do immediately. I say we secure the house, get some sleep, and talk about it in the morning."

"Well, thank you for waking us up, freaking us out, and then trapping us here for a bit longer. That plan makes perfect sense."

Some days, I want to throttle Hart. "Excuse me for being freaked-out myself." My hands flex into fists and loosen again. I'm not known for my patience, but I'm not known for running scared either. The deep, stubborn part of my center is adamant about digging my heels in and showing this asshole that I'm not afraid of him, even if he did pin me to the bed with next to no effort. I can't say that didn't fuck with my head, didn't make me feel vulnerable and powerless, but there's one of him and three of us. The odds are on our side.

Well … I eye Hart. *Two* of us. And Kennedy is big enough that he could probably take Wilde on his own.

I swallow all of that back as I set a withering glare on Hartwell. "Help us secure the house."

"Why? This place would go up like tinder. If someone wanted to kill us, that's all they'd need to do." With that cheerful note, he spins on his heel, and a moment later, I hear him on the stairs again.

"I hope you don't like being a twin," I tell Kennedy, glaring at the place Hart was. "Because I'm going to kick his ass one day."

Kennedy sighs and pushes away from the counter. "Let's get moving. There were boards over the windows when we got here. We'll put them back up."

I'm apprehensive about going outside to dig them out of the

junk pile, but thankfully, the street is as deserted as it normally is. We make fast work of securing the house, and it's not until I collapse back into bed that I really let the tension take hold. I can still feel him in my room.

I refuse to be scared though, and I punch my pillow as I roll over and put my back to the window, falling into fitful dreams about killer cats and Viking men riding them.

There's something about the sun that reaches into your soul and clears out any lingering worry. Morning comes around, and already, last night's visit feels like something I might have imagined, which makes the decision my subconscious came to so much easier to handle.

When I told Wilde we're not leaving, I meant it.

There's a chill on the air like there always is before the sun is high enough to heat the town, and a low haze of fog hugs the trees around us. I don't think that will ever not be creepy, and as I sit by our makeshift stove, I study both sides of the street for movement.

I blow on my mug of bitter coffee as the twins emerge, first Kennedy and then Hart, summoned by the smell of caffeine.

Kennedy pauses by one of the camp chairs, hands on hips as he looks toward the forest like I was doing, while Hart brushes by him like last night never happened.

"Good to see you're both alive," he says snidely.

"Right back at you." I refuse to let him get to me. "While I'm in town, I'll make sure I pick up some guns."

Hart's attention snaps to me from across the table, and surprise fills Kenny's face.

"Guns?" Kennedy asks, breaking first.

"Yeah. We need a way to defend ourselves, and that seems the most practical."

Hartwell ignores me in favor of his coffee.

Kennedy rounds the burner to take the chair closest to me. "But none of us know how to shoot."

"Good thing we have all this room for practice."

"Practice for what? Shooting *people*?"

It's not something I'm comfortable with either, but if my life is at risk, I doubt I'd need more incentive than that. "I thought you wanted to stay here."

"I do."

"Then we need to come to terms with the fact there are things living out here that aren't friendly. Not just people. Wild animals too."

His fingers drum an anxious rhythm against his knee. "Right. Okay."

"You know," Hart says lazily, "I'm beginning to feel like this Wilde guy doesn't exist. You bring some shrooms with you, brother? And you're not sharing?"

The low blow is supposed to get under my skin, and with the way Kennedy's face reddens, he's ready to jump immediately to my defense. I haven't touched anything since I was hospitalized in high school, and Hart doesn't need to know that his comment was dangerously close to the reason I wanted to get away in the first place.

I stand slowly and move to settle in front of him. He's not expecting my bright smile. "That supposed to annoy me?"

"It's a valid question."

"If it was fifteen years ago, maybe."

He blinks hooded eyes up at me, and I stare him down.

"Are we going to have issues?" I ask.

"Oh, I think we're way past that."

"You signed up for this too," I remind him. "You could have said no."

"Why? It's not like you ever listen to a damn thing I say."

Getting a rise out of him doesn't feel as good as it should. Instead, it sets my teeth on edge. "Because you never have anything productive to say. All you do is bitch."

"Then stop giving me shit to bitch about."

"Like fucking what?"

Hart laughs bitterly and gestures to the street. But before he can say anything else, his movement brings my focus up, and I catch a glimpse of someone who's not supposed to be there.

*Wilde.*

On that fucking lookout.

Standing in plain sight like he doesn't care if we see him.

I'm only feeling partially vindicated after Hart's accusation, because a flair of stubborn irritation takes over instead. I leave my brothers, crossing to the center of the street to make sure he can't miss me.

Then I cup my hands around my mouth and shout, "Yo! Wilde! I've got your answer for you." My voice bounces down the deserted street five times over.

And feeling more reckless than I have in years, I lift both my middle fingers his way.

This is our town now.

# CHAPTER
## SIX

WILDE

That motherfucker. I seethe at his audacity and turn to stalk back to the truck. Ziggy is waiting, eyebrows at his hairline, and I huff as I take the driver's side while he slides into the other.

We sit there, but I don't start the engine.

"Guess asking nicely doesn't work anymore," I say around my clenched jaw.

Ziggy taps his lips three times quickly, and it's an effort not to roll my eyes. Sure, sending Rooney probably would have been the smart thing since he's a thousand percent better with people than I am, but this is a situation I can't be nice about. We don't have time to play into these games because the longer those brothers are here, the more chances they have to find out about the rest of us.

"Rooney would have been *too* nice about it."

Ziggy uses his fore and little fingers to make horns above his head.

"And Lynx wouldn't have been nice enough."

My thoughts are impossible to catch as I focus ahead at the tops of the buildings that are barely in view above the elevated tree line.

I tried to be nice. I tried to break it down for him and give him an easy out.

If he won't take it, then he's forcing my hand.

"These boys want to play wild man? Let's show them exactly how hard it is to live out this way."

Ziggy's expression darkens.

"Relax, I won't hurt them," I say as I coax the engine alive. "But we are very, very remote up here. And there's only one way in and out."

When Ziggy turns his attention out of his window, I take that as a sign I won't be getting his help with my plan. I have more than enough people in town who'll be happy to do the heavy lifting. We Wenders stick together.

I drop Ziggy off and then head home. I'm supposed to be making my way out to the furthest side of our land to check that we've done everything we can to prevent fires this summer, but that will have to wait.

Like everything else this week.

I've set all training aside too, and with our monthly fight night only a week away, I'm feeling rusty. That's something Foley will exploit in his favor, and we could really use the cash from a win this month. It's nearly time to refill the guzzler with gas, and the old fire engine parked alongside my house could use a battery replacement.

I have more than enough money for both, but I try to avoid spending it on everyday supplies where I can. That money is for emergencies, and I hate touching a cent of it.

If these brothers wanted to live here and follow our way of

life, we'd have no issue with welcoming them to our neighborhood. But as one year bleeds into the next, I've learned to read people, and those guys are trouble. They've got plans, and I highly doubt their plans match up with what we want for Wilde's End.

It's not even about me.

I didn't make this town. I didn't claim it. I was welcomed here, same as everyone else, and it gave me a new start, which is why I renamed myself after it.

I've been here for so long now that most people forget the town came first.

I need to do whatever I can, whatever I have to, in order to protect our home.

At least one of the brothers leaves every day around eight, and if I want that road blocked before he's back, I don't have time to waste.

The first person I hunt down is Rooney, who joins me without question before we head down to the doctor's place together. It doubles as a med clinic and surgery space and we jokingly call this place the chop shop because Dr. Booker has an off-putting fascination with blood.

"This is a pretty sight," Booker says when we pull up. He's about the same height as Rooney and has messy brown hair and brown eyes that always have a sadistic spark to them. He turns those eyes on me. "Who's injured?"

"No one, but I'm sure you've heard by now about the brothers in Old End?"

"I have. Been thinking about paying them a visit."

This is exactly what I don't want. Wilde's End is reasonably cut off from the rest of the world, and some of the people who live here, like Booker and Lynx, never venture out into civilization. I only do when I strictly have to. Because of that avoidance, they're … different. We understand it around here, but guys from the city wouldn't, and the last thing we need is for rumors to get out about the town and the people who live here.

We're left alone. Allowed to exist.

That's literally all we want in life.

"No need," I say, cutting that thought off before it can form. "I did last night. Told them to get out of our town, and from the looks of it, they're not going to take my warning. So we're going down there to barricade the road."

I can feel Rooney's gaze on my face because I hadn't told him that part yet.

"We have Peril next week," Rooney points out. "How will people get here if they can't use the road?"

"The brothers won't last that long. Once they're gone, we'll remove the barricade again." My mind flashes back to the man's answer this morning. "Otherwise, Booker will have to get the word out that we'll be using Hobby Straight this time."

"You want people driving that road in the dark?"

"We don't have a lot of other options."

Booker's face is delighted. He's got chubby pink cheeks and this childlike air of innocence about him, which is at complete odds with the way I've seen him cut through skin like it's butter. "If anyone goes off Hobby Straight, you know I'm happy to help."

"Oh, we know." I point to the truck. "Get in. Between the boulders by the hill and those two trees the Pickards brought down the other day, we should be able to cut off access from that road completely."

"You know how I feel about manual labor," Booker says, but he climbs up into my truck anyway. Rooney follows him, and once I get back in on the driver's side, we're off.

It takes us an hour to fill up the back of my truck, and I worry that it's dangerously overweight, but it holds out as we make our way to the lookout. The car is gone from Old End like I knew it would be, but missing is the sound of people hard at work, echoing up the hill. Did they all go? I strain for any sign of life, but there's nothing.

I get back onto the dirt road that leads to the sealed one and drive through the old town, taking note of how everything is shut up tight. I'd almost think that they'd come to their senses if it wasn't for the three camping chairs, sitting vacant around the foldout table cluttered with a cooktop and a range of utensils.

I stop the car suddenly and unclip my seat belt. "Hold on a second," I tell the others before climbing out.

No one confronts me, so I walk straight over to their things, grab the cooktop, and toss it into the passenger-side footwell. I'd like to see them wanting to stay with no way to cook their food.

"You good?" Rooney asks, voice suppressing a laugh.

"That's mine now."

"Glad to see you're not taking this personally."

He can make it into a joke all he likes; Rooney's never understood our need for secrecy, and I'm not about to break it down for him. He came to Wilde's End with a past, like the rest of us, so I'm doing this as much for him as the others.

Sure, we could give up Old End to these guys and steer clear, but it won't stop here. It never does. They'll destroy the town before moving on to the areas around it. There's only one reason they'd be gutting the houses, and that's to give them a revamp. And the only reason to do *that* is money. Which tells me that they're planning to modernize and sell.

Then who knows how many people we'll be dealing with?

We need to cut it off while there are still only three of them.

I follow the road out of Old End until we reach a point about a half mile away. Then I pull to the side, cut the engine, and turn to the others.

"They're normally gone for a few hours, but I've never seen them all leave before. We should work fast. Just in case."

"Too easy." Rooney climbs out and follows me around to the back of the truck. Booker is just behind us, and while most people underestimate him because of his sweet face and chubby frame, I know he's one of the strongest men in town. Like he's proving that point, he hoists a huge rock onto both of his shoulders before carrying them easily to the front of the car, where he sets them on the road.

"Does here work?"

"That's perfect," I tell him.

We're far enough from Old End that walking from here would be annoying, but bringing in supplies would be near impossible. I need these brothers to work out that we're not playing. Once they leave, I'll be able to go back to my quiet life again.

# CHAPTER
## SEVEN

## HUDSON

I slam my foot on the brake, bringing the car to a sudden and dramatic stop that throws the three of us into our tightening seat belts.

"Jesus, Hudson," Hart snaps from behind me, but he stops there, and I assume he's seen what I've already spotted.

The road back into town has been completely blocked off.

I focus on the wall that looks made up of rocks and tree trunks, stretching from the trees on one side of the single-lane road to the other, unable to work out where the fuck it came from. It has to be at least chest height too, which makes the whole thing even more unbelievable.

"Uh ... who's that?" Kennedy asks, and I follow where he's pointing to the faded red pickup truck parked behind the roadblock. There are two men sitting in the cab, and leaning against the hood is Wilde.

"That mother*fucker*." I thump the wheel before throwing the car in park and shoving out the door. I'm trying to stamp my anger down, because I don't want this asshole knowing he's gotten to me, but it's not an easy thing to do when it feels like my brain is boiling.

"Hudson!" Kennedy calls after me, but I ignore him.

I wait until I'm close enough to the wall to speak with forced nonchalance. "So, this is new." As calm as I'm trying to be, an edge still creeps into my voice.

Wilde straightens, and it reminds me of how he did it last night. He's not that much taller than me, but he has this intimidating presence that radiates from his every movement. He's solid muscle and broad shoulders, with a beard that almost completely hides his face and curls that cover his forehead. His intense stare watches me from between both. "That's the wilderness for you. Unpredictable. Things change with no warning."

"Yes." I gesture to the wall. "And who could have predicted this?"

"Complete anomaly."

"How the fuck are we supposed to get through?"

Wilde shrugs like he's unconcerned. "Guess that's your sign to pack it up, city boy. If you can't handle this, you can't handle Wilde's End."

I force a smirk that even I can tell is strained. Irritation is rattling at my bones, but I refuse to let him win. "Never said I couldn't handle it."

Something behind his forced friendly gaze snaps. "Don't test me."

Him dropping the act only gives me more confidence. It's rare that I'm not the one to break first. "Why not? I've always loved a good challenge." I lean in closer and grip the top of his fucked-up wall. "Looks like fun. Nothing else I'd rather spend my day on."

"You've caught me in a nice mood," he bites back, sounding distinctly *not* nice. "But that won't last."

"Your nice looks a lot different to where I come from."

"Then go back there!" He leans closer, right in my face like he was last night. If he thinks his size and wild-man glare are going to do anything but make me more stubborn, he's going to learn the hard way. "Take your brothers and fuck off."

"So much for small-town hospitality."

"We don't do that around here."

"But your house visit was so wonderfully welcoming." I swear I hear his teeth crunch.

"This *isn't* a game."

"You sure?" I drop my voice. "Because I'm having the most fun I've had in years." Fun is a stretch. I'd like nothing more than to pick up one of these boulders and cave his face in with it, but I keep my fists locked at my sides where they can't do any damage. Wilde can warn us away until he's blue in the face because I have a feeling it's all talk. He won't hurt us, and the two people he's brought with him won't even bother to get out of the car.

The most they can do is this.

Make our life hard.

Well, I'm used to a hard life, and if they want to start this, I'm going to meet them at their level.

"Lack of self-preservation skills won't do you any good out here," he says.

"We'll see, I guess." I tap the top of the wall and take a step back. "See you soon, cutie."

Wilde bristles, and I bottle that victory for later. Big, burly mountain man doesn't like being called cute. I'm not sure if it's the nickname that got him or that it came from another man, but it doesn't matter. I can use it.

For now, I have to deal with *this* fucking mess.

My mind is spinning out with solutions as I storm to the car and throw myself back into the driver's side. I sit there, trying to keep the anger from my face as I glare across at Wilde. He hasn't moved, and I know he's waiting for whatever the hell I'm planning, but even I don't know what my next step should be.

We need the wall moved.

Technically, the three of us could shift it piece by piece, but despite how long it will take, I get the feeling Wilde isn't going to sit pretty and let us work. I'm still confident Kennedy could take him, but given my wimpy brothers also stayed planted in the car, I can't rely on that.

I need to solve this. And it needs to be in a way that doesn't ask for Wilde's permission.

"Thanks for the support out there," I snap.

Anxiousness rolls off Kennedy's buzzing limbs. "That man is terrifying."

"He's just a man."

"He looks like he wants to murder us all with his bare hands."

"Well, until he does that, why don't we focus on how to get the stupid road clear?" I glance back at Hart, but he's lying across the back seat, Kennedy's hat over his face. "Hartwell?"

"Sleeping."

"You're the smart one. Think you could attempt to be helpful once in your life?"

He sighs like my request is inconveniencing him. "We don't have a car built for this."

We don't … ohhh. That gives me an idea. This SUV is technically able to go off road, but there's no denying it's a city car, not a work car. The trucks we drove back home could have handled this easily, but since we don't have time to make the day-long round trip, we're going to have to make do.

And I have an idea.

I throw the car in reverse, jerk the wheel strongly to the right, and when we're facing the other way, I step on the gas.

"We should have bought those fucking guns," I throw Kennedy's way.

He ignores me, and I'm forced to make the long drive back the way we came.

"You sure about this?" Kennedy asks, white-knuckling the handle above his head as I stomp on the gas so hard it feels like I'm trying to put my foot through the floor.

"Nope."

He lets out some kind of sound, but I ignore him. For what it's worth, this *should* work. I checked and double-checked with the guy who fitted the grille guard, and while I share Kennedy's worry, I'm holding it off for now.

Fuck Wilde.

And fuck that stupid barricade.

It comes into view maybe fifty yards away, and I spend every one of those yards making sure I'm lined up perfectly and braced for impact. Kennedy's free hand flattens against the glove box, and my grip on the steering wheel gets bruising.

A split second before we hit, I almost chicken out, but then it's too late.

The front of the car collides with the towering pile of debris, and the grille guard makes easy work of it. Chunks of rock and timber burst out of the way, some rolling over the top of the hood and leaving huge craters behind in the metal. We screech to a stop, my lungs burning with how hard I'm breathing, and

Kennedy lets out a long "aaah ..." that doesn't stop as I shake the impact from my arms. Thankfully, the wall gave out easily enough that it didn't set off the air bags, but fuck me. My heart is racing so hard I might be sick.

I have a lot of act first, think later moments, and this has probably topped the list.

Through the dust cloud, the faded red pickup comes into view, and a moment later, so does Wilde. He's only a few feet from my front bumper, and if I'd hit the brakes any later, I would have taken him out.

We size each other up for longer than I can measure, and the only thing that breaks our eye contact is the rumble of a motor bringing up the rear. The dirt bike Hart is riding slips through the gap I made with a loud *vrooooom.*

Wilde watches as Hart flings up dirt and rocks as he shoots by, and then the sound of the motorcycle fades into the distance.

I crack my window until it's low enough for me to lean out. "What else do you have for me to handle?"

Wilde ignores the taunt, thank god, because I'm still struggling to breathe. He climbs back into his truck as the big guy in the middle waggles his fingers my way.

I wait as Wilde backs up and pulls away, and only once they disappear behind a bend do I let myself fold forward over the steering wheel, like all the fight has whooshed from me. "Fucking hell ..."

"Petition for us to never, ever do that again," Kennedy says. "Ever. My heart is still trying to jump out of my fucking chest."

As much as I'd love to reassure him that it's over now, I also refuse to lie to my own brother. "I get the feeling we haven't even started. Wilde doesn't seem like the kind of man who loses easily."

Kennedy mutters something under his breath.

"What was that?"

"I *said* I know the type."

I lift my eyebrows his way, wanting him to elaborate.

"*You*, Huddy. If this guy is anything like you, I'm scared for whatever comes next."

# CHAPTER
# EIGHT



ooney lets out a long whistle. "That was hot."

"Why, because he can drive a car? I drive one all the time. I don't see the big deal."

"We both know it had nothing to do with him driving."

The one hand I have on the wheel clenches tighter as I drum my free hand on the window frame. Getting rid of these guys might not be as easy as I'd like, but I'm not giving up.

Fucking Hudson.

I turn the name over in my mind. It sounds like a city boy name. He was no less handsome up close today than he was last night, but at least in the daylight, I could make out his imperfections. The dark shadow at his jaw, the uneven set to his lips, the way his dark blond hair curled back from his forehead, showing off his bushy blond eyebrows. And those dirty green eyes …

Rooney can be impressed by the driving all he likes, but there's something else tugging at me. Something grudgingly like

… not respect. Never that. But the way he met me head-on makes me want to go another round with him.

With *Hudson*.

We pass through town, and I'm half tempted to drive off the road and into the dirt bike parked near where the car normally sits. The bike prickles the warning center of my brain, but I'm already past it before I can make up my mind, and the glimpse of their white car in my rearview mirror makes me refuse to turn around.

We need to keep our distance from the brothers while making sure that everything here is as hard as possible for them.

If I need to break them, then so be it.

The next day, the smallest brother heads into town and comes back with a new burner, two gas bottles, and a bunch of construction equipment. They chain their gear up and move it inside at night so I can't steal it again.

I guess city boys do learn.

Monday, we intercept a delivery of timber heading for Old End. Rooney doesn't love the idea of meddling, but he comes with me and convinces the driver we're meeting him because his truck is too large and heavy for the small road. He unloads it all and leaves. Watching the brothers find the timber and have to strap a few beams to the roof of their car at a time gives me a thrill, and I'm half convinced Hudson will come up to confront me. He doesn't, which means I need to try harder.

Tuesday, I let the air out of their tires before they wake, and seeing the little one kick a camping chair halfway across the street almost makes me happy.

Wednesday, I break into the houses they're dismantling and steal every nail and screw I can find. It puts them half a day behind, but they buy more and keep going.

It's hard to know who's more irritated: them at all the setbacks or me at how fucking resilient they are.

By Thursday, I have to let it all out. They've forced me into playing a game that I don't have time for, a game they're set on winning. I'm not used to being out of control, and I hate every second of them existing in my town.

So I take a sledgehammer to the windows of the houses they've already gutted, and the sound of shattering glass has Hudson storming outside. He's half-dressed, and his expression darkens as muscles strain on either side of his wide jaw. Vicious satisfaction spikes through me to see him finally ready to snap.

"What the hell are you doing?" he shouts, red in the face, still struggling into his T-shirt. "That's destruction of property!"

"What is?" I smash the nearest window for good measure.

"That!" He starts toward me, but I lift the sledgehammer toward him in warning and wait for him to stop. Once I'm sure he's not going to come any closer, I set it over my shoulder.

"Says who?"

"Says the *law*."

I take a slow step closer to him, loving the way my proximity riles him up. "There are no laws out here." Then I swing hard at the house. Timber splinters under the blow, and my muscles work to tug the metal head out of the shallow hole. "Call the cops. Go on."

Hudson spends a moment chewing on his words, glare cutting deeper into the timber than my sledgehammer did. "What the fuck is your problem?"

"I don't like you."

"I dunno ..." A twisted smile crosses his face, and he steps so close he slams his chest against mine. I rock back a step from the impact. "You had no issues pinning me to the bed the other night."

He's trying to get under my skin, and unfortunately, it works. My teeth grind together, and I have to unlock my jaw to reply. "I pin a lot of people to a lot of beds. Liking them isn't a requirement."

"Well, don't I feel special?"

"Fuck you."

He bats those obscenely long eyelashes at me. "Are you offering?"

"I'm not fucking playing with you," I snap. "And if you stay here, I promise I will make every day a living hell."

"Might want to try a bit harder, then."

"Don't act like I haven't gotten to you."

Hudson reaches up and pats my scruffy cheek, but I jerk away from his touch. "Of course you have. You've made it *so* much more fun than I thought."

"Fun?" I set the head of the sledgehammer against his sternum and give it a little shove. Hudson's the one who staggers back this time, even as he tries to stubbornly hold his ground. Movement out of the corner of my eye tells me his brothers have stepped outside too, but neither of them comes closer. No. Those two are scared of me … so why isn't Hudson?

"Yeah," he answers. "Fun. Ever heard of that before? Or is it all hunting animals and building mud huts out here?"

"You won't be around long enough to find out the answer."

His eyes flash, dangerously green in the sunlight. "Why do you want us gone so badly?"

"We don't like outsiders."

"What about the people who owned this place before we did? Did you try to drive them out too? Is that why they sold?"

The fact that he didn't do even the most basic research before buying Wilde's End only pisses me off more. "Bert's owned this place since before I moved here. He came in, did maintenance, and then he went straight back to where he came from."

"You want us to maintain this place, for you, for free, while you get to live here all you like?"

He's deliberately twisting my words, but I don't know how to argue against it. That was the arrangement, but it's not like we ever asked for it. Bert just showed up and moved on.

I'm done with getting off track.

"I *want* you to take your brothers. And leave. I've been very clear about that."

"But what you haven't been clear on is why. I'm a curious guy. I can't walk away without answers."

I'm ninety percent sure he doesn't actually want to know why, but I ignore my better judgment and answer the question anyway. "We like Wilde's End the way it is. We've worked hard to make it into something special, and we don't want people coming up this way and ruining what we've built."

He looks genuinely surprised by that. "Ruining? This place is falling apart. We're making it *better*."

"And then what will you do once it's better?" I push. We're less than a foot apart, staring each other down, and I swear I can see a debate going on behind his eyes. Hudson might be attractive, stubborn, and impulsive, but he's not the type of man I will ever see eye to eye with. Pretty, rich, self-destructive guys were my weakness before I moved here, and I've done everything in my power to distance myself from men like him. Not only are they a threat to Wilde's End, but Hudson is a very real threat to the person I've become.

His internal debate comes to an end, and he steps forward, clearly expecting me to retreat, and when I don't, his face lights up. "When we're done here, we'll sell the dream. Remote luxury for people with more money than brains. My brothers and I are onto a gold mine, and nothing you say is going to stop us from making bank."

"The last people who moved here after a windfall are all gone. I was here long before, and I'll be here long after you and your brothers realize this is a fruitless effort. You want money?" I sneer in his face. "Buy a lotto ticket. Our town isn't for sale."

"Considering I bought it, I strongly disagree."

If I ever see Bert again in my life, I'm going to have words for that man. "Fine. Name your price."

Surprise lights up his face. "Ah … what?"

"Name your price. What will you sell it for?"

His eyes do that thing where they search each of mine, like they're looking for answers. It's instinctive to look away, but I force myself to meet his piercing stare. "You're serious?"

"Yes."

"You really think *you* can afford this place?"

"I can."

Amusement takes over as he turns his head to look at the buildings, and my focus drops to his scruffy jawline. He's far too close, but stepping back will look weak, and I refuse to give him the upper hand. "Ten million dollars."

"What?"

"No, you're right," he says on a laugh. "That doesn't divide three ways equally. Let's go twelve."

"Twelve?"

"Yes."

"Million?"

"I can change it to a B if you like."

My hand tightens on the handle of the sledgehammer. "It's not worth that."

"You asked for my price. You've got it." Then the bastard blows me a kiss. I jolt away from him, and like that, I give Hudson the win.

He tugs his sunglasses out of his shorts and slides them onto his face. "When you have an answer, you know where to find me."

The damn city boy turns on his heel and makes his way back to his brothers. Rage is rushing through my ears, and while I have a reputation for being quiet and grumpy, I never actively lose my cool.

Not anymore.

Not since …

I swallow the regret and anger down, then grab the sledge-hammer in both hands and swing it back over my shoulder. I bring it down on the stone front steps again, and again, and again, until all that's left is rubble and a dust cloud that clogs my lungs.

I'm breathing heavily, shoulders straining, and as the sound ringing in my ears fades, another echoes toward me.

Hudson's … clapping.

I turn my hard look on him, and he stops, but his smile doesn't shift.

"Thanks for that." His words echo in the distance between us. "Removing those was our next job. You saved us the effort." He glances over at his smaller brother. "What do you think? He saved us … a day? Makes up for all the time we lost shifting the lumber." Despite his light words, he returns my hard eye contact.

I bite my tongue through the insults I want to hurl his way. "These houses will never be sold."

I'm too mad to stick around, so I turn my back on them and leave. My truck is parked where the road meets the gravel, and I gun the engine as I take off into the trees.

Hudson's lack of reaction has me rattled. It's only been a few days though, and while we've hit them hard in a lot of ways, problems are easy enough to ignore when they're short-term. Give me days, weeks, months if they last that long. I'm going to wear them down.

I'm going to be here every day, making sure they know they're not welcome.

Old End is a graveyard of memories, and if I need to burn the place to the ground, I will. Given how easily fires get out of control out here though, that will be a last resort.

But I'll do it if I have to.

Because Hudson confirmed exactly what I knew he would.

They're in this for the money, and once they're done, they'll sell the places off to an influx of strangers, and Wilde's End will never be the same again.

I'll be dead before I let that happen.

# CHAPTER
# NINE

## HUDSON

Today is off to a fan-fucking-tastic start. Waking up to a message from Sutton saying *I'm horny, where are you* and having to explain that I really moved here should have been the low point, but then the smashing started. Not even pacing to one end of the street and back again is enough to shed the irritation rattling inside me.

This week has been a fucking disaster.

Hartwell's watching me through lazy eyes as he sips his coffee, and Kennedy's anxiousness has him on the move. He's cooking breakfast on the cooktop we've chained to a pole and avoiding talking to either of us. Out of the three of us, Kennedy is most excited to be here, but after spending the day yesterday getting air back into our tires, even he's starting to question why we're sticking around.

My gaze skims over the glass glinting in the squat front lawns, and I force myself to exhale. The windows had to be replaced anyway. Sure, they were keeping the weather out, and now we're going to have to board those up too, but this isn't a complete disaster.

What happens when they *are* replaced though? Will Wilde smash those too? Will he destroy the progress we make again and again and again? And when we're selling, is he going to show up during walkthroughs and threaten all our buyers?

I lift my fist to my mouth and bite down on my knuckles with all the pressure I can handle. My scream smothers in my chest, and it takes way too long for me to shove all this shit with Wilde out of my head. No matter what, I'll take it as it comes. I'm not backing down from this.

My phone vibrates in my pocket, and I pull it out, Sutton's message back at the forefront of my mind. Not only am I here for my brothers, but I also needed to get away. His text is a perfect example of why.

If I'd still been home, I definitely would have woken up to his booty call, and I definitely would have slept with him. Because I'm terrible at making decisions, especially when my cock is involved.

The smell of eggs reaches me as I open the message Sutton has sent back. It takes me a second to make sure I'm reading the words I think I'm reading.

SUTTON:

Wait. That was serious? You're actually there?
This is the dumbest fucking shit I've ever heard.
Don't text me when you're back. You were last
on my list anyway.

My grip on my phone gets so hard I swear I'm one squeeze away from shattering the screen. We were far from exclusive, and I know he's only saying that to piss me off, but somehow, it still works. I contemplate texting him back a thousand and one insults, but I get control of myself and put my phone away instead.

Ignoring him only makes him madder.

I know. We've played this game before.

At least being here means that I won't be the first to give in.

Kennedy holds a plate up toward me, and I shove everything that's already happened this morning aside to join them.

"What did your wild man say?" he asks cautiously.

"The usual." I pick up the fried egg with my fingers and take a bite. "It's his town, get out, blah blah blah."

Kennedy sends a searching gaze Hart's way, but our brother ignores us both. "Maybe we need to listen."

"Or not."

"He broke all our windows. What are we supposed to do now?"

"Board them up."

I can tell Kennedy's torn. He's clinging to any little hope I can give him, and lucky for him, I can talk through my ass like no one else.

"Another setback, though?" He doesn't sound convinced.

"And I doubt it will be our last. Look, I know it's shit. I know this is a pain in the ass, but he doesn't get to push us around. We worked hard for this. We deserve it. Think about how excited you were when we first got here."

He pokes at his eggs. "Maybe we could get our own chickens?"

That's not at all where I was going with this, but it's a start. "Now you're thinking. We'll set up a coop next to the house, and then we'll have all the eggs we need."

Hart groans. "Don't we have enough to do around here?"

"If Kennedy wants chickens, he can have chickens."

"Cool, so you want to be here, and Kennedy wants chickens, and I want to throw myself off the roof. Does that mean I'm next?"

If I thought Hart cared enough to actually kill himself, I'd have him in a psych office before he knew what was happening. He's not suicidal though; he's just an asshole. "You're always complaining you don't have purpose in life. Well, here I am, trying to give you something. But I can only get you partway. You need to do the rest yourself."

"And you need to get laid. Heard from Sutton recently?"

I almost throw my phone at him. How is it that I know when people are deliberately trying to get a rise out of me and they're successful anyway? I really need to work on my anger issues.

"I have, actually," I say through a grin that feels painful and probably looks it. "We fucked before I got here, so I should be okay for a while. Thanks for being worried about me, brother."

Kennedy huffs and shoves a full egg into his mouth. "He's an asshole," he grumbles around his food. "He doesn't deserve you."

"Him being an asshole is kind of the whole point." I wave a hand over myself. "Gay, remember?"

His half smile makes his mustache tremble. "I don't mean the literal kind. I mean that he's horrible to you, and you shouldn't have to put up with that."

"It's sex," I say, trying to brush it off. This is why I don't talk about Sutton with him. My brother is a romantic, and I don't think he's slept with someone he hasn't fallen madly in love with. "It doesn't matter how he treats me. It only matters that I get off."

"Your life makes me sad."

"At least I haven't been through three heartbreaks already this year."

The smile slips from Kennedy's face, and Hart murmurs, "Cold, bro."

He's right. "Sorry," I say to Kennedy. "Wilde's got me frustrated."

Kennedy, always a better person than me and Hart, lets me

take the out. "What do we do about him? We can't let him keep messing with our stuff. It'll bankrupt us before long."

"Could hire security," Hart says.

"We could, but that would cost a fortune."

"Put fences up to keep them out?" Kennedy suggests.

I run my gaze along the perimeter, from one end of the street to the other, then along behind the houses where the trees slope up the hillside. "That's a lot of fencing."

Hart drums his fingers on the canvas chair. "And I doubt a little thing like a fence would stop that guy."

"Back to the guns, then?" I watch Kennedy for a reaction.

He kicks at the dirt, still thinking. "Where does this guy even come from anyway? And the others? I've counted three people other than him, you can't tell me they're all just … just … living in trees or something."

I catch on fast. "They have to have a house somewhere."

"Probably close since they're up there watching us every day."

I look from Hart to Kennedy and back to Hart again. If they have a home, they're as vulnerable as we are. Maybe even more so. None of our personal items are here; it's only tired old buildings that we're trying to breathe life into. Mountain man or not, he'd have belongings. Things he likes or needs.

"That's it."

Kennedy's eyebrows jump up. "What's it?"

"If they want to wreck our things, we're going to wreck theirs."

"That was not at all where I was going with it."

"I'm in," Hartwell says before Kennedy even finishes talking. "Let's break some stuff."

"We're not breaking anything." Kennedy stares us both down.

"We're trying to deescalate here. Not escalate. What do you think they'll do to us if we mess with their belongings?"

"No clue." I look at Hart, and for a tiny second, there's life in his eyes. "But we're going to find out."

"*No.*"

I jump at Kennedy's whiplike word. At first, I think he's joking since he's the most easygoing guy ever, but his expression matches his tone. "Excuse me?"

"Please don't do this. We're onto a good thing here, and I'm tired of waking up and wondering what the fuck is going to set us back today. I want to focus on the three of us and our plans for this place. That's it."

I can't blame Kennedy because that's all I want too. "Unfortunately, these guys aren't giving us that option."

"I don't want to make things worse. This was supposed to bring us together."

Hart cackles. "This? Really?"

We both ignore him. But I can't ignore what Kennedy says next.

"I've been so worried about both of you. Back home, we were lucky if Hart showed up for work, and if you weren't making yourself depressed by fucking Sutton, you were drinking to forget about him. I was worried you'd ... you know, *relapse.*"

It's hard to hold those thoughts against him when I've been having them myself. I'm completely caught off guard that it's something he picked up on. "I'm over that. It was shortsighted teenage stuff. That's it."

His gaze is unexpectedly shrewd. "*Was* it?"

We're not going there. I pick up the helmet and hold my hand out to Hart. "Keys?"

He fishes around in his pocket before he tosses them to me. "Where are you going?"

"To find Wilde."

"Hudson—"

I cut Kennedy off before he can worry. "To *talk*. To make a truce. You're right, this is all stupid and needs to end."

"Promise you won't start anything?"

"I promise." He gets a real smile from me. "I'm an easy guy to get along with. All Wilde needs is a bit of the old Bellamy charm." And a kick up the ass.

"Don't go too far," he says. "Your phone location is on, isn't it?"

I don't bother reminding him how shit the reception out here is. "Of course."

"Then be safe. And, Huddy? Good luck. We kinda need this."

That's the whole reason I'm doing this. For my brothers. The two people who mean more to me than anyone in this world.

# CHAPTER
# TEN

## WILDE

'm rippling with agitation as I head around the property, checking for fire hazards and testing to see if the perimeter fence is still intact. I'm no less annoyed by the time I get back to my place, so instead of spending the day pissed off, I grab my post—a polished stick that's about three feet tall and an inch thick—from inside and make my way down to the Lair. We only officially built this place ten years ago, and just like the Cutty— our town bar—we keep it pristine. The external timber is oiled and polished to a gleam, standing ten feet tall all around, and whenever I'm here, it's like everything else falls into place.

Wilde's End has survived through luck, and we're not the only remote community out here. The Dale is closest and the biggest, but there are plenty of others that need money to keep going as well. It's where Peril originated.

It started as illegal fighting rings. People would show up once a month to place bets, beat the shit out of each other, and then leave. The problem with angry people in an arena is that the matches were fast and dirty. There were also injuries severe enough that if we didn't change something, people would start asking questions.

So the podiums were added. Like an obstacle course to fight on, with the main objective being to knock your opponent off instead of beating them to within an inch of their life. In order to get close enough to knock someone off though, it also gives them the chance to pull you down with them, and matches ending in a draw aren't profitable.

That's where our posts came in.

The Lair is roughly the size of a lecture hall, with seating on all four sides and a sunken floor in the middle. The floor is padded to prevent serious injury, but the tiered platforms in the middle and the bars hanging overhead are shiny, unrelenting metal.

No matter how many fights I win or lose here, it feels like home.

I cross the padded floor to reach the starting platform and climb up onto it. My post is heavier than what most people use, but it's perfect for what I need today.

From the first swing, my muscle memory takes over. The effort I have to pour into each strike and movement focuses all my thoughts into my training and helps drain the frenetic energy from my limbs. I move from one platform to the next, testing my balance as I hit and attack imaginary opponents, all of them looking exactly like Foley.

By the time I'm heaving for breath and have sweat running down my back, I've almost forgotten about Hudson. Almost. I don't think his thorn will ever leave my side. I'm overheated, sore, and probably pushed way too hard, but at least I have a second's peace.

A small break from all the stress and worry about what

happens next for Wilde's End.

It's a fifteen-minute walk back to my place, and every one of those minutes drags. It's been a long time since I lost control of myself like that, and my muscles are making me pay for it now. Even with the pain, I love this walk. It's peacefully quiet, the breeze is cool against my sweat, and everything smells like trees and dirt and earth.

Who wouldn't want to protect a place like this?

There's a secluded swimming hole I normally bathe in not far from my place, but I opt to use my outdoor shower instead. I avoid it when I can because I hate to waste water, but after that workout, I'm starving, and I refuse to eat smelling like this.

I strip off and shower, scrubbing the horrible effects of the day from me. The world as I know it hasn't ended yet, and I need to keep focused on that and nothing else. There's still time to stop the worst from happening.

As soon as I'm clean, I switch off the shower, dry in the sun, and then climb my back stairs. The Wenders and I built this place with our bare hands, and I've never been prouder of anything than when we finished and I had a place all of my own.

It's my sanctuary, and I've never had another person step foot inside.

Until now, apparently.

Sitting on my couch, leaning back against my grandmother's patchwork quilt, is Hudson.

He grins when he sees me, like he hasn't invaded my personal space, and then his gaze drops from my face … to my dick.

One side of his mouth stretches higher. "Well, that's unexpected."

"What the hell are you doing in my house?"

"Returning the favor."

The heart-pounding irritation from earlier returns. I'm not sure which part frustrates me the most: that his face can do that so easily or that I worked my ass off to get rid of this feeling for nothing. "Get out."

"But you didn't say please."

"Get out. *Please*."

Hudson laughs, and the scratchy sound is too appealing. "I would, but I'm really enjoying the view."

I huff and cross the small room to pull the quilt out from under him. I'm not modest—I don't give a fuck who sees me naked—but I'm in no position to make demands when he can't keep his eyes off my cock. Once the quilt is wrapped securely around my waist, I glare menacingly down at him.

"Show's over. Get out."

"Just one thing first." He reaches for the clay pot on the coffee table in front of him. I don't have much in here, but the few things I do have are personal. Gracie Raylon made that for me when she was six, and it was the first gift I'd gotten in years. I'm about to snatch it out of Hudson's grubby hands when he tosses it into the air.

My heart drops.

"No!" I try to catch it, but the pot slips past my grip, and I watch as it drops, fast, and then hits the floor. All I can do is stare as it shatters, the tiny pieces exploding out in all directions.

I barely hear Hudson over the pounding in my ears.

"Ooops," he tries, but there's no apology behind it. "I guess we're even for the windows now." He stands, and as he steps around me, he pats me on the shoulder, but I'm still staring at the wreckage in shock. "Just wanted you to know I'm always happy to visit. In case you get any other ideas."

My indignation is roaring in my veins, and Hudson doesn't

make it a step before I grab his shirt and throw him halfway across the room. He's ready for me, and I get an elbow to the face for my efforts. He takes another swing that I block, and before he can tackle me, I grab him and shove him face-first into the wall. I need to use my whole body to keep him pinned, even as he thrashes against me.

He's strong for a city boy.

"How fucking dare you," I snarl.

He tries for a hard shove backward, and when that doesn't work, he lets out a chuckle instead. "Coming from you."

"You can get new windows. I can't replace that."

"Maybe you shouldn't have started this shit with us, then."

"I wouldn't have had to start anything if you'd listened in the first place."

His breathing from our scuffle slows down. "Did you ever stop and think that maybe I'm not leaving because what I left behind is a thousand times worse than whatever you have to throw at us?"

That question hits me in a way it shouldn't. It's the same reason so many of us wound up here to begin with, and all I can do is ignore it. I don't *want* to understand him. I can't risk it. "Did you ever stop and think that maybe I don't give a shit?"

"That would require me to give a fuck about your opinion."

"So how does this end, huh?" I ask, barely able to hold back from slamming him into the wall again. "I burn down your shit, so you burn down mine?"

"Sounds like a good time."

"I'd kill you before you got the chance."

I can only see one side of Hudson's face, but it's enough to make out his smile. "Nah. You already told me that you don't do that."

"Maybe I was lying."

"I'll take my chances." He shoves back hard but can't throw me off him.

What he does do might be worse though. His jean-covered ass rubs over my bare cock. I lost the quilt as we wrestled, and as much as I hate everything about Hudson and the reasons he's here, it doesn't change that he's a stupidly attractive man.

Before he can do it again, I angle my hips away, but it's already drawn my attention to how close we're standing. He smells like something sweet, and his skin has warmed the thin T-shirt he's wearing. The T-shirt I can feel every muscle in his back through.

"Why don't we make a truce?" he asks.

The word disgusts me. "Never."

"Don't think you have much choice." I'm waiting for him to shove me again, but he doesn't. "I found your place easily enough, and anything you do to us, I'll do right back. Which reminds me … I hope you weren't planning on going anywhere today."

Going … it only takes me a second. "What the fuck did you do to my truck?"

"Don't know what you mean." His dry tone makes it very clear he knows what I mean, the same way I know what he's hinting at.

He let the air out of my fucking tires.

Unlike him, I have easy access to an air pump.

"Fine, then," I relent, hating myself for doing it. "Let's negotiate. What will make you leave town? And don't say twelve million dollars."

I'm not expecting him to push back this time, but he only manages enough space to turn and face me before he's pinned again. My forearm presses against his throat, but Hudson accepts every bit of pressure I give him. He gazes steadily at me, and for a moment, all there is between us is hoarse breathing and warring eye contact.

He takes his time to answer me, and when he does, it's not what I expect. "What happened to your eye?"

He doesn't need to be specific; I know he's talking about my scar. He won't be getting an answer though. "That's my business. Answer my question."

"I would, but I don't think you'll like my answer."

I huff and shove against him again before stepping away. Being close to him and his arrogance makes me uncomfortable, and I can't keep looking into that irritatingly sly expression. We're getting nowhere fast, and I'm running out of options. "That's it, then? We keep going until one of us is destroyed?"

"Or we just stop."

"I can't stand by and let you sell off Old End."

"Old End?" He tilts his head, and the lock that curls up above his forehead falls to the side.

"The town," I grit out.

"Let me? I'm not asking for your permission."

I swear every time that he opens his mouth, it makes me want to punch him in it a little more. "Get out."

"Or what? You'll manhandle me again?" Then he bites down hard on his bottom lip and shamelessly runs his eyes over me. I'd been wondering if his taunts were purely to piss me off or if there was truth behind them. The way he's looking at me solves that mystery. I wish I could say I was immune to him, but him blatantly staring at my cock is making it think it needs to put on a show.

I scoop the quilt back up off the ground and wrap it around my hips before I can get hard.

"Pity …" Hudson sighs on his way to the door. "If we'd met

under any other circumstances, you could have manhandled me all you liked."

He leaves, and I slam the door after him, hotter and more irritable than before I showered.

I've never met someone who makes my blood boil like he does.

# CHAPTER
# ELEVEN

## HUDSON

The whole way back, I can't shake the image of Wilde from my brain.

Beefy, lightly hairy chest, big arms—who the fuck am I kidding? All I could concentrate on was his cock. I've seen plenty in my day, but the way it was hanging there so confidently thick even while soft is burned into my mind.

Of course, my current biggest headache would have a perfect dick, and *of course*, all I want is to suck that perfect dick. I couldn't have come out here to the middle of nowhere and met someone emotionally well-adjusted to get horny over, could I? No. As usual, the biggest asshole in a five-mile radius has caught my attention, and I'm tempted to make all the same mistakes I always do.

I've stopped paying attention to where I'm riding. This deep into the forest, all the tracks and turns look the same.

I'm swamped on all sides by trees, and my reception is dipping between one bar and out of service. Wilde's place had been easy enough to find since the gravelly road led me close enough by it that I could make out his faded red truck through the forest. The house hadn't been what I expected either.

In my mind, I'd been looking out for maybe a tent or a shack made out of a hastily put-together collection of junk. Wilde's house was … nice. Small, timber, with a living room, a kitchenette, and what looked like a bedroom, but it was immaculately built and cozy enough inside I would have thought it belonged to his grandma. It put a wrench in my first opinion of him.

Not that any of that fucking matters when every time I blink, I get a flash of his dick.

Damn, to have him press me into a wall again …

I shake that off and look around, picking a random track and gunning the bike down that way. The *nrrr nrrrrr* of the engine is echoing through the forest and probably scaring off any animals I would have found out this way. So far, the only house I've seen is Wilde's, but there has to be more. We've seen three people since getting here, and that place wasn't big enough for them all. Since I'm out here, I might as well explore and figure out what the hell else is happening on our land.

It's a mission to navigate the tree roots and random boulders sticking up out of the overgrown grass. I barely spot them in time before having to veer sharply, but other than that, it's a nice ride. Everything is so green out here, the trees are blocking out the harsh sun, and as I ride, I can almost, *almost* stop thinking.

It isn't something I've been able to do for … I don't fucking know how long. Between running Bell Building, being on the construction site, my shitty sex life, and, most importantly, my brothers and their issues, I'm tapped out. It's no wonder I have a short temper when I can't breathe half the time.

Now, I have Wilde to add to my list.

Well, Wilde and his dick.

Because those are two very different problems.

I try to picture what Wilde's reaction would have been if I'd gotten on my knees and offered him a blow job. Sure, it would have been hard to resist the temptation to bite the fucking thing right off, but picturing his hatred as he stalked closer is enough to wake my own cock up.

Between the naked wrestling and Sutton's message reminding me of the degrading sex I missed out on, it won't be long before I'm tempted to head home for a few days to get off.

Good decisions? I don't know him.

Some days, I wish I could be more like the twins. Kennedy has his head on right in everything except relationships, and Hart's so damn switched off to the world that nothing gets to him. The things that make me worry about them are also the things I envy. How the hell did Kennedy end up so well-adjusted? Then, on the flip side, what would it be like to not feel a single thing beyond a vague hum of emotion?

Sometimes I feel things too acutely, and with no idea how to handle it, I explode.

Thanks, Mom and Dad, for the awesome upbringing.

I shouldn't complain though. There are plenty of people who had it worse than us. At least with Mom popping one too many benzos every day and Dad sticking his dick into every woman he came into contact with, it meant they were both too busy to be abusive.

So ... yay for us?

My grip on the handlebars tightens, and I give the bike more gas. It feels fucking incredible to tear through track after track, kicking up dirt and leaves and leaving the breeze behind me.

Along with all thoughts about my parents.

Those stupid, fucking—

Shit. A tree cutting into the track all but lurches out at me, and

I only just manage to avoid it in time. The redirection throws me off, and I swerve for another tree, braking hard, tires shredding through the dirt before the back end curves out and collides with *fucking something*, and then I'm launched into the air.

My gut flies out through my ass, and then I land, colliding with the unforgiving ground before I slide a few feet. There's a second for me to catch my breath—and then my bike catches up with me.

It smacks into my chest before taking me out. I lose track of what's where as the bike goes over the top of me; there's just pain and the urge to scream that doesn't come out.

The bike hits a tree and finally stills, and it's only in the echoing silence that stretches out around us that I let out a *"fuuuuck!"*

When I try to sit up, pain spikes so sharply up my side that I almost pass out. My shirt looks wet, stuck to my side, and it takes me a really fucking long moment to realize it's not blood. It's a burn from the motor.

I try reaching for my shirt, but my fingers are too stiff. My hand's shaking; it takes my swimming vision a second to notice my fingers are swelling up.

"What the fuck ..."

I roll onto my side, teeth clenched so tightly my jaw might break, and after what feels like forever, I struggle to my knees. I'm sweating, even though it's cool down here, heart thumping loudly in my ears, and if it wasn't for my helmet, I'd swear I hit my head with how disoriented everything feels.

My left arm is okay, and I use it to steady myself as I climb to my feet. My right leg takes my weight, but when the left joins in, a throb pulses through my ankle.

Well, that's a fucking problem.

While my hand and ankle hurt, it's nothing on the burn. My

skin feels like it's on fire, and I'm doing everything I can to concentrate on literally anything else.

I shove my good hand into my pocket and find my phone thankfully unharmed, but when I bring the screen alive, I see exactly what I'm expecting to.

No service

No *fucking* service. I almost throw the useless thing against the tree.

I can't call anyone, I can't walk, and I can barely fucking breathe with how harshly my breaths are coming. My vision is swimming in and out, and the burn is making me want to curl over on myself, but I limp for the bike instead.

Do I want to get back on this damn thing? Fuck no. But I'm hoping and fucking praying as I lift it upright, throw my shitty leg over, and then try to turn it on. At first, I think it's fucked—there's only silence where there should be an engine—but maybe it's in as much shock as I am because after a moment, it chugs to life.

I rest my helmet on the handlebars for a second, relief taking over as I try to clear the haze swamping my brain. The most difficult part is getting the bike balanced while on my shit leg, but after a few attempts, I get going.

My adrenaline is through the roof, and the dizziness is making it hard to focus, but I somehow manage to find a track and follow it. It leads to what looks like the gravel road that leads to town, and I urge the bike faster, needing to get where someone else can take over. I need painkillers and the ability to not think for a while.

It feels like my brain is swelling, and I have no idea where I am, but I swear it keeps darkening and lightening.

I jerk the bike to a sudden stop and almost fly off the damn thing. I'm struggling to hold on, and after a second, the bike drops as I stagger painfully to the side.

I'm at a house with a red truck. It feels familiar. Like relief. I'm sure I was just here, but my thoughts are snatches of images too hard to reach through the pain.

My vision swims so hard I almost throw up.

"Hello?" I croak. But I don't know if it's out loud or in my head. I'm tired. So damn fucking tired. I try to get closer to the house, but it only moves further away. *"Hello?"*

"Hudson?"

I turn at my name, and it takes me a second to focus on the bearded man. As soon as I do though, it's like all the strength drains out of me. My knees crash to the ground, and the rest of me follows. I'm not even sure where I hurt anymore, other than everywhere.

I'm panting so quick and sharp that it's burning my chest, and I squeeze my eyes closed against the … well, everything.

I need the pain to stop.

Once it stops, I'll be fine.

Just fine.

And maybe some sleep.

All I know is that the bearded man will fix it. I know him, and I know I know him, but my brain is moving too slowly to pick from where. The mixture of fear and interest promises me that he'll make this better.

Even if he kills me.

At least that will take the pain and nausea away.

# CHAPTER
## TWELVE

WILDE

Well, this is fucking perfect.

I stare at the very unconscious asshole lying on my property. Technically, if I nudge him over a little to the left, he's on someone else's property and therefore not my problem. With a sigh, I look around to check we're alone, even though I already know the answer to that. Then I move closer, half-convinced he's going to jump up and stab me.

I don't trust anyone from the city.

The closer I get though, the less likely it looks as though he's going to be doing anything but bleeding out.

For fuck's sake. Why is this my problem?

It figures that he'd come here and force me to deal with him. He's bleeding all over, arms cut up, front of his shirt covered in dirt and shredded in places, and even in his sleep, he's shaking. Then my gaze finds the nasty burn on his side.

Guess he came off his dirt bike, then.

My head drops back toward the canopy as I whine at the universe for bringing him my way.

Too much of my day has already been dedicated to this fucking guy.

Completely against my will, I stalk to my truck, throw open the back, and head over to Hudson's sprawled body. He's lucky I refilled my tires with air while he was gone, otherwise we wouldn't be going anywhere.

I crouch beside him, and I'm gentler than I should be as I tug the helmet off and toss it into my truck. Then I slip one arm under his knees and the other behind his back, then haul him against me and stand, cursing his name the entire fucking time. Hudson says something incoherent right before I dump him in the back, lock the tray into place, and then round the truck to climb into the cab.

This proves exactly what I've been saying. These guys don't get it. They don't respect what it's like to live in a remote place, they don't understand how different and dangerous it can be, and they definitely don't take accountability for any of the bullshit they bring our way.

I slam my palm into the steering wheel as I drive, cautious not to take the corners too sharply and avoiding the bumpy tracks where I can. Not that he wouldn't deserve a few extra injuries. It only takes a few minutes to reach the chop shop, and Booker must have heard me coming because he's waiting on his front steps.

The second the engine is off, I climb out and slam the door a little too hard.

"What are you doing here?" he asks.

I don't answer, just walk around and open the back so he can see where Hudson has been thrown in there.

Booker hums as he approaches. "Didn't think you had it in you."

"*What* in me?"

"Murder. Is this mine now?"

My eyes close for a brief moment as I ignore what he could mean by that. "I didn't murder him. He came off his bike."

"Pity." Booker looks him over. "Bring him inside."

"You're the doctor, you do it."

"You're the one with the muscles."

Like that means anything. "You're more than capable."

"Oh, I know." Booker shrugs, chubby cheeks creasing as he smiles. "It's more fun this way. Pick up your pretty boy and follow me."

Booker doesn't wait for me to argue. He goes back inside, and I'm left to grit my teeth and reach for Hudson. I grab his ankle and haul him closer. He's a dead weight, and it would be easier to toss him over my shoulder, but that burn looks nasty, and even *I* don't hate him that much.

As I carry him inside, I ignore the way his head lolls against my shoulder, how heavy and solid his body is, how he mutters something in his fitful sleep, and still manages to smell sweet, even covered in filth.

Booker has cleared off the examination bed for me, and I dump Hudson onto it as soon as I can. The chop shop is attached to Booker's house, and for us being in the middle of nowhere, he's well stocked. The place has been lined with white vinyl on the floors and walls, and there are metal racks on one side filled with who the fuck knows what medical equipment, a locked industrial-sized fridge for medications, and a computer on a movable desk right next to the bed.

Booker clucks his tongue against his teeth as he leans in and inspects the burn. He gets close, breathing deeply as he studies it for a few minutes, before he looks up suddenly and catches my eyes. "You're too good to me."

There isn't much I can say to that. Our Peril matches keep

Booker in business and well funded; I think it's the main reason he landed in Wilde's End. Having an actual doctor close by is definitely a win, but that doesn't mean I like everything about it.

The way Booker's eyes sharpen, innocent face lit by some deep glow as he inspects Hudson's injuries, creeps me the fuck out. I haven't and won't ask about his past since it's our unspoken rule, but there's also a part of me that doesn't think I'd like what I found out.

Booker holds out a pair of scissors. "Want to do the honors?"

"Nope."

"Your loss."

I watch as he cuts Hudson's shirt off and peels the material from his body. He cuts around the burn with more care than I'm used to seeing from him, and then he tosses the scraps of shirt into a bin at his side, pulls on a pair of medical gloves, and sets something cold over the burn.

I've been treated by Booker a lot in the past, thanks to Peril, and he usually relishes seeing me in pain. He never tries to hide his excitement as injured fighters turn up to see him and he has to deal with stitching skin back together or setting broken bones. He's in his element, and while he might make me uncomfortable, I also know we need him. As long as he doesn't do anything inappropriate to patients, he can enjoy what he does all he likes. Some people would argue that enjoying your job is a *good* thing.

While Booker works, my gaze strays back up to Hudson's face and the unnaturally long eyelashes that look out of place with his other, harder features.

Everything about him plain pisses me off.

An inhale hisses between his teeth, followed by a groan going in the other direction. Those eyes of his blink open, squinting against the bright light above him, and it takes a second for reality to kick in.

Hudson flinches away from Booker, gaze shooting to the racks of medical equipment to the ceiling and then to me. "What the fuck did you do to me?"

Booker sets a gentle hand on his shoulder. "You need to stay still."

"Fuck that. Where the fuck am I?"

"I'm a doctor. You've taken a nasty fall on your motorcycle, and I'm popping you back together again."

Some of the tension leaves Hudson, and his eyes screw up as he presses his hand to his temple. "Everything fucking hurts."

"Oh, shoot. Painkillers. Silly me. So forgetful. Give me a moment." There's something in his tone I don't believe.

Booker disappears into the large refrigerating unit, and Hudson shoots me a suspicious look. "What really happened?"

"You're a shit rider."

"Fuck you."

"Next time, I'll leave you on the road to die."

He manages a painful, unamused laugh. "Why didn't you?"

"You were too close to my house. Your body would have attracted bears." It's not a complete lie, but as much as I want to never see his face again, my conscience wouldn't let me leave someone—anyone—to die. Not even Foley.

So Hudson isn't special.

"Bears. Right." He lets out a long, painful noise. "Why does everything hurt?"

Booker takes that moment to return with a catheter, and I don't miss the upward tilt to his lips as he slowly slides the needle in. "There we go," he says, sounding sympathetic and not at all like a sadist. "The pain will disappear relatively quickly. I'm going to clean you up to see if anywhere needs stitches. Then we'll deal with your burn, which won't be fun—for you—and after that, we'll move on to anything else that's annoying you. The good news is that I think it's all cosmetic. Well, except for the concussion, but that'll only scramble your head for a couple of days." He turns toward Hudson's chest. "Oh. But if you have sunglasses, put them on. I'm keeping the light angled away from you, but I need it to see what I'm doing."

It doesn't look like Hudson followed any of that. "Sunglasses," I snap at him.

He pats down the pockets of his shorts, but he still looks confused.

With a huff, I stalk closer, reach into the same pocket he pulled them from earlier, and slide them out. One side has a deep crack in it, but they're mostly in one piece. "There."

He takes them without a thank-you and shoves them onto his face. Thankfully, they hide his eyes from my sight, but even that isn't enough to relieve my bad mood. "I'm going," I say. "You've got it from here, Booker."

"Actually, you can't," he says in that annoyingly singsong voice. "I don't have a car, and he's going to need a lift home once I'm done with him. It's not like I can discharge him in this state— what kind of doctor do you think I am?"

I glare at him, and he smiles innocently back. Then my gaze moves on to Hudson.

He smirks in my direction, but it sounds like it hurts to talk. "Doctor's orders."

The challenge in his tone has my hands curling over into fists. Give me my post, and we can settle this like fucking Wenders— until one of us can't stand up again. I'd like to see Hudson smirk then. "You really trust me not to dump you in the middle of the forest?"

"Trust? You?" The heavy pain in his voice is fading. "I'd rather take my chances with the bears."

"Funny …" Booker glances at me. "Isn't that what men call *you*?"

"Fuck off."

Hudson settles his head back against the bed. "You gay?"

"You fuck off too."

"That means yes." Even with painkillers kicking in, his voice is slurred.

"I don't care. It's none of your business anyway." I'm ready to ignore him for the rest of the time Booker is treating him, but he keeps talking.

"I'm gay. Kennedy is bi, and Hart is … something."

"Something?" I ask and then want to kick myself for caring.

"Don't know if he dates. Or hooks up. Won't talk to us."

"Guess you should go back to the city, then, so he can meet someone."

"Ooh, nice try." He spares me an appreciative look, and I assume his pain must be gone now. "But it's still a no."

Booker leans in and whispers, "He's always been like this. Very serious. One-track mind."

"What did I say about fucking off?"

He lifts a shoulder and goes back to cleaning melted skin. "It's true. If you're not looking after the town, you're in Peril matches, and if you're not in Peril matches, you're down in Wayward once a month, hooking up."

"That's my business."

"Nah, can't see it," Hudson says.

"Can't see what?"

"You hooking up."

Bold claim, considering I had him pinned to the wall earlier. "I do just fine."

"Don't believe you."

"Don't care."

Booker looks gleeful. "You might have met your match, Wilde."

I glare at them both and head for the door. "I'm going to wait outside. Hurry the hell up."

I don't know which of them it is that says bye because the door slams behind me at the same time. So what that I have a simple life? It's the whole point of moving out here. It's hard work, way harder than life in the city, but it's quiet, cut off, and I'm free to focus on the important things. Make sure the town is safe. That we have everything we need. Then, once a month after my fight, I go and get a release.

It works for me.

And this weekend, I'm going to need it more than ever.

# CHAPTER
# THIRTEEN

## HUDSON

This is the weirdest fucking doctor's office I've ever been in. Considering where we are, I should probably count myself lucky that they even have one out here, but now the pain is gone, I'm feeling less lucky and more irritable.

I have no fucking clue what happened. I'm getting snapshots of broken windows and Sutton's text and grabbing the bike to find Wilde. Did I find him? I mean, he obviously found me, but … I might not be in pain anymore, but thinking fucking hurts.

"Why can't I remember what happened?"

"Concussion," the doctor says.

"No way. I would have been wearing a helmet."

He clucks his tongue against his teeth. "Helmets don't prevent concussions. They prevent your head being cracked into two." His eyes look a honeyed brown through my sunglasses as they roam from my chest up to my hairline. "You avoided a lot of blood in that lovely blond hair."

As much as the words should sound like a good thing, there's something in his tone that makes me take him in again. He's a larger guy with fluffy brown hair and round, pink cheeks, like he sunburns easily, that give the impression of him being much younger than I'd assume for a doctor. "How old are you?"

"Thirty-six," he answers, turning back to my chest. There's a gash concerningly close to my nipple that he pokes his finger into. "Need stitches for this one."

"Okay …" This guy is definitely weird. "I'm thirty-three. By the way. Except I look older than you. You barely look twenty."

A smile curls at his lips. "That so?"

"You can't tell me no one has said that before."

He stabs me suddenly with the needle, tugging the thread through before leaning in close to my face. "First rule about the End is not asking questions about our beginning."

I search his eyes for any sign he's joking. "Your beginning?"

"Our backgrounds. Where we came from, who we are, who our families are, why we're here. None of that matters."

Too many words for my swimming head. "It matters. What if you have a murderer move in next door?"

"More people for me to patch up?"

My eyes widen. "Was that a joke?"

"No." But he's still smiling. "The only thing that matters is what you do once you're here. And what you've done is cause drama."

"That was Wilde."

"Was it?"

I scoff, unable to believe that's actually up for debate. "Yes. He …" My brain feels like it's squeezed too hard, and I press my hand against it while the doctor finishes stitching me up. "He threatened us and ruined our things."

"His things."

"What?"

"This is his town."

My blood pressure creeps higher as that familiar need to explode takes over me. "*My* town. I bought it."

"And?" The doctor cuts off the thread and then runs his thumb lovingly over his work. "Ownership isn't a piece of paper out here. Wilde will never give this place up without a fight, and unless you're ready to go to war with him, you should probably leave and save yourself the headache."

"Oh, I'm ready," I say through clenched teeth. None of these people intimidate me.

"Really?" He gently takes my right hand and strokes over my fingers. It's the first time I notice how fucked-up they are.

"The fuck?"

"Broken. I could set these for you … but I'm very protective of Wilde."

I wheeze a laugh. "You fucking him?"

The doctor squeezes down on my fingers, and I'm sure that would be painful if I wasn't drugged. "Never. I have my own mountain to conquer."

"He did this to me, didn't he?"

"No."

I'd been ready for the lie, but it doesn't piss me off any less. "I don't believe you."

"You can trust me. I'm a doctor."

I snort to let him know what I think of that. "Can I go yet?"

"If you want your fingers to set in all different directions."

I forcibly relax back into the bed. "Make it quick."

All up, I have three broken fingers in a splint, a large burn that needs the dressings changed for a few days, seven stitches I have to come back to have taken out, a concussion, and a sprained ankle, which luckily is only mild. As much as Wilde hates me, I don't think he did all this. I *want* it to have been him so that it fuels my resentment some more, but it doesn't make sense. Where would the burn have come from? And why would he have brought me here?

My head is tight and unsteady from trying to think, and I spend the rest of the time on that bed, ignoring all the things racing through my mind.

"I don't have crutches for you, so you're going to have to hobble home. Keep your weight off of your foot for a few days, and keep it elevated. Lots of rest."

Rest. Right. That's exactly what I have time to do. The worst part is that I can't even blame Wilde for this setback. I don't *think*.

What was I even doing out here?

"Is it normal to not remember what happened?" I ask as Dr. Booker helps me off the bed and supports me to the door.

"Very. You're concussed. Your brain has had a little reset while you slept, but there's a good chance those memories might not come back. Go home. Stay in a dark room. No screens for at least forty-eight hours. And keep that damn leg up."

I'm actually surprised when we get outside and Wilde is waiting, leaning against his truck, arms crossed tight and jaw clenched in a way that forces his beard wider at the sides. "Done yet?"

"Your patient is released. Next time, bring me a real challenge."

Wilde grunts and climbs into the driver's seat while the doctor helps me to the passenger side. "What two main things do you need to do to recover?"

"Darkness and elevation."

"Good." His eyes drift down to my bare chest. "Don't forget to bring those stitches back to me."

My face scrunches up, and I nudge him away so I can slam the door between us. I'm going to take these damn stitches out myself. "Thanks," I mutter through the open window as Wilde guns the engine and pulls away.

I wait until the doctor is out of sight before I ask, "What the fuck is wrong with him?"

Wilde doesn't answer me.

"He seems like the kind of guy who'd slice and dice a man and enjoy it."

At first, I think he's going to keep ignoring me. "Booker's harmless."

"I don't know what to tell you, but that's a lie."

Silence wraps around us again, and I fucking hate it.

"You sure you didn't get a bit too angry?" I ask, just to push him. "A little slip of the fist, a little squeeze of the hand …"

From his profile, I see his jaw clench again.

"Maybe you thought it would be an easy way to get rid of me." It hurts to think of words, but running my mouth is second nature.

I swear his nostrils flare, but he's still acting like he can't hear my bullshit. His knuckles are little white hills, standing out against his sun-battered skin.

"Nah … I'm pretty sure I could take you."

Nothing.

"Bet you're all talk, no action."

Still nothing.

"Were you the one who tore my shirt off? Wanted a closer look?"

"You're so fucking irritating. I should have punched you."

"Then why didn't you?"

Nothing *again*. I almost groan in frustration. What the hell is with this guy? I glare at him and his messy beard, the wild hair, the way he barely fits in his seat. In addition to the scar through his eye, he's got tiny white ones all up and down his arms, but the sleeve tattoos on one arm make them harder to see. "What are the scars from?"

"I already told you that isn't your business."

That makes me frown. "When?"

"When you broke into my house. Right before you took off and broke yourself."

I was in his house? Apparently, that was caught up in the memories I knocked from my head. I'm squinting behind my sunglasses as I try to remember, but everything from today feels like soup, and the harder I try, the more it makes me want to punch something. "Tell me *something* about you."

I'm fully expecting him to ignore me again, but he answers. "I don't like you."

"That's fine, no one does."

He goes back to boring silence.

"I got this scar," I say, pointing to the gashes across my chest, "when I fell off my dirt bike."

Wilde throws me a disgusted look. "What the fuck are you doing?"

"This is called getting to know each other."

"I don't want to know you. I'd be happy if I woke up tomorrow and never saw your face again."

My resentment only grows, so I do what I usually do when someone is pissing me off. I use my body against them. I flex my pecs, drawing Wilde's attention, and the reluctant interest in his eyes is exactly what I'm after. "My face, maybe. But the way you're looking at my body tells me you want to see a whole lot more of it."

His bullish snort is music to my ears. "Says the man who couldn't keep his eyes off my cock earlier."

His ... "*What?*"

"Don't get all shy about it now."

"What do you mean I saw your *cock*?"

When he glances over, it's less angry and more guarded. "You don't remember?"

I moan and cover my face with my good arm. "No. Bring it back … bring it back …"

"Don't worry," he says dryly. "You were very impressed."

And now, I'm very *pissed* that I don't remember it. Considering my fuck buddy is hours away and the fingers on my jerking-off hand are broken, it's probably a good thing though. "I wouldn't feel too smug about it. I find any dick impressive. Especially when they're attached to an asshole."

He does that no-answer thing again, and it makes me want to scream at him. I don't like the stoic and silent type. I need him to meet me on my level. To give me attention. Be petty.

The truck crosses onto the gravel road, where the trees are spread further apart, making it easier to drive.

"Where's my bike?"

"I'll drop it off later."

"When?"

No answer.

"Your doctor thinks this is your town. Might want to correct him on that."

Still no answer.

I rack my messy, injured brain for something, anything I can use to draw him into conversation. Asking to see his cock again will probably get me punched in the face. I'm tempted to ask about his past since Booker said that was off-limits, but something else the doctor said flits in and out of my memory too fast for me to catch. "He said something about Peril. What did he mean? Peril what? Something about that and hooking up. Is it a kink thing?"

He's way too good at ignoring me, but I can tell I'm getting to him.

"You might as well answer because I'm not going to stop asking."

"You might as well stop asking because my answer hasn't changed. It's not your business, it will never be your business, so stop worrying about it and fucking leave already."

I exaggerate a yawn. "New topic, please."

"Lynx is going to kill you, and I'm not going to do a thing to stop him."

"Mhmm. 'Kay. Who or what is Lynx?"

Still nothing.

"Has anyone ever told you that you're fun to talk to?"

I swear I hear his teeth grind together.

The familiar bleed of gravel to sealed road comes into view way too quickly, and as soon as we're in town, Wilde stomps on the brakes and almost sends me through the front windshield.

"The fuck? I've already been in one accident today, thanks."

He puts the car in park, then turns to me faster than I thought he could move. He grips my thigh so tightly I'm pinned to the chair and leans into my space.

"You might not remember this, but if you ever, *ever* so much as touch something of mine again, this pain will be the least of your worries. Got it?"

"I have no idea what you're talking about."

His hold tightens, gray eyes looking like heavy storm clouds before the rain breaks through. "You purposely destroyed something important to me. Something irreplaceable. If you do it again, I'll break your fucking neck."

I lean in too. "I don't believe you."

"Believe what you want. I might not kill you, city boy, but don't make the mistake of assuming that means I'm not dangerous. I learned to survive out here. And I'll do whatever I need to for that to continue."

The way I see it, we're in a no-win situation. Wilde is ready to protect this place with his life, and I'm getting to feel the same way. Financially, we need this place to work, but deep down, I know it's more than that. We could sell the town on again and be fine. *Financially.*

But there's nothing waiting for us back home but disaster. Kennedy is one bad breakup away from turning into Hart. Hart's so empty I'm scared for whatever comes next. And me? I've been so, so tempted lately. Tempted in a way I've never been before. All I can think about is high school and the way I escaped. The way popping a pill or snorting a line or licking a tiny bubble of liquid could make everything shut up again.

It's not cravings. It has nothing to do with need.

Mentally, I'm tired. It's an easy out, and it's one that's been slipping into my mind too often lately.

"Maybe a little danger is what I've been missing."

We're so fucking close, and the anger radiating from him wraps around me in a comforting way. There's no doubt in my mind that he hates me and believes everything he says about never wanting to see me again. I'm just so fucked-up that it's his hatred that turns me on. He's giving me attention, and it doesn't matter what kind it is because while he's staring at me like this, I'm the only thing on his mind.

He's not even attractive. Intimidating, yes, which I like a lot, but his hair and beard are a scruffy mess, so it's not like you can see much of his face anyway. Not my type. At all. Sutton, in comparison, is a fucking swan compared to Wilde, and yet here I am, my dick getting hard anyway.

I'm fucking disgusted with myself.

But I'm not surprised.

"Get the fuck out of my truck."

"I can't walk."

"I don't care."

When I don't move, he swears, throws off his seat belt, and climbs out. I'm waiting for him when he flings open my door, but I'm not expecting him to reach over me, unclip my belt, and then lift me off the fucking seat.

I grip Wilde's neck as he carries me across the street, and this is doing nothing for how hard I am. All I can feel are his muscles working against my side and the way his bodywash, so strong in the cab, is even stronger on his shirt.

"You just wanted to feel me up, didn't you?"

"I already did enough of that when I had you pinned to the wall earlier."

My jaw drops. How the fuck could I forget *that*?

"Erotically?" I ask, making sure I sound teasing and not at all like the image of that is too much.

"*Aggressively*."

"Pity."

"Even though I was naked when I did it."

Then he dumps me on the front steps of the nearest house and stalks away without a goodbye. I know I'm supposed to say something back, to tease him or piss him off or …

He's back in the truck before I can think of a damn thing, and all I can do is watch him drive away.

# CHAPTER
# FOURTEEN

## WILDE

thought I got rid of this agitation already, but I storm into my house, cross the living room, and then slam the bedroom door closed behind me. I'm too worked up to get far, so I thump back against the door, shove my shorts below my balls, and then fist my cock. It's painfully hard, and jerking off dry doesn't do anything to calm me. I'm just so … so … I grit my teeth against thoughts of Hudson, but like in real life, the memory of him is determined to torture me.

His lips have this natural curl to them that I want to sink my teeth into. Anything so I won't have to look at it some more. I hate his mouth so fucking much.

Giving up, I spit into my hand. My thrusts into my fist are easier, and I sink into that place where I stop fighting the orgasm. It doesn't matter if Hudson is the one I'm jerking off over. All I need is a release, and then I can kick my ass over it later. If I fight where my mind wants to go, I'll only end up fucking up my high, and I need this frustration inside of me out. Not to make it worse.

My cock is oversensitive, and I lean back into the wall as I fuck my fist harder. Hudson never fucking shuts up. He never knows when to back down. His constant pushing and challenging is getting under my skin in a way that both makes me horny and also makes me want to punch him. It's been … well, since before I first got to Wilde's End that I've had someone challenge me like he does. We all make an effort to get along here, to talk out the drama, and when that can't be done, to put it to rest in a Peril match. Nobody tells me no. Nobody fronts up to me. Nobody enjoys the way I hate them.

Then on top of that is his antagonistic flirting. I know he's using it to get under my skin, but I don't think he knows how far under it burrows.

My balls tighten, and I lift the bottom of my shirt with my free hand to clamp the hem between my teeth. I'm getting close. My body feels feverish with how much I need to get off, and I let the images of Hudson take over.

Of the pretty city body, perfect chest made sexier by the map of gravel rash over it. Of the heavy way he breathed through the pain, and my brain mixing that with him breathing through something else. Of that curl to his lips. Watching it slowly disappear as he spreads his infuriating mouth and wraps it around my cock …

My dick jerks in my hand before I'm ready for it, and relief sweeps over my shoulders as I unload into my fist. The tension in my body uncoils, orgasm draining from my balls, and as I come down from it, I sag against the door, panting like I've just finished a workout.

Then my brain kicks in.

*Motherfucker.*

I choke on the sound in my throat as I yank my pants back up, and I throw open my bedroom door. As good as that felt, it's not at all what I wanted to happen. Giving in to those thoughts about

Hudson is a terrible idea, and if I'm going to succeed in running him out of town, I need to be smarter than that.

I wash my hands off in the sink, then head back outside to load up the bike and take it back again. The thing really doesn't look good though. I take a minute to inspect it, noting the oil staining the ground beside where it was lying. The bike isn't my problem, and Hudson has two brothers who can fix the damn thing while he's injured, but once I load the bike onto my truck and strap it down, instead of taking the road toward Old End, I make a right and head for Ziggy's place instead.

I pull up out front of the old mine shaft and lay on the horn for a second before climbing out of my truck.

It only takes a moment for Ziggy to stroll out, hands in his pockets, eyeing me with interest.

He rubs a hand over his clean-shaven jaw before pointing toward the bike.

"It's the brothers'," I say darkly, loosening the bike straps before unhooking the back of the tray and setting it down. "Think it has an oil leak."

He walks over to help me get the bike down, but I can feel his eyes on me the whole time. I try ignoring him, but it doesn't last.

"The faster this is fixed, the faster they can use it to fuck off."

His stare doesn't let up for another long moment, but then he drops it and shakes his head.

"Don't."

"Didn't say nothing," he mutters so quietly I barely hear him. Ziggy takes the bike and wheels it away from me.

We're down the bottom of the hill that leads up to Hobby Straight and the main road that passes by. It's helpful having Ziggy live here because he's usually the first to hear if someone's come off the road or—like with Hudson—if we have unwelcome visitors in town. And because he's more isolated than the rest of us and I actually trust him, right by his place is where we keep the supply carriages.

The old train cars have been repurposed to house anything and everything the town could need. There are five of them standing side by side, towering over me and pockmarked by years of being beaten by the elements. What were once steely gray are mottled red with rust and browned by years of being blanketed in dirt. Grass and weeds anchor them to the earth, and I don't think there's a soul alive who could move them at this point.

Ziggy parks the bike by the nearest one and pulls out his keys.

"What do you think is wrong with it?" I ask.

He shrugs and unlocks the carriage before pulling the heavy metal door aside. Rows and rows of light bulbs, screws, nails, bolts, brackets, pipes, wiring, and just about anything else you could possibly need for repairs or construction line the internal shelves.

Ziggy grabs a bucket and a handful of other things, then gets to work. I probably could've fumbled my way through it, but you don't fuck around with safety, and when it comes to anything electrical or mechanical, Ziggy is the expert around here.

The silence is broken only by the occasional birdcall, rustle of leaves, or a lone car passing by on the road somewhere far above us.

Normally, this peace is exactly what I need. It's part of the reason I chose to stay out here. Today though, my thoughts are like scurrying mice, and I can't help letting one escape.

"What if they don't leave?"

Ziggy's heavy sigh scatters the mice in my mind. He pauses for a second, one hand resting on the bike, the other on the bucket, and studies me with pity.

"It's not like I can give up on this place."

Ziggy keeps working, but I sense the guardedness from him

too. If we give up, we lose Wilde's End. We lose everything we've built. And losing this place means losing who we are.

It's hard to remember who I was before I came here, and the longer I go not thinking about it, the murkier the details get. Forgetting is something I want, but the more I go into Old End, and the more I consider what the brothers' plans mean for this place, the more those past demons creep out of the holes I've stuffed them into.

I'm close to bringing it up with Ziggy. I know he'd understand, but we've all leaned so heavily on the "don't ask" rule that I don't know whether I could talk about it if I tried. Once it's out there, it's done. Ziggy will know more about me than I know about him, and while I trust Ziggy more than anyone in Wilde's End, even more than Rooney, I know I can't trust anyone with this.

It's the kind of thing I'll take to my grave.

I rub absently at the scars on my arm, and before I can bring up anything else, I ask, "You have everything you need to fix it?"

Ziggy nods and gets to work, leaving me to deal with too many thoughts alone.

# CHAPTER
# FIFTEEN

## HUDSON

When Wilde came back with the bike, I'd perked up, looking for another chance to tease him and draw him into … well, whatever the fuck we have going on. But he only dumped the bike in the middle of the street and took off again.

It's been days, and I haven't seen a glimpse of him. No one has been watching us from the overlook. No one has been messing with our stuff. And when I wake suddenly in the middle of the night, expecting to see him lurking in my room, it's empty.

I'm not saying that nighttime stalkers are a good thing, but you can't set a man up to expect one thing and then take it away completely.

It's fucking rude.

A week ago, I would have said this was a good thing. Now, it's like someone dragging claws down my back. No way in hell am I letting him ignore me like this.

Thankfully, the doc was right about my ankle, and after a few days of taking it easy, I'm able to put weight on it again.

Hart is pissed off that I scratched up the bike, and he's only talking to me because I'm injured, whereas Kennedy won't stop flapping around me like some kind of mother hen. I have to remind myself, daily, that I love my brothers. That the majority of the reason we're here is for them.

Doesn't make it any easier when Hart refuses to hand over the keys to the bike so I can go and hunt down Wilde again. It takes me a few days to acknowledge that was a good call. It's not until my concussion wears off that I realize how bad it was.

"Need anything before I head next door?" Kennedy asks, sticking his worried face into my room.

"I can walk again. I'm fine."

The reassurance doesn't do anything to shift the tight lines by his eyes.

"Just go."

"Okay, but if you need me, yell out. I'll keep the music off."

Despite myself, the way he cares gets to me sometimes. It's one of those rare moments that I remember we really are in this together. The second he disappears, I yell out to him again, and Kennedy's back, eyebrows perked up like a puppy waiting for a treat.

"Sorry I brought up your exes. It was a dick move."

Some of his eagerness fades. "Yeah. I get it."

We're quiet for a moment.

"Is it really that bad that I want to find someone?" he asks, thumb stroking over the wooden doorframe. We both watch as his nail digs an easy groove into the soft timber.

Is it so bad? Objectively, I guess the answer to that from most people would be no. Seeing him hurt again and again is the part I have an issue with.

"It's not you wanting to settle down that's the problem. It's the way you don't care who it's with. You deserve someone who's worthy of you, Kenny. I don't say this enough, but you're a cool guy."

His lips try to pull into a smile, but there's still something getting to him. "Why don't we make a deal, then? If I give up dating for like … six months, you're not allowed to message Sutton in that time either."

That deal catches me off guard, mostly because Sutton has been the last thing on my mind. "Ah … okay."

"I mean it. Even if he messages you, don't respond. Block him if you have to. I'm not the only one who deserves better."

Now I'm following. If I don't reply, Sutton will move on. Even telling him to fuck off keeps him interested because that's exactly how messed up our relationship is. The trade-off is having Kennedy protect himself. Maybe if the three of us focus on nothing else but this place for six months, we'll come out the other side less of a mess than we are now.

"Fine. Deal. No contact."

His hope is hesitant but there. "This will be good for us."

"Now we have to find a way to get through to Hart."

Kennedy widens his eyes doubtfully as he digs further into the wood. "Sometimes I think he enjoys being miserable."

"Maybe. Or maybe he's forgotten how to be anything else."

"That can change, can't it?"

"Of course," I lie, because if there's one thing I don't want, it's for Kennedy to lose that eternal optimism. Plus, I want to believe it too.

There's the sound of a car outside, and I sigh and ease myself to my feet. "Speak of the devil."

"He's hardly the devil."

I pat Kennedy's shoulder on the way past. "He's your twin. You have to say that."

We get to the front door, and I'm expecting Hart to be waiting, attitude radiating from him like always, but our car's not in sight.

I glance back at Kennedy. "You heard a car, right?"

"I thought I did."

I'm embarrassed by how eager I am when I turn the other way, expecting to see Wilde parked on the edge of the forest. He's not there either.

Sunset has already started, and night is creeping in, casting long shadows over the town. It might be a ghost town by name and was slightly creepy when we first got here, but I've seen no evidence of actual ghosts. Is it possible Kennedy and I both just hallucinated the same thing at the same time?

"Weird …"

"Maybe Hart forgot something," I suggest.

Kennedy pulls his phone out to check it. "I've got service, I'll call him."

Then he stays really still so he doesn't lose reception as he clicks on Hart's number and puts the phone on speaker.

"What?" he answers.

"Oh, hey. Just curious when you'll be—"

Headlights flash in the distance.

"Is that you now?" Kennedy finishes.

"Is what me now?"

"Coming up the road?"

From the sounds coming down the line, he's driving.

"No, I'm still an hour out."

"Then …"

I descend the front steps as the car draws closer.

"What's going on?" Hart asks.

"Someone's here."

"What?" It sounds like he hits the gas. "Who is it?"

"Not sure. The car looks black, but I can't see it properly from here."

It's growing closer quickly though. The sun seems to set fast out here, where the hills surround us on three sides, which makes this place darker earlier than it should be. It only takes another minute until the sleek black SUV tears into town and then slows suddenly. The headlights wash over me as it creeps closer, and then the passenger window slides down.

There are four men inside, from what I can see. The one in the passenger side stares me down, and when they're close enough, they slow almost to a stop.

"Ah, hey?" I try, but the man doesn't answer me, and the driver leans over a little so I can see him properly. The lights from inside the car light up his face. He's handsome with a lot of black hair, empty eyes, and teeth tattooed across his mouth and onto both cheeks. Like a skeleton mouth.

"Cool tattoos," I manage, trying not to recoil from the car.

Skeleton man lets out a quick laugh, then stomps on the gas. I watch them leave town and hit the gravel road before their brake lights disappear into the trees.

Who the fuck were they? Based on the whole five-second interaction, I doubt they're here by accident. Are they friends of Wilde's? They didn't *look* friendly, but how the hell would I know. Wilde doesn't exactly look friendly either.

"What's happening?" Hart's voice coming from Kennedy's phone snaps me back to the present.

"Who the fuck were they?"

Kennedy looks like he isn't sure of anything. "Think they're lost?"

"No way. Those weren't the faces of people who were lost."

"Can someone please tell me what the fuck is happening?" Hart demands.

Kennedy turns back to his phone, but my attention is still on the road. Should we *warn* Wilde? I might not like the guy, but I don't want him dealing with whoever the fuck that was alone. Our relationship is a complicated mix of incompatible goals, unhealthy sexual tension, and neither of us being able to stand the other, and yet, I want to go anyway.

Only partially because this gives me an excuse to seek him out.

I stalk over to Kennedy and take the phone from him. "Where are the keys to the bike?"

Hartwell's disdain comes loud and clear down the line. "None of your business."

"Where the fuck are they?"

"There's no way in hell you're getting back on that thing."

Kennedy pulls a face at me that immediately looks guilty. "You've got broken fingers."

"Don't need them to ride." I hold my hand out to Kennedy. "I know you have them."

His eyes flick to the phone, and Hart groans. "For fuck's sake, Kenny. You can't keep a secret to save your life."

"He doesn't like to lie," I defend. "That's not a bad thing."

"Whatever. I'm still over half an hour away and can't stop you from being reckless. Go for a ride. Kill yourself. See if I care."

I hold my hand out to Kennedy, and he looks like he wants to argue for a second before he pulls the keys from his back pocket. The thing is, Kennedy could easily stop me if he wanted to. We've wrestled before for fun, and while I'll never admit it, I really did try to win. He's just a strong motherfucker.

Luckily for me, he's also too sweet for his own good.

We all fall silent as another car approaches, and this one does the same slowdown to stare at us before taking off again.

"Was that another car?" Hart barks.

"It was." I head for the dirt bike. "I'll be back as soon as I can."

They don't bother to argue with me. I guess they know me too well for that.

My ankle doesn't love holding my weight for as long as it has been, but as soon as I get the bike started and take off, it gets relief at last.

I have no idea where I'm going as I hit the dirt path, but I figure if I found Wilde's house once, I can do it again. It's almost completely dark now, and as I round another bend, I spot something glowing through the trees. Like lights, but a fair distance from the gravel road.

I pull to a stop and try to judge the distance, wondering if that's where those cars ended up.

Well, I won't find out from up here.

I take the first track to the right and follow it as far as I can before it branches off again and again. I'm going deeper into the forest, loudly announcing my approach and trying to keep the lights in sight while I deal with the trees and strangled bushes blocking my view.

The closer I get, the less it looks like cars and the more it looks like something bigger. I finally find a wider path, wide enough for a car, that looks like it will lead me in the right direction.

I slow as I approach, taking in the solid, dark timber wall that's maybe fifteen feet high and the chaos of bulky SUVs, trucks, and vans parked right beside it.

*What the fuck is going on?*

I park the bike and climb off, pacing closer until I find a break in the wall that must serve as the entrance. Two people are standing there talking to Booker, and as I watch, he nods, and they pass, entering the weird building.

"Hey, Doc," I say, stepping out of the shadows. He doesn't look at all surprised to see me.

"Sorry, Hudson. It isn't time to remove your stitches yet. Come back later."

"You know I'm not here about that." My gaze climbs the large exterior wall. "What is this?"

"What is what? Life? The universe? Our creation?"

I pin him with a glare. "What's going on inside? Just behind you. Why are all these cars here? Is it a party or something?"

Booker's lips tremble. "Or something."

"Want to be more specific?"

"Not especially."

"Can you anyway?"

That sweet face lights up. "It must be so irritating for you not to know."

Unable to stop myself, I say, "Considering I should know what's happening in my own town, yeah. It's fucking irritating."

His eyes narrow a little while his smile stays in place. "Wilde's town."

"Where is he anyway?"

"If he wanted you to know, he would have told you."

He can't exactly tell me anything if I haven't seen him. "He hasn't been around since I got injured." I force a casual shrug. "Maybe he's backing down."

"I wouldn't hold your breath."

I'm putting an end to this. I go to step around Booker and walk inside, but he immediately blocks my path.

"You're not on the list."

"Check it again."

"Don't need to. I wrote it."

I bite back the need to swear at him. I'm going to get through this conversation without getting angry and insulting him. I can do it. "Then it shouldn't be so hard for you to add me. Hudson Bellamy. Two *L*s."

"Damn, forgot my pen."

I go to sidestep him again, but Booker's hand snaps tight around my right wrist with a strength I'm not expecting. He lifts my injured hand in front of my face. "Don't make me hurt you again," he whispers.

"I don't see the big deal with letting me past." My voice is bordering on anger and pain, but I somehow keep it steady.

"The big deal is that this is a closed event. You were not invited. So I suggest you leave before things get nasty." He releases my wrist with a shove backward, and I stumble a step.

"Can I at least talk to Wilde, then?"

Booker studies me. "No."

My fingernails are digging into my good palm as I talk myself out of punching him.

"Not here," he adds, and that gets my anger under control. "But I can tell you where he'll be after this."

"And where's that?"

"Wayward. As soon as he's done, he'll head down there. He does every night that we have a—one of these *events* on—for as long as I can remember."

Wayward. It's two hours away.

Still, it looks like I'm not going to get anything out of Booker, and the town is bringing back a memory.

Wayward is where Wilde goes to hook up. It's a weird bit of information to retain, but I'm glad I did because I have an idea forming.

And Wilde is going to hate it.

# CHAPTER
# SIXTEEN

## WILDE

'm sorer than usual after a Peril match. Foley managed to beat me tonight, but not before he got a good shot to my shoulder with his post and left a huge welt on my thigh as he shoved me off. I don't take losing lightly, but I take it even worse after a week where my focus hasn't been where it belongs.

I have no one to blame for the loss but myself. Even the last two days of nonstop practice didn't have me ready to beat that asshole, and it's a spit on my pride to see him take money we could have used in Wilde's End and leave with it.

The only thing that will save tonight is a good fuck, and it's not going to be pretty. Wayward isn't exactly a huge queer town, but a lot of the people who come to the Peril matches tend to head there afterward. The bar we built in Wilde's End, affectionately called the Cutty, isn't set up for hundreds of people, and we keep its existence quiet from non-locals because it's our little sanctuary. So the Wayward Traveler bar ends up filled to the brim, which draws in the locals on the third Saturday of the month to drink up a storm with us.

It also means I have a steady group of discreet men to choose from. We're all good with doing the no names, just sex thing, and it's what I need more than anything right now. Someone who will let me take this pent-up aggression out on them and then forget about them once we're done.

I pull up in the already full parking lot and leave the paved parking spaces to find a place on the grass beside it. Inside is as busy as I'm expecting, and I order a beer to give myself something to do while I take stock of who's here.

Foley and his friends are over in a corner, surrounded by a ring of hangers-on from some of the other towns. He likes attention—I'm assuming that's the explanation for his face tattoos—whereas I'm happier to go unnoticed.

A few familiar faces pop up in the crowd that I recognize from Peril, and I turn my back on most of them. I'm not here to analyze the matches or talk favorites or to have people commiserate with my loss. I *should* have lost. I deserved it. My focus has been too split lately.

"Almost didn't see you there."

I nearly choke on the sip I've taken, but I refuse to turn toward the voice. There's no fucking way Hudson is here, and even if he is, I'm not going to acknowledge it.

"Are we playing the quiet game again?" he asks. "It's okay, you can give it up. I'm never going to win, so you might as well take pity on me."

*Eyes forward, eyes forward, eyes forward.*

"So what were all those cars doing in Wilde's End tonight? I know you had some kind of event on, and I'm a little offended that I wasn't invited."

I need strength. Unfortunately, after draining my drink, I can confirm it isn't in the bottom of the glass. "And why would you expect an invitation?"

"Good manners."

"Not out here." Before I'm even aware of it, I give in. I turn toward where Hudson is leaning, one elbow on the bar, his body turned toward me, and I'm caught off guard by how close he's standing. He's one inhumanly good-looking man, and I don't need him in my line of sight when being in this place makes me horny enough as it is.

He doesn't back up out of my space though.

"Go away."

He grins, and I hate that by sitting on this stool, it makes him slightly taller than me. "I will once I have my answers."

"You don't need answers. You need—"

"To leave. Uh-huh. Let's pretend like that's even a possibility and move on to something new."

The way he so easily brushes me aside has my teeth on edge. "Why are you here?"

"I followed you."

I'd assumed as much but didn't think he'd admit it. "*Why?*"

"Because this is where you come to hook up, right?" He leans closer, that smug look turning to something hungrier. "Figured that's enough incentive to trade for my answers."

"What is?"

"The fact I'm going to cockblock you all night until you tell me what the event was."

I'd call his bluff, but there's nothing in his expression that would make me doubt him. He's only a few inches away, holding my gaze, and so, instead of playing into his tantrum, I give him what he wants.

Because I'm not walking out of this place before I've had an orgasm, and the sooner he's out of my way, the sooner I can make that happen.

"Fine. Once a month, we have our Peril matches. People come from out of town because it's the largest illegal fighting event where we don't have to deal with the authorities getting too nosy. And we make a lot of money out of it. It's how we keep the town supplied with what we need."

"And that's where the skull face man was going?"

*Skull face*? "You saw Foley?"

"I dunno, did I?"

I point through the crowd and Hudson's gaze follows. "Yep, that's skull face. He drove through town."

"Then yes. He was here for Peril." I lean in, tilting my mouth by his ear and ignoring that bubble gum smell he's always wrapped in. "Now, get the fuck out of my face unless you're planning to suck my cock yourself."

I'm expecting Hudson to retreat, to tell me to get fucked and storm away, or get angry like I've seen him do more times than I can count. But instead, his cheek skims mine as he turns his head, and then we're face-to-face with nowhere to go. I'm not expecting the raw challenge written all over his expression.

"Let's do it, then."

"What?"

His tongue wets his lips as his voice drops. "Fuck me."

I sneer and go to push him back, but he forces my knees wider and steps between them.

"I'm serious. If you hate me that much, think about how good it will feel to let that hatred out on me. To fuck me so hard it hurts. Or use my mouth until I can't breathe."

I can already picture doing exactly that. My cock is making its interest known in a more demanding way now, and I have to reposition it away from my fly.

Hudson clocks the movement, and his gaze stays locked on my groin.

"Why would I do that when there are plenty of willing guys in the bar who I can trust not to bite my cock off?"

He smirks at the question. "It's because you can't trust me—that makes it fun. It's because you know I won't make it easy for you. I'll fight you every step of the way, and I'll make sure you know I hate it as much as you do." This time, his mouth finds my ear. "But you'll make me come anyway. Because of how raw and fucked-up it is."

"Why the hell would you want that?" But I think I know. It's the same reason I want it too. I'm hard, and I'm so fucking tempted by the images he's putting in my head. Dominating Hudson, finally feeling like I get to win with him, has an appeal greater than sex.

"Fucking someone who hates you is the best kind of sex."

"Done that a lot, have you?" I ask dryly, but is it any better than fucking someone who doesn't even know my name? Both ways get the outcome I came here for. I've never been all that picky about where I stick it.

"I don't think I've ever fucked a guy who *does* like me, honestly."

"Sounds like all the men you know have good taste." Like my body knows we're doing this before I've even made up my mind, I widen my legs and pull him in closer.

There's no hiding how hard we are from each other. No covering up that our hearts are racing like a fucking madman's. No hiding that deep, destructive want in his eyes that I'm sure is filling mine as well.

That fucking bubble gum scent makes me want to lick the man's skin, but I hold back because I know better. He wants it quick and dirty? That's my fucking specialty. I'm roaring with the need to get out all this frustration on him. He's dangerous, a threat to my town and my life, and yet he's so fucking hot I can't focus on doing what I need to. Maybe fucking him will change that. Maybe showing him exactly how much I despise him will make him think twice about the town.

Or maybe we'll just fuck. And get off. And then tomorrow, we'll be back to being unable to stand the sight of each other.

At least leaning into the tension will make it snap. The fun of the pursuit is finally over when I know I can get what I want, and for right now, that's Hudson. It's been a long, long time since I've wanted someone the way I want Hudson.

"This is what's going to happen," I tell him in a low voice. "You're going to go into the bathrooms. You're going to let yourself into the last stall, and then you're going to prep your ass for me. I have no interest in touching you. No interest in kissing you. I'm going to have one more drink, then I'm going to use your hole and leave."

He's breathing heavier. "And how do I know you're not going to run out on me?"

I try to ignore the rasp in his voice. "You don't. Remember? The fun is that we don't trust each other." Then I take his uninjured hand and set it over my straining cock. "But whether it's you or someone else, I'm taking care of this in there. Might as well give me an easy option."

"You wish I was easy."

"Guess we're about to find out."

He rubs me through my jeans, and it's a mission not to moan. The bar is so crowded that no one is paying attention to us, but if I start making obscene noises, that will change pretty fucking quickly.

I don't think I've ever done this before, and I'm surprised how much I'm into it. I might not know Hudson well, but I know him outside of this bar, and that's usually something I avoid. And while my dick might be hard, it doesn't change that I really do, all the way to my core, hate the sight of him.

Being attracted to him only makes that hatred deeper.

Because I hate *myself* too for being this weak over him.

"Who knows?" Hudson breathes, sounding half a second away from coming himself. I'm so tuned in to his every breath, every movement, every little twitch of his face. Like he's the only one who exists. "Maybe I'll be the one to stand *you* up."

Then he takes a sudden step away. The sounds and colors of the bar come rushing back to me, and I'm panting as I look around.

Hudson backs up again, that raw want and taunting smirk plastered on his face. "Better drink fast," he says, and then the crowd swallows him up, and I'm left to work through what the fuck I'm doing.

And even though I can't answer that question, I know I'm doing it anyway.

# CHAPTER
# SEVENTEEN

## HUDSON

Of the two lightbulbs hanging from the bathroom ceiling, only one of them works. The broken one pulses and dies every few seconds, and I personally think this place looks better when you can't see it at all. The dark gray stalls suck the light from the room and remind me of an office block, the mirrors have tarnished in the corners, and the tiles above the sink have come away in places. Then the whole room is graffitied so heavily it could almost pass as street art. If it weren't for the word *fuck* repeated more times than I can count.

I let myself into the last stall and lock it behind me. It's going to be a tight fit once Wilde joins me, and my heart is racing over the thought. I'm shamefully hard over him, and it's this weird mix of horny and hatred as I wonder how many men he's been in here with.

My pants are uncomfortably tight over my cock, and I press down on it, warning it to behave. It doesn't matter how many transactional fucks he's had here because I'm determined to be the one he doesn't forget. I want to rot his brain.

The main door opens with a slight scrape and a temporary burst of music before it's cut off again. It's followed by footsteps that have heady anticipation twisting my gut so hard I'm lightheaded.

A firm rap on the door and then a reluctant, "Open it, Hudson."

I stare at the lock for a moment before I reach for it, and almost the second I have it open, Wilde pushes through the door, then slams and locks it again.

My cock is unprepared to have his focus on me.

"You don't look ready."

I hold up my injured hand between us. "There was a problem with your plan." And even if there wasn't, I would have come up with some excuse. He wants to use me? He's going to have to work for it.

Wilde eyes my broken fingers with disgust. "Use your other hand."

"It's just not the same."

He turns, like he's about to leave, so I shift until I'm leaning against the door. Then I open my pants. Wilde watches as I fumble with my button, then slowly tug down my fly. Having his eyes on me is heating me from the inside out, and while I told myself I was coming here to get answers, the fact that I didn't put on underwear makes it hard to deny my real plan.

As soon as my fly is down far enough, my cock pushes through the gap.

"Still want to leave?" I ask, voice deeper than it normally is.

"Never said I did."

"Then get to work."

He's fighting himself, but his gaze is hungry, and it only turns me on more. "Turn around."

He should know me better than that. "No."

"No?"

I kick my left leg out of my jeans and set my knee on the stall wall. "No."

The same anger that usually fills me crosses his face, but I don't wait for it to take hold. I grab his hand and lift it to my mouth, then suck two fingers inside.

Wilde's silent as he watches me suck on them, getting them nice and wet before I release him, tongue dragging from his knuckles to the tip of his index finger. He doesn't make a move, and this time, I keep my mouth shut too. As much as I love playing with him, I'm not forcing him into anything, and with the way Wilde is looking at me, I doubt he needs any more convincing. So I give him all the time he needs to debate over doing it my way or forcing me to turn around.

I'm caught by surprise when he settles a heavy hand above my head, gripping the top of the door, and steps in. My nerves rush in my ears as his glare meets mine and his wet fingers brush my hole. I'm expecting him to be rough, maybe painful, but even with a look that clearly says he wants to hurt me, his touch is soft. He massages the area around my hole until I'm relaxed enough for him to press one finger slowly inside.

"How many times have you had sex in here?" I ask.

He grunts, and his thick finger fills me completely. "Plenty."

"That's not a number."

"I don't have a number. Keeping count is ridiculous." His tone tells me to back off, so of course, I do the math.

"Every month. That's twelve times a year. For … how many years?"

"Too many."

"Ten?"

"*Too many.*"

"Let's say at least ten. So a hundred and twenty times. One hundred and twenty times you've been in this same spot with who knows how many men."

Wilde's glare deepens, but he doesn't stop fucking me with his finger.

"And it will be this time that's burned into your memory for the rest of your life."

He actually chuckles. Dark and smooth, the confidence of it takes up space in my chest. "That's a bold claim."

"Doesn't make it any less true."

He's only a few inches away, and when he adds a second finger, a relieved *huh* puffs from my lips. The gleam that fills his eyes is delighted to pull that sound from me, but it's all I'm planning to give him. Just enough so he knows how into this I am, but not enough to satisfy. Not yet.

"Me though?" I continue. "I don't think I've ever been more bored. Strange way to make it memorable for me."

He shoves both fingers into my hole, hard, choking a second's breath from me as I adjust to the burn. He stretches me open, brushing my prostate without giving it any real attention, and I'm vibrating at how good it feels.

"I expected better," I have to force through my teeth because if I separate them, I might do something as stupid as moan.

"Tell that to your cock."

"Why? It's not picky."

Somehow, the distance between us has tightened, and Wilde's gray eyes are the only things I can see. They're darker than I'm used to, and his black eyelashes are enough to shield most of what he's thinking from me. Except the very clear message he's projecting: I'm the last person he wants to fuck and he can't help doing it anyway.

I pick up on that thought easily because it's the exact same one I'm having. Being able to admit that my attraction to him is surface-deep is something I can thank Sutton for. He never tried to be anything other than an asshole, and I still remember the day I distinctly realized that I didn't like him. At all. There was nothing about him as a person that appealed to me, but he was hot, and that's apparently all my dick cared about.

I can't even claim that Wilde's hot. His beard hides too much of his face.

But that huge body, steady glare, and refusal to take things easy on me is a new low for my cock to sink to, and I'm letting it get away with the shitty standards anyway.

A tiny twitch meets the corner of his lips. "You're riding my fingers hard for someone who's bored."

Fuck. I didn't even notice the way my hips were grinding back into him. "Just getting impatient for you to give me more."

"You'll get more when you shut that fucking mouth of yours."

"Guess your cock is going to be disappointed because I don't plan on that happening."

He yanks his fingers from me, spits on them, and then places them back at my entrance. This time when he pushes inside, he uses all three, and my balls tighten as I force myself to relax into the stretch.

"Look at that. Quiet."

"You try talking while someone shoves three fingers up your ass."

"Maybe I will one day." His nose almost brushes mine. "I'll be sure to let you know how I go."

I manage a husky laugh. "Try not to think of me when you do. The poor other guy will never live up to this."

"This?" The word sounds amused. "Me fully dressed while I finger you up against a door? I don't think I've done this since high school."

"You're the one too scared to stick your dick in me."

"You really think a lot of yourself."

"Well, I'm ready. You know I'm ready. What other reason would you have for still playing with my ass?"

"Maybe the fact you haven't stopped riding my hand since I started."

God fucking damn him. He has a point, but can he blame me? This tiny cubicle has me feverish, and with next to no room between our bodies, I'm close to begging him for more. The fingers aren't enough, and every time I tilt my hips forward, the material from his shirt brushes over the tip of my cock, leaving it too needy for me to see straight. I'd be jerking off by now if I didn't need my good hand to keep balance.

"You know what?" Wilde says. "I think it's going to be the other way around. You're the one who won't be able to forget me."

I open my mouth, but he cuts me off before I can talk.

"And don't give me that bored bullshit. You're fucking my fingers like you've been sex starved for years."

"Only weeks. Weeks is enough."

He strokes in again before slowly withdrawing all the way and leaving me empty.

I grunt. "Now will you fuck me?"

Wilde lets go of the door and steps back, then pulls a condom from his pocket. "Since you made me prep you, it's your turn to work for it. Pull me out, put that on, then lube up my dick."

"I have broken fingers, you jerk."

"Only three. The other seven have no issues."

I'm torn between arguing the point and wanting to be fucked, but I already know which one will win. I carefully lower my leg back to the ground and test putting weight on it before I snatch the condom he's holding out to me. If I could get my dick out, his shouldn't be a problem, and it's lucky that my thumb and forefinger were the two that escaped injury.

Wilde's jeans are older than mine, which means the buttons along the front loosen easier than the one on my pants. I get them undone, shove his jeans down to his thighs, and then work on getting his briefs to follow. His dick springs forward, heavy and eager enough to make mine throb. It's big—not huge—but big enough that I'll feel him for a day or two after this.

There's nothing I want more. The hunger I have for him has unseated anything rational that might have been lurking in my mind, and no part of me wants to back out of this now. I tear the condom wrapper open with my teeth and pull it out. I'm ready to feel him, to wrap my hand around his cock and stroke him until he forgets he hates me, but I'm not going to give in to that urge. Instead, I roll the condom down his shaft, lingering for that bit longer than I should.

He hands over the lube next. I squeeze the packet out into my hand, then finally get the chance I've been waiting for and take him in my palm. Fuck, I hate how sexy his cock is, and my only hope now for him being a terrible fuck is that he has no idea how to get a man off with this thing.

Because if he's as good at using his dick as I think he might be, I'm in a world of trouble.

Forget Sutton. I think I've found a new bad habit.

# CHAPTER
# EIGHTEEN



Hudson's hand is enough to make me want to blow. Even through the condom, I can feel the warmth of his palm, the confident, almost cocky, way he strokes me like he's somehow got the right to touch me the way he is.

I hate that it's a turn-on, even more so when he gives up the pretense of rubbing in the lube and takes a firm grip around my shaft. His eyes flick up my way, those long eyelashes carving out shadows in the dark, and I can't stand it anymore.

I grab his hips and turn him, then press him against the door. My cock rests in the delicious groove between his cheeks as my mouth finds his ear. "We're doing it my way."

"Aww, what's wrong?" he taunts. "Don't want to look into my eyes as you fuck me?"

"If I did that, I wouldn't be able to pretend you were literally anyone else." As much as I'd love for that to happen though, I already know it would be impossible. His sweet scent is so distinctly him, and I don't believe for a second that he'll shut up long enough for my imagination to take over.

"Who's your fantasy man?" he asks, purposefully taunting me. "Who do you wish you were fucking right now?"

Those are two very, very different answers. I don't have a fantasy man. I have no idea about celebrities—both on purpose and as a result of living out here—but I also don't like the thought of building someone up in my head only to be disappointed. I'm not built for settling down, so it's never been something worth thinking about.

As for who I wish I were fucking? I grab my cock and reposition it between his cheeks. Given the way he's stirred me up to a point where I'm torn on whether I want to fuck him or fight him, I might as well get one of them out of the way to find my answer. Process of elimination or whatever.

He pushes back, trying to take me, but I refuse to let him. Denying Hudson what he wants only makes my dick harder, and it really is a mystery how I've been able to hold it together so far. If I weren't playing with him, I'd already be well on my way to an orgasm.

"Since you love talking so much," I say, teasing him as I rub my tip over his hole, "I want you to say something for me."

"My mouth doesn't work like that."

"Well, it'll learn if you want to be fucked tonight."

He grunts, and I wait him out. Wait for the eventual agreement I know I'll get. "What is it?"

"I want you to tell me how much you need my cock."

"I need your cock."

The monotone almost makes me laugh, but I wrap my free hand in his hair instead. I tighten my grip, tilting his head back until his eyes find mine. "Tell me."

The defiance in his gaze is maybe the hottest thing I've ever seen. "If you don't give it to me," he rasps, "I'm going to go out of my fucking mind."

The lust coursing through me hums at that, and I reward him by pushing inside. I don't go deep, and it's torture for me as much as it is him. The way he molds around my tip is firm, heavenly pressure, and it takes every bit of strength I have not to give in and rail him.

"What else?" I release his hair and plant both hands on his hips to stop him from taking any more.

"*God fucking dammit*, you're an asshole."

"Tell me."

"I'd rather you stopped playing games."

"But I thought you loved games?"

The noise in his chest sounds angry. "Fuck me already."

"Unlucky for you, I'm the one in control here, and it's my cock you need. So give me what I want, and I'll give you what you want."

His head *thunks* against the stall door. "You're going to use this against me, aren't you?"

"Possibly."

"Fuck you." He tries to shove back again, but I'm holding him too tight. "*Urg*. Fine. I'm going to die if you don't give it to me. If you don't stick your cock inside me, I'm going to be so goddamn frustrated that I walk out there and punch every fucking person in this fucking bar. Now, give me what I need, Wilde, before I go from wanting to hate fuck you to just hating you, and that's not going to get me off."

I'm not expecting my chuckle, but I fill his ear with it as I give in and sink into his desperate hole. There's nothing better than fucking someone. Than feeling how their body gives way to mine and my cock is sucked in by some undeniable force that makes it impossible to want to stop. Hudson's ass is firm and round, and under any other circumstance, I'd take my time to appreciate it, but this is about getting off, and that's it.

I'm balls-deep inside of him when I hook my arm under the knee of his injured leg and lift it. "Better hold on," I warn him.

Hudson grips the top of the stall door. "Hurry up before I fall asleep already."

I pull back and snap my hips forward, hard enough to send a jolt through him. He cries out, and it fills my gut with this deep, feral need that is so far beyond what I'm used to that I don't know how to handle it.

I do it again. And again. Faster and harder each time until Hudson's arm muscles tense under his skin as he white-knuckles the door.

"Awake yet, city boy?"

"You better have more than that."

His breathless reply spurs me on. I set a punishing pace on his ass, my cock thrumming in his tight hold as I grip his thigh and his hip and give him everything I've got. I've heard people fucking in here more than enough times that I don't bother trying to keep quiet, and with the way our skin is slapping together, it would be pointless anyway.

It's getting humid in the small cubicle. A mix of our proximity, the heavy breathing, and the way I haven't slowed down in my mission to get him off. Now we've started, I want this to be over with because as soon as the high wears off, I know what comes next.

Complete disappointment in myself and my standards.

But who needs standards when going against all your morals feels this good?

Sweat prickles my back, a steady rattle fills the room with each thrust that sends Hudson into the door, and when I glance down in the dim light and watch the way my cock pulls out and then sinks deep back into his body, it's the kind of high that makes me lightheaded.

My cock is in bliss, and I'm getting so damn close that my balls have filled with that tingly pressure I've been chasing.

Fuck, I needed this.

An orgasm.

With anyone.

I've almost forgotten it's Hudson until he talks.

"Touch me."

"Touch yourself," I throw back.

"I'm worried if I let go … that I'll go face-first … into the door … and break my nose."

"Risk you'll have to take."

He impatiently pushes back to meet my thrusts. "Fucking asshole."

"Not new information."

"You're the worst fuck I've ever had."

I ignore him. I'd be offended if he wasn't moaning like he can't get enough.

"I thought that cock would split me open. Can barely feel it."

We both know that's a lie. I can see exactly how stretched his hole is around me.

He goes to say something else, but I've had enough. I pull my shirt over my head and press against his back. Then, grinding my cock deep into him, I reach up and stuff my shirt into his mouth.

"You say one more word and this ends," I warn him.

His groan reaches his chest, and I swear it vibrates through to me. I wait for his teeth to clench down on my shirt before I release it.

The plan is to back off again, but this close to him, feeling the heat radiating off his back, nose full of his scent, hard chest under my palm … it all takes over and wipes my mind blank. My hand finds its way up his shirt to his nipple, fingertips trailing over the tiny peak, thrusts picking up pace until I'm pounding into him like I've been dying to. My heavy breathing is right by his ear, and he's working double time against all the words he has to keep inside. I can only imagine what would be coming out of his mouth if he could, and I'd bet that all of it would both irritate and turn me on.

Instead, I'm left to listen to the muffled noise of the cubicle rattling against us and the slap of skin on skin as I drive into him, wanting and needing more. My pants around my thighs have me locked in place, but this isn't going to take long enough to bother taking them off.

Hudson's aggressive as he rides my cock, muscular body moving so fast I've forgotten where I end and he begins, and as we fuck, I slowly dip from that place where I'm attached to what's happening and give in to the orgasm wanting to take over.

That rippling feeling filling my limbs and shuddering down my spine. It's too much and not enough all at once. I can't get there fast enough. I'm driving toward the edge, mind blank of anything but the full-body pleasure coursing through me, and then the pressure snaps all at once, and I unleash. I gasp with sudden relief, thrusting slower, more purposefully as I fill the condom. It takes a second for me to become aware of my heavy breathing, and my forehead drops forward onto his shoulder as I steady myself.

Hudson's frustrated grunt reminds me he's still there.

What sounds like a smothered *touch me* comes from around my shirt, and I'm still fuzzy enough that I pull out, put his back to the door, and then drop to my knees.

I wrap my mouth around his cock and sink down on it until he breaches my throat. Hudson's fist thumps against the door, and when I look up at him, his arms are bowed back and gripping the top again, while his eyes are locked on me. With my shirt gagging him, he's never looked sexier.

The precum flooding my taste buds tells me he's already close. I work his dick with my tongue, sucking hard, and then slide my fingers back into his hole.

Hudson groans, and it only takes a few thrusts into my mouth before he comes. I swallow every drop and lick him clean before I push back to my feet.

Looking at him is a mistake.

His eyes have that glossy look of a good orgasm, and he still hasn't spit out my shirt. My heart is beating wildly from everything that happened as I wait for the reality to sink in. I step closer. Hudson's watching me curiously, and I almost want him to say something that's going to piss me off, but all he does is release the door and flex his unbroken fingers.

I reach for my shirt, and it takes a second of staring at each other before he lets it free.

Hudson's panting too, cheeks flushed red and usually smart mouth settled.

The cubicle feels so much smaller now.

I pull my shirt back over my head, remove the condom and tie it off, then do up my pants.

Hudson doesn't move until I lift his hand and drop the used condom into it.

"I'm sure you can handle this," I say, and then I unlock the door and pull it open before he's even had a chance to reply.

There's no point hanging around any longer.

I got what I came here for.

# CHAPTER
## NINETEEN

## HUDSON

I will never admit it out loud, but I think that was the best sex I've ever had. Considering it was in a bathroom that looked infested with bacteria, that's really saying something. It's been hours since I got home, the sun is well and truly up, and I can still feel that deep ache from Wilde's cock filling me to the point I can't feel my legs.

Considering how much pain I've been in lately, it's an improvement.

I stretch out across my bed, feeling like the stress of the past few weeks has been sucked from my body, and when I think about it, it sort of has. Wilde did *something* with that blow job. Something that dried up every word I'd ever spoken and left my mind blissfully blank.

My fingers are still stiff from my deathlike grip on the door, and even as I climb to my feet and hunt down some clean clothes, flashes of the sex we had keep filling my memories.

The way he took control, the way he manhandled me, the way I could barely breathe with how hard and fast he was fucking me.

I go to pull on my shorts when I'm distracted by the bruises on my thigh. Four circles, perfectly in line to match Wilde's large hand. A smile tugs the corners of my lips as I run my finger over them, remembering the way he hoisted my leg from the ground. I want to believe he held my weight to make sure I didn't reinjure my ankle, but knowing him, the most likely reason was so that I couldn't run away.

Like I was going anywhere.

In fact, I'm desperate for it to happen again.

I'm only partially disappointed in myself as I do up my shorts and tug a T-shirt on. I really should be used to making terrible decisions by now, and yet every day, I wake up hoping I'll have suddenly changed.

If anything, I think I'm getting worse.

Sutton might have been a dick, but he never threatened me, and yet thinking of Wilde makes Sutton fade into disinterest.

Guess it'll be easier for me to keep my word to Kennedy, even if this is the exact opposite of what he wanted.

I follow the smell of coffee to the kitchen, a twinge hitting my ankle with every other step, and find Hartwell pouring himself a pot as Kennedy's whistling comes from outside.

Hart turns his glare on me. "Make him stop. No one should be so happy this early."

"I dunno …" I match Kennedy's whistling for a second. "Seems like a great day to me."

He scowls, hugging his mug between his hands as he leans against the counter and watches me pour my own cup. Somehow, he's wearing a hoodie with his gym shorts, even though it's already warming up. "I hate you both."

"And we love you very, very much, pumpkin."

"You're happy."

"I'm always happy."

I feel the searching gaze from under his hood as he drags it from my head to my feet. "Nope. This is actually happy. Not that fake shit you think we don't notice you putting on."

Even though I know I shouldn't say anything, I also don't see the point in keeping secrets from him. We all know the worst parts of each other, and this will only reinforce what a fuckup I am. "I got laid."

"About time." He tilts his head. "You weren't gone long enough to head home though, so I'm guessing it wasn't Sutt-fuck."

"Nope. I promised Kennedy I'm done with him."

Hart snorts his disbelief, which would irritate me if I hadn't said I was done with Sutton a hundred times already.

"It was Wilde."

Coffee shoots from Hart's mouth as he chokes on the sip he just took. I thump him on the back through his coughing, and it's not until he stops that I realize we're not alone.

"Wilde?" Kennedy echoes.

Something twists in my gut, but I force the smile to stay in place. "Yeah. Shocking, huh? I knew that asshole wanted me."

My brother studies my face, and I try to ignore the disappointment I can feel directed my way. "You knew why I wanted you to block Sutton."

"Yeah, he was a dick."

"And you deserved better! How is Wilde *better*? I'd actually argue that he's *worse*."

The problem is that I agree with him. "It was a one and done. Relax."

Kennedy and Hart might look almost identical, but I'm not

used to the glare coming from my sweet brother. "It's *never* one and done with you."

"Last I checked, that was my business."

"He has a point," Hart backs me up, sounding like he's already over the conversation.

He's on the receiving end of Kennedy's glare this time. "So you're just going to support him through this stupid idea?"

"I'm here, aren't I?" He takes another sip of his coffee. "I think that proves I support you both through stupid ideas."

Okay, so maybe I *shouldn't* have told them about fucking Wilde. Next time, I know to keep things to myself, no matter how badly I want to talk about it.

"Forget I said anything."

Kennedy pinches the bridge of his nose. "I'm going for a walk."

Neither of us answers as he leaves.

"Interesting plan," Hart muses. "Every time Wilde tries to run us out of town, you're just going to bend over and distract him?"

"Fuck you."

"Valid question from where I'm standing."

The most irritating part of it is that I can't even be mad at him. Maybe if I at least regretted it, I could argue the point, but I don't. I loved every second his dick was inside me, and if he showed up for another round, I'd be ready for him.

Hell, I'm *hoping* for it.

I've been fucked until I'm raw and possibly blew out one of my stitches, but I don't even care. I want to be back in that fucking bar again.

Every month. He's there every month.

So even if Wilde tries to pretend like it never happened, I'll be able to find him there and convince him to do it again.

I'm hopeful I won't have to wait that long. There's no way

Wilde didn't leave there feeling as satisfied as I did, and if that's the case, I give him a few days, max, before he comes looking for it again.

I can wait him out.

Like I told Wilde, I'm having fun with his games.

The demolition of the houses went quickly, and now we're up to the annoying part: moving walls, rewiring the electrical, shifting and updating the plumbing. This is the part we normally get tradesmen in for, and while the plumbing is something we can do ourselves, none of us are good with electrical, so that, minimum, we'll need to hire out.

Our problem is that even if we can find someone qualified in Wayward, we'll be paying them to drive there and back again each day. It's not like we have somewhere livable that we can offer them for the time it takes to get these houses right.

That's the worst part about being so fucking remote. Where we can market it in our favor when it comes to selling, getting us to that stage might take longer than I originally planned.

Maybe we can convince one of the electricians we've worked with in the past to bunk with us for a few weeks and eat the difference in offering them more money.

I need to trust that we'll find a solution like we normally do.

We work our asses off for the next few days, and even with my broken fingers, I try not to let it slow me down. I'm stupidly restricted and still can't do any heavy lifting, but I'm stubborn enough to push through it. The harder I work, the less time there is to think about things … like the reason Wilde hasn't shown his face once.

We're still being watched, but it's never him. I catch sight of someone up on that outlook every morning and afternoon, and because I know they'll be reporting back to that asshole, I always offer them a friendly wave.

Yes, we see you. No, we don't give a shit.

Nothing they do or say is going to stop what we're working on, and every day, I wake up expecting to find some new shit to deal with. It doesn't come.

I'm not sure why that throws me so much. Has Wilde given up? It would be a good thing if he had, but I doubt he's the kind of guy who throws the towel in that easily. Which makes me think he's planning something bigger than stolen hot plates and broken windows.

And how fucked-up is it that I want him to hit us with it already?

Not so I can get whatever it is out of the way, but because I'll have his attention again. Three days of being ignored have me working my way out of my skin.

It has nothing to do with the sex.

I can get that anywhere.

It's not important.

But him thinking he can fuck me and then act like I don't exist after making my life hell for the last few months? Yeah, I'm not letting him get away with that.

"You getting them out today?" Kennedy asks, pointing at his chest. He's been more reserved since our argument, and I'm trying to ignore the guilt that jabs at me whenever we're in the same room.

It takes me a second to realize he means the stitches. "Huh. I totally forgot."

The thought of visiting Booker to have them removed is unsettling, but going back into the forest means getting closer to

Wilde, and who knows? Maybe the sound of the dirt bike so close will bring him out of hiding.

"It's been a week."

I nod at the reminder. "Yeah, I'll head down when we're done here."

"I can't believe they have an actual doctor out here."

I think calling Booker an *actual* doctor is pushing things, but I can't deny that he knows what he's talking about.

Kennedy reaches over and takes the drill from my hand. "I'm breaking for lunch, and there isn't a whole lot else for us to do today. Go down now, and at least you'll be back before it's dark."

I don't want to leave him with it, but I take the dismissal for what it is. Kennedy is one of those people where you genuinely feel like shit for letting them down. I want to fix things and get his happiness back, but the only way I can think of to do that is by promising him that whatever happened with me and Wilde is done.

But it would be a lie.

Because even with Wilde disappearing on me, I'm almost positive it will happen again.

You don't have sex like we did and then walk away unaffected.

# CHAPTER
# TWENTY



stay focused. Every day, I have my list, and I get to work. Fixing fences and repairing houses, checking the land for any areas that are prone to fires once the peak of summer hits. I train in the mornings, and late afternoons, I visit the Cutty and try to be social. I work myself to exhaustion until it's late, and the only things I want to do are eat and pass out.

So far, it's working for me.

But it's only been three days, and there's no way this is sustainable.

I stop my truck along the side of my house, tired from a long day helping the Raylons with the extra bedroom they're adding to their place. JJ has just turned fourteen, and he's past old enough to have his own room, so Rooney, Ziggy, and I lent Paul and Arleen a hand with getting the frame built properly.

It was on the tip of my tongue, so many times, to ask Gracie to make me another pot like the one Hudson broke. She's always been such a sweet kid, but asking for a gift doesn't feel the same.

So I'm left to stare at that empty place on the table where it should still be while I deal with all these mixed feelings Hudson brings out in me.

I climb out of my truck, cursing that it's still too early for bed. The sun is high enough that I have a few hours to fill before I can realistically sleep, and for half a second, I debate jumping back in the cab and heading to the ridge that overlooks Old End.

But I'm not going to give in to that temptation because I know exactly two things will happen.

One, I'll remember every moment of the night I'm trying to block from my memories, and two, that curdling anger and frustration at them selling off the town will grow. There's no winning at this. Sex was temporary relief from the irritation Hudson fills me with, but that can only put it off for so long. Because he's set on destroying my home, and that's not something I can forgive.

I lock my truck—not something I ever do—because it gives a strong signal to myself that I'm not going anywhere else tonight. There's a flurry of birds in the trees overhead, a breeze almost strong enough to keep the spring heat away, but otherwise, everything is quiet and still.

Like it should be.

I throw a quick look out at my house to make sure no one is lurking inside, and then I strip off my shirt and head for the swimming hole. It's one of the reasons I decided to build my home here. It's about a hundred yards away, through the trees, and where I like to unwind after a long day.

The swimming hole has craggy rocks around three sides, with trees towering over it. The sun is low enough that it's not hitting the water anymore, but I know from experience that it'll be warm from the day.

A steady trickle of water falling from rock bounces around the small space, and I check that there's no wildlife hanging around before I strip off. The last thing I want is a bear taking a drink while my dick is out.

It doesn't matter how attractive Hudson is; I'll never understand someone like him. I stride deep into the water, letting myself feel every drop, every shift in the breeze, every rock under my feet. This, right here, is the real prize. It's not money or success. It's this. Taking in the surroundings and appreciating how incredible it is.

I dive under the surface, cutting myself off from everything as I swim to the other side.

In a lot of ways, I feel sorry for the people who live in big cities and don't know what they're missing out on. I never did. And it shouldn't have taken something traumatic for me to understand what the difference is between living and existing. Living will always be a work in progress, but I'm getting better at it.

Movement catches my eye up on the shore, and my heart rate spikes as I see Hudson pause by the place I left my pants. His gaze flicks from them to me, and like he's making up his mind, he strips off his shirt.

I'm treated to an eyeful of his body, chest and torso a road map of pinks and browns as he heals from his accident.

"Hey," he says, lifting his voice enough for me to hear him. "Didn't know there was a dress code."

Then he shoves his shorts and underwear down in one.

Heat rolls over my head and passes south. I'd been careful not to look too closely the other night, but as Hudson walks lazily to the water, there's nothing stopping me this time. You'd think common sense would do its part and catch up, but it's apparently deserted me as I drink in everything from Hudson's broad shoulders to his trim waist, slightly eager cock, and thick, long legs.

He kicks at the water, sending it in an arc across the surface.

I'm already moving slowly closer before I tell myself to stop.

"What are you doing here?"

"Thought you might like to admire your hard work," he says, dragging his hand over the line of bruises on his inner thigh. "I know I have been."

I chew back my reply, not wanting to give him the satisfaction of knowing how sexy they are.

"Why didn't you ever tell me this was here? It's awesome. I'm going to have to bring my brothers."

"No."

Those permanently curled lips part in glee. "You want to keep it our little secret, huh?"

"No. Only Wenders get to use the pool. Get out."

Instead of getting out, he surprises no one by walking in deeper. I watch the exact moment his dick disappears from sight and try not to feel disappointed.

"What's a Wender?"

"Someone who lives in Wilde's End."

"I live here," he points out. "And I own the place. Does that make me King Wender?"

"Nope. Still makes you a pain in my ass."

He laughs and strides closer. "Are you ever not grumpy?"

"Always. When you're not around." I move to the side, intending to go around him and leave, but Hudson drifts casually back in front of me. "Move."

"I *am* moving."

"Out of my way."

Hudson only ducks his head under the water and comes back up, flicking the wet blond strands back from his face. He's wearing his cracked sunglasses, and droplets dot the bronzed lenses above that perpetually mocking smile. Light from the water reflects back onto his face, and out here, his features are even sharper. The discoloration on his skin, the line of moles by his left eyebrow, the way his top lip is a shade darker than the bottom.

Fuck, I hate how good-looking he is.

"Why are you here?"

He splashes me, and I blink the water out of my eyes in shock. "*Why* are you so obsessed with that question? I followed you here. Like I follow you everywhere. Just assume that from now on and move on."

"Fine. Then *why* are you following me?"

"What else am I supposed to do when you're avoiding me?"

"Take the hint?"

A small *heh* parts his teeth. "Nah. Not me."

"You're probably fucking with your stitches," I point out, trying to find an excuse to put distance between us.

Hudson straightens out of the water and lifts his arm, showing off the jagged scar on his midsection. "I already went and saw the good doctor. I'm all cleared for skinny-dipping with you."

"There's no way he said those words."

"Fine. Not exactly." He pauses for a long moment. "He's the one who told me where you'd be Saturday night."

"Good. Now I know who to murder."

The bastard splashes me again. "We've covered that already. You're a kitten."

What the fuck is wrong with him? "A *kitten*? I've been through more shit than you'd ever imagine. You think it's *fun* to taunt me and get me worked up when you're here threatening my whole fucking world?" A scowl ripples over my face. "*Kitten*."

He drifts closer, and I can feel his eyes on my face. "I do think it's fun. Believe it or not, my life hasn't been all peaches either. My brothers think I'm fucked-up. Especially for sleeping with you."

"You *told* them?"

"Didn't see a reason not to."

My anger has moved higher, making my neck feel uncomfortably hot and tight. "I don't want anyone knowing about that."

"Too late."

I have to remind myself that I can't drown the guy. "Do you go out of your way to be the single most annoying human to exist?"

"Sometimes. I really don't know what you're so worked up about though. It's not like it won't happen again."

"There is no fucking *way* it's happening again." The words are out before I can stop them, and I see the exact moment Hudson recognizes my challenge.

"So if I tell you that you have my full permission to fuck me anytime and anywhere you wanted, that would mean nothing to you?"

The way my gut swims with those words is ridiculous. I don't want to be reacting to him this way, but with that permission, with Hudson only a foot in front of me, completely naked, my cock is already hardening. It's not getting away with this twice though, and at least for right now, I'm still in control of myself. "I'd have to want it for it to mean anything."

"Pity." He backs up a bit. "Lucky I still have Sutton back home, then."

That floating in my gut tightens. "*Who?*"

"My ex. Kinda ex. He was more than a booty call, but we weren't exclusive. They really should come up with a name for that."

"I think it's called dating." But what would I know? I don't do it. The only person I know who actively does is Queenie, and the stories I've heard from her are more than enough to know I never want to get involved in any of that.

"Either way, it doesn't matter. If I text him, he'll come. Then we'll *both* come. Catch my drift?"

My jaw is tense when I say, "Have fun with him, then."

"Not him. *Sutton.* Two *T*s. Best fuck I ever had."

Before he can move any further, before I've ever had a chance to think it through, my hand flies out and grabs his neck. The water makes it easy to drag him closer. So close that if I were breathing any deeper, our chests would probably touch.

"I'm the best fuck you ever had. Don't pretend like you weren't begging me."

This close, I can make out the shape of his eyes behind the sunglasses. "I was horny. I beg when I'm horny. That has nothing to do with you."

"I know what you're trying to do, and it isn't going to work."

His pink tongue drags over his bottom lip, and he tilts his head a little higher, showing off where I have hold of him. "Isn't it?"

"Go and fuck Sutter—"

"Sutton—"

"I don't care. Because I know the entire time he's with you, you're going to be thinking about me. That's the reason you followed me out here. But I'm not going to give you what you want."

"What *we* want."

I hate that he doesn't know when to shut up because right at that moment, his leg brushes against my cock underwater, which tells him exactly how hard I am.

There's no point denying the obvious, so I use a different tactic. "I'm used to not having what I want. Can't say the same for you, city boy."

"You're right. Because I always get what I want, and you're not going to be an exception."

# CHAPTER
# TWENTY-ONE

## HUDSON

When I wake up to find the front door busted open on one of the houses we've torn apart, I know Wilde is back. Apparently, our sex only held him off for so long.

I creep inside the gutted building, all exposed wooden frames and stripped-back flooring, to find the line of tools we'd had yesterday is no longer sitting where I left them. And it's no great mystery where they've gone.

Fucking Wilde.

I kick the toe of my boot into the filthy floor. What do we do now? With no tools, there's no work, but those fuckers were expensive. Maybe Wilde thinks he's being cute, but this game is wearing thin, and when my brothers see what we're missing, they're not going to be happy. It's bad enough that I banged up the bike we bought; now the guy I fucked less than a week ago has stolen our prized possessions.

They're going to kill me.

Before they wake up, I duck back into our house as fast as my sore ankle will let me move, grab the bike keys, and take off again. The motor kicks to life with a low rumble, and then I'm off. My first stop is Wilde's house, but it's empty, and so is the swimming hole I followed him to the other day. I check down by Booker's place, the giant building where they have Peril matches, and get lost more times than I can count. How they keep track of where anything is out here is a mystery, but I keep following trails that lead to other trails, and thankfully, the bike is loud enough that it scares off any wildlife before I come across it.

Apparently, it also scares off humans because I don't catch sight of anyone. No Wilde, no Booker, and neither of the other men I've seen with him. The forest is exactly as deserted as it's supposed to be, and it's the first time I wish it wasn't. If I don't get back with all of our tools, I might as well not come back at all.

I've traveled further down toward the river, judging by the sounds of birds and softly moving water. It's the deepest I've come yet, that I can remember, and even if I have no clue where the hell I am, I'm pretty sure if I follow the river, it will take me back to Old End.

And just, I dunno, let my brothers take a swing at me, I guess.

Maybe this will be the thing that finally makes them pack the car up to go.

Because we can replace the tools, but if we have to keep replacing everything that we buy, this place will bankrupt us. Borrowing against the business, again and again and again, will reach a point where it's not sustainable.

This place was supposed to save us. Not ruin us.

Maybe Hartwell is right.

Maybe life was as good as it was going to get for us.

I turn to follow the river, but the second I look up, I almost jump out of my fucking skin as I pull the bike to a fast stop and land heavily on my sore ankle.

But that's not what catches my attention.

"Holy *shit*."

There's an enormous cat blocking the way. It's spotty, with tufts on its ears, golden eyes, and lips pulled back to expose tiny, razor-sharp teeth. It's on all fours, and the fur along its back is prickled as it watches me through the light mist that clings to everything around here.

I think it's a bobcat, and I have no idea if those things are dangerous or not, but I'm not in a hurry to find out.

Especially when it takes a menacing step forward and lets out a demon sound, halfway between a hiss and a yowl.

"*Fuck*." My heart is thrumming against my ribs as I yank the bike around and hit the gas. I tear through the trees, paranoia creeping over me that the thing is hot on my heels and too chickenshit to glance back and check.

I refuse to be scared, but the instinct to put distance between me and that thing fills my head as I beg to find the gravel road without another accident, and somehow, luck is on my side for the first time since I moved to this hellhole. The second the front wheel hits gravel, I lean on the accelerator and take my first real breath since I saw the beast. We're in the middle of nowhere. Wilde even talked about bears. But knowing there are things out there that could eat your face and actually seeing one of them are two very different things.

And that cat definitely wanted to eat my face.

I reach town, heart thrumming, and burn rubber against the road as I slide to a stop in front of our house. It's not until I climb off the bike that I let myself look backward and confirm the road behind me is clear.

Because of course it fucking is.

"Where have you been?" Kennedy asks, almost like he doesn't want the answer.

I rest the helmet on the handlebars before I can launch it into the wall and dig my fingers through my hair instead. I'm fucking pissed that the stupid animal scared me off. I'm pissed I couldn't find anyone. Pissed that the tools are gone and I didn't get them back.

Pissed that we're dealing with all of this in the first fucking place, and there's nothing I can do about any of it.

"They stole our fucking tools. All of them. Gone. And I couldn't find a single person to fucking scream at, until a stupid bobcat got in my way and practically chased me out of there."

"Our tools?" Kennedy asks, looking at the house we're renovating with concern, but before I can answer him, Hart takes over.

"A bobcat chased you? Really? That's what you want us to believe?"

I stare at him for too long. "That's what happened."

"Sure. That's why you're a mess and not because you fucked Wilde again."

I want to strangle him, so I turn away sharply and toss him a "fuck you" instead.

"Did you at least trade a hammer for a hammering?"

"I didn't fuck Wilde, so stop being an asshole. I tried to find him to get our stuff back."

"And I believed you until you brought up a bobcat. They stay clear of people, so there's no way in hell one chased you."

"Maybe it had rabies."

"Doubtful."

I throw the motorcycle keys at his fucking head, but Hart knows me too well and catches them before they can hit. "You go for a ride, then. I hope it finds you and bites a hole in your neck."

He gives me a rare smile. "Think there's a chance?"

"Maybe instead of fighting again," Kennedy says, like his patience is about to snap, "you could focus on the fact that with no fucking tools, there's no work."

Guilt that I really shouldn't be feeling trickles its way past my anger. This is all on Wilde, and sleeping with him hasn't changed that he doesn't want us here. I lean face-first against the shiplap building, like blocking out the sight of everyone will somehow make this latest disaster disappear.

"Are we finally at the point of going home?" Hart asks.

"No," I grumble, wood eating my word.

"I don't want to," Kennedy admits. "But how much more can we take? Maybe we need to cut our losses."

"Or maybe," I say, pushing back and turning to them, "you could both back me up for once. I'm fighting these guys single-handedly, and you two want to give in. No wonder they're walking all over us."

"Nothing would make me happier than them driving us out of town," Hart says, but Kennedy looks rattled.

"I don't know what we're supposed to do."

"Not let them walk all over us would be a start." I cross my arms, using it as a way to keep my anger inside. I'm supposed to be the one leading them, and all I've done is lead them into a fucking mess. All of this was supposed to help us. To be good for us. I'm scrambling to try and save this experience, and it's rapidly going downhill, and while I'm directing my anger their way, I know it's only because it's easier than being angry with myself.

I fucked up.

And I can either admit that and go home, eat the losses, and splinter further away from my brothers, or I can dig my heels in and fight Wilde to the last breath.

It's no choice, really.

"I've never been good at that." Kennedy sighs and tilts his

head back, like he's looking at the sky, but it's something he does a lot when he's trying not to cry. "I don't want everything to have to be a fight. I only wanted to come here and work and spend time with you both."

His confession helps dull my anger, but it does nothing to Hart. Not that I expected it would. "It must be nice to believe in fairy tales."

"It is. And it makes me sad that you'll never understand it."

"Don't be sad for me, brother. Be sad for yourself," he says as he gets up and makes his way to the other house. Kennedy follows him, and it tears me up to see him so … flat. I have to do something about it. Something to bring the spark and hope back to him, but I'm so lacking in both of those things myself.

All I know is that unless we work together, this place is never going to happen.

We end up wasting too much of the day in Wayward, picking up a new drill, some screws, and the groceries we'll need to get through the week. We spare time for lunch at the diner, and maybe it's because we've been living off anything we can cook on a hot plate, but it's the best meal I've had in a long time. None of us is in a hurry to get back, and I'm dreading what we'll find when we do.

I'm relieved when, after a check of the site, I confirm that we haven't come home to more headaches. We spend some time going over the shopfronts and making plans for what to do in there, and then it's late afternoon, and I want nothing else but to escape the tension between the three of us. There was a man with longish black hair watching us today, who takes turns with Wilde, but he's gone when I make my way back across the street to the house.

"Weird," Kennedy mutters, and I turn back to see what's

caught his attention. He's paused by the dirt bike, and as I watch, he reaches out to run a hand over the seat.

"What is?"

"Someone's cleaned it."

My gaze flicks to Hart, who looks equally as confused. "They cleaned the bike?" I confirm.

"Yeah, look. All the dirt is gone."

He's right. Other than the scratches in the paintwork, it's gleaming as happily as the day we bought it. "That *is* weird."

Hartwell laughs, scattered and hollow. "Fuck this place."

I bound up the stairs before he can get into another one of his rants and head inside. Somehow out here, the days feel stretched thin, and while I'm not hungry and dinner is still a few hours away, I'm exhausted through to my bones.

I kick my shoes off as soon as I get back to my room and slam the door behind me. There's no way I have the energy to deal with anyone else tonight, so I'm going to play mindless games on my phone until it's dark and then hopefully knock myself out for the night.

The sun is beating straight into my window, so I cross to close the makeshift curtains when something catches my eye. The man who's been watching us from the outlook all day is gone, and Wilde has taken his place.

The sight of his scruffy beard, red flannel shirt, and crossed arms makes me want to head over there and scream at him. Which will get me exactly nowhere because we've done that one too many times.

The restlessness in me grows, and if I can't fight him, I can do the next best thing.

It *was* Hart's suggestion to trade a hammer for a hammering after all.

So instead of feeding into his game with anger, I reach back and pull my shirt over my head. I hug it to my front, almost one hundred percent confident he's watching me as I let it slip off my arms and onto the floor.

Then I hook my thumbs into my gym shorts and push them slowly from my hips. They stick around my thighs before dropping, and while he's too far away to make out the expression on his face, I don't miss the way he shifts his weight. Don't miss the way one of his crossed arms pops free so he can rub at his mouth.

And if he can't see me, who the fuck cares? There's no one else around. I lose my briefs next and wrap my hand around my cock. I'm not hard, but with Wilde, it doesn't matter because I'll get there soon enough. And once I am, I slide the window all the way open, then step back and do what I first planned to do. I close the makeshift curtain to cut off the sight and hope Wilde took my invitation for what it was.

# CHAPTER
# TWENTY-TWO

## WILDE

really should have lasted longer than this. I'm pissed off with myself, but not enough to turn and walk away. Critters rustle and titter through the trees around me, and as I approach the old house, a darkness settles over my chest. I promised myself I'd never step foot in one of these relics again, and here I am doing it for a third time. And all because of Hudson's red-light district window show.

Even if his brothers were watching out for anything suspicious, they wouldn't see me as I drift from shadow to shadow until I'm standing right beneath his window. It's my last chance to walk away, and the ringing in my ears is screaming at me to do it. My feet are planted though, my gaze steady on that open invitation, my dick already hard at the promise of what's waiting for me.

I wish I could pretend to be considering this, but when I reach up and grab hold of the windowsill, I know Hudson won't be at all surprised to see me. Which only makes me more annoyed with myself.

It takes two steps up the side of the building before I'm able to haul myself through the window and get my feet back on solid ground. The sheet nailed to the wall above my head cuts off my view, but when I shift it aside and step into the room, I find Hudson on his mattress—a normal one, not the inflatable one this time—sitting against the wall, wearing nothing but a victor's smirk.

His bare feet are planted on the floor, legs casually parted so his heavy balls hang between them. My gaze lingers on them for too long before skimming higher, following where his cock is lazily resting against his lower belly, to the rippled, pinkish-red burn, to his cuts and grazes and pretty nipples, before I reach his face.

We lock eyes, like Hudson is waiting for me to say something, but I only cross my arms and lean back against the wall. I'm as far from him as I can get, but it's still not far enough. I don't trust myself not to touch him.

I'm kicking myself for being in his room in the first place. It's a clear signal to him that I'm weak. That he's winning. But when he brushes his fingers along his shaft, I can't help wetting my dry lips.

City boy or not, Hudson is delicious.

"Oops," he finally says. "If I'd known you were coming over, I would have thrown on something decent." The natural curl to his lips hitches higher as his fingers ghost a trail over his balls. "Silly me. Being all exposed like this. There's no telling who'll creep through an open window."

He tugs his balls down casually before slipping both hands behind his head. He's laid out, offering himself up for whatever I have in mind, and it's like a drug the way it makes my brain fizzle.

I want to stride over there and swallow his cock whole. The taste of his cum is never far from my thoughts, and my mouth is watering over the thought of enjoying him again. But I've already given him the upper hand once. He wants me to go to him.

It's not going to fucking happen that way.

I drop one of my hands to readjust my cock into a more comfortable position, but I know it won't be comfortable until it's inside him, and tonight … I really want his mouth. That sexy mouth that never shuts up won't have a choice when it's full of my dick. I'm aching for it, and there are so many ways we can do this that I'm struggling to choose where to start.

Hudson draws circles around the bruises on his thigh, the purple already seeping away and leaving a greenish-yellow tint. "You're not even going to say hello?" His innocent tone isn't fooling me.

I don't humor him.

"It's polite, you know," he pushes.

"I'm not polite."

His narrowed eyes light up at my response. "Love when your voice sounds like that."

"Like what?"

"Like you haven't used it all day, and now you're fighting yourself over replying, but you want me too badly to shut up."

Every part of that is unfortunately accurate. I can go days without talking to people, and it suits me fine, but Hudson knows how to bring it out. How to taunt me until I don't stop to think, just speak, and I need to get better at controlling myself.

Hudson shifts his legs wider, and I have to force out a deep exhale to stop from giving in and closing the distance between us.

"Don't you want to touch me?"

He knows I do. Being here tells him that, but so does the way my gaze can't stop roaming over his body. He's not a hairy man, and I don't know if that's natural or on purpose since he's shaved his balls since we were together the other night. I don't understand the obsession with manscaping. Give me hairy and rough and masculine any day.

Not gorgeous city boys.

My standards should be higher than this.

They never are.

I finally give in to rubbing myself through my jeans. "Come here."

Surprisingly, he doesn't argue, but before he can stand, I stop him.

"No." We lock eyes. "I want you to crawl to me."

A beat passes with only the twitch of his mouth. "Crawl?"

"Yes."

"You want me to crawl?"

I widen my stance, getting comfortable. "What's wrong? Don't know what that word means?"

"No, I do."

"Then get on with it."

His attention drops to where I'm massaging my palm into my dick, and when it lifts back to my face, he's glaring. Hudson has obviously figured out that I'm not playing with my request. Now it's up to him to decide how badly he wants it.

Will he give in and do what I want?

Or will he test me?

It doesn't matter how much I want this, if he tries to push back, I'm gone. We'll try again another day until he works out that I'm not giving up control for anyone. What I say goes, and he might enjoy testing that in general, but he's going to figure out that when it comes to sex, I don't relent.

We watch each other for too long. I'm already intimately acquainted with those cute moles by his eyebrow, with that pouty top lip, and the way his mouth gives everything away, even when there's no sound coming out of it. I'm sure he's waiting for some hesitation from me. Some sense of doubt.

I give him none.

And his mouth tells me the second he's made his decision when his lips flatten into disgust and he leans forward onto his hands.

"You're fucked-up," he gets out between his teeth.

"You knew that when you invited me here."

Still, I'm not forcing him to do anything. And when Hudson gets onto his hands and knees, back dipped into a sexy curve, something hot and consuming fills his eyes. He stalks toward me like a predator.

I expect him to get it over with, but he takes his time, shoulder blades rising and falling with each pace as his rounded ass, high in the air, draws my gaze, and I wish I could see more. I desperately want him to crawl away from me next, but I already know I won't get away with this twice. So I enjoy every second of him giving in to me.

My cock hardens the closer he gets, and when he comes to a stop at my feet, he rests on his knees and reaches for my fly. Hudson's narrowed eyes dare me to stop him, but I drink in every movement instead, clutching my crossed arms tighter so that I don't reach for him.

That hair is begging me to thread my fingers through it.

"Good boy," I taunt.

"Fuck you." He gets my pants open, then tugs my briefs down under my balls. The heady sound he lets out before leaning forward feels almost as good as his tongue flicking over my slit. The puff of warm air against my heated skin has my body begging for more, but I know better than to let any of those thoughts out.

"It's a crime this cock is attached to you, by the way," he mutters, mouth brushing my tip.

"Why don't you punish me by sucking until it hurts."

"I will … if you promise to give our tools back."

That sentence brings me up short. He's about to close his mouth around me when I give in and rest my hand on his head. I turn his face so he can see me and tighten my grip in his hair.

"I don't negotiate during sex. If you want something, you're going to have to resort to more than blow jobs to get it." My grip in his hair is a warning. "If you suck it, you're sucking it because you want to."

I loosen my hold but leave my hand where it is. We trade glares, and I wait for him to call this off, but after a second, Hudson leans in. Those plump lips seal around my dick, and no matter who the hell is on the end of the blow job, this is fucking bliss. He sinks down onto my cock, wrapping it in wet warmth, tongue massaging the underside as he attempts to drive me out of my mind.

I've been horny for days, and he's not taking things easy on me.

Hudson looks so fucking pretty with my dick in his mouth.

"You have stupid eyelashes," I tell him, rocking forward into the sweet suction.

His glare lessens for a second as he bats them at me. It has no right to be so seductive, has no right to hold my attention the way it does. I look down at him, wishing I was looking at literally anyone else, while knowing this wouldn't feel as good if it were.

The permanent irritation only heightens the way I have to have him. Hudson makes my whole body hum completely against my will, and I thrust deeper into his mouth each time he swallows me down.

There's something about towering over him, using him, knowing he's as conflicted over this as I am that really turns me on. We're so attracted to each other that nothing else matters. Not when it feels this good.

The suction and the way he hums around me work against each other until I can't see straight. A heavy *"fuck"* shivers from my lips before I can stop it, filling the dark and quiet room with evidence of my need. Hudson could be an asshole and pull off now, leave me aching and blue-balled, but he answers me with a moan and moves faster.

His uninjured hand is between his legs, stroking himself, eyes having long fallen closed, and I greedily drink in the sight of him in the darkness of his room, panting, spit covering his chin, tufts of hair sticking out between my fingers as he sucks on my cock like he'll die if he stops.

And thank fuck for that because I'd die if he stopped too.

A deep groan forces its way from my chest as I thrust into Hudson's mouth. I'm twisting close to that edge, and all I want is to topple off it so I can get out of here. To give in to that high, knowing how good the last one was.

I've never had an issue with anonymous sex before, but I've also never come in my life like I did with him. There's something about putting this unnerving man in his place that I can't get enough of, and I'd hoped it was a onetime thing. I'd hoped—pointlessly—that the second time would be missing all the intensity of the first, and I could walk out of here disappointed but free.

If anything, the tension tugging at my skin is worse.

My whole body is flushed, sweat prickling at my shirt as

Hudson works me over. He lets go of his own cock to wrap his fist around mine, and it's exactly the friction I need.

I forget everything except this. The pleasure, the way my veins are humming with it, the way my balls are pulling tighter and the end is creeping over me.

I fuck his face as I meet each pass of his lips until I can't take it anymore. A long moment stretches out like the vibration of a band before it snaps. My orgasm rushes over me, cum pumping into his mouth and making him splutter, but I only twist my grip tighter. Hold him there, both of us suspended in a moment where nothing matters except this high before it all crashes down again.

My hand snaps away from him like I've been burned, and Hudson pulls off my cock. His sinful lips are red and puffy, and cum has mixed with the spit on his chin, leaving him the most beautiful version of himself I've seen yet. Then he leans in and wipes his face on my shirt.

I huff and pull away, but Hudson doesn't let me get far. He holds tight to my hips as he stands and presses me into the wall.

"I'm not done yet."

"I am."

He ignores me as he takes my hand and slides his cock into it. Then he wraps his hand around my hold.

I don't want to like this as much as I do, but instead of backing off, I grip him tighter.

"Your turn to get me off," he says.

"And if I don't want to?"

Hudson's eyes laugh at me, so close it's impossible to not think of them as tiny gems glowing in the dark. "Then I'm sure you'll have no issues pushing me away."

We stand there, locked in a game neither of us really wants to be playing but that neither of us can resist. He gives me all the time I need to end this, and I don't take it.

Because I don't want to take it.

Hudson thrusts into my fist.

"My left hand isn't the same," he confesses. "I've tried jerking off so many times, but it never hits the spot."

"You need more practice."

"Or maybe it's not my hand that's the issue." His hips pick up the pace, lips barely an inch away, so every needy breath that passes them tickles mine. "You're the last person I want to do this with."

"Right back at you, city boy."

"So why won't my dick get the message?"

Our gazes clash, that same question echoing back to each other. It's no surprise I'm attracted to him; that charisma is hard for anyone to resist, but what's the appeal for him? I'm a no one who lives in a nowhere town, with little to my name, and I'm not even interesting to look at. It's all on purpose too. All choices I've made. I don't *want* people to look at me. I don't want anyone to give me more than a passing glance and an occasional orgasm. Life is better when you live it alone.

Hudson is a complication I didn't see coming. A twisted, confusing complication. The type that's wormed its way under my skin, and since I can't beat the shit out of him, we've resorted to this. Filling the ache in different ways. Weak. Horny. Stupid.

His head tilts back, body pressing tighter against me as he chases his own orgasm, and I'm fixated on the curve of his thick neck. On how quickly his chest is chasing air. Hudson is an erotic dream, and I want the dream to end. I want my quiet peace back.

"Oh, *shit*," he rasps, and his release floods my hand. I'm too slow to let go, and Hudson has me milk him through it, drawing out each little wave of pleasure until he slumps against me.

All he does is breathe for so long that I forget I'm supposed to be moving away. He's gripping my T-shirt in both hands, and when he pulls back—not enough, never enough—he looks up at me through his eyelashes.

I want to shove him aside, but my body won't listen.

"You know we're doing that again," he promises.

"I don't know that at all."

"And again. *And* again. I can see it in your eyes." Is there any point arguing with him when we both know he's right? Hudson's like looking into a mirror sometimes. He doesn't accept my bull-shit, and we're locked in this struggle of who is going to come out on top. I can't let him win, but I'm worried I don't have the edge to keep fighting.

"Why can't you just *leave*?" My voice breaks on the word.

Hudson's eyes dull as his gaze searches mine. I catch a glimpse of the demons he's trying to keep buried. "Because I'm scared of who I'll become if I do."

His answer strikes me silent, and while we watch each other, no response I have fits. I'm too lost in the echoed ghost of screaming and scent of metallic blood to acknowledge that I understand that fear. I know without asking that was probably the most real thing he's ever said to me.

He saves me from deciding on a reply when his face splits into a sudden grin, and he pats my messy hand. "I'm sure you can handle that," he says, echoing my words back to me from the first time.

Then he backs off, tugging his underwear out of a drawer before he steps into it.

I don't move, and it catches his attention.

"If you're hanging around for postorgasm cuddles, you're wasting your time," he says.

I grunt and head for the window. Nothing on Earth could make me want that.

# CHAPTER
# TWENTY-THREE

## HUDSON

can't say I was thrilled to trade sex for tools, so when Wilde turned me down, it was almost a relief. Almost. Because now I'm out of ideas.

I'm not sure what happened last night, but after we got off, there was a moment there where things got a bit too real. Where I looked at him and saw an actual person through the wild-man beard, which isn't something I want to happen ever, ever again. I'd like to continue to view Wilde as a walking dildo and the source of all of my frustrations.

I have a rare bar of service, so I use it to call through to our building manager and get the rundown on what's happening back home. I'm almost holding my breath as I wait for him to tell me the world is on fire, but all the tension whistles out of me when he confirms it's business as usual.

"Hart's got me everything I need," he says, and it pulls me up short.

"Hart?"

"Yeah, he's been checking in every day. If he doesn't call, I'll have an email or two. He scored us a contract that starts next month, so I'm in the process of sourcing everything for it now."

I'm still not sure I'm understanding, but I also don't want to make my lack of faith in my brother obvious. "That's good to hear," I answer vaguely before we say our goodbyes.

Then I hover in the middle of the street, looking at where our car is usually parked. Hart leaves with it most days, and I thought it was because he wanted to spend as little time here as possible, but apparently, he's actually … *doing* something with his time.

I shouldn't be this surprised.

I shouldn't.

Because if he's being productive and Kennedy is being responsible, then *I'm* the disaster brother.

Fuck me, I did not see that coming. Our move here was supposed to stop that from happening. I listen to the whirl of the drill as I pace. I've cleaned up as much of the site as I can with one hand partially out of commission, and now we're trying to move on to the next stage, but it's such a long fucking process. None of the electricians we've reached out to have been interested in working up here, and we're running out of options. Do I go and become a qualified electrician myself? We don't have the years to waste on that.

I'm close to pulling out my hair when I turn toward the sound of something … squeaking?

The road is clear, and Kennedy's drilling has stopped, but it doesn't sound like it's coming from inside the house.

*Skeek. Skeek. Skeeeek.*

It sounds like … a busted wheel. Maybe.

I loop around the nearest house, ears pricked for the sound. It's stopped, but I know there has to have been someone here. Our site is clear, and I'm beginning to think I imagined it when I make it back to the street and almost run headfirst into a man.

He's tall and lanky, has a lot of messy black hair, and his dark eyes fly wide under pierced eyebrows. I'm pretty sure this is the guy who's been helping Wilde keep an eye on us. It takes one look from his startled expression to the cart full of our tools before my shock disappears.

I shove him into the building and press my arm to his throat. "*You* stole our tools!"

There's sound inside the house, probably Kennedy, but I'm too fixated on the man in front of me.

He throws his hands up between us, head shaking madly, almost like he's scared, and maybe I'd care more about his feelings if I hadn't busted him with our shit.

"What the fuck are you doing?" I demand.

He doesn't answer me, just keeps shaking his head, pressing back against the building like he'll somehow disappear inside it.

"Hudson?" Kennedy asks, pausing at the bottom of the front stairs. "What's going on?"

"Look at what's in the cart."

"It's … our tools?"

"Exactly. I caught this motherfucker with them!"

The man tries to wriggle away from me, but I press my forearm tighter. His gaze is fixed somewhere on the ground, and the only thing he's doing is shaking his head nonstop.

"Jesus, Huddy," Kennedy says as he approaches. "At least let him explain."

"Explain how he ended up with our things? It's pretty obvious to me."

"I mean it." Kennedy grabs my arm. "Let him go."

"We can't be weak with these people!"

"I'm not being weak." He glares at me. "You told me to stand up for shit, so now I'm doing it. Let him go. You're hurting him."

I'm definitely not hurting him, but Kennedy being so direct makes me back off. I slowly release the pressure on this guy's throat, and he slumps back against the wall. My heart is still racing, an insistent, stubborn reaction to literally everything that's going on with me.

"Don't even think about running," I grit out.

Kennedy shoots me a warning look but turns to the man. "Are you okay?"

He hasn't looked away from the ground, but after a moment, he nods.

"Sorry about Hudson. We're all a bit stressed."

He nods again.

Kennedy shifts closer. "I'm Kennedy. Who are you?"

The man drags his gaze from the ground to brush over me before settling on my brother's face. There's a long stretch of nothing, but the man lifts a hand and makes two fast, slashing movements over his mouth.

"You … can't talk?" Kennedy asks, and I look back at the guy, waiting for confirmation.

Instead, he sighs. It's one of those full-body ones that has his shoulders sagging, and then he clears his throat and drops his gaze somewhere around Kennedy's throat.

"Ziggy." It's barely a whisper.

"Ziggy?" Kennedy confirms, and when the man doesn't answer, my brother's natural smile shines through. "Did you steal our tools?"

The man shakes his head.

"Do you know who did?"

A nod.

I finally catch on to what Kennedy is doing. This guy can talk, but he clearly doesn't want to, at least around us. "Was it Wilde?" I cut in.

Ziggy's gaze flicks my way, but he stops short of looking at me. He doesn't confirm it either, just shifts his weight to the other foot and kicks at the dirt.

"I'm going to take that as a yes," I say, and still there's no answer.

"Did …" Kennedy squints toward the cart of tools. "Did Wilde tell you to bring them back to us?"

Another pause, then another nod.

Well, fuck.

I attacked the messenger.

Both hands rake back through my hair. We're in a new place, but I'm still the same me. When does this end? "I'm sorry. I'm fucking sorry."

He doesn't acknowledge me at all, and I can't say I blame him. What was supposed to bring out the best in us is bringing out the worst in me, and I don't love it. I'm so tense and on edge, and you'd think after that muscle-melting orgasm last night, I'd be in a way better headspace, but it's worse. It's so much worse. Because I already want it again, and that's driving the guilt in deeper because it should never have happened at all.

"This can't keep happening," I say, more to myself than to them. "This whole fucking thing is so fucking stupid."

Kennedy ignores me. "You like it here?" he asks Ziggy.

Once again, the guy wordlessly confirms it.

"Is Wilde giving the tools back as a peace offering?"

A shrug is the only answer.

"Did he also clean the motorcycle?"

Ziggy shakes his head quickly, then glances at me like he's worried I'll come for him again, before turning all his attention on Kennedy. He points at his chest.

"*You* did it?" Kennedy's expression softens. "Thank you. That was really nice."

Ziggy goes on staring at the ground.

I exchange a look with my brother because I don't know what we're supposed to do now. All I know is that I want to be done with this. The short fuse is nothing new, but I don't want to make everyone into my enemy, and if Wilde is giving us these back, it makes me think that whatever that thing was last night, he felt it too.

Maybe he's realized I'm not a walking dildo either.

That doesn't feel like a good thing.

"This is going to sound random," I warn them both. "But I think I need to talk to Wilde."

"Talk?" Kennedy repeats, sounding wary.

"Yes. *Talk*." Because with all the times we've griped at each other, we've never actually tried that. It sounds offensively boring, but I'm willing to try anything at this point. Who knows? Maybe if Wilde knew how desperately I need to tear his town apart, he might suddenly be okay with it. Doubtful, but he can't say I didn't try.

"Is he home?" I ask Ziggy.

Silent treatment again. I deserve it, but that doesn't make it any less frustrating. I give Kennedy the *help me* eyes that he clearly finds amusing, but he does it anyway.

"If Hudson goes to Wilde's house, will he find him there?"

Ziggy lifts his shoulders again.

"Fuck it, I'm going anyway."

Kennedy trails me to the bike. "Don't fight him."

"I won't."

"Your fingers are still broken."

"Well aware."

He hovers in front of the bike as I climb onto it. "Don't sleep with him either."

I tug on the helmet, already hating myself. "Don't need to. He got me off last night."

"Hudson!"

"I know, I know. Stupid choices are nothing new for me. But I'm really going to talk to him and hopefully get to some kind of resolution."

Some of the worry leaves his face. "Do you think that's possible?"

"I dunno." I start the bike up, the loud growl of the engine filling the street. "But I need to do something."

He pats the handlebars. "Good luck, then."

Something tells me that I'm going to need it.

# CHAPTER
# TWENTY-FOUR

WILDE

The sound of the motorcycle isn't unexpected, but I'd hoped it wouldn't come. I don't want to see Hudson.

Giving the tools back was an ... error in judgment.

*I'm scared of who I'll become if I leave.*

It's like Hudson plucked those same words from my mind seventeen years ago and made me face them. The person I am now would look very different if I'd headed back to LA and stayed there.

I push through my front door and wait on the porch for him, not wanting to risk him inside with any of my things. There's enough room on my porch for the two chairs to the right of my door, but I ignore those and set my arms on the railing, hoping that I give off *I'm not here to talk* vibes.

He pulls up behind my truck, and something twists in my gut as he pulls off the helmet. His blond hair is a mess from being covered, and that same lock kicks up in the front, just as obstinate as the rest of him.

The T-shirt he's wearing shows off his arms, the shorts hugging his powerful thighs, and even though I tell myself not to, I can't stop my mind from filling with images of him naked.

Hudson attempts a smile as he approaches. "I got your present."

"Don't know what you're talking about."

"My tools." He tucks his hands in his pockets. "You gave them back after all."

I drop his gaze and refocus on the trees behind him. "Changed my mind about needing them."

He paces a few steps forward, and I want to tell him to stop, but I lock my jaw anyway. "You know what we're going to use them for, don't you? The whole reason you took them in the first place?"

He already knows the answer to that, so I don't bother responding.

"Wilde ..." The crack in his voice tugs my attention back to him. "Why did you give them back?"

"Better things to do with my time."

"Than look after your town?"

He's baiting me, and it almost works. I bite down on my tongue because the more I talk, the more he'll stick around, and I'm ready for him to go now. He couldn't take the return for what it was, could he? Then again, *I* don't even know what it was, so it's a bit much to expect him to.

All night, I was unsettled, overly aware of the tools I'd hidden at Ziggy's place and knowing that when it came right down to it ... they didn't matter. The brothers would get more. They'd keep coming and coming, mindlessly focused on their end goal, and while I could delay them as much as possible, the end result would be inevitable.

"Can we talk?" Hudson asks suddenly.

"Isn't that what we're doing?"

"No. I'm talking. You're ignoring me."

That sounds about right to me, but I still maintain that's as close to talking as we get. I don't want anything more than that, especially not from someone determined to ruin my whole life.

He knows better than to wait for a response that won't come, but instead of cutting his losses and heading back to his bike, Hudson climbs my front stairs. He passes by close enough that a wave of sweet scent fills my nose, and then he drops into one of the two chairs sitting behind me.

I refuse to turn toward him, but having my back to him doesn't feel smart.

"I have a shitty temper," he says, and it makes me snort. I knew that about two seconds after meeting him. "I don't know why. My parents weren't ever angry people, and my brothers aren't like that either."

"Maybe you're just an asshole."

"Maybe. I got mad at your friend. Ziggy."

That makes me whip around. "What did you do?"

"Nothing." He eyes me suspiciously. "Got angry and shoved him into a wall. Our foreplay, basically."

If he weren't sitting, I'd probably do the same to him now. "Ziggy had better be okay."

"He is. I apologized." Hudson slumps down further in his chair. "Made me feel a bit bad about it, actually."

"Good."

He looks me over. "And how many times have you manhandled me?"

"Yeah, but the difference is that Ziggy is a sweet guy. Unlike either of us."

Hudson doesn't argue because he knows I'm right. As much

as I don't want to admit it, there are similarities between us that stretch deeper than us both ending up in Wilde's End.

"How did you know his name?" I ask, hating that I'm extending the conversation.

"He told us."

Ziggy willingly speaking to people he knows is rare; him willingly speaking to strangers … I almost don't believe him. "You didn't beat it out of him, did you?"

"No." He has the audacity to look offended. "Kennedy is *also* a sweet guy. Ziggy told him."

That sounds closer to what I'd expect. "Why are you here?"

"That question again …"

"If you'd stop showing up, I'd stop asking it."

Hudson pats the chair beside him, and it's natural instinct to refuse. I'm curious though, and I know it will shock him if I take his offer, so on a whim, I do. I shouldn't move closer; everything in my body, from my racing heart to my unsettled gut, lets me know it. I settle back in the chair, the creak of the wicker a warning that I'm way too close. Which is ridiculous when I literally had my dick in his mouth last night.

He glances over at me, and I'm struck again by how close he was as we jerked him off, how those same eyes burned into mine.

"How many of you live here?" he asks.

I answer truthfully, which I think surprises me as much as him. "Twenty-seven."

"That many?"

"Yes."

"I was expecting you to say, like, five …"

"What does it matter?"

Hudson shifts in his chair, gaze flicking away. "Wanted to know how many lives we're ruining."

I don't have an answer for that, not that I think he's looking for one.

"What do I do?" he finally says.

My eyebrows pull tight, and I study the side of his face. His lips are quirked as usual, but he somehow manages not to look happy. "About?"

"The town." He glances my way, and our eyes meet for a prolonged moment before he looks away again. "If we sell the place, you're going to end up with the same issues you have with us. Anyone who buys it will want to redevelop the town to make money."

Unfortunately, he has a point there. "I said I'd buy it."

"How do you have that kind of money? No offense ..." He taps the side of my house. "But this doesn't scream luxury."

"I have everything I need. And the rest isn't your business."

"Can you try to meet me halfway? I'm giving you honesty. You could try to do the same."

"I was being very honest."

He props his hands behind his head in a way he likes to do and a way that I like him doing. Probably too much. "We're not going to get anywhere, are we?"

"I made you an offer." One I can't help but notice he didn't jump at, so that tells me Hudson doesn't actually want to sell.

"We didn't come here to develop the place."

"Just a lucky coincidence, then?"

"No, like ..." He huffs. "That was the purpose I told Kennedy and Hartwell, but ..."

"But?" I kick myself for asking when what I should be doing is getting him off my front porch.

Hudson taps one of his booted feet against the wooden deck, an erratic, uncertain pulse like he's echoing the thoughts running through both of us. "Kenny's a lover. Literally. If it was him you were fucking, you would have come home to a house full of flowers and him ready to feed you chocolates. He comes on … strong."

"Damn," I monotone. "Picked the wrong brother."

Hudson flips me off with his good hand and keeps talking. "I swear it's every other month that I'm having to pick him up after he's had his heart broken."

I have no idea what any of that has to do with me.

"Then there's Hartwell. You've probably already put together that they're twins. And it's like Kennedy got all the feelings and Hart got none of them. He's just empty. All the time. Loves to joke about dying, and I know he's not serious, but I also think there's a small part of him that doesn't care either way. I'm lost on how to reach either of them, and I've tried. I've tried to fix things for them and make it easier on them, but I've reached the point where I don't even know what that is."

"And you?"

He lazily looks my way. "Me?"

"You've told me a whole lot about your brothers, but last night, you said that you're the one who's scared to leave."

He almost looks like he's going to shut down, but this is a challenge, and Hudson meets those head-on. For all he says about having a short fuse, he's not scared of anything. "If I can't help them … what's the point?"

"What do you mean?"

He lightens his voice like that might somehow make what he's going to say easier. "I'm fucking powerless. I see them hurting all the time, making the same mistakes all the time, and I can't do anything about it. It's … exhausting. And if I'm that fucking useless, then—" He bites off his words like maybe he went too far. "I used to have a problem. In high school. I made a bit of a name for myself at parties as being able to get … stuff."

*Stuff.* I stiffen where I'm sitting, the lightness to the conversation pulling tight in an instant. Too quickly, this feeling of dread washes over me, and whatever he says next, I can't take in.

"One thing led to another, and it wasn't good. It felt like the more I could get my hands on, the more people liked me, and then when they got whatever they were after, they disappeared too. Anyway, usual sob story: I started partying too hard, moving from one high to the next and—"

"*Leave.*"

Hudson's head snaps my way, all fake lightness gone as confusion kicks in. "What?"

"I don't know what the fuck you thought you were doing by coming here—" I'm struggling to keep my voice level. "—but you need to fucking go. *Now.*"

"I'm *trying* to … to … connect with you. To make you understand that I'm not here to purposely ruin your life. That I—"

I shoot forward in my chair so fast I'm not even aware of moving. "I don't fucking care! I don't want to know you or who you were or any of this shit. Now, get the hell out of my house!"

Hudson's gaping, blinking at me like he's not sure what's happening, and I'm honestly not sure myself. My heart is thudding, face building with emotion that's trying to force its way out of my eyes. Every little scar on my arms and chest and back feels like they're trying to burn through my skin, and as he glares at me and I glare at him, it feels like all the oxygen around us is growing thin.

His shock melts like a snowflake in spring, and he whispers, "I never want to go back to that. So no. I'm not leaving Wilde's End. Just wanted you to understand."

And I know I should say something, but the rippling hurt I keep locked away in my chest is threatening to make itself known. I keep my jaw clamped shut, my hands in fists on the armrests of the small chair.

Hudson stands, and there's emotion trying to beg its way out of his eyes as well, but all we can do is glare at each other until he leaves.

I hear the engine long after it's stopped echoing through the trees.

Then the scent comes back to me. Oil and fuel and blood. Fresh rain. Pain everywhere.

I swallow thickly before his name can slip past my lips, and so it fills my head instead.

*Kyran ...*

# CHAPTER
# TWENTY-FIVE

## HUDSON

refuse to cry. I'm used to assholes. I'm used to being ignored, to being brushed aside and my feelings minimized. Sutton would do it all the time. Listen to me rant about something, then sigh and ask if I was done yet. Kennedy says I can't let that anger take over me, and Hart says it's pointless to even worry about it.

So I've gotten used to not talking at all.

It figures that the one time I'd try again, I'd get … that.

If Wilde had been dismissive, I probably could have handled it better, but that sudden, explosive anger knocked the carefully restrained box of zero fucks over, and I'm struggling to wrangle them again. It's like he's unleashed a beehive in my chest, and I can't calm it down.

This shaken feeling probably isn't normal, but I'm long past caring.

Hart still has the car, so I can't even take off in that, and I have no clue where Kennedy is, but it's better this way. I don't want to talk. I don't want to think. I just want to … *break* something.

I guess it's a good thing we have a lot to break.

I grab the sledgehammer from our cart of tools and head for the nearest shop. It's almost completely destroyed inside, either from vandals, age, or the multiple water leaks that have found their way inside. My anger is burning hot as I kick the busted-up door in, and then I ignore the wailing squeaks of the boards as I reach the service counter and lift the sledgehammer back over my shoulder.

Unlike when Wilde was giving our house love taps, I don't hold back. I swing and swing, moving from the counter to the walls to the door that leads into a back room. I'm panting, sweat pooling on my back, broken fingers burning, and shoulders aching with the effort that I have no plans to stop.

*None of this is fucking fair.*

I grit my teeth against the thought, not willing to go there. Too many times, I gave in to the building despair, but I'm still determined to fight it. No matter what Wilde thinks, or Hart says, or Kennedy feels, none of that matters. I'm the only one who's ever looked out for myself, and that's never changing.

The weather is wet heat baked into concrete and timber, and we get the extensions added to house two with no sabotage. Every day that ticks by without a sign from Wilde doesn't sit right, and now that my initial feelings of betrayal have calmed the fuck down, I have space to consider why he reacted like that.

It was extreme. And maybe it was building to the point where he really can't stand my presence, but I find that hard to believe when he actively sought it out to get off. People are complicated. I hate people. And I hate complicated.

I especially hate that my feelings are as complicated as his.

Even with my growing resentment, I can't help feeling like I deserved it. I'm always the one exploding on people, and all he did was give it back to me. I did *not* need to look so directly into the mirror to know how fucked-up I've become, but he forced me anyway.

I guess I should thank him.

Not that I've seen him in over a week to be able to do that.

There have been too many times I've considered going to his house and demanding an answer, but I need to let it go. I *know* I need to, even if that gnawing confusion won't move past it. Wilde is giving me what I want: to be left alone to work. That's all I've demanded since I got here, and now that he's doing it, it's … it's …

The familiar need to lash out rises swiftly, and I have to physically brace myself to push it away. I have a short temper, I've always had a short temper, but maybe I don't want to have one anymore.

Maybe controlling it is the *one thing* I can get out of this place.

The *zzzt zzzt* of my drill meeting wood almost drowns out Kennedy's words.

"Is that Ziggy?" He's got his hand shielding his eyes from the sun, and I turn my attention toward where he's looking. There's a tall, lanky man leaning over the open hood of our car.

"What the *fuck* is he doing?"

Kennedy shoots me a look, and I remind myself to take a breath and settle my tone.

I try again. "Why is he looking in our car?"

"Dunno. Let's go ask him."

Considering how well that went the last time, I'm not interested in talking to myself again. "You go. I'll finish this."

He hurries off, and I do my best not to be bitter about how easily I slipped right into that headspace of suspicion and aggression. In my defense, he could be doing who the fuck knows what with our car, and—I forcefully cut that thought off too. Normal people don't react like this. Ziggy has done nothing to deserve me being an asshole again, and I'm going to stick with that.

I get the last crossbeam in place and then walk toward the group. Hart has drifted out from somewhere, and he's standing behind Ziggy, watching his every move as Kennedy talks enough for the three of them.

"Yeah, I wouldn't have even thought about getting it serviced, but with the miles we've been doing lately, that's a smart call."

I'm good with houses, but when it comes to cars, I couldn't even tell you where the oil goes. Dad wasn't around to show us things like that, and Mom probably wouldn't have been able to remember where she left the car, let alone locate the oil tank.

Ziggy's unsurprisingly working silently, and I have to hope that my brothers know more about what he's doing than I do because, for all I know, he could be cutting our brake lines.

Feels shitty to bring that up if the guy is only here to help us.

"You a mechanic or something?" I ask, keeping my voice low enough that he can pretend not to hear me.

It's too late for that when his back stiffens, and he throws a look around Kennedy at me. My brother shifts—on purpose or not, I don't know—and blocks Ziggy's view.

After a few seconds, the guy taps the battery.

"You know about … batteries?" Hart guesses.

That prompts Ziggy to tug at the red wire beside his hand, slightly more aggressively each time as he watches Kennedy.

"Power … wires … electrician?"

Ziggy nods, and Kennedy immediately turns to me, eyes wide in a way I can read his every thought.

*No,* I mouth, but he ignores me.

"We need an electrician. We've been trying to find one to help us here."

Ziggy takes an immediate step back from the car.

"Don't," I warn Kennedy. "None of them want us here in the first place. You really think he'd *help*? You really think *Wilde* would let him?"

"It's not up to Wilde," he snaps back. "I'm sure Ziggy can decide for himself if he wants work or not."

And apparently, he can, because Ziggy closes the small box he's brought with him, then turns and walks away.

"Hey, wait!" Kennedy calls, but Ziggy doesn't stop.

He's about to go after him, and I have to catch Kennedy's T-shirt to stop that from happening.

"It's his choice," I point out. "Looks to me like he made it."

"No. Like you said, it's Wilde. He's probably scared."

It's an effort not to roll my eyes. "Or he doesn't want to see his town overrun, just like everyone else here." What did Wilde call them? *Wenders?*

"Then why is he helping us? Why is he checking the car over and washing our motorcycle?"

Those aren't answers I have for him either. "Maybe he's bored."

"I think he wants to make friends."

"With you, maybe. Definitely not with me."

"Yeah, well, that happens when you throw people into walls."

I don't bother to point out that's basically Wilde's and my mating ritual. Or it was. Before … whatever happened.

"We do need an electrician," Hartwell says, not bothering with the rest of the conversation. "What's the luck that one happens to live right here?"

Considering the luck we've had so far, I'd say it's slim. "Is he actually qualified, or does he just know about it? Or *thinks* he knows about it."

Kennedy's still watching where Ziggy disappeared. "I believe him."

"Of course you do," Hart says. "You think everyone is a good person."

"Not Sutton." He gives me a pointed look. "Or Wilde."

Sutton, I'll give him. Wilde … none of us knows anything about him. The guy made me fucking *crawl* to him, which is evil enough, but … I can't move on from his anger when I last saw him. There had to have been something deeper there than general pissed-offedness.

"Maybe you could try talking to him again," Kennedy says without looking at me. "We really need an electrician."

"You don't even know that Ziggy wants to do it yet. He literally turned his back on us."

"Whatever." Kennedy throws his hands up. "We'll go back to complaining that we have nothing."

He leaves, and I feel Hart's heavy stare on me.

"I do so love to complain," he drags out.

"Wilde doesn't want to talk to me."

"You mean you *don't* trade sweet nothings while you fuck? Enlightening."

I turn and close the hood on our car. "You are so irritating."

"I am. You remember that when I'm the only one who can find us an electrician since Kennedy is usually too busy to leave this place and you refuse to make friends."

Refuse to make friends. Fucking hell. "First I was getting too friendly with him, now—"

Hart's snort takes over my words. "We both know you don't have to be friendly with someone to fuck them."

"I really love how you're both suddenly coming for my private business."

"Kenny says this is caring," he answers, sounding like he doesn't care at all.

"It's not."

He watches me, and I pointedly don't watch him. "Anything you need to talk about?"

"Nope."

"Thank fuck for that." He heads in the same direction Kennedy went, really cementing that it's them against me. Like it's always been. I'm left to figure it all out for myself.

# CHAPTER
# TWENTY-SIX

WILDE

When I get to the swimming hole, I don't need the sight of the bike or the dirty old boots to tell me there's already someone there. I can feel it in the ripples through the normally still air, in the way something inside me braces for a fight. I swear, even from here, I can make out the ever-present bubble gum scent.

"You kept me waiting," he calls the second he sees me. I can't help noticing the clothes lying innocently by his boots.

I'm not sure how to feel about him showing up here. I've calmed down after the other day, and as long as our conversation stays clear of that, I have no issues. None beyond the general fact that he's in my town at all. Which is the real kicker. I'm not used to being out of control, and the way Hudson manages to stir me up so easily should have me turning and heading in the other direction.

I count to three in my head, giving myself a chance to walk away. When that doesn't happen, I strip off my shirt instead.

Hudson watches every movement, and I hesitate for a second over taking off my briefs. It's not something I've ever thought twice about, and I have to shake off that stupidity as I kick out of them in annoyance.

The water's warm like I knew it would be, and I stride out into it, ignoring that Hudson is there at all. Except if there's one thing Hudson can't do, it's be quiet, and as soon as I'm close enough, that mouth of his opens again.

"You have a lot of scars."

It takes me a second to remember that the first time he saw me naked, he supposedly doesn't remember, and the second time, I was half-submerged in the water. Instead of answering, I dive under the water, eyes screwed shut as I float there for a moment just to get away from him. When I come back up for air, he's moved closer.

"I pissed you off the other day," he says.

"Probably will piss me off again if you bring it up now."

The water brings out the blue and gold tints in his green eyes. "I'm sorry. I mean, I'm clueless exactly what it is that I said, but … something got to you."

"Nothing got to me."

"Uh-huh. That's why you chased me away. No reason."

"I didn't chase you."

Those pretty lips of his almost reach a smile. "I like it here …"

"Enjoy it," I can't help but throw back. "It won't be this way for long." I don't need to spell out my meaning for him to follow what I'm getting at.

"It might not be as bad as you think. Maybe whoever we sell to will barely be here at all."

"Will you stop with Old End?" I ask him, but I can already

read the answer before he has one for me. Old End is the start. He owns this place, and he's planning to make as much out of it as he can.

"I don't know."

"Probably should figure it out, considering you have twenty-seven of us reliant on your decisions."

His blond eyebrows flex into a frown. "I'm not the bad guy."

"Good guys usually don't have to say that."

"Good guys usually don't have wild men questioning their character."

"Good guys don't give wild men a reason to."

We've drifted unconsciously closer, and I'm barely aware of the magnets tugging us together, only the aftereffects that leave us face-to-face with a few feet between us.

I want to ask why he's here, but I know I'll only get his usual smart-ass response. After how we left things, I thought he'd be as content to ignore me as I was to ignore him. The urge to fuck him again has been strong, but I've been able to push that down whenever I remembered the sickening feelings he left me with.

"You're here hoping I'll lessen your guilt?" I prod, hoping it will get me answers. "Not going to happen."

"Good thing I don't feel guilty."

"You want something, then?"

I'm almost hoping he'll say he wants sex because it will put an end to talking, but then I'll have to figure out if I want to go there. Well, actually, *want* isn't the issue. I know I want it, but I also know I shouldn't.

Which one will win today?

"Is Ziggy an electrician?"

The question throws me. "Why?"

"He told us that he is."

Again, Ziggy telling them anything doesn't make sense.

"Did you get that out of him the day you threatened him?"

"No." Hudson's smile finally tugs upward. "Today. He was working on our car, and I thought, you know what? If Wilde wanted to get rid of us, all he'd have to do is get one of his Wenders to cut our brake lines." Hudson watches me for confirmation.

"Now, why didn't I think of that?" I ask flatly.

"So he wasn't there because you sent him?"

"Believe it or not, everyone here runs their own lives."

"Good to know." He's still inching closer, and I haven't backed up yet. "Then you won't care if he helps us out with a little wiring?"

"Wiring?"

Hudson tilts his head from one side to the other. "Some wiring. Lighting. Then the full electrical needs for the place."

Bile creeps up my throat at the thought of him using one of my Wenders for his job. "Ziggy can do what he likes."

"Good to know."

"Doubt he'd like that though."

A little *ha* leaves him. "Don't be so sure. I think Ziggy-zag has a soft spot for us."

"Considering the way you're destroying all our homes, don't bank on it."

"If that's the case …" He gets close enough to drop his voice. "Why do you have a soft spot for me?"

"You're confusing a horny need to shut you up with being soft."

"I don't think I am." Hudson settles within a foot of me, eyes roaming my face. "Do you ever shave off that filthy beard?"

"No."

"Clean it up, at least?"

"No." The most I do is messily trim it when it gets too long. "I noticed you shaved your balls."

His whole face lights up. "Waxed. And I knew you were checking me out."

"Bit hard not to when you're putting on a display." My lips are burning with another question. "Is that the only place you wax?"

"Nope." He grins. "Ask me where."

"Where?"

"My chest and stomach. Men like a smooth surface to play on."

"Not me."

"Haven't heard you complain yet."

If he gets any closer, he'll feel how hard he's made me, so I keep those few inches of distance in place. It doesn't matter though. Hudson's steady gaze has tension wrapping around us like thick humidity before a summer storm.

"Your hair could use a trim too." He reaches out, fingers tipping into the hairline above my ear before I snatch his wrist in my grip.

"Was Ziggy all you came here for?"

"Yes." His voice dips lower, hand dropping until I release him from my grip. "But he's not why I want to stay."

The clear plea for sex makes my pulse inch higher. Fuck, it's ridiculous how much I want it. How he can infuriate me and leave me desperate for more. It's been two weeks since we fucked. Normally, I go a whole month without getting off with another person, and it isn't an issue. Now, we've done it twice in two weeks, and I know, without a doubt, that I can't wait another two weeks to be in Wayward again.

Hudson's making me insatiable.

"Why do you want to stay?" I push him.

"Because you're fantastic fucking company."

"Liar."

He laughs again, the small type of laugh that gives his lips purpose. "I haven't seen you all week."

"I know."

"It pissed me off."

"You? Angry? I'm shocked."

"I left my window open and everything."

I have no way of knowing if he's telling the truth or playing with me. "You'll let all the bugs in."

"Not what I was hoping to catch."

The question that's been burning on my tongue since last time comes out before I can stop it. "Why? I know what your appeal is, but why the hell are you bothering with me?"

I've obviously shocked him. "You think I'm appealing? I thought I just annoyed you to the point of orgasm."

"I never said you didn't."

"Fine. Here's a deal. I'll tell you if you tell me."

I shift that offer around in my head. Do I want to know badly enough to confess how attracted to him I am? It should be obvious by how often I want to fuck him, but wanting sex and being attracted are two very different things in my experience. And when it comes to Hudson, what we're doing, it's not only about getting off. I don't need to come this often. I never want to come this often.

This frequent boner is all him.

"Fine," I grunt. "You first."

"Deal. I'll trust you." The challenging look he levels me with taunts me not to follow through. "You intimidate me. Everything about you is designed to look scary. Untamable. And I know that when we fuck, neither of us has to deal with feelings afterward. Getting to you makes me feel powerful. Unstoppable."

Like I thought, sex is a game to him, like everything else in his life. Considering it usually isn't anything more than a transaction for me, I can live with that. He can feel as powerful as he likes as long as he knows I'm in control.

"Now you," he reminds me.

But after hearing what he said, confessing that he's the most beautiful man I've ever met doesn't sit right. Being a pretty face isn't something he had to work for or even something he did on purpose. It just is. And so I keep that side quiet and say, "It's the only way I can make you do what you're told. And the controlling side of me really fucking loves to see someone so stubborn give in, all because I told you to."

An exhale shivers from him. "Both of our reasons are fucked-up."

"They are."

"I don't care though."

I didn't think he would, but those four little words feel like they're saying more than they should. "What now? We fuck again, then pretend it didn't happen until we give in the next time?"

"No." He moves so fast I don't have time to move away. Hudson's chest and torso press to mine, hard cock slotting against my own, and my hands find his hips under the water. There's nothing that gets my blood pumping like a solid man against me. "I say that we fuck again. Then instead of pretending like it didn't happen, we do it again." He nips at my earlobe. "And again. And we give in to the fact that as long as I'm in this town, we're going to want each other, no matter whether we actually like each other or not. My body wants your body, and your body wants mine. We need to stop fighting it. Just give in. Enjoy the one good thing we can get out of crossing each other's paths."

I'm so used to fighting. I'm so used to being in control of

everything in my world. What he's asking for: open-ended sex that will end when he leaves isn't something that can be controlled.

"Why can't I stop wanting you?" I groan.

"It's chemistry." His lips tease mine. "Now, do you agree to the deal? Or am I walking out of here?"

# CHAPTER
# TWENTY-SEVEN

## HUDSON

'd been prepared to leave—with a lot of whining and pain—but Wilde doesn't take that option. Is it cocky of me to say that I knew he never would?

Maybe we should be talking more or sorting through the landslide of issues that exists between us, but talking can come later when I'm able to concentrate on anything other than how good this feels. His confidence and the way he knows exactly what he wants and isn't worried about demanding it does things to me that I probably shouldn't feel, but I'm not going to fight it. Not when my dick is so enticingly hard.

Wilde maybe has an inch on me, if that, so we're almost eye to eye as we breathe through this intense arousal, and I watch his face for any sign of doubt.

He's backing me up, hands a steady presence on my hips as we head back toward the shore. Our cocks skim under the water, and all it does is tease me harder.

"I think I hate your beard as much as you hate my eyelashes," I tell him.

Wilde pauses where the water reaches mid-shin and briefly squeezes his hold tighter. "Lie down."

I do as I'm told, half on the rocky shoreline while the water laps at my calves. Wilde's big body covers mine, and the heat of the day and light brush of the breeze means nothing with his body warmth taking over.

He dips his mouth by my ear. "One day, when my beard is scraping your inner thighs, I'll ask you what you think of it then."

Just the thought of it sends phantom ripples along my legs and into my balls. Wilde buried between my thighs sounds like heaven, and I'm tempted to ask for it now—even if it means crawling all over this fucking place—but then he thrusts slowly on top of me, and that need settles. His body against mine, our wet cocks rubbing together, the way his biceps bulge from where he's holding himself up on his forearms … this is what I need.

"Look at us, face-to-face," I tease, trying to pull his attention to me. His eyes stay locked to the ground beside my head. "Didn't even need to force you this time. You're addicted already, aren't you?"

"Can I get through one orgasm without hearing your voice?"

"Never. I know it gets you good and riled up."

He thrusts down harder, one hand taking my leg and hitching it up to give him more room to move. Our wet bodies slide together easily, and the weight pressing me into the ground, combined with the gentle water lapping at our legs, makes this feel like a fever dream.

I take hold of his sides, hands running up to his shoulders and back down his back. His skin is almost dry from the sun, burning up and addictive under my palms. I reach the dip in his lower back before moving on to his ass. It's all muscle. Steady muscle from days of hard work that flexes sluttily in my grip with every roll of his hips.

"Fuck …" I breathe into his ear.

I think this is the first time we've been completely naked together, and having him flush against me is heating my blood. His beard scratches at my cheek and neck, and for all my taunting, it only nudges my senses higher. Makes my brain wander to the thought of kissing him and how it would feel. Would my lips end up reddened, like a walking advertisement to everything we're doing, or would it be soft enough to avoid leaving me raw?

Wilde's never shown interest in wanting to kiss me though, so I'll never know, which is a pity since I find kissing so fucking hot. Being in control is important to him, and while I'll push him with some things, I'm okay with letting Wilde take the lead.

His steely cock ruts against mine, our balls pressing together, making the whole area alive with want. It's bliss, and I could lie here all day having Wilde move on top of me like this, but there's an itching need that's become impossible to ignore.

He hasn't looked at me once, and I crave his attention more than I crave blowing my load.

Before Wilde can stop me, I grab hold of him and flip us so Wilde's back meets the rock, and then I settle up on top of him.

There's confusion and unasked questions in his gaze, but I ignore them as I sit on his thick thighs, cock to cock, skin prickling tighter under his heavy focus.

Our eyes meet as I spit into my palm and then wrap it around us both.

He's trying to look unaffected, but every tightening of his throat, every time his lips part or his hips thrust up into my fist, seeking friction, I see the control chip away bit by bit.

"Do you like what you see?" I ask, fucking my fist, frustrated that I can't get a good grip in my left, but it's only dragging this on longer. Keeping my need skimming along the surface, holding out for that moment until the wave collides and it's over. With our beyond-rocky relationship, I want to hold on to these moments for as long as I can, hoping they'll drug us with endorphins and ensure there's no end in sight.

The more we do it, the more I'm finding my attraction to him growing. It's not just the danger and wanting to best him; it's the scent of pine trees and salt water that clings to his skin. It's those deep gray eyes that try to hide what's going on behind them and failing. It's the road map of scars that tells a story he's keeping close to his chest.

I've never met anyone like Wilde, and I have no idea yet whether it's a good thing or a bad thing. I just know that this is another one of those stupid choices I'm so good at making. This will either end with an all-out town war or me leaving once my job here is done. As long as we stay in it only for the sex, that works for me, but when Wilde lifts a large, calloused hand and sets it over my pec before dragging it down my torso, it brings my whole body alive.

This euphoric high that I can't get enough of.

I want him to look, to touch, to burn me from the inside out. I want to be Wilde's sole focus. I want to consume his thoughts, all day, all night, like he's been doing to me. My balls tighten with the idea of him becoming addicted. With him *needing* me.

"You didn't answer," I push. He's bucking underneath me, seeking the relief I am. "Do you like what you see?"

I'm not expecting an answer, so he surprises me with his deep rasp. "You're too fucking sexy for words."

Lust shivers down my spine.

Wilde's thumb flicks over the stiff peak of my nipple. "If I could reach, I'd sink my teeth into this sexy nipple."

"You like my nipples?" I ask as they prickle tighter under his praise.

"I unwillingly like every fucking inch of you. How can one man be so irritating and look so fucking …"

I lean forward, planting my hand near his head, and Wilde wraps his hand around us. My left hand gets caught in his grip, and he crushes our cocks together in a way that almost makes me come.

"So fucking what?" I manage to choke out.

His teeth clench together.

"What were you going to say?"

"Nothing. It's the orgasm talking."

"Then let it talk." I lean my face in closer.

It takes a whole minute of panting before Wilde pulls his stare to mine. "So fucking *perfect*."

The praise, the appreciation, it's too much for my little mind. I fuck his grip like I'm losing control, and I can feel him unraveling beneath me. With every second of desperate hunger that passes between us, I'm expecting him to look away. I wait for the connection to drop. For me to lose his attention.

But those gunmetal eyes are locked on mine, gaze focused and penetrating. Our labored breathing meets in the few inches between us, and I don't know what Wilde sees when he looks at me, but for those few razor-sharp seconds, he lets me see too much.

Something tugs deeper inside my chest than I've ever felt before, but it doesn't last long. The pleasure rippling at the base of my spine takes over, and I'm done for. I fuck our fists, lost in the glide of our precum as my balls tighten almost painfully, teasingly, and then … the release I need hits. The orgasm melts away every thought I've ever had as I sink into the high and finally have the relief I've craved all week.

Wilde follows me over the edge, and feeling his cock pulse against mine is something I want to experience for too many more moments to count.

Before I can follow that thought too far along, I roll off him, back against the hot rocks, water on my legs feeling cool against my overheated skin. Wilde's chest is rising and falling as fast as mine, and when my gaze dips lower, I'm treated to the view of our cum mixed together in the hair sprinkled over his torso.

He doesn't look at me, so I have all the time I want to look at him. He's … unpolished. It's not something I ever thought I'd find hot, but on him, it feels raw and honest in a way I've never considered before. The only thing out of place is his sleeve of tattoos.

"You don't strike me as a tattoo kind of guy" is the first thing I say.

He goes on staring at the sky, ignoring me, before he extends that arm between us, tilting it over so I get a good view of his inner arm. And the scar that runs almost from wrist to elbow.

I don't waste my breath asking about it, just roll onto my side to get a better look. It's an old one, probably as old as the smaller ones that cover his torso. Most of them are uniform, like little nicks, but here and there, one is deeper, more twisted. Whatever happened, his arm caught most of it.

He got his tattoos to hide it. The twisted linework does well to incorporate the milky skin into the design.

And Wilde willingly shared that with me.

"I like it."

He tugs his arm away, then pushes to his feet. "I'm going to clean up."

I watch him stride into the water, gaze locked on his broad

back, wondering about all the things he won't talk about. There's more to him than the growly mountain man I first encountered, but I have a good feeling I'll never get those answers.

I join him in the water, not in a hurry to leave and, for once, not having much to say. It's a weird sort of silence, heavy with curiosity, but peaceful too.

It lasts until we both get dressed and leave.

# CHAPTER
# TWENTY-EIGHT

## WILDE

The tarp that covers the entrance to Ziggy's mine shaft is open, so I take it as an invitation to walk inside.

"Where's your shaver?"

He glances over from where he's brushing his teeth at his sink and taps the set of drawers next to it. Ziggy's whole place is one room. His bed is down the furthest end, almost swallowed in the darkness of the tunnel, and a stuffy couch closest to the entrance sits next to his fridge, with a small table holding a boxy old TV in front of them. Then his bathroom is lined up along the opposite wall. Sink, makeshift shower, toilet. All plumbed in at some point. The only thing he's missing is a kitchen, but Ziggy doesn't cook anyway.

The building storm outside has thrown his place into shadows.

I retrieve the razor from the drawers next to where he's standing, ignoring his shrewd gaze in the tiny mirror.

"Thanks. I'll bring it back tomorrow."

He spits out his toothpaste and turns to me. Ziggy can say way too much with absolutely no words, and I know the searching gaze is looking for a clue about why I'm here when scissors have always worked just fine.

"I'm due for a trim. Beard's getting a bit long." Unfortunately, I catch a glimpse of myself in his mirror, and I don't like what I see. It's not only long, but it's … impossible to tell that there's a face under there. My grip tightens around the shaver.

"So …" I wasn't planning on bringing this up, but I need a subject change. "The brothers want you to work for them."

He goes unnaturally still, and his lips pull tight.

"Do what you want."

Ziggy rolls his eyes and crosses over to his couch. He drops onto it, body sagging forward, elbows on knees as he drags his hands through his thick hair.

"Hey … what's wrong?"

There's a moment of indecision before he speaks. "Kennedy is … he's, umm …" The flush that creeps up Ziggy's neck finishes that sentence for him.

"You're attracted to him?"

He scowls, but the way his body tenses tells me I'm right and he's as happy about that as I am about my thing with Hudson.

"At least he's not an asshole." I sigh my way through. "Apparently."

Ziggy's gaze hesitantly finds mine.

"I'm fucking Hudson."

The judgment in his eyes echoes everything I've been thinking.

"Yes, he's a dick. I get it." That said, after yesterday, I don't know if I completely believe my words. I have a lot of issues with his confession about dealing drugs—prescription or otherwise—

because I have no time for that. It's a very hard line I've set for this town, and we've had two people leave because they wanted to bend those rules.

From everything he said before I got thrown back into the past, he's stopped that life, but knowing he was so close to going back to it before he came to Wilde's End has me wary. If things get hard here, will that be his solution?

"I'm conflicted," I finally admit. "I know what they're doing here. I know that their goals go completely against ours, and if they succeed, everything that we've built here will disappear. But I can't turn off that little voice telling me to go see him. To draw him out. To fuck him again." I don't even know what I'm hoping to get from this conversation. "I'm just saying that I know what it's like to be torn. If helping them with those houses gets you time with Kennedy, well, you won't get judgment from me."

He taps the place over his heart, and I do the same back.

It's not exactly an I love you, but an I appreciate you. I see you. Thank you. All rolled into one.

"Right." I look down at the shaver. "Guess I should probably …"

Ziggy stands suddenly, strides toward me, then takes my arm and tugs me back over to his mirror. It's only just large enough to make out my whole face in it. I can't remember the last time I looked directly into a mirror. I don't own one. Checking my reflection isn't something I think about anymore, and the first thing that hits me is that I don't recognize myself.

There are lines by my eyes where there didn't used to be lines, and that's basically all I can see of my face.

Ziggy opens the second drawer I pulled the shaver from and grabs an attachment that he sets on the end. Then he plugs the thing in.

"You're going to shave me?"

He nods, slings a towel across my chest, then grabs a pair of scissors. He turns my head back toward the mirror and tugs my beard down with one hand. It reaches past my collarbones and might be the longest it's ever been.

Ziggy sets the scissors against the end, maybe an inch from the bottom. It's probably around where my choppy job would have started. Still long, still hidden, not enough of a difference for anyone to notice.

I huff, hating that I'm this torn over something so insignificant.

"Shorter."

Ziggy moves the scissors up.

"Shorter."

He keeps moving until the scissors are just below my chin. A "there" makes it past my lips before I can talk myself out of it, and Ziggy brings the scissors together. He cuts a rough line across the front, removing all the excess, and I have to look away.

I don't watch as he works, the *bzzz* of the shaver filling the air. We have solar batteries hooked up to the grid here, something that took years to accomplish, but while we have access to electricity, no one in Wilde's End uses it much. The point of being off the grid is to live off the grid. Most of us don't have TVs. Don't bother with lights when candles work just as well. I use my stove when I don't have the time to start a fire, but that and my fridge are basically it. We have a lot of freedom out here, and doing things manually, providing for ourselves, is a part of Wilde's End.

His gentle fingers turn my face from side to side as he works, and once he's done with the shaver, he moves on to a small razor. Hair falls away from my cheeks, and I tell myself not to look, but I do it anyway.

The difference is huge. He rubs something over my face before gesturing that he's done. I tug my hair back from my forehead, taking in the person I haven't seen this much of in years. In tidying up my beard, Ziggy has revealed the majority of my face. The effect makes me feel naked.

I regret it instantly.

He smiles at me, and I glower back.

"It's very noticeable."

A laugh slips from him.

The stark difference is a lot to take in, and I'm almost nervous about Hudson seeing me like this. He'll think I trimmed my beard for him when I didn't. At all. I was just ready to tidy it up again. I do it every few months, and him being around doesn't change that.

Even if this is a bit more than a tidy up.

I run my hand over my jawline, marveling at how smooth and short it is. This is going to take some getting used to. I eyeball the messy curls around my head, remembering how Hudson's fingers slid into them, and I shake my head.

I'm not cutting my fucking hair.

"Thanks."

He cleans the shaver equipment and tucks it all away.

I cross my arms and watch him work, remembering what Hudson told me about his brothers. "Kennedy's bi. By the way."

Ziggy flicks me an unimpressed look.

"Thought you might be interested. Bit of a romantic from what Hudson says."

The side of Ziggy's mouth creeps higher. "You two talk?"

For someone I've known for years, this might be the deepest conversation we've ever had. Normally, I talk and he listens about crops or fire safety or whatever else the town needs to keep chugging along. Sometimes it's rants about Foley. But it's occurring to me now that all the friendships I have here, that the family we've all built together, it's been based on a need to survive. Not necessarily because we know and like each other.

That's not the case for everyone, of course. Rooney has no issues with people. This is on me and my need to keep things surface level.

So I refuse to do that this time, as hard as it might be.

"Sometimes. Not a lot and not about much. Actually, Hudson is the one who usually does all the talking."

The glint in Ziggy's eye tells me he's not surprised by that.

"Maybe I could try harder, but I don't actually want to like him. I don't want to be attracted to him at all, but I can't control that. Being friends with him is something I still have a say in."

The hooded-eyes look he gives me makes it clear he doubts that.

"I don't want to be friendly with someone purposely ruining our lives."

He shrugs, and I know exactly what he's saying. Sometimes we don't have a choice. Sometimes things just are. It's the reason so many of us ended up here.

Ziggy whispers so quietly I have to strain to hear him. "Maybe friendship will make them stop."

I blink at him, processing the words because that's not something I ever considered. It's not something I think I ever *would* have considered. Why build a friendship when I can try running them out of town instead?

Except that running them out of town didn't work.

Maybe this is all I have left.

I'm not good at being friends though, and trying it with someone like Hudson, who's a minefield of bad ideas, makes the whole idea even worse.

But this is Wilde's End.

This is my *home*.

I refuse to go down without a fight, but maybe I've been using the wrong weapons.

"You going to help them?" I ask him.

After a moment, Ziggy nods.

"Okay then. I'll give you a ride down there."

# CHAPTER
## TWENTY-NINE

HUDSON

Feeling happy shouldn't be this off-putting, but there's literally nothing that could have brought it on. It's like I have this little spark in my chest, and whenever I try to fall into bad thoughts, the spark jolts me back to this sense that good is coming.

There's no other way to explain it, so I'm going to hope it means something and that I don't get let down.

The external frame of house two is done, which means we really have to decide on whether we're going to commit to bricking the whole thing or going with a more modern finish like metal. Wilde's End gets hot in summer but is supposed to snow in the winter, so we have to make sure we cover all bases. Insulation is a must, but we can't fucking decide on what to do first.

"Did you hear that?" Kennedy asks, cutting through my thoughts.

I look around the gutted room. "What?"

There's a pause as the three of us strain our ears for a sound, but there's nothing other than the birds outside.

"What did it sound like?" I ask.

"Hmm … An animal, maybe?"

"We *are* in bumfuck nowhere," Hart reminds him.

"No, but *in* the house."

I stop to listen again, and my brothers do the same. There's still nothing. I'm about to call Kennedy out on making up the sound to distract us from what to do on the exterior walls when deep *rwwwoal* beats me to talking.

"Okay, *that* I heard."

"Sounded like a cat," Hart murmurs, turning back to the plans.

A cat? That tickles the fight or flight in my brain when I remember that feral bobcat I came across. What if there's a whole feral family of them and they came to eat our faces?

I get up and head in the direction the noise came from. It was more toward the front of the house, I think, and I strain my ears over my heavy footsteps in case it comes again. There's nothing.

Until I open the front door. With the snick of the door, a gust of cold breeze rushes inside. The dark storm clouds are sitting low and heavy above us, and on the bottom step of the house—

A bobcat.

I have no idea if it's the same one or not, but considering it's larger than I've ever heard of a bobcat getting, there's a good chance it is. As soon as it sees me, it shifts upright, fur prickling around its shoulders, little razor teeth bared as that deep *rwoal* vibrates in its chest.

"Fuck off!" I tell it, one eye on the animal as I search either side of me for something to throw.

Its tail twitches in agitation.

"Move." I stomp forward, trying to scare it. The giant cat doesn't react. "Get the fuck out of here!"

I hear my brothers approaching behind me, but they lose my attention when the cat isn't alone.

"That wasn't very hospitable." The voice comes before the man. Devoid of emotion, but not in the bored way that Hart has perfected, it's the kind of voice that makes that spark in my chest die.

The man who steps into my view doesn't make me feel any better either. There's nothing friendly in his tight expression. My gaze runs from his red hair, shaved on one side, long and wild on the other, to his tense arm muscles, to the knife he's holding. Though I'm not sure that thing can be called a knife when it's as long as my forearm.

My arms fly out to grip the doorframe on either side of me, trying to block my brothers from view.

"What the fuck …" Kennedy squeaks.

"What do you want?" I ask the man.

"I thought city boys were supposed to have manners." His voice is low and hums with the tension of keeping it there. "First, you scare poor Bob. Then you shout at him. And now you haven't even bothered with introductions."

I have no idea what game he's playing, but as long as he stays down there and I stay up here, I'm going to play along. "Hudson. Who are you?"

His smile is chilling. "Lynx."

I've heard that name. Where have I heard it though? Probably from Wilde, and the way it spiked worry in my gut means whatever he said wasn't great.

"Ah … you've heard of me."

"No," I lie. "But I remember Bob."

Lynx's gaze drops to the bobcat. "Most people do. He's not very friendly."

"I've noticed."

"Not like me." Lynx's eyes are cold when they meet mine.

I swallow thickly, fingers aching with how tight my grip has gotten. "You're friendly?"

"Life of the party, some would say."

"Funny. Most friendly guys don't carry around machetes."

"Occupational hazard." His head tips to inspect my brothers. "You're twins."

"They are," I say before they can answer. When it comes to this man, I want my brothers left out of it.

"Ominous."

While I want to ask why, I also don't want this conversation to go on longer than it needs to. "Why are you here?" Now I sound like Wilde.

"The three of you have stirred up Wilde's End. I wanted to see what all the fuss is about."

"Well, you've seen. Now you can go."

Lynx's eyes narrow, and Bob makes a warning sound. "You don't make the rules in the End, little boy."

"This is my town." I sound a whole lot more confident than I am.

"You think money and some deeds get you ownership out here?" His laugh sounds all wrong as it's eaten by a rumble over-head. "I tolerate Wilde. I won't tolerate you."

Lynx steps onto the bottom stair, and Bob moves toward me to give him room. I'm coiled and ready for any sudden movements when a sheet of light rain breaks free of the clouds.

"Go away and you won't need to tolerate me at all."

Lynx taps the machete against the stair rail. "What are you doing in this town?"

"Renovating."

"Why?"

"That's our business."

Lynx looks down at Bob. "Did you hear that? His business, he says." Cold eyes meet mine again. "It would be a shame to have to get my answers by cutting them from your head."

I'm done with this. I'm about to shove my brothers back inside and slam the door on Lynx—though what we'd do after that I have no fucking clue, considering the whole back of the house is missing—when the sound of an engine makes us all turn.

Wilde's faded red truck comes into view, rolling to a stop on the road just down from us. He climbs out of the driver's side when Ziggy climbs out of the other.

"Lynx," he calls. "I thought I forbade you from coming here."

Lynx spins his machete with impressive confidence. "You did."

"Then why the fuck didn't you listen?"

"Because you failed at getting rid of them. You can't expect a teddy bear to do an animal's job."

"This teddy bear is doing fine."

I'm still tense, still holding my brothers back, but having Lynx's attention off me, even if that demon cat is still staring my way, makes it a fraction easier to breathe.

"Fine?" Lynx cackles, but it cuts off too fast, and when he speaks, that chilling nothingness is back. "You were both looking *very fine* down by the swimming hole yesterday."

It takes me a moment to realize he saw us. I could hope it was only while we were swimming, but the pointedness to his words makes me think it was more than that. "You were perving on us?"

"You were out. In public. I assumed you wanted me to stay for the whole filthy show." He lifts his machete my way. "You're lucky I didn't trip and land this in your back."

"What we did was none of your business."

"This whole town is my business. See, I'm the pest control in these parts. And you …" He sneers my way. "*You're* the biggest pest we've ever had."

"That's enough," Wilde snaps. "I told you I'd handle it, and I *will* handle it."

"Tick tock …" Lynx whispers through the building rain. "I don't play well with patience."

Wilde stalks toward him. "You don't make demands of me."

"Indeed, my liege, but don't forget. The only demands you make are the ones I let you get away with."

"Threaten me one more time—" Wilde's hands close over Lynx's shirt, and before he can finish his sentence, the cat pounces.

It smacks into Wilde's side, jaw locking over his neck as it takes a swipe at his face with one large paw.

I'm moving before I notice I am. My shoulder slams into Lynx's back, throwing him from the bottom step into Wilde and the stupid cat, and the three of them hit the wet road. I haul Lynx away, tossing him to the side before he can take a swing at me with the machete, and Wilde snarls as he throws the cat off him.

Then he looks down at his outer thigh and the blood seeping through his jeans.

My gut bottoms out, and I'm about to drop down beside him and make sure he's okay when Wilde pushes unsteadily to his feet.

"For fuck's sake. I have Peril next week!"

Lynx straightens, body coiled like an animal about to pounce. "The city boy pushed me."

"If I catch you here again, I'll be calling a town meeting."

"Call a town meeting," Lynx spits, and the careful detachment is gone, replaced by a feral growl. "And I can't promise you'll wake to see it."

They stare each other down, and surprisingly, Wilde is the first to let it drop.

"I've told you to control that stupid thing," he grunts, pointing at Bob.

"And I've told *you* to try controlling a wild animal."

I'm panting as I look from Wilde to Lynx and back. Bob's golden eyes are locked on Wilde, and I'm not so sure it isn't going to attack again.

Lynx's head snaps my way. "You get one warning. Don't make me come back here."

"That sounds like a you choice."

His eyes narrow for a second before he leaves, Bob lingering for too long to be comfortable before he follows Lynx off the road and into the trees.

As soon as they're gone, I turn to Wilde, but Ziggy has beat me to him. Ziggy is shoving Wilde back toward the truck.

"I told you I'm fine," Wilde hisses.

"You don't look so fine," Kennedy argues. "You need that doctor of yours."

"Lynx hardly got me."

But his jeans are soaked through with rain and blood, so it's impossible to know. Even though Wilde doesn't sound like he's stressing, the way my heart is racing makes it clear that I am. "I'll drive you," I say, which gets a sharp and short laugh from Ziggy.

"What?"

Wilde glowers at his friend. "No one drives me anywhere."

"You're injured."

"*Barely.*"

We glare at each other, and like with Lynx, Wilde cuts contact first.

"Fine. I'll see Booker. But I'll drive my damn self."

He turns, leaving us all behind as he tries to hide the way he's limping for his truck. He's not getting away that easily.

Wilde's just closed his door behind him when I reach the passenger one and pull it open. I'd feel bad for dripping all over his truck's seat if he wasn't bleeding all over his.

"I'm coming with you," I tell him.

He huffs. "Just when I thought this day couldn't get any worse."

I'm about to remind him that this isn't my ideal day either when I notice something for the first time.

His face. His *actual* face.

"You shaved."

Wilde ignores me as he pulls away.

But I can't stop looking at him. At his pretty bowed lips, at his jawline, at the way his whole face feels open and the more I look, the closer I'm getting to his secrets.

That little spark in my chest comes back alive.

# CHAPTER
## THIRTY



Fucking Lynx. I should have known he was going to pull something like this. My injuries are burning against my rain-cooled skin, and it's almost a relief that it's all I can focus on and not Hudson's unwavering attention.

The whole time I drive, his eyes are on me, and I knew cutting my beard was a stupid fucking choice. I can't tell if my hands are clammy from the attention or still wet from the rain.

"Stop looking at me," I give in and say.

"Sorry. Still trying to process that a human lived under all that hair."

I want to let it drop, but his eyes are needling at my consciousness in a way that makes sitting still uncomfortable. "I told you to stop looking at me."

From the corner of my eye, I see Hudson turn to look out his window. Not that he can see a whole lot. It's mid-afternoon, and the sudden storm has darkened everything to a point that I need my headlights on as we rumble through the trees. These storms sweep in often and usually sweep out again just as quickly.

"You know," Hudson says, voice fogging up the glass he's leaning against, "if you weren't so hot, I wouldn't keep looking at you."

I huff, trying to play it off like that's the most ridiculous thing I've ever heard, while my face warms. I'm not deluded. I know I'm not hot, and I'm okay with that. I'm a grumpy, damaged shell of a human who focuses on nothing but the town so that I don't need to think about anything else. Twenty long years I've built myself into exactly that type of person, and it was going well.

Hudson's the worst thing that's happened to me since I moved here.

Because Hudson makes me think.

Makes me remember that maybe a human lives under all this deflection.

I pull up beside the chop shop, and before I've even cut the engine, Hudson jumps out into the rain and rounds the front of the truck. His figure cuts through the headlights, brightening momentarily and giving me this weird moment of … he's *here*. This man with bright eyes and a big personality. Someone who could be anyone.

Worry lines his forehead as he pulls my door open.

I snap out of my … whatever … and switch the truck off.

"What are you doing?" I eye him suspiciously as I climb out, and he hovers.

"Didn't know if you needed help. I can carry you like you carried me if you want?"

Like he could get me off the ground. I don't even bother pointing that out as I wait for him to move and let me past. Hudson doesn't get the hint.

"Move."

He studies my face for a moment. "Thanks. I know it was lucky timing, but if you didn't step in when you did … I dunno. He gives me the creeps."

"Lynx has that effect on people. He's a necessary evil. Keeps the bears and mountain lions away, farms the crops we use to feed the town. We'd be in trouble without him here. But he's … his own version of law and order."

"And his cat?"

I reach for the bite at my neck, still feeling the way those teeth shredded through flesh. "It showed up one day and hasn't left his side since. He's waiting for the day it turns on him, but given how overprotective it is of Lynx, I don't see that happening."

Hudson's lips part and close again. "A bobcat *adopted* him?"

"That's the story."

He finally steps back and gives me some room. "Does that hurt?"

"Would you like to be bitten by a wild animal?"

"I saw that thing once. A few days ago, when I was looking for you, it cut off my path and scared the shit out of me."

"You didn't say anything."

"Didn't know I had to." Hudson's ankle is obviously feeling better because he bounds ahead of me and knocks on the side of the chop shop. Normally, Booker hears anyone coming and is out the front waiting, but the storm must have covered our approach.

Booker opens the door, leaning against the doorway as he looks from Hudson to me. "Why are you both standing in the rain?"

"Because it's fucking raining?" I point out.

He steps aside to let us in, and I don't miss the way his eyes linger on my neck. "My, my. What fun have you been up to today?" He walks across to the bed and pats the top of it. I hate sitting in here, despite Peril sending me here more times than I can count. Especially in the earlier days when it was all fists, blood, and broken bones.

"Ran into Lynx."

"Ah." His gaze snags on my leg. "Pants off."

I huff and shove painfully out of them before climbing up onto the chair. I'm confident the cut wasn't deep, but that doesn't mean it's easy to walk on; every flex of the muscle sends a spasm through my leg and into my hip.

"I'm not used to you having an audience," Booker says, pulling his gloves on and walking closer.

"I'm not used to it either." I glare at Hudson, but he only grabs a chair and drops into it.

"Repaying the favor." He grins, like he's enjoying this, but something makes it feel fake.

Booker tilts my head back and runs his fingers over the bite. "Bobby tore you right up."

I grunt as Booker lingers over the wound. I don't have time to play his games today. "Can you get on with it? Not a fan of how much it hurts."

"Oh, I bet it does." He leans closer. "I know better than to offer you painkillers though. I'll need to clean it up and give you a shot—don't argue with me." He breathes in deeply before moving on to my leg. "This will require stitches." He peels the wound back so far it makes Hudson gag and look away. "The clever man reached muscle. What were you doing playing with his knife anyway?"

"It wasn't intentional." For all his faults, Lynx is as much a part of this town as I am, which makes me add, "From either of us."

Hudson snorts. "What other reason would he have for carrying that huge thing around? Even if he didn't want someone to get hurt, he wanted to intimidate us into thinking we would."

He'll never understand things outside of that narrow social consciousness he grew up with. Everyone out here coexists—even Lynx knows that—and we all have a purpose that makes the town work. The way things happen where he comes from and how they happen here don't align. "He uses it to clear paths. Lynx explores further than the rest of us, and most of the paths you ride on were created by him. Plus, he travels deep into the forest, to our borders, making sure his deterrents are set up and there's nothing around that will attract unwanted animals, so he uses it for protection as well." As much as I'm hurting and want to bury my fist in Lynx's face, it's important Hudson gets it. "He never leaves the house without that thing. To him, it's safety. Freedom. An extension of himself. I'd wager money that he had no idea it was scaring you."

"We'll disagree on that."

Apparently. I go back to ignoring him, which really is what I aim to do most of the time. It doesn't play into my *make friends with the guy* plan, but I figure that can wait for my leg to be stitched back together. Injuries always make me grumpy, and this is no different.

Booker gets to work, cleaning the wounds on my neck and face and patching me up as best he can. Then he gives me a shot for the bite before starting on my leg. I have no idea why he'd leave the worst for last, but a hunch tells me he wants more time to enjoy his work. So long as he fixes me, I don't give a shit, but I wait, teeth locked together as he tugs the needle through my skin, over and over again.

I do my best not to let the pain show, but fuck, it hurts. Almost enough that I consider relaxing my rule and accepting the pain relief, but I can get through this. I've gotten through worse.

"You're going to struggle to sleep through the pain tonight," Booker warns, cutting off the stitches and sealing the area with gauze. "You need to keep those clean. No swimming. Come to me if they bust open again … or just if you want me to look after them for you."

"I'm sure I'll manage."

I climb off the bed, leg stiff and already causing hell, and before I can reach for my pants, Hudson beats me to it. He kneels, pants held open and waiting, and when his eyes flick up my way, there's a silent challenge in his gaze to deny him.

But having him kneel at my feet is making the need to deny him the last thing on my mind.

I step into one side, then the next, and Hudson slowly drags my jeans back up again. He's careful not to hurt me, even though I'd expected him to do it on purpose. It's not like we haven't made each other's lives hard.

He stands, only a few inches between us as he fastens the top button. "Time to get you home."

"Oh, I bet it is," Booker interjects, reminding me he's in the room.

I stride away from them both.

# CHAPTER
# THIRTY-ONE

HUDSON

Wilde tries to leave without me again, but he should know by now how persistent I am. Apparently as much as he is because he also refuses to let me drive. We reach his place, and he gets out before I can open his door, but it doesn't make a difference to me. It's not until he climbs up to his front porch, me right behind him, that he hesitates.

It takes a moment of indecision before he turns and holds his keys out. "Drive yourself back. Ziggy can take the truck to get home and come see me tomorrow."

"Yeah, no."

"You can't walk in the rain."

"I'm not planning to."

It takes Wilde an embarrassingly long time to get to the point I'm making. "Well, you're not coming inside."

"Yeah, I am. I have to get you settled."

It's like he takes that as a personal offense. "I can settle myself."

"Can but won't."

His jaw locks like he's praying for patience. "No one is allowed in my house."

"But I've been in there before."

"And I didn't allow it."

I climb the last step so we're both standing on the little porch. "What's your problem?"

"Well, the one and only time someone has been in my house since it was built, they broke one of the few things that are special to me. So maybe that has something to do with it."

I … did what? Guilt tries to shrivel up my gut.

But while I feel bad about that—even if he did smash our shit up—this rule was clearly in place long before me. "I promise not to mess with anything else. Happy?"

He doesn't answer, which means I'm wearing him down. Testing that theory, I step toward his front door and rest my fingers on the door handle. Wilde doesn't try to stop me, so I turn the knob and push my way inside.

It's as small as it looks from the outside. One room that holds a kitchen, living room, and small table to eat at. There are two doors opposite me that I'm assuming are a bedroom and a bathroom.

The place might be small, but I'm taken off guard by how cozy it is. He's got a teapot that's covered in something knitted, and there's a patchwork quilt thrown over the back of his couch. I walk closer, running my fingers over the stitching. It's soft and well loved.

"This is nice."

He limps closer. "Nan made it."

"Where is she?"

"Dead."

Well, that's a fun answer. "Mine too." And because we're already here, I figure I might as well push my luck. "Your parents?"

Wilde's gaze latches onto the quilt. "Dunno."

"Sometimes I wish I didn't know either," I confess. Thunder punctuates those words, but it sounds further away than before. "Dad's fucking his way across Canada. I think he's trying to bone every woman in North America." Wilde has no reaction to that. "Mom's so high half of the time she legitimately has no clue where she is."

"High?"

"No one noticed she was abusing benzos until it was too late. She ended up in the hospital during my senior year, which scared me enough to make some changes myself." It's almost a cute family story, how we went to rehab together. I walked away okay, but when we got out and Dad was in a different state instead of waiting to pick us up, I think she lost all motivation at that point. She doesn't want to be better. "Anyway, it's gotten to the point where whenever she tries to give them up, it's more pain than it's worth, so she's stopped trying. She's happy, living in that fog. Or at least I assume she is." The way she's so unfocused and slurs her way through any conversation makes it difficult for me to even want to be around her. Not that I don't love her, but with how weak I've been lately, she makes me feel guilty for having those thoughts at all.

"If she's that messed up," Wilde says, "why would you be tempted to go back to …" He's struggling through every word. "That?"

"Most people assume it would be the opposite. And maybe it's true for some, but my issues and her issues have always been separate in my mind. Even though we both just want to escape."

I expect him to ask about that, but he doesn't. Wilde slowly pushes his jeans off and throws them through one of the open doorways. "My favorite pair," he mutters. "Figures."

"Buy some new ones."

"City boy …" he throws back, but there's no bite behind it for once. "Most people around here know how to sew. Someone will patch them up for me. Just gotta work on getting the blood out of them first."

"Shouldn't you do that now, then?"

"Probably, but it will have to wait until morning." He grimaces as he eases down on the edge of his couch. "Driving took it out of me."

"I told you I could drive."

"And I told you *no*."

"But you were happy to let me take your truck …" I try to figure out the difference. "So, it's not your truck you're protective of … it's yourself?"

"No."

"Then—"

"I don't trust anyone else to drive. Now, drop it."

I drop it, even though I really, really don't want to. I'm slowly collecting pieces of Wilde that I didn't know existed, and one day, I'm convinced I'll have enough to make a whole picture. His lack of trust, the way he hated me drawing attention to his beard, but he shaved anyway. And I know why he shaved. Because I said I hated his beard. So he did something to impress me without wanting me to be impressed.

If I stand around for much longer, I'm going to keep pushing him for answers, which is a fast way to be shown the door. He's given me way more already than he normally does, and I get the feeling that where Wilde is involved, I have to be patient. So I leave him behind and follow his jeans into the other room. I automatically hit the light switch, even though I'm not expecting anything to happen, and when the small light overhead flickers on, I stare at it.

"You have *electricity*?" I shout.

Wilde grunts, which I'm assuming means yes. This is perfect. All this time, I thought there was nothing up this way, and they've been living comfortably while we've been suffering through cold showers or driving into Wayward and booking a motel room just to get clean.

That asshole.

I swipe his jeans off the floor in a huff and glance around the small room. There's a toilet, a basin, and a washing machine in here, but that's it.

"Where's your shower?" I ask. "Bath? Whatever."

"Outside."

Of course it is. I sling his jeans over the basin, grab the soap, and set to work getting as much of the blood out as possible. Probably should have left these things with Booker since I have a suspicion he would have loved this job.

"What are you doing?" he calls out, like he can't help himself.

I lean around the doorframe to meet his confused expression. "Washing out this blood before it sets. Can't let it ruin your favorite jeans." Him having a favorite pair of jeans is weird. It's not something I expected, and Wilde having an attachment to anything makes me even more curious about him. He doesn't have a lot of stuff, so I'd assumed things were worthless to him, but that's obviously not the case.

I'm getting the feeling that whatever I broke wasn't on the same level as some old windows.

I shut off the water when it runs clear and then sling the jeans over the edge to dry. They'll do for now.

I wash my hands before heading back out, and instead of

settling him in and leaving, I join him on the couch. "What did I break when I was here the last time?"

Silence stretches, and I know that I have to give him time to fight over answering me. It's a personal question, and Wilde isn't a personal man. "A pot. Vase. Thing."

"You don't even know what it was?"

"It doesn't matter what it was. Gracie made it as a gift for me. I don't get gifts often."

"Who's Gracie?" I ask, picturing some leggy mountain lady.

Wilde must pick up on something in my tone because he laughs. "She's a child. One of the few who live here." He leans back against the couch, and after a second, I mirror him.

"How many kids are there?"

"Currently seven, though Matt's about to turn eighteen."

"Do you know everyone?"

"Yes." He stretches his sore leg out. "Matt was the first kid born after I moved here. We're an extended dysfunctional family, but we work."

"Even Lynx?"

"Even him. Everyone has their place."

I know I shouldn't ask, but I do anyway. "What about me?"

His steely eyes meet mine, and there's regret there as he answers. "Every society has its disruptor."

I rip my gaze away. I'm sitting there, telling myself that as soon as the rain stops, I'll leave, but this conversation doesn't feel finished. I just have no idea where to take it from here.

"Do you want to meet them?" he asks. "The others?"

The question is so unexpected that I can't believe Wilde asked it at first. He's been determined to keep everything hidden from me, and this is the exact opposite of that. Has he had a personality transplant?

"When?"

"Today? Now?"

"You're injured."

He bites back his clear irritation at me pointing that out. "Fine. In the morning, then."

The fact that he's offered this at all feels like a turning point. A definable moment where he's making an effort, so I'm going to make one right back. "Will you show me around as well? I want to know more."

"Why? So you can see what you're ruining?"

"So I can understand why you love the place."

There's a pause, then a soft "Why?"

"I don't know. I just want to."

He's conflicted, but when he drags his gray eyes back to me, they're unguarded. Almost vulnerable. "Don't make me regret this."

The worst part is that's not a promise I can make.

# CHAPTER
# THIRTY-TWO

WILDE

Hudson returns in my truck early the next morning, just cementing the *what the fuck am I doing* thoughts that I've been having all night. And I do mean *all night.* The pain in my leg was a constant throb that made getting comfortable impossible.

He doesn't even bother to knock. Just walks in, whistling, then tosses my keys my way. "Morning, sunshine. Need anything before we go?"

"For you not to call me sunshine."

Amusement tugs at his lips. "Ah, but that's the one thing that I can't do."

Figures. I push up onto my feet, ignoring the twinge that happens with every step. I'm determined not to limp because I don't want the attention that comes from an injury. "Let's go, then."

"Did you have breakfast?"

His question stops me before I reach the door. "Yes. I'm not a child."

"You *really* struggle with help, don't you? Believe it or not, that's a normal question to ask someone who's been hurt and can barely walk."

"I have no issues with walking."

The bastard bops me on the nose on the way past. "Sure you don't, sunshine."

"We're not doing sunshine."

"One day, you'll realize that you can't control everything."

My glare shuts him up, at least temporarily, because I'm not planning to realize that ever. "Get in the truck."

"You didn't say please."

"If you're waiting on that, you'll be standing here all day." I leave the house and cross my leafy yard. Everything is still wet from last night's storm, but the sun is rising fast and hot, so I don't expect it to stay that way for long.

Hudson follows me, and when he climbs into the cab, he smells fresh and sweet like always. I have to remind myself that today isn't about fucking; it's about trying to create some kind of friendship and respect for this place that will change his mind about destroying it.

"Who are we visiting first?" he asks.

"Thought we could go and see Gracie so you can tell her about what you did to her vase. Pot. Thing."

"And I'll make sure to tell her you call it a vase pot thing as well."

I rub my temple, already knowing it's going to be a long day. The worst part is that Hudson is literally just giving the attitude back to me, so there's nothing I can do but take it on the chin.

I've been dreading this morning since I suggested it, but driving around with him is surprisingly easy. I keep silent, he talks, and as we move from person to family to person, they soften to him. *I* know he's impossible to resist, but that's mostly in a sexual way. Everyone else seems to … like him.

I wave goodbye to Queenie as I climb into my truck and then sit there for a moment.

"Who's next?" Hudson asks, oblivious to the raging thoughts flying through my mind. "This has been great. I'm pumped to win the next person over."

Slowly, I cast my gaze his way. "How are you so personable? You're a fucking asshole, but the Wenders love you."

A little darkness shadows his green eyes. "I need to be able to talk to people at work. Unlike when we met, I usually have no issues with first impressions. It's not getting people to like me in a surface-level way that's the issue. They work out there isn't much substance behind my smiles, and that's when they want nothing to do with me."

"No substance?"

He plays it off like he doesn't care, but I'm confused.

I speak before I'm aware of even thinking it. "No substance is one of the last things I would have said about you."

Hudson meets my gaze, and I don't know why he looks so surprised. It's just a fact. A man doesn't uproot his entire life and move to the middle of nowhere because he's worried about his brothers if he has no substance. He doesn't stand up and meet every challenge I throw at him head-on if he has no substance. He also doesn't get that flicker of sadness when he talks about shitty past relationships if he has no substance.

There's more to him than he wants to admit, and I don't want to know any of it.

So I turn my car on and get driving again.

"That way is the Lair," I tell him. "Booker said you've already seen it."

"The Lair?"

"Where we host Peril matches."

He glances back the way I pointed. "Do they always happen here?"

"Yes. There was talk about some of the other towns hosting, but it's convenient. Especially with Booker. He organizes the matches, the betting pool, and is ready for any injuries."

"The betting pool?"

I'm still hesitant to tell him details about the town. It requires a level of trust he hasn't earned and, if I'm honest with myself, he probably never *could* earn. It goes against all my natural instincts, but I have to give him something. "It's how we make our money. There are matches throughout the afternoon and into the night, and people bet on who they think will win, whether there are any injuries, how long each match will take … there are endless options. Booker takes a brokerage fee, and the winners take a percentage of the betting pool and door charge. It's where we make our money. Especially when it comes to a fight like mine and Foley's."

"Who's Foley?"

"He's the mayor of Dale and my sworn Peril enemy."

"You?" Hudson chokes back a laugh. "You have a sworn enemy?"

"We're two of the best, and every month, we challenge each other. The wins have been fairly even, but I lost last time"—it takes all my restraint to not point out that the loss was from dealing with Hudson every day—"which means I lost a big chunk of cash the town needs. And now I'm injured, so it's unlikely I'll win next week, which means I'll lose us even more money."

"Someone else can fight for you this time."

"Sure. But they'd lose. Foley and I are the best."

"And then you use your winnings for the town?"

I nod, steering down a narrow road before I pull to a stop within eyesight of the crop fields. "Capitalism isn't a thing here. We share resources. The electricity is solar and we have a battery farm in the containers down there." I point toward the shipping containers that are locked up tight. "Our crop fields are managed by Lynx, and in exchange for food, people help tend the land. If something's broken, we fix it together. Living shouldn't cost an arm and a leg. You need a house? We'll build it for you, but you're going to work hard for it as well. Nothing is free, but it doesn't cost money. Time, energy, teamwork—those things are more important out here."

"Then why bother with Peril?"

"Because the rest of the world doesn't work that way. We can get a lot that we need out here, but things like building supplies, hygiene products, Booker's medicines … that's what the Peril fund goes toward. I earn the money, Rooney takes it and gets whatever we need." I glance at him as he turns it all over in his mind.

"You have it all worked out."

We *did*. The kind of frictionless community that can be built when no one wants for anything. When things like *more* are talked about, it's only the difference between Ziggy having an old TV or the Raylon kids having phones with internet. Both of those things aren't a need, and most of us aren't interested in them. These brothers though … I'm not being dramatic when I say how delicate the arrangement up here is.

New people coming into town, wearing brand labels and driving Range Rovers and posting pictures of Wilde's End all over the place, could easily be the tipping point. It doesn't take much to turn the most level head envious, and while most of the families moved here willingly, the kids have grown up only knowing this, and they're the ones who are vulnerable. They don't know what the rest of the world is like.

And the rest of the world definitely doesn't know what we're like.

But Hudson and his brothers have a plan, and I don't have a workaround for them. They have money tied up in the place, and they need a return on that money.

Even if it makes him the bad guy in *my* eyes, he's right. He's not a bad guy. This is all a matter of circumstance.

"Viv wants to meet you next," I tell him, pulling back out onto the road. "Don't worry, she'll love you. She's the adoptive mom type who loves everyone."

Plus, if today has made one thing clear, it's that Hudson is apparently an easy guy to like.

# CHAPTER
# THIRTY-THREE

## HUDSON

'm buzzing. All day, so many faces and too many names, every single one of them with personalities too big to hold in one tiny town. The way Viv took me under her arm and showed me around her house and land, the obvious pride in her voice, really smacked me in the face with … something. Something I'm not smart enough to recognize. Gracie and her intense curiosity about everything. Jean and Cookie and their exhibit of wooden sculptures. Bashful Nixon and his five younger siblings. Queenie, who insisted on reading my tarot cards. Nox, and the chess game they challenged me to.

I give my head a shake as I work through the muddled feelings that are warring for space in my chest.

No matter how different these Wenders are from each other, they have one thing in common. They're *happy*. Not the type of happy I put on to cover the crushing disappointment of life. The kind of happy that is bursting out of them. And when Wilde is around them, it softens him. Those hard edges melt, and the tension in his shoulders relaxes.

I'd been expecting hostility and intense questioning, not being made to feel welcome.

It's probably the worst thing I've experienced here so far.

Wilde's watching me over the hood of his truck. "Come on, I'll buy you a drink."

"Shouldn't I be the one making that offer?"

"Not this time." His leg is getting stiffer, so I let the argument go and frustratingly let him drive. I'd argue if I thought it would get me anywhere, but Wilde has made it clear that he won't get into the car with anyone driving but him.

It's a peaceful sort of silence as we trundle along, pulling up out the front of a decent-sized building a few minutes later. It has a wide front porch overlooking the river and tall front windows, and through them, I can make out large ceiling fans circling sluggishly.

"What is this place?"

"A Wilde's End secret." His lips pinch like he's unsure whether to keep talking. "We call it the Cutty. It's our bar. No one but Wenders knows about this place."

Again, that odd feeling tries to take over. "Why do you call it the Cutty?"

"Because the drinks have a way of cutting you down." He strides toward the building, doing his best to hide the pain he's in. "Come on. One drink. Then I'll drop you home."

The reminder that I have to go back there dulls my good mood, but I push it away for now. Any extra time I get to spend with Wilde is extra time I'll take. I'm determined to piece him together, to figure out his mystery, even as he does everything he can to stop that from happening.

We get inside, and it's nothing like I expected. Most of the homes I've seen today were small and modest, whereas the Cutty is the complete opposite.

It has high rafters and a long gleaming bar down the right, and there's a seating area down the left with a pool table and jukebox at the back. I turn to Wilde with wide eyes. "This is fancy."

"It works. We built it."

"From a professional standpoint, it's really good."

He grunts because he always grunts and then rounds the bar to pour two beers.

"You help yourself?"

"Yep."

"Like, *anyone*? But … what if someone steals it? Or drinks too much? Or …"

So help my fucking heart, he chuckles. I didn't know he could do that. "Can't steal what's free, and we're all adults smart enough to run our own lives." He hands me a glass and joins me back on the customer side. "The rule is once you're done, you leave whatever money you can spare, if you can spare some."

"But if people aren't paying for it, how do you afford to keep it stocked?"

"Who said they aren't paying for it?" Wilde shrugs and takes a sip. "This shit isn't expensive, and the money left is usually more than enough to replace what we drink. What you're thinking of is profit. We don't do that here."

It's embarrassing how hard it is for me to wrap my head around that. Ever since starting our business, I've been driven by money. Money to cover costs, then money to get ahead, now money to make my brothers' and my lives easy.

I follow Wilde to a table toward the back. There's no one else in here, and I don't know if it's because it's still early in the day or because there are so few people in the town to begin with.

Our chairs are side by side, and I have a long drink of the sweet-tasting beer before leaning back and looking at him.

"You have a pretty cool town," I admit.

His lips twitch. "Yours now."

"Ask anyone around here and I'm sure they'd disagree with that."

"True." His jaw twitches to the side. "Not my town either though. People look at me like a leader because I do so much, and truthfully, I don't think anyone else wants the responsibility."

"People always want power."

Then Wilde shocks the hell out of me when a smile catches his lips. It stretches his jaw wide, and these little creases spread from the corners of his eyes. "You are *such* a city boy."

I smile back, but mostly because I've run out of things to say. I don't think I've ever seen him smile before, and that's probably a good thing because Wilde with a sexy trimmed beard and a smile that warms his eyes is enough to make everything inside of me short-circuit.

It slowly slips off his face again. "What?"

"You're smiling."

It disappears completely. "And?"

"And … I …" You're beautiful. I'm in shock. It made something in my chest go *ping*. "Didn't know you could do that."

"I have a mouth, don't I?"

Before the amusement in his eyes can totally fade, I change the subject. "My dick is well aware of that fact."

Life flares into his dark pupils. "That one time was nothing. Barely a blow job."

"Can't wait until you give me a real one, then."

He shifts around, arm resting across the backs of both chairs. "You'd never recover."

"That might be the best challenge you've given me yet."

"We'll see." He finishes the last of his beer. "Drink that, and I'll take you home."

Instead of draining my glass, I take a small sip. His eyes narrow, and it brings my combatant side out. "I'm enjoying myself right here."

"Because we're talking about blow jobs?"

"Because I'm talking to you."

Wilde looks like the one who goes offline for a moment. "That's … no one …"

"How long have you lived here?" He can bumble his way through denying he's fun to talk to all he likes; I'm not going to let him get away with it. Sure, he's a minefield of grunts and nonanswers, but the way I feel with his attention on me is too addictive to walk away from.

"Twenty years."

"Oh, wow. That's a long time."

He doesn't immediately answer, but I can sense one coming. "It's gone faster than you'd think. Things like birthdays and dates don't mean much to me. It all just … passes."

"How old are you?"

"Thirty-seven."

That means he was only a teenager when he got here. Did he come alone? What happened when he was seventeen that had him land here? I know better than to ask, especially with that contemplative look playing across his face.

"What are you thinking about?"

His large hand scuffs at his beard. "When Ziggy shaved it for me, it was the first time I've looked in a mirror in … a long time. Looked older than I was expecting."

"Old isn't a bad thing."

He laughs softly. "I didn't say old. I said older. Jesus."

I reach up and run my knuckles over the short facial hair. My nerves are in my throat as I wait for him to bat my hand away, but he only watches me, curious. "Older looks good from where I'm sitting."

My voice is huskier than I expect it to be, and instead of disagreeing—or hell, even saying it back—Wilde lifts my glass and holds it out to me. "Finish."

I guess I've pushed my luck enough with him today, so as much as I want to keep teasing him with small sips, I do what I'm told for once. The cold liquid disappears, and then I set the glass down again.

Wilde takes them both, and I follow him to the bar, where he washes them up, dries them, and sits them on a rack. Then he stuffs five dollars into a jar full of cash.

I'm about to ask if it's ever been stolen, but I think I already know the answer to that.

"Truck. Now."

I assume he's had enough of me, but halfway back to Old End, Wilde stops suddenly. Trees hug us on both sides, and there's no one else in sight, so I'm only partially surprised when he reaches for his fly and tugs down the zipper. His hardened cock springs out.

"Suck it."

He doesn't need to tell me twice.

Something about being in each other's presence all day to the quiet moment in the bar has me needy for it, and I suck his cock like I've never sucked one before. I'm careful of his leg, but otherwise, there's nothing holding me back from giving in to the way I want to taste him more than I want anything.

It doesn't take long, and when Wilde floods my mouth with his cum, I swallow every last thing he gives me.

He sighs, sitting back in the chair with his eyes closed as I sit up and wipe my mouth.

"That was unexpected."

There's a scratch in his voice when he speaks. "Was it?" His eyes flick open and catch mine, a spark of light in the muted green cab. He's right. Whenever we're together, I can't deny that sex is high on my list of wants, and today is no different. Actually, today probably only made it worse.

Most of the time when I get to know someone, I resent how much I want them. How I crave that high that's always followed by a crash brought on by how disappointed I am in myself.

But here, with his taste fresh on my tongue, I wait for disappointment that doesn't come.

"Want a turn?" he asks, nodding to my dick.

"Nah, I'm good." I'm not good. I very, very much want a turn, but I also don't want him to have the pain that will come with him giving me head. That bite looked nasty, and there's no way he'll deep-throat me without reinjuring himself. I know better than to give him the real reason though.

"Suit yourself." He turns the car back on, and it's frustratingly short minutes before we're back in Old End.

I climb out without saying goodbye, and Wilde doesn't bother either. Before I can ask when I'll see him again, he takes off, and I watch the truck disappear down the dirt road.

"How was it?" Kennedy calls from a doorway as soon as Wilde is gone.

*How was it?*

At first, my brain leaps to the blow job, but then I remember everything else from today. All those indecipherable feelings come racing back, and I don't know where to start. Do I tell him about the people? The Cutty? That I just blew Wilde in his truck after a moment of actual conversation between us?

Fuck me, I'm really settling for scraps, aren't I?

Even acknowledging that, a smile forces its way onto my face and doesn't give up until I feel like I'm shooting rainbows out of my eyes.

"It was interesting" is all I say before I clap him on the back and get to work. It's the best mood I've been in since I got here.

# CHAPTER
# THIRTY-FOUR

## WILDE

The blow job should have been enough to get me through, but here I am, being pulled toward Old End against all my wishes with one destination in mind.

Hudson.

I can't pinpoint exactly where this pull is coming from either. Is it the sex? Or those teasing lips I can't scratch from my mind? The way his eyelashes flutter as he comes? How he looks me over like he's waiting or hoping for something that only I can give him?

I groan and rub a hand over my face, wishing I could walk away, but the pull toward Hudson grows deeper by the day. Even the pain in my leg isn't enough to deter me when I reach the old house and jump up to grip the window. It's not as easy as it usually is, and I tell myself that I'm only climbing up here for sex, but there's something in the back of my head telling me that's a lie.

Even the reminders that he's here to ruin my life don't hit the same way.

I step out from behind the sheet to find Hudson blinking awake, cute frown weighing down his eyebrows.

"I wasn't expecting you tonight."

Considering we saw each other a few hours ago, he had no reason to. I'm glad he doesn't call me out on it, doesn't question me, because I'm not sure what I'd tell him if he did.

For once, I can't keep my questions inside. "Then why was your window open?"

His teasing lips curl upward. "Because I'm always hoping anyway."

In the dark, I can't make out his eyes, but I'm sure they're watching me like I'm watching him. My gut is all twisted, and for one strange moment, I picture myself climbing into his bed beside him and … talking?

What the fuck kind of thought is that?

I'm not a selfish man. I'm not someone who thinks about anything but the check box list of things I have to do for this town. I've protected the people here for years, and sleeping with someone who's actively ruining our town is out of character for me. My needs have always been an afterthought, my monthly visits to Wayward all I let myself have out of necessity, so this burning need for more, the way I can't resist Hudson even though it's the smart choice … it doesn't make any sense.

So I stop thinking about it completely. I focus on the sex.

Because that's the only thing between us that I understand.

"You showered?"

"Yeah, why?"

Nerves attack me, but I ignore those too. "Get on your knees."

He doesn't even question me, just rolls over and does what he's told. I watch the way his shadowy muscles move, giving myself a moment to really appreciate what a work of fucking art he is.

The way his long back curves in a delicate arch, the round slope of his ass, the tension in his strong thighs, and his soft, sleep-rumpled hair—growing out but still longer on the top and back than the sides—begging for me to slot it between my fingers.

The fact that he's taken to sleeping naked, always ready for me, warms my blood in the most delicious way.

I strip off my T-shirt and shove my shorts to the floor. I didn't bother with underwear because I knew I wouldn't be wearing them for long. I'm here for sex, and that's it.

My cock hardens as I stalk toward the bed, Hudson watching me from where his head is resting on his crossed arm.

He's offering himself up for me on a platter, and damn if it's not the most irresistible sight I've ever seen.

I kneel on the mattress behind him, barely able to make out his ready hole in the darkness. Only a small amount of moonlight is peeking in where I didn't close the makeshift curtain properly, but it's enough. Enough to throw these nights and what we're doing into the illusion of a hazy dream.

It means that come tomorrow, I can pretend like it didn't happen. Pretend like I'm not weak and becoming obsessively needy for him.

Fuck it. I'm here now. There's no pretending when my cock is full and I'm staring at his ass like it might disappear if I look away.

I dive right in.

He twitches at my touch, and I bury my face between his cheeks, tongue swiping his hole. The way Hudson shivers under my palms only encourages me, and I kiss and suck at the sensitive skin. As much as I'd love to fuck him tonight, even I know that my leg will get in my way, so I'm going to be content to eat him out.

Apparently, Hudson has no complaints as a long moan leaves him.

Hearing him so vocally enjoying himself is a turn-on, and I double down on softening his hole. I tease the sensitive flesh, lick and stroke until he's ready for me to slip my tongue inside.

He's tight but pliant, relaxing around me and giving me more room to move. I bury my tongue as deeply as I can, and then I start to fuck him with it.

I'm not gentle. Not when I'm this hungry for him. My tongue spears into him over and over as I eat his hole like a starving man. Spit runs down his crease, and I reach up to cradle his tight balls as he rocks back onto my face.

"You like that, don't you, city boy?" I tease his rim again. "You like riding my tongue."

"Touch my dick," he begs. "I need it."

I slip my hand from his balls and up between his legs to grip his shaft. He's got such a beautiful dick, and feeling the weight of it in my hand is addictive. I keep fucking his hole as I stroke him, hard and fast, needing him to come before my jaw aches. Even like this, my leg is getting stiff, but it's not going to stop me from making him feel good.

"You were right," he says, thrusting into my hand. "The beard stays. Forever. *Oh fuck*, it feels good. So good. Shit. I ... I ..."

He's deliriously rambling, but it only takes another few seconds before his cock thickens in my hand and unloads. Each throb of his release against my palm turns my brain to mush.

I wait for him to finish before I release him and straighten, ready for my own relief.

I slip my length between his cheeks and squeeze them together. My gaze is locked on the sight of his ass cupping my cock as I thrust. The pain in my leg is almost blinding, but I can't stop myself. It's a race between what will give out first: my orgasm or my thigh, and I'm so simmeringly, frustratingly close to the edge that I can't give up now.

Not when it's Hudson in front of me. Not when the muscles in his ass are shuddering around my cock with every thrust. Not when I'm homed in on the sight of my swollen tip poking out the top of the muscles and being swallowed again between them. It skims his wet, gaping hole, and Hudson's pushing back, hand on the wall in front of him, trying to stop us both from toppling off the bed.

Slowly, the pain sinks into oblivion as my orgasm clouds my mind.

"Come on me," he rasps. "Cover me in it."

My eyes roll back at the request, and everything gets to be too much. I thrust against him, animal urges taking over as my brain goes offline and I barrel toward the finish line. I'm too sensitive, too tight, skin burning up and heat building in my cheeks until the rippling from my spine fills my balls and I come.

I've lost track of anything other than how amazing I feel, and when my muscles lose their tension and I'm able to blink the fog away, I look down at my work. At the glistening cum streaking his back and running down his crease.

I peel myself away from him, and even with the shadows, there's no hiding how well used he is. Hole stretched, cum dripping down his balls, prickling rash building from my beard against his skin. It's fucking beautiful.

Satisfaction surges so deep and fulfilling through my body that it catches me off guard.

I back away, not sure I'm even breathing properly yet, and limp on weak legs to where I left my clothes. Now that I came my brains out, my leg is punishing me for what I put it through, but I ignore it as I get dressed and head for the window.

Hudson's watching me. He's always watching me. And while I don't feel right to come and leave, the hesitance at all pisses me off. I've never had an issue with it before. It's what I've been doing for years. Sex and then go separate ways. It's easy.

It's *supposed* to be easy.

I pause when I get to the window, and of course, Hudson can't leave it alone.

"Will I see you tomorrow?"

*Yes.* "No."

"I'll be ready the next night, then."

I bite down on my lip because as much as I want to deny it, what's the point? By then, I'll be just as out of control as I was tonight. It'll be a goddamn miracle if I don't end up here tomorrow night anyway. I ignore the pull to stay. I ignore the pull to answer.

I climb back out of his window and limp my way back to my truck.

The pain is throbbing so badly I'm tempted to go to Booker for painkillers, but I won't. I've gotten through broken bones without them before, so I'll get through this. I don't want any of that shit in my system.

Besides, no matter how much it hurts, I don't regret it.

That was worth every bit of pain I'm going through.

# CHAPTER
# THIRTY-FIVE

## HUDSON

Between my days working and my nights being railed by Wilde, I can't remember ever feeling this settled in one place. What started as a creepy town in the middle of nowhere is becoming more familiar, more real, and I can't deny that I've got a connection growing to this place that I never would have expected.

Which I obviously can't let happen.

One morning, after having my guts thoroughly rearranged the night before, I leave on the bike before the sun even comes up and go and visit someone I've only ever met once.

Gracie Raylon is already outside, filling a bowl with blueberries from the bush beside her house, and she immediately recognizes me when I pull up and take the helmet off.

Her eyes narrow a little, but she doesn't run off. I've never had much experience with twelve-year-olds, but I would have expected one as sheltered as her to be a lot more skittish than she is.

"Want me to grab my parents?"

"Actually …" I walk closer but keep a safe distance between us, conscious that while we've met, she doesn't actually know me. "I came to see you."

"Me?"

I nod, wishing I could turn around and leave this stupid idea behind me, but all it takes is the memory of Wilde saying he has a favorite pair of jeans to keep my feet planted to the ground. "I have a favor to ask."

"Okay?"

"I broke something of Wilde's. A vase. Pot. Thing."

"Not following."

"He said you gave it to him, and he was really upset that I wrecked it."

She moves the bowl to the other hand as she thinks. "Wait, the clay bowl I made him when I was little?"

I don't point out that she's still little. "Yep. It was one of his favorite things."

Shock fills her features. "It was?"

"Yeah, so I was hoping … could you make another one?"

She thinks for a moment. "No."

"Oh." I try to hide how my hopes crash out.

"*We* can."

"We?"

"Yeah. Mom said Wilde was showing you around the other day because he wanted to stop you selling off Old End. Like if you knew us, it would soften you to us."

"I assumed as much."

"I don't think it will work though."

"You don't?"

She shakes her head, long brown hair spilling over her shoulders. "An outsider will never understand what it's like to live here, but you can be taught the basics, and in Wilde's End, if you want something, you work for it. Every Wender knows that."

"If I make the pot—uh, *bowl*—you'll help me?"

"Sure. And if you're lucky, it might look as good as the one that you smashed."

"You think I can't do better than a six-year-old?"

"No way, man. You're a city boy through and through. I'll run these into the house and let Mom know where I'm going."

"She won't care that you're walking off with a stranger?"

"Oh, no, I'll be bringing my hunting gun. But I can handle myself."

Given I think Gracie might be more mature than I've ever been, I don't doubt it.

Wilde pulls out of me and flops onto his back on the mattress, trying to hide the way he stretches out his leg. My hole has taken a beating this week, and while it probably needs a few days to recover, I have absolutely no complaints.

The last two nights, Wilde has lingered longer after sex than I'm used to. There's a hesitance to him, like he wants to touch me or talk, but he never lets himself get there, and eventually, he gives up and leaves.

Tonight, I'm determined for it to be different.

"Your leg still sore?"

I'm assuming he won't answer me because that's kind of his thing, but then his voice fills the silent room. "A bit. He got me deep."

"Should you have Booker check it again?"

"No, it's healing fine."

"Good."

I can feel the way he wants to say more, and for once, he gives in. "Don't know how I'll go in my match on it though."

"Peril?"

"Yeah. If Foley senses I'm injured, he'll target the spot."

"Foley sounds like a dick."

"I'd do the same to him."

Okay, so they're both dicks. But Wilde is sort of kind of *my* dick, so I'm going to assume Foley is the bad guy in this scenario. "I'm still going to hate him."

He snorts. "Why?"

"Because I'm loyal like that." I think back to everything he's told me. "If you lose, will the town have enough money to get by?"

"I have my personal funds, so we'll always be okay."

"You spend your own money on this place?"

"I don't like to touch it at all, but I won't let people go without."

"Why don't you like to touch it?"

He turns, eyes catching mine, and I don't back away from his stare. "Every cent of it is tainted."

A sentence like that has my curiosity through the roof. I want to question it. Peel open his thoughts and dig for all of the nuggets he keeps hidden. But for someone who's obviously not used to talking about himself, the fact that he's given me this much has to be enough.

And now, it's time to give him something.

All day, I've been nervous about seeing him tonight, and as I remember why, those nerves come back in force.

I climb up on shaky legs and clean myself off with the T-shirt I was wearing earlier before crossing to where I left Wilde's gift.

Really, all I'm doing is replacing something that I broke, so I shouldn't be feeling so weird about it, but even when I get back to my bed, I still feel like I might vibrate out of my skin.

"I, uh, have something for you."

Not only was Gracie right and it turned out horribly, but she insisted on scratching both our names into the surface before it dried. Seeing the uneven HUDSON on the side when I'd picked it up today only made the nerves even fucking worse.

Wilde sits up slowly, like he's worried this is a trap. "You what?"

"Have, umm … well, I owed you it. After fucking with your things. It was wrong, and I shouldn't have, so …" Before I can lose my nerve, I pull the *bowl* out from behind my back. "Sorry, it's sort of dark in here."

He doesn't take it. There's a long moment stretched tight where Wilde looks at it and I wait, my gut twisting tighter and tighter until I can't stand it anymore.

I grab his hand with a huff and press the bowl into it. "It's yours. Don't make this weird."

He clears his throat gruffly. "I'm not."

"Good."

"Great."

I'm caught between what I want to say and denying that I want to say anything at all.

He stands before I get a chance to decide and tugs his clothes clumsily back on. The disfigured little bowl is still balanced in his hand, and the longer he doesn't say anything, the more stupid I feel.

"Night," he throws out as he stalks toward my window.

I flop back on the bed as he pulls open the curtain, questioning whether that could have actually gone any worse.

Except he doesn't disappear right away.

When I turn to him, he's looking back at me, moonlight flooding his expression and making something catch in my chest.

I almost don't hear his whisper before he disappears.

"Thank you."

Then he's gone, and I'm left more confused about Wilde than ever.

# CHAPTER
# THIRTY-SIX

WILDE

I try to keep my distance and focus on training for the next week, but injury or not, it doesn't stop me from climbing through Hudson's window every second night. He's too hard to resist, and the more time we spend together, the more sex we have, the longer I stay afterward.

At first, it was seconds. Then minutes. And last night, I couldn't make myself get up and leave for a full half an hour. Even though my brain was very clearly telling me it was time to go, there was something instinctual anchoring me to the spot.

That same something I'm ignoring right now as I turn the bowl he gave me over in my hands. Gracie + Hudson. I've seen how much Grace has improved with her pottery, so I know she didn't make this.

Hudson did.

He made it.

For me.

I swallow thickly and set it aside, my gaze catching on the

small closet in my room. For the first time in … I don't know how long, my fingers itch for rough strings, a steady hum, a soft, scratchy voice that I haven't heard in so long. And never will again.

Yeah, I'm going to ignore that too.

Peril is tonight, and while I'm healing well, I know that Foley will target my injuries for a win. It's stupid to even go because I'll walk out of there with wounds reopened and in worse shape than I am now, but it's not like I can skip this one. If I'd won last month, it wouldn't be an issue, but with nothing last month, probably nothing this month, and then next month not being a guarantee, I don't want to throw away a chance.

I'm only mildly embarrassed about talking Hudson's ear off about it last night.

I've spent the morning warming up and the afternoon taking it easy, so once night rolls around, I grab my post and head toward the Lair. With all the extra cars making their way into Wilde's End, I leave my truck behind and take the distance by foot like usual. The walk there and back helps clear my head, and afterward … every single month for too long, I've gone down into Wayward. Technically, there's nothing stopping me from doing it again tonight, except for this off feeling. Hudson and I aren't exclusive. We're not anything to each other. We gripe at each other and sometimes get off, and once or twice, he's brought out an emotion that wasn't total irritation, but none of those things are reason enough to stop doing what I've always done.

None except that I don't think I want to.

"*Argh.*" I scratch the thoughts away and try to focus on the upcoming match. Last time, the match went longer than they normally do, and Foley seemed like he didn't even feel some of my bigger hits. His torso was full of mottled bruises by the time we were done, and the only reason he won was because of a sneaky shot right to the armpit. It was so unexpected I didn't brace for it and lost my footing too easily.

This time, I'll stick to the bigger, lower platforms and not let Foley draw me up higher.

Booker's at the door to the Lair, and he eyes me as I approach. "This should be interesting. Like watching him play with roadkill."

"Don't count me out yet."

He waits until I pass him and reach the door to speak again. "Your boy came to watch."

"The fuck." I swing around to him. "This is a closed event. Why did you let Hudson in?"

"Because I invited him." I'm about to lose my cool when Booker goes on. "Interesting, though, that you immediately knew who I meant."

I think back over his words, insides shriveling as it hits me that Booker never said his name. Goddammit. I storm inside before I can give him any other wrong ideas and go in search of Hudson.

People already fill the tiered seating, ready for the first match that has just been confirmed. I watch as money trades hands, gaze searching out the one man who shouldn't be here.

He's closer to the floor, irritating blond lock flicked up over his forehead as he looks around like he's never seen a room so full of people before. There will end up being a few hundred once everyone arrives, and while the Lair is big enough, it's not huge. The noise gets deafening, and the heat bakes into your skin by the time you walk out of here.

I take the seat beside him. "Why are you here?"

"Wanted to know what all the fuss was about." Hudson turns his bright expression on me. "Where's Foley?"

It only takes a quick glance around the room to spot him. He's tall, bigger than I am, with smooth black hair and a skeleton mouth tattooed over his own. "Over there."

"He looks like even more of a dickhead in the light."

"Agreed."

"Fucking hot though."

I cut a look Hudson's way, hating the darkness that hits at those words. "When he wins, why don't you offer to fuck him then?"

He leans in, almost nose to nose. "Maybe I will."

"Good luck with that." The words barely make it past my teeth. Looks like I'm going into Wayward after all. I stand, intending to put as much distance between us as possible, but Hudson tugs me back down next to him.

"Not so fast. I need you to teach me the rules."

"Why?"

"I want to know what I'm watching. I've never seen one of these matches before."

I huff and point to the platforms at all the different heights in the middle of the room. "The aim is to stay on those and use this" —I tap my post—"to knock your opponent off."

"So you run around hitting each other with sticks?"

"Basically."

"Sounds like how my brothers and I used to sword fight when we were kids."

This is nothing like that, but I don't bother pointing it out. Just wait for the first match to begin. The people new to Peril are up first, but even with their inexperience, they're good to watch. A man and a woman take their starting points on the floor, and once the buzzer sounds, they launch onto the platforms. There are ten in total, with bars hanging overhead that I like to use to evade Foley's long reach, but most of the novices ignore those. These two are the same, jumping from one platform to the next, mostly keeping their distance until one of them gets confident and moves in for a hit. The first *thwack* echoes over the cheering around us and has Hudson jump in his seat. "Whoa, that sounded hard."

"It was."

He takes the post from my grip and inspects it. "Heavier than I thought."

"Most people prefer the lighter ones because they're whippy and easier to move with, but the heavier ones mean every strike counts."

"This could do some real damage."

"It's why hits to the head are banned."

"Good call." He hands my post back to me as the two people we're watching draw to a close.

The man has the woman cornered on the top platform. It's one of the smallest, barely enough room for one person to stand on, and any experienced fighter avoids being cornered there. The man sends a slashing hit her way. She blocks the blow and charges forward, but right as she jumps, he redirects and takes a swing at her legs. His hit collides with them both, sending her off course, and her post drops as she grabs the platform instead. The metal slips through her fingers, and with a *foof,* she hits the padded floor, and the buzzer sounds, ending the match. The crowd is an equal mix of cheering and booing at the result.

"Huh," Hudson says, looking around. "It's like American Ninja Warriors."

"I have no idea what that is, but I'm sure I'd hate it."

"The match was cool, though."

And because I can't stop myself, I add, "Wait until you see mine."

"Even though you're injured?"

"Even then." I'm in for a world of pain, and my chances are slim, but that's not going to stop me from trying. I test straightening out my leg, and the stretch sends frustrating fissures of pain through my thigh. "I'm going to *kill* Lynx."

"Still hurt?"

I refuse to admit it out loud, but I guess that's what happens when a machete takes a chunk out of you.

The next fighter stands and challenges an opponent. There are a few minutes before each match for side bets to be placed, and Hudson leans closer to me.

"Can you challenge whoever you want?"

"Yep."

"Interesting …"

We don't talk much after that. The stands fill with so many people in close quarters, the voices and cheering echoing in my ears. One match bleeds into the next, and Hudson is hooked on it all. As the night goes on, the more experienced fighters come out, and it's a whole other level. The more familiar we are with the place, the more the arena is used like an extension of our abilities. There's no regulation when it comes to our posts, other than being made of wood. Some are long and thin, used like whips. Others are short and heavy. Some people use one, and others use two. It makes every match so different.

It gets late fast, and the match we're watching wraps up.

Foley shifts, like he's getting ready to stand, and it catches my attention.

"Here we go," I mutter to Hudson, nodding Foley's way.

But almost as soon as the words are out of my mouth, Hudson pushes to his feet.

"I challenge Wilde."

At first, I don't think I've heard him properly. Then the pitch of the crowd rises over the way my name keeps repeating through my mind.

"*Me?*"

He looks way too cocky. "Your name is Wilde, isn't it?"

"You don't even have a post."

He shrugs. "Lend me one."

"You don't know the rules."

"Now you're tricking me. There are no rules."

I stare at Hudson like I'm trying to figure out how to turn him down, but people are already placing bets. Bets on me.

The bastard tweaks my beard. "Scared, are you?"

"Only of hurting you."

"I'm tougher than I look."

I slowly stand, looking down slightly to meet his eyes. There's no hesitation there, and who am I to tell him what he can and can't do? I just have one question. "Why?"

"Wouldn't want you to lose two months in a row, would we?"

The answer shocks me. I'd been expecting something stupid like finally getting the chance to sock me in the face, but he fully expects to lose. For me. I shake that thought from my mind. "Guess we better find you a post."

Booker is only too eager to organize one for him, and while I wait on my side of the arena, Foley leaves his seat to settle by my shoulder.

"This is interesting."

Unlike Hudson, I know that if I ignore Foley, he'll get bored and leave.

"Must be hard to know you're not as good as you once were. Though taking to matches with rookies is a little extreme, isn't it?"

The obvious antagonism isn't going to get to me.

Booker approaches, a post held up in question. His gaze flicks to Foley, and I hear the man beside me exhale sharply.

"Booker," Foley says slowly. "Guess I won't be coming to see you tonight. That rogue has taken my fun away."

The cold look Booker levels him with should be studied. "Oh no. Damn. I'm so sad."

Foley approaches him, towering over Booker as he pinches his chin between his fingers and forces Booker's attention to him. "I was prepared to get good and bloody for you."

"And even that wouldn't interest me." He turns his back to Foley and addresses me. "How's this?"

It's not too heavy and has a good reach on it. "It'll do. He might actually get a hit in with that."

"We can only hope," Booker says angelically.

He leaves to take the post to Hudson, and I glance over at Foley, who's watching Booker with hunger in his eyes. He's never hidden his attraction for Booker, but from what I can tell, Booker doesn't return it. I'm not surprised. The man is tall and heavily muscular, so I can understand why Hudson finds him attractive, but his face only makes me want to punch him in it.

"Move."

Foley's bright blue eyes lock on mine for a second before he turns and walks back to where he came from.

The swell of bodies in here has me stripping off my tank top, sweat already prickling at my skin. The gloves stop my palms from slipping against my post, but I prefer fingerless ones to grip better. Each of my fingers is wrapped with tape to stop friction burns, but Hudson doesn't have any of that. He's completely unprepared, has no idea what he's getting into, but when I look across the area at where he's following along with whatever Booker is saying, there isn't a hint of nerves about him.

He passes the post from one hand to the other, testing the weight, before he looks over and shoots me a grin.

That fucker.

Booker moves away, the cheers fill the stifling room, and I block all of it out.

Hudson lifts a hand in a wave to the people around us, and then the buzzer goes off.

He hurtles forward, springing up onto the first platform with ease, and I move a second later.

It's enough to give him a head start, but there's no way I can let him block me from getting up there, otherwise I'll be disqualified before we even get started.

I'm not letting Hudson win this by default.

I'm on the second platform by the time I take my first swing at him. The end of my post skims his stomach as he jumps backward and then takes off to the next podium. He's like a mouse on the run. Skittish and unprepared, easily backed into the corner.

But Hudson looks like he's having the time of his life.

I refuse to take it easy, but when he takes a sudden lunge to the left, he gets a sneak shot in on my calf. The fact that he could have easily hit my thigh and didn't makes it more obvious with every passing second why he was the one to challenge me.

Hudson's prepared to get his ass kicked in order to save mine.

Which makes it so much harder to hurt him.

But this is Peril.

And Hudson's going to learn it's all or nothing.

Where Foley and I fight with weight behind us, Hudson's got agility on his side. He avoids my hits by narrow margins, and the ones he sends my way are sneaky backhand shots that I don't see coming. It's been so long since I fought someone new that it takes me longer than I'm comfortable with to adjust.

The next time Hudson swings at me, I'm ready for him though. His post connects with my palm hard, but I refuse to let go, even as he tries to tug it from my grip. His blond hair has darkened with sweat, cheeks flushed, but there's a brightness to his eyes that I've never seen before.

"Do it," he goads.

I let go of him roughly, which almost throws him off his plat-form, and his only option is to jump across onto the next one. The highest one. I box him in, and when we lock eyes, I smile.

"Lesson number one: you're standing on what we call the suicide platform. The only place you're going now is down."

"But you so love it when I go down." Hudson winks, and then before I catch what he's doing, he jumps, catches the bar over-head, and swings himself across to a large platform in the middle, out of my trap.

I chase him around the arena, platform to platform, and every blow of mine leaves a shocking red mark in his skin. I know from experience they'll turn into bruises, and even though I said I wouldn't hold back, I definitely am.

That can't last long though.

It feels like we've been fighting half the night, but in reality, it's probably only been a few minutes. Mine and Foley's record was twenty, and that ruined me for a week.

Both taking and throwing the hits have more impact on your body than you'd think; then add the agility on top of that, and it's a whole-body workout.

Hudson tries changing course, but I'm already expecting it. He gets his post up too slow as I go in for the killer blow, and as soon as my post collides with his chest, I take the wind from him.

Hudson pitches backward, losing grip on his post as he slips. For one second, he catches the edge of the platform, but it's not enough.

He drops. The *foof* of the padded floor bursts out, and then the buzzer sounds.

Like that, Hudson's first Peril match is over.

And I won. Which secured a nice cash bump for the town.

All thanks to him.

# CHAPTER
# THIRTY-SEVEN

## HUDSON

"'m going back to your place," I tell Wilde before we've even stepped foot out of the Lair. "I'm sore. Don't make me go all the way home. No arguments, just this once, okay?"

My whole body is burning up and covered in welts, but damn, that was fucking fun. I don't think my adrenaline has run so high in … forever. I'm bouncing on my toes, ready to go another round, even as my shoulders are bunched up and tightening uncomfortably with all those hits I made.

I'm going to be *sore* tomorrow.

"I didn't drive," he warns, but that sounds like a yes, which I wasn't expecting.

"I'm okay with walking."

He takes off into the forest, and I follow him like a good little puppy. My blood is pumping after tonight, and the last thing I want is to go home and sleep. I want to fucking skydive. Or sing karaoke. Or … Or … "Shit, I'm buzzed."

"Why do you think I always end up in Wayward after a match?"

I catch up to him, understanding better than ever. "Good thing you don't need to go that far tonight."

Wilde doesn't agree, and I give him more time than my patience wants me to.

"Right?" I demand.

"Haven't decided yet."

It's a fair answer. I know it is. We haven't promised each other anything, and nonexclusive has been the name of all my relationships … maybe ever. Doesn't stop my jaw from clenching though. "Why? You wanna fuck, and I wanna fuck. Why waste the fuel?"

"The fuel?"

"Exactly."

He stops, barely visible in the dark, but maybe he can see better than I can because I can feel him watching me. "You're worth more than a tank of fuel, Hudson."

Nerves launch in my gut as he keeps walking. "So you'll stay?"

"I didn't say that."

I have to bite down on my lip to stop from arguing with him. Wilde isn't going to give me more, so I have to give him something he can't say no to. Tempt him into staying. Make sure that Wayward doesn't even cross his mind.

I'm still scrambling for a plan when we reach his house, and something catches my eye in the moonlight.

His outdoor shower.

I'm sweaty and gross from our match, so I have a good reason to use it. A good reason other than wanting to get naked in front of him and drive him out of his mind.

"Enjoy your night," I tell him, breaking from his side and

approaching the back of the house. It's a nice night, and a warm shower sounds like fucking heaven.

I pull my shirt up over my head, then switch the shower on. It doesn't take long to heat up, and I decide then and there that I'm not suffering through any more cold showers at home when he has this one right here.

"What are you doing?" Wilde asks as I kick out of my shorts. My dick is already at half-mast, and if he *does* still try to abandon me, I don't trust myself not to chase his car down. I haven't needed him to fuck me as badly as I do tonight.

Sex after a fight is something I haven't tried before, but with how I'm already humming, I'll bet it's intense.

"Showering," I tell him. "You got me so filthy back there."

I step under the water, facing him, and I tilt my head back under the spray. Even without looking, I can feel his eyes on me, and damn if that doesn't make my dick thicken in an instant.

I refuse to look over at him, but it's hard to keep my resolve when Wilde stays completely silent. When there are no hands on me or the sound of clothes hitting the floor. Wilde is still the most stubborn man I've ever met, and while it's annoying, I also wouldn't want that to change.

Slowly, I blink the water out of my eyes and look over at where I left him. He's settled on a chair, watching me, and a spark of triumph flows through my veins. If Wilde wants a show, I'll give it to him.

My hand follows the water down my chest, over my abs, until I wrap it around my thickening cock. Fuck, I love being horny. I love sex, and I love the high that comes with it, even if every time I'm with Wilde, I expect things to crash right after. It never happens, but I can't shake that feeling.

It's like shame and regret are built into my DNA, and I'm questioning how to function when that familiar flood of emotion doesn't happen. It's not like I've upped my standards with Wilde, but I don't completely hate myself for sleeping with him.

Is this what respect looks like?

I'm not about to analyze that when the feel of my hand moving over my needy shaft is taking all my focus. He's watching me, blatantly taking in my body, gaze moving from my pecs to my abs to my dick and back again. Something about the predatory look in his eyes has my gut heating more than the hot water has been able to.

The throbbing, lusty need pouring into me is begging for Wilde to get up and join me, but he only shifts lower in the chair, legs widening, hard cock standing proudly beneath his loose gym shorts. The sight of that rigid outline makes my balls ache.

"Thought you were leaving," I mutter.

"I was."

"So go."

His tongue appears to swipe over his lips. "You know exactly what you're doing to me, Hudson."

Then he fishes out that magnificent cock. We lock eyes, maybe six feet apart, silently stroking ourselves and wishing one of us would cross the distance. I could come like this. From him watching me and getting turned on by the sight of my body. I might not do a whole lot right, but I look after myself, and feeling in his stare how much he appreciates my efforts bubbles a flood of happiness to my brain.

"Come here," slips out before I can stop it.

With barely a shift in his expression, I can already tell he's going to deny me, so I get in first.

"Now."

"Now?"

I nod, uncertain but determined. "I really need your cock in my mouth."

Wilde's harsh curse spikes me with victory, and he tugs his shirt aggressively over his head. He pushes onto his mouthwateringly strong legs, shoves his shorts down, and then he's naked in the moonlight, muscle and hair and skin and scars, all on display for me.

Something new trickles through the lust.

Something raw and unexpected but equally as exciting.

Does anyone else who's ever been with him know what they missed out on?

He approaches slowly, like an easily spooked animal, and once he's close enough, I step back to give him room under the water. He grabs a bottle of soap from behind me and pours some out into his hand before passing it over. Then we wash ourselves, mouths saying nothing while his eyes tell me everything.

He wants to devour me.

I wait until he's finished, until he runs his head under the spray, loose curls flattening under the water, and then those eyes pop back open and hook me.

"Your *eyelashes*," he grits out as his hand cups my jaw. "I want to see them all wet like that while you look up at me from your knees with your mouth stuffed full of my cock."

I shiver with need. "Is that an invitation?"

"Take it as a demand."

I should be embarrassed by how much that turns me on, but instead, I play right into his fantasies. I lean under the shower, making sure the water hits my eyes, and then I sink down to my knees.

Wilde towers over me; that solid body built through decades of hard work makes me feel small and powerless like this, and I don't think I've ever experienced that sensation before him.

I look up at Wilde through my eyelashes, watching his chest

shudder under a sudden breath. Then, with the most innocent look I can manage, I lean forward and suck him into my mouth.

He's already salty with precum, tip smooth against my tongue, but I don't stop to enjoy it as I hold his gaze and slowly sink down onto every inch. I massage the ridge and his swollen vein with my tongue until his tip nudges at my throat, and I relax, letting him push forward into it.

Wilde's fingers tangle in my hair as he pulls back and feeds me his cock, again and again, teasingly at first but then less controlled.

And as much as I'd love for him to blow in my mouth again, I need him to fuck me. Need it like I might fall apart if he doesn't.

So I pull off before he can get too excited, then push to my feet.

"Not tonight," I tell him. "Tonight, I want you in my ass."

He switches off the water and grabs a towel. I watch as he dries off as fast as he can, then tosses it at me.

"I'll be back in a second. Start prepping yourself."

"With no lube?"

"You'll figure it out."

His long, heavy strides take him away from me, and I've already scrubbed as much water as possible off my body by the time he gets to the house. I spit onto my fingers, then reach around and press a finger into my hole. I'm experienced at bottoming, and sometimes spit is enough, but if it's up to me, I'll ride his cock for hours, and spit doesn't last that long.

If Wilde doesn't come back with lube and at least three condoms, he's going to be wildly unprepared.

I've just pressed a second finger inside my hole and started stretching myself open when he walks back outside. He's carrying the lube, and it takes me a moment to realize he's already wearing the condom, and his dick is glossy.

"Started without me?" I ask, pointing to it.

His gaze casts over the yard. "Come with me."

He leads us over to an orange-and-beige striped hammock strung between two thick tree trunks.

"There's no way this will work."

He holds it open and tosses the bottle inside. "Get in and move to the other side."

I'm still doubtful, but fuck it. I've done worse things to get laid.

Wilde holds it steady while I climb in, and a moment later, he follows. The hammock gives a concerning swing before it settles, and then … then I don't hate this idea so much.

Wilde's body presses in snug behind mine, the tension in the hammock forcing us together in a way that makes my gut swim. His nose brushes behind my ear, and he hooks a leg up to rest on my hip.

"You good?"

I quickly nod, even though I'm suddenly not sure I am good. Something about the way we're wrapped together, his breath on my neck, warm skin pressed flush with mine, feels so different from all the other times. It's not until Wilde's fingers press to my hole, already covered with lube, that I realize I checked out for a second. Like I'm trying to separate from all the emotions swimming inside me.

I relax into his intrusion, loving the feel of his thick fingers entering me. It's not hurried or rough, just a gentle stretch as he adds a third that I take easier than I normally would, thanks to starting the prep before him.

He doesn't seem in any hurry, alternating between stroking my entrance and sinking his fingers in deep. He's stretching them open, teasing that spot that sends tingles racing through to my balls, and then he does something that makes my heart fucking stop.

He presses his lips to my shoulder.

It's so unexpectedly tender that I turn to look as he does it again. It brings us nose to nose, close enough that his exhale plays over my lips, tingling with the need to meet his. Wilde's eyes dance between mine, frown pulled tight like he's as caught off guard by this moment as I am.

I inch forward, expecting him to retreat, but after a terrifyingly long second, Wilde leans in. Our mouths meet and the contact sends zaps shooting through my gut.

His lips are soft, his beard scratchy, and he kisses like he's testing me. Like he's curious if he'll want more. My curiosity disappeared the second his lips touched mine, because I definitely want more, and I show him how much.

My tongue swipes his lips, and they crack open, just enough for me to take the chance. I push forward, creating room to let out all these unwanted emotions, wanting to feed them into Wilde instead of me, but the moment our tongues connect, those emotions explode. This crater fills my chest, digs in deep, a knuckling, scrappy, happy pain that has me kissing him deeper like I'm mining for more.

Wilde's fingers leave me empty, and then his cock is pressing against my hole. I'm ready for him, and the whole time he's pushing inside, he's peeling me open and leaving me exposed.

I don't need this because I'm horny.

It's a new, fresh type of need that horny comes second to, and when he snaps his hips forward and fills me to the brim, the hammock shudders beneath us, rocking us together and making everything feel so damn right.

My kiss deepens, a desperate frenzy to hold on to this connection we've never forged before. He fucks me slow and deep, careful not to move against the hammock, and the gentle spearing, the pressure on my prostate, it's bringing my orgasm alive.

He's a hot weight pressed flush to my back, coarse leg hair bristling against mine, arms a heavy anchor as he wraps them around me and holds me tight, like any small gap between us would be a disaster.

Wilde deepens the kiss, spearing in my ass, deep and lingering in an almost uncontrolled way. His whole body is coiled tight like he's holding back, and his strength has me leaking.

I give in to the need to touch myself, lapping up every one of Wilde's moans as I press back onto him and then thrust into my hand. We're tangled together, and I've lost all details other than naked skin and a propelling high.

He's consuming me, all my senses overwhelmed as he fucks me into a coma. I'm so used to fast and dirty quickies that this slow, sensual pounding is rearranging my brain chemistry. We kiss until my jaw aches and my neck twinges. We writhe together until I wouldn't be surprised to see the sun kissing the horizon.

I have no idea how long we're cocooned in this hammock, have no idea how long our bodies seek each other out, his cock dipping in and out, until I'm a frustrated, panting, sweating bundle of need.

My balls tighten, and the groan I feed him is unhinged.

"I'm close," I rasp against his lips.

Wilde growls, and his feral need really does something for me.

"Come," he demands, shallow thrusts speeding up. He buries his face in my neck. "Fuck, Hudson, *please* come."

Who would have thought that Wilde begging could be the hottest thing I've ever witnessed? I strangle my cock, jerking myself hard and fast, needing to get there. My balls are aching for release, and I need that little more. That little nudge closer … closer …

Like he knows exactly how close I am, Wilde reaches up and pinches one of my nipples. The simmering pressure releases, a burst of pleasure, rolling through my shoulders, out to my limbs, causing my back to arch as my cock throbs out my load into my waiting hand.

I'm so shiveringly checked out that Wilde's hard thrusts and deep grunts take a second to reach me.

"So tight … fuck … it's fucking beautiful … the way … you come on my cock."

It's more affirmation than I've ever heard from him, and he stills, muscles locking up as he twitches behind me and milks out the last of his orgasm.

He slumps against my back, head bowed forward on my shoulder, damp hair twisted into tighter curls, and eyes closed as he catches his breath. I reach back and stroke my fingers through his hair before I realize what I'm doing, and Wilde arches into my touch before he picks up on it either.

I know the moment between us is fragile. That we're kissing the edges of what we are, dangerously close to ruining everything. But if this is what ruin feels like, maybe I want it.

Maybe I want this more than I've ever wanted anything.

"I'm staying here tonight," I whisper.

Wilde doesn't respond.

But for the first time, I can understand his silence.

*Yes*.

# CHAPTER
# THIRTY-EIGHT



'm not sure what last night was, but I carry it with me through the day. I dropped Hudson home earlier, and it's hard to wrap my head around the way I've gone from no one being allowed in my house at all to him staying the night.

I mean, fuck. I can still taste his mouth. Still feel the way it curved under mine. Those tiny sighs that cooled my wet lips.

I should have gone to Wayward.

I'm sitting in the back of my truck, tray down, guitar I haven't touched in over a decade sitting ignored at my side, looking out past the trees toward where the swimming hole is. Somehow, even though the view is exactly the way it's always been, it feels crisper today. The sun that's filtering through the trees is hot, and after dropping Hudson off, I got to work checking our land is ready for summer. It's a demanding job, but I love it.

I love everything about Wilde's End.

Even thinking that allows a sliver of darkness to creep into my good mood because how long will this be Wilde's End?

An engine slowly picks up through the happy insects and bird-calls I've been listening to, and it doesn't take long for the dirt bike to come into view. My immediate instinct is to smile, but I keep it locked away as the bike pulls to a stop.

It's only been a few hours since we've seen each other, and I'm not going to start acting like this is a regular, expected thing for us. Sleepovers are not on the table, despite last night, because when it comes right down to it, he still wants to destroy my whole life's work, and we haven't found a way around that.

The man climbs off the bike, and his size immediately alerts me to the fact that it's not Hudson. I don't need him to remove the helmet and set it on the bike for me to know which brother this is.

Kennedy ruffles his damp hair as he approaches, uneasiness crossing his face when he catches my eyes.

"Hey, Wilde. How are you?"

I watch him curiously, eyebrows peaked, but don't bother to answer the pointless question. Kennedy shifts to his other foot, struggling to keep his happy expression under my unwavering gaze.

"I, uh, wanted to catch you, actually," he says. "Have a quick chat."

"About?"

He points to the spot next to me. "Can I ..."

I don't answer, and after a moment, he seems to take that as a yes because he moves closer and pulls himself up beside where I'm sitting. It shouldn't be a surprise to me, considering how easily Hudson makes himself at home.

He doesn't say much for a man who wants a quick chat. I study him from the corner of my eye, taking note of all the differences between him and his brother.

Kennedy is less guarded; it's immediately obvious in his expression and how he holds himself. He's got a larger build, a mix of muscle and softness, a thick mustache, and normal-length eyelashes instead of the ridiculously long ones that Hudson has.

"You know," I say, taking pity on him, "conversations usually require words."

His laugh is edged in nerves as he bites his thumbnail. "Yeah, sorry. Guess I'm not really sure where to start."

"Instead of stressing about it, give me the reason you're here."

For all the differences they have, Kennedy's eyes are that same speckled green as Hudson's. "My brother."

"Figured. And does he know you're here talking about him?"

"Nope. He'd kill me."

Good to know that I'm not the only one Hudson has a shit attitude with. "Why risk it?"

"I'm worried about him." Kennedy casts his gaze away. "I don't know what he's told you about himself or our upbringing, so all I'll say is there was a lot of stuff he shouldn't have gone through that messed him up a bit."

My thumb immediately finds one of my scars. I know about being messed up.

He props his elbow on the side of the tray. "Hudson doesn't have a lot of respect for himself. It's like he always thinks he deserves to be treated like shit. He's had boyfriends over the years, who were …" Kennedy clenches his jaw before releasing it again. "Not good people. His ex especially was a complete asshole. If you heard the way he'd talk to Huddy, I'd just … I'd … *gah*, I hated that guy!" Kennedy rubs at his eyes like he's trying to push the frustration back inside. "Hudson always makes fun of me for wanting to find love, but I don't think he even knows what that is. All he knows is that any attention is good attention, even when the guy he's supposed to be seeing video calls him while he gets off with some random because Hudson was too busy to meet up."

My gut takes a dive at that. "Is that something that happened?"

"Yes. He was always pulling this manipulative bullshit. Telling Hudson they weren't exclusive because Hudson had nothing to offer except a pretty face. Whenever they're back *on* again, I refuse to go to Hudson's place in case I run into Sutton."

That name rings a bell.

"He acts like it doesn't get to him, but I know it does."

And as Kennedy's tone drops, I get a hint of the real reason why he's here. "You think I'm treating him like shit too?"

The side-eye I get is all attitude. "Aren't you?"

There's no good way for me to answer that. I treat Hudson the only way I know how to treat someone I have mixed emotions over. He's taken over my thoughts more than any person has a right to, but that doesn't change the very real fact that there's nothing long-term there. Not only am I an emotional black hole, but Hudson is fast to remind me this is only sex, and we both know his time in town is limited. I know better than to get emotionally invested in people, and if I can't even have real relationships with the friends I've known for decades, what hope do I have of creating anything meaningful with the man I've started screwing? Even if it's harder to hold on to everything that annoyed me about him in the past.

Now, when I think of Hudson, it's less of an angry storm cloud and more like the still water of the swimming hole before it's disturbed. Calm and waiting, hidden depths there for anyone willing to dive down and find them.

Am I willing? I look around my land, that sharp clarity gone, the view as familiar as the trails I walk.

"There's nothing between me and Hudson," I finally say.

"I know you're fucking."

"Sex is sex. He's not looking for more, and neither am I."

It's clearly not the answer Kennedy wants. "Then why is my brother walking around the site, whistling and singing and not rising to Hartwell's snark?"

"I …"

"He's the happiest I think I've ever seen him."

Well, that's a humbling fucking thought. So why does my gut immediately drop out through my ass like it's a bad thing? Knowing that Hudson's been walking around with that same extra boost I've been feeling all day should be good, right? It should be a sign that whatever path we've started down, we're onto something that could be good for us both.

But whenever I try to mentally follow the path and see where it ends up, I can't get past the darkness.

Kennedy slides off the truck and turns to me. "I know you don't owe me anything and that you hate us for what we're doing. So I get it. I do. But … He deserves a break, Wilde. He deserves to stop hating himself and for someone to show him what a great person he really is."

"And you assume I don't do that?"

"I have no idea what you do. All I know is that I've seen a few interactions between you both that didn't look healthy, and now he's all happy, and I'm scared this is Sutton all over again. That you're treating him like shit and he doesn't even know the difference anymore. Hudson's a good person. He deserves to be treated like one."

"Right."

"I'm just saying, if this thing goes on … please don't be an asshole. If you can't promise that, then … well, maybe you shouldn't be around people at all."

That makes me snort, and I'm not at all amused. "Literally my whole reason for moving here."

Apparently, Kennedy has said everything he needs to because

his expression falls. The disappointment seeps from him into me before he turns and heads back toward the bike.

I still haven't worked through that conversation by the time he leaves and the bike dulls to a distant hum.

Kennedy wants Hudson to have what he deserves.

And that will never be me.

Where my gut sank earlier, something in my chest follows it. I sit there, trying to rub life back into my sternum, as I figure out what the fuck I'm supposed to do now.

Ignore the warning and enjoy this thing while it lasts.

Or listen to Kennedy. The problem is that I've forgotten what not being an asshole even looks like.

# CHAPTER
# THIRTY-NINE

## HUDSON

The *thump* against the side of the house comes later than usual, but I'm not about to complain. I only saw him this morning, so technically, he isn't due tonight, but there was some kind of shift between us last night that I can't deny feeling. Maybe this is a sign he felt it too.

I sit up and wait for him to climb through the window, cells prickling with the expectation of his touch. I'm not sure when exactly I stopped hating the sight of his face; all I know is that seeing it now sends quakes through my gut that I can't control.

It's an off-balanced type of feeling, the thrill of the high and sheer terror of toppling over the edge. I'm stuck on the terror side of things when he pushes the curtain out of his way and straightens, something *chinking* in my chest that catches me off guard.

Fucking is not supposed to make me feel like *that*.

Instead of immediately stripping off, Wilde crosses his arms and leans back into the wall. Fuck, he's so ... *fuck*. Those thick arms. His broad chest. The way he holds storm clouds in his eyes.

I have this strong urge to walk over there and kiss him, maybe strip him down myself, but this incessant need to get off with him, to feel his skin against mine—no fighting, no low-lying anger—it's not normal.

"Hey." I lean back into my hands. "Forgot your way to my bed?"

One side of his mouth looks like he wants to smile, but he stops it. "What are we doing?"

Is that a trick question? "Talking."

"No." He waves a finger between us. "This. What is it?"

His gaze searches mine, even in the dark, and I look away. Whatever is going on in my head isn't something I want him to witness. There are way too many gaps between what I think and feel and want. Wilde is … he's made to be alone. I know what I am to him—relief—and that was exactly what I wanted when this whole thing started, but something has shifted. Something in the way he got uncomfortable when I mentioned how hot Foley is. Something in the way he planned to go to Wayward, and I *had* to stop that from happening.

The thought of him fucking some other guy wasn't a tease like it was the first time. It hit deeper, this familiar sickly feeling I'm so used to, the type of feeling I didn't notice was missing until it came flooding back.

He's still waiting for an answer I don't have.

"What do you want me to say?"

It's the shock of the damn century when he doesn't answer. Because while he expects me to let everything out, Wilde keeps it all inside. He tears open this wound of a conversation and then leaves me to deal with it, while he watches me, unsettles me, for what? His amusement? A way for him to feel superior to me?

I stand up, the irritation only he can bring spurring me into action. I cross the room until I rock back on my heels in front of him.

"Conversations go both ways," I tell him.

"They do."

"Well, if you're so interested in this topic, maybe you should be the one to lead it."

Wilde's throat bobs under a swallow, something I've never been able to witness with his beard in the way. "I asked first."

"And I'm asking back."

"Kennedy came to see me. He's worried about you."

"He's always worried."

"He thinks I'm mistreating you."

I study Wilde's eyes. "And are you?"

"I don't know." His hand comes up to trail the bruises over my chest, left from his post last night.

"I have no complaints."

"Yeah," he huffs and pulls back a little. "That's part of the problem."

"And what's *that* supposed to mean?"

"It's supposed to mean that you don't know what it's like to be treated well, and I'm the last person who can show you that."

"I never asked you to."

"No, but I think Kennedy's right that it's about time someone did."

Anger trickles into my veins. "Why *the fuck* is he getting involved at all? It's not his business."

"He's worried."

"About what? We're having sex, who fucking cares?"

"He does."

That's rich. The second Wilde leaves, Kennedy is going to know exactly what I think about his interference. "He doesn't know what he's talking about."

"Maybe he does."

"Great. So you're on his side?"

Wilde drives his palms into his eye sockets. "There are no sides. I'm lost, Hudson."

Hudson. Not city boy.

We're right back to that place where we started. On opposite sides of the same argument. It hits me, very fucking suddenly, that for the first time in my whole fucking life, I expected more. How stupid am I?

Wilde is fierce and passionate and driven ... just not when it comes to me. It's no secret that whatever we had was going to end eventually, but eventually wasn't supposed to be right now. Is it so bad that I wanted a guy who was only interested in me for a change? To live in some ridiculous fantasy that doesn't exist in the real world?

Battle lines were drawn between us early on, and I thought we were well on our way to erasing them. I guess not.

"Do you want this?" I finally ask. Because it's occurring to me, at the worst possible time, that I need him to. If he wants me, the rest doesn't matter. But if Wilde can't even give me a simple word about how he's feeling, at something deeper than his grunts and this town and the vague hints at the man he is beneath his infuriating silence, then maybe I don't want this either.

Wilde's eyes lock on mine and drag me into infinity.

"When I moved here," he says, "I learned to stop wanting anything."

I'm caught off guard by how that simple sentence sucker punches me in the chest.

That's it, then.

I take a purposeful step backward, determined not to let him see how much that's thrown me. "Then I guess it won't hurt you to leave."

Considering how easily he turns away from me and climbs out of the window, I'm right.

My hands roll over into fists as I turn and storm from the room. I thunder up the stairs, two at a time, like I'm trying to race my heartbeat, only slowing long enough to shove through Kennedy's door.

"What the *fuck* is wrong with you?"

He jolts awake, blinking into the dark. "Hudson?"

"What is *wrong* with you?" My voice cracks, and I hate it. "Why did you have to say anything?"

"What are you …" The sleep haze disappears as understanding kicks in. "Wilde?"

"Yes. It's fucking over. And I hope you're fucking happy."

The way his gaze tracks the bruising on my chest gives him confidence. "Yeah, I am."

His words ring in my ears. "Excuse me?"

"You deserve better."

"It's not your fucking choice!"

Kennedy climbs out of bed, not backing down. "You promised me there would be no more Sutton and then went and replaced him with someone just as bad." He jabs two fingers at my chest. "He's hurting you! He's playing with your emotions and making you think this is a good thing, then sending you home covered in bruises. That's *not* okay!"

I'm about to deny the bruises were him at all, but how do I explain the illegal fighting without mentioning the illegal fighting? "This isn't what you think it is."

"Oh, fuck off, Hudson. I've seen this same cycle so many times. I'm sick of it. How am I the only goddamn one of us that gives a shit about you? Or about Hart? We're brothers, and you won't talk to me about things. You find some guy and make him your whole world and ignore every fucking warning sign in existence. I'm worried you're going to be murdered one day, and you're pissed off that I told Wilde you deserve to be treated right? If he can't give you the actual basics of a good relationship, then I'm glad he broke it off."

Even with Kennedy's words echoing a little of the thoughts I was having, I'm too pissed off to agree with him. So much for ditching my short temper. "I'm sorry I don't fall in love with every person I fuck. I don't want that kind of relationship. I don't want the same things you do. Dinner and flowers and love declarations by the third date are the worst fucking things I can think of. You're a loser, Kenny. That's why no one sticks around!"

Instead of getting mad, Kennedy's expression fills with pity. "Wanting respect isn't loser behavior. The fact you don't know that makes me feel very, very sorry for you."

I'm so close to punching those smug words from his smug mouth, but even as I fight that impulse, I'm fighting at the prickling behind my nose as well. Wilde can't give me a single emotion, and Kennedy gives me too many.

Hartwell stumbles through the door. "What—and I mean this in the unkindest way possible—the *fuck* are you screaming about?"

Kennedy leaves it to me to answer.

"Our brother not minding his business."

"And you couldn't hold off being a dickhead until morning so I could get some sleep?"

Of course. Because it's always my fault.

Fuck, maybe it is.

I'm the one who dragged us here.

I'm the one who wanted to make things better and somehow made everything so much worse.

I raise my hands in surrender, biting off all the curse words I want to throw their way as my chest feels like it's been ripped in half. "You guys don't need to worry about me anymore. I'm going home."

"You're what?" Hart asks flatly.

"*Home*. I'm leaving. I'll send someone to replace me and help you guys up here, and I'll go back to running the business. Either finish this place or sell it, I don't fucking care anymore. I'm done. I'm out."

Hartwell's laugh is full of disbelief. "That easily, huh? All those times I wanted to leave and was told no, and you're just going to throw a tantrum and go?"

"No one has ever fucking forced you to be here. Ever. You've whined and complained and been a total goddamn brat, but you never tried to leave. Well, now's your chance. Congratulations. We can all be out. All I know is I'm done."

I can't stand around looking at the torn-up expression on Kennedy's face, so I storm toward the door.

"I'll send someone back with the car," I throw over my shoulder, and then, because shit can't get any worse, I add purely for Kennedy's benefit, "Sutton's going to be *so* happy to see me."

# CHAPTER
## FORTY

WILDE

"You okay?" Rooney asks as I hand over the paper.

I ignore the question. "It's smaller than usual, so it shouldn't take you long."

Rooney scans the list of what people in town need, and I silently will him to hurry the fuck up so I can go back to … well, nothing. Since yesterday, I've been planted on my couch, Nan's quilt tucked under one arm, guitar locked back in the closet, wishing for the first time since I moved here that I had a TV. Instead, I was left to stare a hole into my wall as Hudson's face filled my mind, no matter how many times I shoved it away.

"Yeah, this is easy," Rooney says. "Now, are you going to tell me why you look like you're about to cry?"

My gaze snaps back to his. "Fuck you, I do not."

"I can pretend to believe you, but then we'd both be lying. Might as well get it off your chest."

Funnily enough, that's exactly where all the pressure seems to be sitting. Opening my mouth and saying the words is hard though, and I let the silence stretch too long for Rooney.

"Is it about Hudson?"

I scowl at how easily he read me. "Why?"

"Gossip says you guys have a thing."

Of course it does. Even here, it's impossible to avoid people spreading stupid rumors. Even when those stupid rumors are true. I told myself that I'd make more of an effort with the people I consider friends, and here I am, still locking the words up tight. It's too easy to slip into the comfort of keeping everything inside after doing it for so long, especially knowing how much it hurts to make an effort and have it all be for nothing.

"Use your words, big guy," Rooney says, and something inside of me breaks.

"It's over. The shit thing is that I don't even know what *it* was, but when Kennedy asked me if I could treat Hudson right, I didn't have an answer for him. I don't know how to treat people—I avoid them for the most part—so how the fuck am I supposed to promise him something that feels impossible?" I pace closer to my truck and kick the goddamn tire. "It was *supposed* to be nothing. Just some weak moments of fucking until … until … Hudson's so … he's …" None of the words I have feel big enough.

"Kinda perfect for you?" Rooney suggests.

"Fuck off."

"Sorry." He tucks the list into his pocket. "People said he was nonstop flirting with you the other day. Looked good on you, apparently."

"Well, it was pointless because it's over now."

"Shit …" Rooney steps closer to give my arm a squeeze. "I'm so sorry."

I don't want sympathy. I want to shove any lingering emotions down so deep they're hidden from scrutiny. "It was a fling."

"Sure. You're still lying, by the way."

"Lying." I scoff and tug my arm away.

"Why did it end?"

That's the part that's still cycling through my brain because I can't figure out how it got to that point. When I climbed into his bedroom, my whole purpose was to figure out if he wanted more out of this thing to give weight to Kennedy's concern, and then ... it exploded.

It wasn't until Hudson asked me what *I* want that my thoughts ground to a halt.

Because it never occurred to me that would matter.

I wasn't lying when I told him that I'd stopped wanting anything, because somewhere along the line, I've woven myself so deeply into the town that it's all I know. What do I want? Whatever is best for Wilde's End. I want safety. Protection. For this place to thrive. I want all my Wenders to live in peace. Those are the only wants I've had for twenty years because if the town is okay, then I'm okay.

It never occurred to me that I could want Hudson too.

Not like this.

Wanting him for an orgasm is more of a primal urge.

Wanting him for *me*, that's deeper. Intentional. And it's the wanting on purpose that scares me.

"I think I have feelings for him." The words are a slow drip of confession.

"*That's* why it ended? He didn't want that?"

I shake my head because I'm still not sure of the exact reason for it. "No. I didn't tell him."

"Why not?"

"Because what if he doesn't feel the same?"

Rooney's mismatched colored eyes turn sympathetic. "Then he doesn't feel the same. But at least then you know. It's the not knowing that tears you up inside."

Apparently, because I'm feeling fucking torn right now.

"So I'm supposed to walk up to him and … say what?"

"Exactly what you told me. That you think you have feelings for him."

Even the concept of that makes me lightheaded. "I can't do that."

"It's a very normal part of dating."

Is it? I rub at one of my scars, trying to remember that time in my life. Everything from before Wilde's End is shoved down tight, and pulling out each slip of memory takes effort. Like picking the scab off a wound. A flash of a face. The press of lips during a first sloppy kiss. Nerves and heartbreak and nerves again.

The intensity of it all makes me feel sick.

"I used to think you weren't scared of anything," Rooney says.

"I'm not."

"Then why are you scared of Hudson?"

That quirk in his lips, his never-ending words, those eyelashes, and the confidence he wears like armor. The way it all slowly breaks down under my palms and I'm treated to the truest him I've seen yet. "Because he could hurt me."

"Kurt—"

I look up sharply, breath hissing between my teeth at a name I haven't heard in forever. It grates at my heart, and I want to demand he take it back, but Rooney's gaze is unflinching.

"You're already hurting. I don't think you've ever stopped. Maybe, this once, you stop running from it."

"How do you know that name?"

"I know everything. I saw all the articles when it happened, but I never mentioned it because how do you bring up something like that?"

"You know who I am?" My throat is trying to close over.

"The whole time." He looks uneasy as he stuffs his hands in his pockets. "It wasn't my business. We don't ask. But I'm saying that I *do* know you, and I know you can do this."

"I can't promise him anything."

"Then don't. Promises are stupid anyway. All you're looking for right now is where you two begin. The rest can happen when it happens."

"The rest can happen …" I think I'm more saying it to convince myself than anything. I'm getting so caught in by all these next steps when he's right. Promising forever isn't for me. It's not for Hudson either.

I want to treat him right, so will that be enough for me to actually do it? It's too early to tell. Just like it's too early to tell whether we'll ever get through our countless other obstacles. But damn I want to *try*.

Rooney nods at something in my expression. "That's right, Wilde. You've got this."

I really, actually don't think that I do. It's this needling in the back of my mind, reminding me of Old End and Hudson's short temper. Of my demons and refusal to feel.

We're both untethered weights, but maybe we can help each other not to sink completely.

I stride toward my truck, determined to do it now before this courage deserts me. The whole drive, it's like I'm rattling out of my skin, and that's almost enough reason for me to head home instead. I don't like this uncertainty. I don't like the way it rips me from the mundane hum and launches me into overdrive, like I'm facing down with a mountain lion instead of Hudson.

The mountain lion would probably be easier though. They scare in a way I've never been able to scare Hudson before.

Old End appears way too soon, and I almost forget to hit the brakes. The urge to keep driving, long and far, is tempting, and the sickening knot in my gut is almost too much for me. I pull up in front of the house they've been working on, the one where my blood still stains the cement out the front, and I suck down a deep breath before popping open my door.

I climb out as Kennedy and Hartwell get to the front door.

I don't bother with hellos.

"Need to talk to Hudson."

Hartwell crosses his arms. "Good luck with that."

"Just tell him I need a minute."

"He's not here," Kennedy cuts in.

I glance toward where the car normally sits. "When will he be back?"

"Probably never." Kennedy narrows his eyes. "At least that's what he said."

The blood feels like it gurgles from my body. "*What*?"

"Apparently, you and Kenny made him angry," Hart adds. "Nice for it not to be me for a change."

"That wasn't the point!" Kennedy snaps.

"Still happened."

I cut in before they can go back and forth. "Where can I find him?"

Kennedy sets a heartbreaking look on me. "Probably with Sutton."

That name rings in my ears. "*Sutton*?"

"I think he's trying to prove a point."

"I need an address. Now."

Hartwell disappears back inside, but Kennedy shakes his head.

"It's too late. He would have been home for hours by now."

"Does it look like I care? I don't know if I deserve Hudson, but I know that asshole sure as fuck doesn't. If I have to drag him off your brother myself, then I will." I'll snap his fucking dick off if it's gone anywhere near Hudson because this bloody rushing, heart-pounding *fear* isn't something I've ever experienced before.

All because I couldn't answer his goddamn question.

Hart rejoins us and jogs down the short steps to hand me a piece of paper. "His address."

"Thanks."

"Can we …" Kennedy takes a step forward. "Can we come with you? I hate the way we left things."

I glance between their near identical faces, tempted but unmoved.

"No."

Then I climb back into my truck and gun the engine, trying to hold tight against this sickening pit gnawing deeper into my gut.

This is between me and Hudson.

If I have my way, they can sort things out when we *both* get back.

# CHAPTER
# FORTY-ONE

## HUDSON

'm not sure when my mind went numb, but I wish the rest of my body would follow its lead. There's this deep ache in my chest like my heart is eating itself, and I'm not sure if it's Wilde-related or because of my brothers, but at least if it's cannibalized, it will stop fucking hurting.

Yesterday, it felt as though my life had found a track again. That constant anxiety of being lost was missing, and for once, when I looked forward, it wasn't an exhausting fight ahead.

Now, I'm slumped on my couch, phone frozen in my hand with Sutton's name taunting me from the screen. There is only so much I can take. I'm not a strong guy, and after everything that happened with Wilde, I'm not so sure I want to be.

It would be so easy to unblock Sutton. To call him and tell him I'm home so he can come over here and make me forget this deep ache for a while. I'd have to deal with his snide comments and pointing out that my plans failed like he said they would, but it would be worth it. I need to not feel for a minute.

The one flicker of hope I have left acknowledges that even with this shitstorm I've stumbled into, I have no desire to visit Mom. No interest in weaseling away a few pills or hunting down something stronger. I'm struggling to remember why it felt so big and important before I left, and the only explanation I can come back with was that it felt easy.

An easy escape.

But now, the only escape I want is overgrown trails and green trees and the deep sweat that fills my pores after a day of hard work. The pelt of an afternoon storm. A rocky shoreline against my naked back.

I sigh and drop my phone, rubbing the dusty feeling from my eyes. There's nothing left for me back there. What I thought was starting with Wilde was all in my head, and any hopes I had for making things right with my brothers were misplaced. We're too dysfunctional. Too messed up by our pasts to move on to something better.

Did I really call Kenny a *loser*? Am I five?

God, the way that memory prickles at my eyes almost has me lose it again. I thought I was the stable one, but turns out I'm the problem.

Maybe Kennedy and Hartwell will have a better time up there without me, and at least if I'm back running our business, then I'm still contributing. In my own small way.

My apartment is exactly the way I left it. Kennedy and Hart's lease was up before we moved, but we agreed to keep paying for this place to have somewhere to stay when we came home.

Home.

I've lived here for years, but even as I look around at the hardwood floors, semi-modern kitchen, newish furniture, and every goddamn light in this place shining pointlessly against the morning sun, I don't feel the connection that I should.

I want dirt under my nails, the smell of pine trees clogging my nose, a hot sun, and dust coating my skin.

I was right about Wilde's End. Once we're finished rebuilding the town, people will be eager to buy into it. Maybe Kenny and Hart can even come up with an agreement with Wilde. Fence off the land they're using and allocate the rest toward our plans. I think that's what they call a compromise, and it could have worked so well for us.

When I'm ready to apologize to Kennedy, I'll have to mention it to him.

For now, I'm too embarrassed, too drained, too goddamn beaten to deal with anyone. I'll give myself today to mope, then tomorrow, I'll get back to work. It won't take long for this place to become familiar again, and once I'm working to the point of exhaustion, it won't take long to forget Wilde's End either.

Unfortunately, I think forgetting Wilde will take a bit longer.

*Sutton can help with that.*

I glance back over at my phone. A day of endless, degrading sex *would* work, but … the hurt in my chest intensifies. Apparently, this feeling has linked up with sex for the first time ever in my life, and a rebound fling feels exhausting.

Not only that, but it feels *wrong*.

I wish I'd never gone to Wilde's End.

A sudden knock at my front door makes me freeze.

Does Sutton have the place bugged? It can't be my brothers since I sort of abandoned them in the middle of nowhere, and they also have a key. Mom's never visited, which means it has to be him, and even after deliberating over my phone all morning, the thought of seeing him makes me feel sick.

The knock is louder this time. Confident and more insistent. When I don't immediately get up, it comes again, and then again, cluing me in to the fact that whoever it is doesn't plan to give up.

Do I have enough luck in me for it to be an address mix-up?

I showered as soon as I got home last night because the water helped me pretend like I wasn't crying, so at least I don't smell like a dead animal, even if I feel it. As soon as I brush off whoever it is, I might as well go and face-plant on my bed and hope like hell I can sneak a nap in.

"Yes?" I snap as I tug open the front door, but whatever I'd been planning next dies in my throat.

Because the last person I'm expecting to see is Wilde.

He looks so strangely out of place in the clean, white hallway.

And he looks ready to kill.

Rage simmers from every coiled muscle, and somehow, through his gnashed teeth, he squeezes the words "Where the fuck is he?"

I'm still trying to process that his large form is filling my doorway, let alone the words he's saying.

"If Sutton touched you—"

"Wait, *what*?"

"I said—"

"I heard you, but why the hell do you think …" My brain kicks in. "You talked to Kennedy."

He swallows hard, but I refuse to watch his throat move. "Yes."

Did Kennedy go to him? Is that why he's here? Question after question pops up in my mind as I meet the anger burning in his eyes.

"Sutton's not here," I finally say. "I only said that to piss off my brother."

Second by second, Wilde's tension eases, until all that's left is him gripping the doorframe and the ache in my chest burrowing deeper.

The memory of kissing him has burned itself to my memories,

and I can't believe that for a brief moment, I was able to touch him in all the ways I wanted, simply because I wanted, and now the thought of reaching for him is impossible.

The shock of him showing up here is the only thing that's keeping the pain at a manageable level, and no matter how much I try to ignore it, my feelings keep poking at me until I bruise.

He's here, and I don't know why he's here, but I'm desperate to take it as a good sign. Because when it comes to Wilde, I'm not content to take the scraps I've accepted from everyone else.

So I steal the question he's always asking me and hope like hell he's braver than either of us has been in the past.

"Why are you here?"

His voice breaks with an emotion that echoes mine. "You know why, Hudson."

# CHAPTER
# FORTY-TWO

## WILDE

can barely think with the relief rushing through me. No Sutton, no tearing a man apart, just me and Hudson and him looking at me like he did the other night.

Unlike then, I'm not scared. Not after how panicked I was over letting him slip through my fingers.

Ever since we met, Hudson was *there*. An irritating problem that needed to be solved. A roadblock to my happiness. A trailing annoyance, a pretty face, a curious personality, and finally, a persistent needle to my attraction.

I'd taken his presence for granted and assumed I'd always have it.

"I need you to say it though." He's projecting a vulnerability I never would have thought existed inside him, and it's making my hands itch to reach out and cup his face. I keep them planted where they are, gripping the wood tighter, willing my heart to stop beating out of my fucking chest so that I can concentrate.

I can't fuck this up again.

"I'm a mess."

"Okay ..."

"Emotionally, I don't think I have a lot to offer someone, not that I've ever actually tried. See ..." My throat tries to fold over the words, I hate them so much. I hate being here, out of my safety net, giving Hudson my harness and trusting him with it.

But if he needs words, he's going to get them all.

"When I was seventeen, my whole world ended."

Hudson steps aside, pulling the door wider to let me past, and I take the offer without question. The apartment is bigger than my whole house, but I ignore it all, turning my back on the view and focusing on the only thing I currently care about.

"Tell me," he whispers, and I turn my arm over so the jagged scar is between us.

"My brother and I were in a band. It was getting popular really quickly, so we were in LA after signing a big contract for a lot of money. We started recording and through that met a few people ... There was a party, and even though I was only seventeen, I ... I got fucking wasted." Tears haunt my eyes, but I refuse to let them build. "I don't remember much other than Kyran putting me in a car and getting behind the wheel. I don't know *what* he was fucking thinking ..."

Hudson's hand wraps around mine, a shocking warmth pulling me from the blistering cold of my memories. "You don't have to tell me."

"I know." I squeeze my eyes closed and bury the emotion right down. He hardly knew how to drive, and on unfamiliar roads, in the dark, going almost twenty over with coke in his system ... "He was sixteen" is all I can say.

My little brother didn't deserve that. If I'm honest with myself, neither did I. Our parents kept pushing us to do more, go further, and I think they thought they were being supportive. But as soon as we lost Kyran, I might as well have been dead to them, too, with how lost they became. My whole family disappeared in the blink of an accident.

Hudson's green eyes have the sheen of tears. "I'm so, *so* sorry."

"It was a long time ago." A time when I was a completely different person to the one I am now. I don't recognize my younger self anymore, but that kid who ran away from LA, who got stranded in Old End and decided to never leave ... he's still buried deep beneath where I can reach him anymore.

"If that was Kenny or Hart ... no amount of time would be long enough."

Given how it feels like I've ripped my heart open again, he has a point. "I've disconnected from it all. Or, tried to. I changed my life, changed my name—"

"What was your name?"

"Kurt. Blackwood. I named myself after Wilde's End, because I really thought that living there was the end for me."

"Kurt ..."

The name doesn't feel the way it used to. "It's Wilde. Just Wilde. All I'm trying to say is that for the last twenty years, I've trained myself to ignore my emotions. Feeling anything brings it all back again. I can't feel happiness without guilt. Can't feel pride without pain. Can't look at you and feel everything I want to feel without remembering that he never got that chance to experience it. I don't know how to be normal. I don't know how to tell you what I want because I stopped wanting a long time ago. But ... all I know is that the second I came to find you and heard you'd left, it felt like something inside me died. You belong in the End, and I think you might belong with me."

"I told you that I'm not the romantic type," Hudson says,

letting go of my hand to cup my face like I wanted to do to him. "I don't need the grand gestures. I don't need you showering me in affection or going on and on about feelings. All I need is to know that I'm worth something to you. Because I've never been worth something to anyone."

The way he can say that and believe it is almost too much for me. When I look at Hudson, he gives me this overwhelming impression of life. There's fire burning in his soul that draws me in, and I can't stay away. Not from his teasing or his laughter or his determination to succeed even in the things I don't want him to. That fire burns so brightly I swear I feel it inside me sometimes, and if Hudson can bring even my dead soul back to life, he's worth everything.

Slowly, like I'm almost scared how he'll react, I turn my head and press my lips to his palm. "Come back with me," I whisper. "I can't make you any promises other than I want to try. You deserve the world, and I can't give you that, but I can give you my world. Because it's been centering around you since the day we met."

It feels like I'm holding my breath as I wait for him to answer, as he searches my eyes in that way he loves to do, and I can only hope that they show how serious I am. How, if he refused, I don't think that I could ever recover.

"Okay," he agrees. "But first, I need you to come with me."

He leads the way down a short hall, and I trail behind him like he's got me on a leash. If Hudson calls for me, I'm there, and this is no different.

He steps into a bedroom, and as soon as I'm inside, he closes the door and pushes me up against it.

His lips meet mine, warm and consuming, and I melt into his kiss. Everything I've kept bottled up in my chest rattles to break free as I let myself be in the moment, where it's him and me, and everything else can wait. I reach up to cradle his head, soft strands of hair slipping through my fingers. Hudson's tongue brushes mine, and I answer him back with intensity. He kisses like he lives: no restraint, all passion, in a way that drives me out of my mind.

My cock is thickening with every passing moment, but I don't want to let him out of my grip. This moment is fleeting and precious, and while I'd love to believe it's the start of so many more, we have a long way to go yet.

"Bed," he mutters, pulling me along with him, mouth still locked to mine. We stumble across his room, losing items of clothing as we go. When I'm naked, Hudson slows, and his gaze drops to my torso. The searing heat from his stare sets off the usual discomfort at having someone's sole attention, but I'm unprepared for how deep it gets when he reaches up and runs his thumb over one of my scars.

"What are you doing?"

He doesn't answer. His fingers skim further over my torso, lingering on old scars and tracing the remainder of memories I've run from for so long. He leans in, lips dusting over my shoulder, and I can barely breathe, let alone react to him.

"Your skin healed," he breathes, lips drifting to my throat. "Now I'm going to spend the rest of my life helping to heal the scars inside you as well."

"Hudson …"

"It's okay." He pulls me close. "You don't need to think about any of that yet. I've got you."

Hudson's naked body pressed to mine is a familiarity I'll never get sick of, and when we reach the bed and he drops backward onto it, I'm quick to crawl over him.

My mouth seals to his again as I run a hand over his chest. Soft blond hairs that are growing back tickle my palm, and I pause to run my thumb over his nipple. The deep groan, the way it hardens under my touch, I'll never get enough of Hudson and how he responds to me.

His hips tilt up to meet mine.

"I'm going to need you to put me out of my misery here," he says, hands cording through my hair. "Thinking this was over has only made me need it more."

It's like he's plucked the thoughts from my mind. This intensity is nothing new for us, but it has taken on a new edge. Like our bodies are desperate to make us deliver on all the words we gave each other.

I dip my head to taste his neck, and Hudson arches to meet me.

"Fuck, yes," he rasps, that scratchy tone bleeding into his words and making my balls heavy. The sweet scent is almost overpowering, but I breathe every little bit in, trying not to focus on how I almost lost it and focusing on how I get to keep it instead.

Every moan, every sigh, every rock of his hips against mine as I drag open-mouthed kisses down his neck to his shoulder, then from his shoulder to the nipple I'm neglecting.

I grip it between my teeth, tongue flicking over the hardened peak before I suck the whole thing into my mouth. Hudson's so fucking perfect, the way he's writhing under me, uncomfortably hard, dick brushing mine with every upward thrust of his hips.

The urge to grind down against him until we both come is strong, but I want something else tonight. Something I've only ever used my fingers for and am ready to make happen.

"You know," I say, pulling back to flick my tongue over him again before sinking down between his legs. "I really want this …" I suck his cock down to the back of my throat before releasing it. "In my ass."

Hudson's eyes snap open. "Yeah?"

"If you want to."

"So, so much." He points beside the bed. "Lube is in there."

I reach for the drawer, pulling out lube and a condom that I drop onto the bed beside us, and then I hesitate before looking back at him. "I've never done it before. So be gentle, okay?"

The way he looks at me makes me worried he might try to talk me out of it or say something sweet or give me more than I'm ready for, but it only takes a moment for that to pass, and then Hudson tucks his hands back behind his head.

"You're in control here." He thrusts his hips obscenely. "It's ready when you are."

He's not lying. His cock is hard and flushed red, still shiny at the tip from my spit. Having him in my mouth feels so right, and I can only hope it's the same when I ride him.

I cover my fingers with lube, then lean in and kiss him again while I soften my hole. There's nothing like a good jerk-off in the shower while I ride my fingers, so I'm assuming this will be a thousand times better. To be stretched around him, to know that I'm making him feel good, to bring us both to release in the closest way possible, I want that. Fucking desperately.

I swallow my grunt as I slip a finger inside.

"Tell me what you're doing," he murmurs against my lips.

I ignore the request. I'm not sure I could give voice to these thoughts if I wanted to.

His lips curl upward against mine. "Let me guess … you're fingering that sexy hole?"

Lust curls into my gut, and it would be easy enough to say yes, but I can't bring myself to. He skims his cock against mine again, sending a rush of nerves to my balls, which loosens me enough to add a second finger.

"How many have you got in there?" he asks. "One? Two?

You've got such thick fingers, I'm almost jealous that I'm not the one taking them."

I can't play along with this game, not when words are my weakness and he's turning me on too badly to think, but I can give him something. "Two."

"Two …" His lips brush mine. "Bet you could take three. Bet three would get your hole nice and loose to sink my cock into. I could almost blow, thinking about how warm and snug you'll feel."

The arm I'm leaning my weight on shakes with the desire sinking deep in my gut, and even if I'm not ready yet, I try a third finger. I take it slow, letting myself adjust around it, the lube making it easier but not at all easy.

"Hey …" Hudson whispers. "It's okay. You've got it. Just focus on me and breathe."

"I am breathing."

He actually laughs at me. "Breathe *better*, then. Relax. I know that's a hard thing for you to understand, but it really does make it so much easier."

I'm glaring at him out of instinct, but it only pulls his smile wider. And when he looks at me like that, it's hard to even pretend to be mad.

I relax.

The three fingers sink to my knuckles.

"Fine. Maybe you know what you're talking about."

"Pro cock rider. Don't worry, I'll teach you everything you need to know."

My lips meet his softly, because with him, I'm not worried at all. At least not about sex. What comes next beyond the sex is completely unknown, but I refuse to get ahead of myself. I've only just been able to admit that I don't hate the man, so it's going to take me some time.

But looking down at him while he gazes up at me, hatred is the last thing on my mind.

Hudson's making me feel again. Like he's released a wind-up car, tension snapping and propelling us toward this moment.

"You good?" he asks.

"I'm ready."

# CHAPTER
# FORTY-THREE

## HUDSON

never in a million years thought Wilde would be here, in my bed, thick, hairy thighs straddling my waist and steely gray eyes locked on me, like it's giving him strength.

"You don't have to," I remind him, gently holding his hips. My dick is so fucking hard, enticingly close to his hole, and I want to sink inside him almost more than anything. But if he's not into this, I'd prefer he said that.

Wilde grunts and reaches back for my dick. Even through the condom, his grip makes me tremble, and it takes all my damn power to hold still as he lines me up. "I know I don't," he says petulantly before pressing down onto me.

It's torture, all that initial weight before my aching tip breeches him. Wilde's slow, giving himself all the time he needs, but little by little, his ass swallows me, sucking me into that gloriously tight warmth. I keep my damn ass planted on the bed so that I don't give in to the urge to thrust into him. It'll happen. It's coming. I only need to be patient, dammit.

Every inch he takes is satisfying that gut-deep lust, and by the time he settles over me, I'm in heaven.

"Fuck, you feel good," I say, voice deeper and huskier than I mean it to be. Not that anyone could blame me. My cock is buried inside my tough, mysterious mountain man, and he's looking at me like there's nowhere else he wants to be. Wilde might not be great with words, but I think I could learn to live with that if he always looks at me the way he is right now.

He shifts, grinding my cock inside him, and my eyes almost rock back in my skull. There's nothing like having Wilde wrapped around me, his large, solid body towering over me, and that magnificent cock arching up toward his belly button, swollen and needy for more.

I release him with one hand and stroke his shaft gently.

"You good?"

"So good." He rocks back onto me again.

I'm so fucking horny, and he has to be aware of how turned on I am. His gaze is burning into me, filling me with all the attention I crave, and with the way my skin is prickling all over, I've never felt this alive.

Wilde lifts and lowers himself again, the tentative movements giving me exactly what I need to stay on edge. He's like a coiled animal of pure muscle, and the smoother and faster he moves, the closer I get to losing control.

I don't know how I'm supposed to survive it. His ass is squeezing around me, and I love the feel of his cock passing through my fist, but I'm greedy. It's not enough. I want to touch him all over. To feel his hard pecs, and enjoy his hairy torso, and kiss and bite those lips that are finally visible beyond the beard.

His gray eyes shine down at me, full of lust and something deeper, and my free hand rests against his outer thigh.

"You're doing so good."

His lips twitch like he catches himself before he can laugh. "Not a hardship on my end, that's for sure."

Thank fuck he's enjoying it too. He sets a pace above me, and when I'm sure he's comfortable, I join in too. Meeting his movements to grind up into him, loving the way my cock feels as it sinks into his body over and over and over.

All that towering strength, the way his thigh muscles move as he lifts up and down, how easily he's rocking back onto me, it has my mind twisted up into the most overstimulating high I've ever experienced.

He's here. After twenty-four hours of this crushing sadness, his presence is stitching my shattered heart back together one thread at a time. I can't stop touching him, like the realer this feels, the more I'll believe it.

Every scar on his body, that deep one through his eye, knowing the source is like this secret key I have to Wilde that no one else gets to see. What he's been through, what he's lost … it makes so much sense that he'd shut down. Hide away. Focus on his people and never himself, but I refuse to let him keep doing that.

He's so passionate, so faithful, and so deserving of having someone on his side. My thumb circles his tip as I jerk him off, and I'm rewarded with a full-body shudder. But it's not enough. I need him closer. Need him wrapped around me.

I roll us so Wilde's back hits the mattress, and I press back inside him again. My face hovers inches above his, and before I second-guess kissing him, Wilde's fingers are in my hair, tugging my mouth down to his.

I groan deeply into the kiss, working my thrusts harder. His knees come up on either side of my hips, and his free hand grabs my ass, digging bruises into the skin. We move together, and I've never been this turned on, never sunk this deeply into the moment during sex. Normally, I'm too focused on making sure it looks good and half-detached as Sutton rails me and takes what he needs.

With Wilde, I'm finally understanding what Kennedy talks about when he calls it making love.

We might not be in love, not yet at least, but this building emotion is one I never want to let get away.

Wilde's panting heavily as he kisses along my jaw, grip on my hair tight, eyes struggling to stay open as I pound into him like I'm possessed. The flush that creeps from my toes to my scalp makes my bedroom a hundred degrees hotter, and the sweat building between our bodies only turns me on more.

There's no way that we could resist this forever. No way there's a future where we don't share this again. I need him, and I'm scared to need him, but it helps knowing he feels the same.

What we're going through, we're going through together.

We won't always get it right, but as long as we come back to this, to need and pleasure and remembering what we're all about, we'll be able to handle anything.

"Fuck, Hudson, touch me," he commands. "Make me come."

A shiver ripples along my spine. I'll never get enough of him telling me what to do, and nothing will get me there faster than hearing him say my name in that uncontrollable rasp.

My hand dives between and closes over his cock. I match up my strokes with each thrust as he sucks his way along my throat. It's sensory heavy, turning my limbs to jelly, and if I wasn't so fucking determined to feel him tighten around my cock as he comes, I would have blown my load already.

But he's close.

I can do this.

His sticky precum is building between our stomachs, and my balls are getting concerningly tight. I'm so checked out, unaware of anything but his mouth on my neck, his ass around my cock, and his heated shaft fucking the tight grip I have on him.

"I'm close," I warn him.

His teeth sink into my neck as his hips shudder, and his release floods between us.

*Fucking finally.*

He clenches around me, my high mixing with my relief, and then it's all too much.

I come hard, in a vision-shaking, limb-trembling high, and as I unload into Wilde's ass, I remind myself that I get to do this again.

Whenever the fuck I want.

That thought is too much for me, that when I can think straight, I pull out of him and flop onto the side of the bed.

It's funny how, when you're that close to the edge, coming is more important than breathing, and I'm paying the price for it now. I lie there, trying to fill my lungs, satisfaction so deep it's surging through my limbs, and every one of the shitty feelings I was wading through earlier has gone.

Well, almost all of them.

I still have to make things right with my brothers, but for all the faults the three of us have, we've never let an argument cause irreparable damage.

So for right now, I want to take a minute—maybe an hour— with Wilde and do something we've never done before.

I roll over onto my side, looking down at where he's also catching his breath, and hesitantly set my hand on his chest. He doesn't tense or get weird, so that's a good start.

"I was good, wasn't I?"

Wilde lifts his eyebrows. "Not bad for a city boy."

For maybe the first time, those two words don't sound like an insult. "Come on, admit it. I rocked your world. Fucked you good." I lean over him with a teasing grin. "Took you to pound town."

He grunts, face scrunched up, and instead of answering, he tugs me down until his lips claim mine. I want to point out that I know he's trying to shut me up, but when he kisses me, it's like the second hand stops, and we have all the time in the world. A million more endless moments.

"Ready to come home?" he asks.

Home.

It's weird to think that when he says that, he means Wilde's End, but then I think of the pine trees and the trails and our swimming hole, and there's no other word for it.

I don't know what it means for the future, but for now, it feels right.

"I never should have left."

# CHAPTER
# FORTY-FOUR

## WILDE

glower at the shiplap houses as I pull to a stop to let Hudson out. He stayed over in my space again for the billionth time last night, and I'm starting to hate how much I love him in my bed. Maybe billionth is an exaggeration when it's barely been a month since I dragged him back here, but time doesn't make sense when I'm with him.

"I'm going to spend the night with Kennedy and Hartwell, but I'll see you tomorrow?" he checks as he pops the door.

"Sounds good." My eyes stay locked to him as he climbs out, then jogs up to the house to get ready for a day of work. We haven't been able to figure out a solution to what happens next with the town, but we've thrown around enough ideas that we should be able to come up with *something* good enough for us both.

Ziggy will be coming down around lunchtime to help replace old wiring, so I'll pick him up and maybe attempt to spend some time with the brothers. With Ziggy there, he's a buffer between me and Kennedy's distrust since he takes up most of Kennedy's attention.

Until I can grab Ziggy though, I have a visit to make.

I take the back way down to where Lynx's place sits next to the crop fields. It's smaller than mine, all one room with a separate bathroom off the house, and when I pull to a stop on the grass beside it, Bob prowls through the open doorway. His golden eyes settle on me, like a warning not to get too close.

Lynx slowly follows a moment later. "All healed up," he says as I climb out of the truck. "What a relief. And you beat Foley over the weekend, so everything is back to normal."

"It is."

He folds both hands over the porch railing while I cross my arms and lean against the warm hood of my truck. "Didn't think you did house visits," he says.

"I don't. I came to talk to you."

"About what?"

"About watching yourself."

Like he can understand us, Bob makes a low noise in his throat.

Lynx glances at the enormous cat and then back at me. "I'm minding my own business over here. Can't imagine what you mean."

"Hudson and I are together—"

"Dating the enemy?"

"And it doesn't matter what's happening in Old End. You need to trust that whatever happens will be for the best of us all. He doesn't want to screw anyone over, but there are goals he needs to meet as well. So we're working on it."

Lynx tilts his head back, studying me. "And you trust him?"

Trust has always been a hard one for me. It doesn't come easily, and it'll never be my default. I've trained myself to expect the worst, which is great for preventing injuries out here, but not so great for wanting a stable relationship. "I've decided to, yeah."

"Then I guess city boy is a Wender now," he says dryly. "Lucky us."

"It also means he's off-limits. Him and his brothers. So this time when I tell you to stay out of Old End, I mean it."

Lynx looks back at Bob, and I swear the two of them exchange a long look between them. "Can't make any promises."

"I can. You go near him, threaten him, hurt him, and it will be the last thing you ever do in my town."

His hazel eyes stare me down. "How savage of you."

"Don't test me."

The corner of his mouth twitches. "Hear that, Bob? Don't test him."

Bob lets out another warning sound.

I stride forward, close enough they can reach me, but I'm not scared of either of them, and I never will be. "You touch so much as a hair on his head, and no animal or knife will save you."

Bob gives me a feral hiss, but I ignore him.

"Noted." The curl to Lynx's lips makes it hard to believe him, but all we have out here is our word. He's given me his, and for better or worse, I've given him mine.

I told Hudson that I'm not a murderer, and I stand by that, but I am a protector, and I am dangerous. If Lynx comes near him again, I'll do whatever I have to in order to defend my man.

I force a smile that still doesn't feel right on my face. "That last crop of carrots were delicious, by the way."

"Always nice to be appreciated."

I turn and leave them, then kill some time before swinging back to grab Ziggy. He slides into the car and places his toolbox at his feet, and then we're off again.

It's a quiet drive, but he's humming with something I can't place. Something that brightens all of his usually hidden features.

"Crush still going strong?" I guess.

He scowls and crosses his arms over his narrow chest.

"I'd put in a good word for you, but I'm pretty sure Kennedy still thinks I'm mistreating his brother."

That earns me a sympathetic pat on the shoulder.

"It's fine. Bringing Hudson back earned me some points, and I still have a long time to win him all the way over." I could probably try harder to convince Kennedy that I'm not another Sutton, but I'm still working on convincing myself. I'd never treat Hudson like he did, but that doesn't necessarily mean I'm going to treat him right all the time either. Just like Kennedy, I still need time to trust myself that I can do it right.

We pull up in Old End, and I follow Ziggy out of the car. We walk straight into house two, and I trail after him, still not sure if I should stay or go. Hudson's brothers … well, they intimidate. There's no real reason for it other than this deep-seated want for them to like me.

"Ziggy!" Kennedy's voice echoes through the old framework. "Wasn't sure if you'd be here today."

He holds up his toolbox.

"Awesome, let's start over here." Kennedy lightly sets his hand on Ziggy's back and steers him away as Hudson notices me.

"I wasn't expecting to see you." He greets me with a long kiss, hand gripping my ass and long body pressed tightly against mine.

"I can go."

"I never want that," he says against my mouth. "But you never stop in. Everything okay?"

The question catches me off guard as I look into his trusting eyes, feeling the same emotion from him that's been rattling around in my chest for so long now. "Yeah. It's all sort of perfect."

"Perfect is taking it a bit far." He steps back, but his amusement is obvious as he gestures to the house. "Still lots of work to go."

I tug him back against me. "I'm not romantic, so let me have this for a second. I can't remember being happy like I am with you, so yeah. I'm allowed to think things are perfect because that's exactly how I feel."

"I've been scarily happy too," he says, reaching up to play with my beard. "But every time I focus on being happy, I worry it will go away, and then it makes me sad again."

"We've got issues."

"Lots of issues. Lots and lots of perfect issues."

I let out a small laugh and press my forehead to his. "Just taking this day by day, city boy."

"Day by fucking day." He kisses me again. "I'm glad you came by."

"Me too." I pull away a little, looking at all the work they have ahead of them. "Can I help?"

Hudson's eyebrows almost shoot off his face. "Really? But—"

"Yeah," I cut him off because he doesn't need to rehash my thoughts on this. Like I told Lynx, I've chosen to trust him, and part of that comes from not having an answer to our problems and knowing that one day we will. "But we're doing this partner thing, and while I've never had one of those, I'm confident that one partner doesn't leave the other to struggle through something alone."

"Well, I've had plenty of partner-type things, and in my experience, they do." His smile is half sad, half hopeful. "So I'd love to try something different with you."

"Let's get started, then."

And like that, the cute moment between us passes, because neither of us likes to talk about emotions for too long. But the way we feel is still there in every look and every touch. We support each other, and we show up for each other.

That's what's important.

It doesn't matter how many doubts I have that I can do this, because I want it. So bad. So I know we'll make it work.

Me and my city boy.

'Til the end.

# EPILOGUE

## HUDSON

"I should have burned it down when I had the chance."

I choke on my laugh when I turn to Wilde and see the way he's glaring up at house two. As the flagship house of our whole project, we're using it as the prototype for the external facing, and with all the shiplap gone, it looks fucking awesome. We've gone back and forth on whether ultramodern was the way to go and in the end decided against it. We might be giving Old End a revamp, but there must be something in the air out here because it didn't feel right to bring a whole head of steel and cement out here.

In the end, the houses will look like cabins. Well, mega cabins. All timber and stone with wide balconies at the front and huge windows looking toward the foresty hill at the back.

"Admit it," I say, elbowing him in the ribs. "It looks fucking amazing."

"Whoever buys it has more money than brains."

"Let's hope!" He can't bring me down today. With the roof

fully finished, I have a glimpse at how the street will turn out, and it's fucking incredible. Wilde can grumble about the renovations all he likes; if he were really that unhappy about them, he wouldn't be here every other day helping.

It's why, no matter what, I'm determined to find a solution that's going to suit us all.

With the money hole we're in, we can't *not* make money off this place, otherwise … what then? We leave, head home, have our business collapse, and end up with less than we started with?

I try not to picture that devastating future because it's terrifying to even think that's an option.

Especially when I glance over at Wilde, at his curly hair and neat beard and wary gaze, I don't think it is anymore.

We still have a long way ahead of us before we're done here, but more and more lately, I've been wondering about what happens when it is. When this is all tied up and we're ready to move on to the next thing, do I just … pack it up and go home? To that apartment where everything is too loud and too cramped? Or … would he want me to stay?

I dart another look Wilde's way and tug him around until he's looking at me. It takes a moment for the caution in his eyes to fade and be replaced by the way he usually looks at me. The way that makes my chest feel too full.

"I've been thinking," I say, because I might as well blurt it all out there, or we'll never get through a conversation. He's gotten a lot better at communicating, but even now, it's sometimes hard to get the words out of him. "What happens when I'm done?"

"I'm not following."

I wave a hand toward the houses. "Here. With this. What happens when it's finished and I have nothing keeping me here anymore?"

His eyebrows inch higher. "Nothing?"

Even months later, he still brings out the nerves in me. "That's what I'm asking. I came here to work, and obviously, there's still a lot to go, but once it *is* done … will I still have you?"

His features soften as he steps closer. "Do you want to still have me?"

"Would I be asking if I didn't?"

It earns me one of his rare smiles. "I'm not going anywhere."

"Not … not even if we can't figure this out? What if I have to sell?"

He takes a long breath. "Then you have to sell."

"Just like that?"

He shrugs, and I'm worried he won't elaborate. "If I haven't made it obvious, I trust you. I'm here because I want to be, and if I thought you'd get your money and run, that wouldn't be the case. I know you'll do everything you can to find a solution and trust that if you have to sell, it's because you have no other option."

My heart melts that he believes that. That even with all the shit behind us, he knows exactly who I am. He sees me. It's all I've ever wanted. "I love you," I find myself whispering. "So much."

His searching gaze is the same one he's given me a million times before. The one that reads every thought circling through my mind and gives him whatever answers he's searching for.

"I love you so much it's hard to breathe."

I tug him to me, mouth finding his as I pour all the love I'm bursting with into the kiss. Wilde's strong arms wrap around me, and I wish we were alone. Wish we could get lost in each other. We might not be romantic people, but sex is our love language, and whenever we're together, it's like the rest of the world doesn't exist.

He's my solid rock, and he gives me all the attention I never knew I needed.

Whereas I help him relax and open up, remind him that he's a whole person, and it's okay for him to want sometimes.

We work together.

That's all I need.

Ziggy approaches us and nods off toward the forest edge. Slowly, I follow his gaze to see what he's noticed.

"We have an audience."

Gathered by the gravel road is a group of Wenders, watching as the roof is installed. I recognize them all, even if the names don't immediately grab me, but in front are Lynx, Rooney, and Booker.

"They won't come any closer," Wilde says. "They're just curious."

I wouldn't care if they did as long as they left Lynx behind, but I have no idea how my brothers would react to them. Thankfully, I don't need to find out.

"We've got a crowd," Kennedy says loudly as he comes our way. He slings an arm around Ziggy's narrow shoulders, and the man blushes all the way out to his hairline. "Should I invite them over?"

"Nah, leave them."

"You sure?" Hart asks, joining us. "That asshole has his machete again. Maybe I can convince him to land on me this time."

Okay, so things are *mostly* good. I'm happy, Kennedy is protecting his heart, but Hartwell is still the same Hartwell.

I'm not giving up on him yet though.

Just like I won't give up on finding a solution for this place.

Wilde's my partner. He's the one who respected me when no one else ever did.

He's given me everything, and I'm going to do the same for him.

I've finally found what I'm living for.

**THANK YOU FOR READING WILDE'S END!**

Want to spend more time in the End? Good news!
Ziggy and Kennedy fall in love next.

Can't wait for more? Get first access to my next releases, see character art, and indulge in all the bonus content on Patreon.

# Let's get ready for ...

# ZIGGY AND KENNEDY

# BONUS SCENE

ZIGGY

Kennedy's unfiltered laugh balloons in the dilapidated house and my attention unwillingly pulls toward him. He's shirtless, sweating, and my sanity can only handle looking for too long.

It's why I avoid it as much as I can.

Because once he has my attention, it's almost impossible to steal it back again.

He's teasing Hart about something I have no interest in--not that it's possible to have interest in anything when his back muscles are moving under his skin like that. I have a very, very big problem, and it's not a problem I plan on doing anything about.

Kennedy's presence is painful, like a well that's been carved into my chest with infinite depths of pain. I'm torturing myself being here, but I'm drawn to him and I can't fight it because while it hurts, this is the most I've felt in years.

I know Kennedy, full of light and smiles and kindness, wouldn't look twice at a gremlin like me, but that doesn't matter.

I'll admire him from a distance. Want. Yearn. Drive myself out of my goddamn mind. It's worth it for those small beams of sunshine he directs my way.

I huff at where my thoughts have strayed to and yank myself back to reality. I'm here to work. Not perv. Concentrating shouldn't be as hard as it is.

*Pussy.*

*Loser.*

*Weirdo.*

The old voices are frustratingly close to the truth and they've been getting louder than ever these days. It's one of the many reasons I've been showing up to work with the brothers because the alternative is sitting alone at home and letting those voices win.

At least if I'm obsessing over Kennedy, I'm not obsessing over my flaws, so I call that a win.

Probably.

"Hey ..."

I glance up at the familiar voice and watch as Wilde joins me. He looks as cautious as I feel to be here, but there's something lighter in his expression than I've ever seen before. His usually dark and stormy eyes look more like clouds right before the sun shines through.

"Hudson says you've been here a lot," he tells me, and I don't know how to respond to that. I won't say anything, not with the brothers here, but usually Wilde can read my expressions and I don't even know what one I want to wear.

*Yes, Wilde, I know I'm here a lot.*

*Funny thing about working is that you have to work.*

*I'm unhealthily obsessed with torturing myself, thank you for noticing.*

Instead of any of that, I give him a flat look like I don't know what he means.

He very nearly smiles, gaze flicking toward where Hudson has joined his brothers. The look he wears as he watches Hudson casts shadows over the well in my chest, and I can't stop from wondering what it would feel like to be looked at like that.

"He also says that you disappear whenever he shows up."

After he attacked me for bringing their tools back, it's a mystery why I'm not interested in spending time with him.

Wilde picks up on the distrust I send Hudson's way. "Yeah, I get it. He can be a hard man to like."

But not for Wilde, apparently. I search his gaze for the answers as to why *he* likes him.

Wilde shrugs, shifting like he's uncomfortable with the turn our conversation has taken. "I see past the asshole he tries to be. And I get it. The way things in our past shapes who we grow to be."

I'd know about that as much as anyone.

Wilde cuts off there with a shake of his bearded head. "Fuck talking about me. Are you ..." He checks we're not being over-heard and I'm grateful given what he says next. "Still all hot over the other one?"

Instant regret over ever mentioning my crush to Wilde takes over as my cheeks burn. I scowl his way and it earns me a short laugh.

"So that's a yes."

"That's a shut up," I hiss so low Wilde's the only one who can hear me.

He laughs again and this time it gets the brothers' attention.

Hart's frowning at us both. "I didn't think you were allowed to do that."

Wilde and I exchange a confused look. "Do what?" he asks.

"Laugh. Be happy. Forget to scowl. Take your pick."

"Don't be an asshole," Hudson snaps, shoving his shoulder.

"Aww ..." Hart responds. "But I'm just trying to take after my oldest brother who I look up to so much."

"You forgot something." Hudson pretends to pull his middle finger out of his pocket.

"Trust me, I didn't." Hart's voice is thick with derision. "You never let me forget."

Wilde grunts. "I'll be outside."

He leaves and Hart and Hudson keep bickering, but I can't focus on them because Kennedy is heading my way.

He throws his thumb back over his shoulder and a half-hearted grin shifts his moustache. "These two, huh? Never ending."

He's not wrong.

"If you want, we can head next door to work. It'll be quieter there."

That's a common mistake people make. They think that just because I'm quiet, that I prefer it. There's nothing I hate more.

My gaze drifts to his brothers, and actually, there's *one* thing I hate more. Screaming and the anger that comes with it. Thankfully his brothers are just sniping at each other, but after Hudson shouting in my face that day, I don't think I'll ever get that image of him out of my memory bank.

Kennedy's still waiting on a response so I shake my head. Up close, he feels even bigger than usual. We're roughly the same height, or maybe he's a little shorter than me, but he's stocky with muscular arms and chest and a chubby belly. The need to touch him rolls over me and I shove my hands into my pockets instead.

He rubs his chest, like he's suddenly self conscious. "Yeah ... bit sweaty. It's a hot day."

It's only then I realize that I'm shamelessly staring at him and he's picked up on it. I hurry to act like his sweat--and not his skin, muscles, nipples--is what I was focused on.

It *is* hot. I'd know since I'm wearing jeans. I pretend to sniff the air near him and pass out, but unfortunately it only gives me a good nose full of his scent and the musky, manly smell makes me weak.

"Hey." He laughs as he playfully backhands my stomach. "I'd like to see you haul all that lumber and not stink."

I pinch my nose.

"Asshole."

I cup my face like I'm breathing through a gas mask, and instead of it scaring him away, a spark lights up his eyes.

"What's that? You like how I smell? You want more?"

And before I know what he's doing, his arms close around me. Heat rushes from my toes to my scalp as Kennedy rubs his body against mine.

"Now who smells?" He laughs, chest pressed firmly to my back. "Ahh, Ziggy, you're *so* sweaty. And you stink. I'm going to pass out!"

*I'm* going to pass out if he keeps touching me. The contact has my every nerve humming to life, and his scent is making me lightheaded. Fresh sweat and sunshine heated skin isn't a combination I ever thought I needed in my life, but it's wrapping me in warmth and ...

Shit.

My dick is hard.

It's lucky he's behind me and can't feel it, but now my cheeks are burning for a completely different reason. I will my cock to go down, but then Kennedy nuzzles his face into my neck and his bare skin flush against mine, the tickle of his moustache racing down my neck and along my shoulder, pumps lust into my veins so sickeningly fast I almost moan.

I playfully shove him away from me and grab my toolbox, almost upending the thing in the process.

Then I march right out the door.

My heart is fucking *galloping* in my chest, and the fact Kennedy has never met a thing called personal space is going to kill me.

"Ziggy?"

I don't turn around. Partly because I'm worried that as baggy as these jeans are, they're not going to hide the flag pole I'm waving at him, and partly because what the hell do I say? My cheeks are on fire which means they'll be flaming red, and I can barely force words with him on a good day.

Horny and worried about blurting out how hot he is definitely doesn't qualify as *that*.

I'm doomed to scramble home in disgrace and spend the rest of the day alone.

Like so many days since coming to Wilde's End.

I feel safe here, but more alone than ever.

*Selfish.*

*Inconsiderate.*

*Spoiled.*

Yes, Mom, *I know*.

My eyes fall closed against the voices and my dick finally starts to flag. Funny what bad memories can do for a guy.

Wilde's leaning against his truck, just watching the sky, but his gaze falls to mine as I storm from around the side of the house. "You okay?" he grunts.

I'm never okay.

I'm so, so close to telling him that.

But I force a smile and hold up the toolbox. "Done for today."

Then I turn my back on him before he can read the truth and head home.

I'll get through this.
I always fucking do.

# ACKNOWLEDGEMENTS

As with any book, this one took a hell of a lot of people to make happen.

The cover was created by the talented Rebecca at Story Styling Cover Designs with a gorgeous image by Wander Aguiar, and edits were done by Sandra Dee at One Love Editing, with Lori Parks proofreading the bejeebus out of it.

Thanks to Emily Wittig for creating this amazing discreet cover.

Charity VanHuss you're the most amazing PA I could have ever dreamed up. Without you I'd be even more of a chaotic disaster and there isn't enough space to list the many hats you wear for me. Paige and Lara Janz, you round out my team in the most incredible way and I'm always excited to see what fun ideas you both have next.

Eden Finley, thank you for being there for all the doubt spirals and hand-holding. Whether you wanted to be or not.

ACKNOWLEDGEMENTS

My incredible author friends who beta read this book: you've made this so much better than I could have on my own.

Adam Gyllenhaal , you're a gem with his hilarious and thoughtful comments for both of the guys, and Kate Kauri your unhinged feral romance sensitivity reading helped get this plot into something worth reading.

For Gabe: thank you for lending the name Nox to this one (and future books in the series) and for being an amazing supporter of my Obsessed Patreon tier.

And of course, thanks to my fam bam. To my husband who constantly frees up time for me to write, and to my kids whose neediness reminds me the real word exists.

# *More* **SAXON ...**

## What do you do when you're a hit man ... who's terrible at his job?

At first, I thought it would be an easy payday. A few pew pews for bad people, a couple of suitcases of cash for me. People have done worse for an honest living. Probably.

The problem is that after a couple of jobs, I've never actually managed to unalive someone, and not for lack of trying. Apparently, a basic requirement of a hitman is being a good shot.

Despite my constant duck-ups—that my boss knows nothing about—I'm given another name, and I very nearly follow through. Only after obliterating this guy's ear and his fervent pleading to spare him, I've sent him into hiding and collected the cash anyway.

But wanted people are hard to hide, and bad guys don't like paying big money for loose ends.

Now that Van Gogh has shown his face again—sans ear—I've scammed my way into his security team, which is sort of ideal since I'm now highly wanted as well.

Unfortunately, we have some "trust issues" to "work through" from our meet-shoot, and with the gorgeous bastard's brother missing, he refuses to lay low until they're reunited.

I'm not sold on the plan, honestly, but this guy has me questioning my sexuality along with my career path, and I'm at the point where I'm determined to see a job through to the end. Or die trying.

But hey, at least then I'd finally deliver a body.

# More SAXON ...

## Christian

Being invited to my cousin's wedding really shouldn't be a big deal except, oh yeah, I haven't seen my family for a decade.
My parents turned their backs on me and I've done everything since to become successful and show them what they lost. Only, it's kinda hard to be a success when you're a walking trainwreck.
So I'm going to fake it. Hire a guy with an online presence so impressive they'll be desperate to welcome me back into the elitist fold, and roll into the wedding with the kind of confidence I've never felt a day in my life.
The plan's a knockout. Until my fake date cancels minutes before the ceremony.

## Émile

One letter from my dearly departed grandfather, and suddenly I'm on a husband hunt. He's reworked his entire will so I'm set to inherit far more than I'm entitled to, and all because he's asked me to use that money for "good".
In order to get that inheritance, though, there's one stipulation: marriage. Even with his request, I'm tempted to stick to my original plan of getting as far from my wretched family as possible, and letting them fight it out. But then I run into a tall drink of scattered mess outside of a wedding who's in desperate need of a date, and the pieces click into place.
I help him, he helps me. Marriage, money, then go our separate ways.
Easy.
Now all I have to do is stop myself from falling for the guy.

# *More* SAXON ...

## Payne

In search of: room to rent.
Must ignore the patheticness of a forty-year-old roommate.
Preferably dirt cheap as funds are tight (nonexistent).
There's nothing sadder than moving back to my hometown newly divorced, homeless, and lost for what my next move is.
When my little brother's best friend offers me a place to stay in exchange for menial duties, I swallow my pride and jump at the offer.
I need this.
I also need Beau to wear a shirt. And ditch the gray sweatpants. And not leave his door ajar when he's in compromising positions ...

## Beau

In search of: roommate.
Must be non smoker and non douchebag.
Room payment to be made in meal planning, repairs, and dumb jokes.
Since my career took off, I barely have time to breathe, let alone keep my life in order. I'm naturally chaotic, make terrible decisions, and scare off potential dates with my "weirdness".
So when Payne gets back into town and needs somewhere to stay, I offer him my spare room with one condition: while he's staying with me, I need him to help me become date-able.
And while he does that, I can focus on my other plan: ignoring that Payne is the only man I've ever wanted to date.

# More *SAXON* ...

*We're basically Romeo and Juliet. But dudes. And without all the dying.*

## Chad

Being VP of Sigma Beta Psi is wild. I get all the benefits of being in charge with hardly any of the responsibility.
Parties, pranks, and frat politics—college life has never been sweeter.
Until I meet Bailey Prince.
He has the face of a goddamn angel. I don't know where he came from or why I'm so obsessed.
But I do know he's a Kappa. And our houses have a rivalry that's written into legend.

## Bailey

At Rho Kappa Tau, I'm a legacy.
It's a lot of pressure, but I've always been responsible, never had that rebellious need to rock the boat, and I like it that way.
But after a party at Sigma—the jock frat—I meet Chad Doomsen, and for the first time in my life I want to step outside my square.
Our houses have always had a rivalry, but some of the guys seem to hate Chad specifically, and I don't know why.
He's surprisingly sweet and kind. At least to me.
I need to stay away. A relationship with Chad would be betraying the very legacy that brought me here. But I can't help myself. And it seems, neither can he.

# More SAXON ...

## Roo

Five years ago, I walked away from Sunbury, Oregon, and left my best friend behind.  The move was supposed to get my life on track. I even had a list.
Life changing epilepsy surgery. Check.
See the world. Check
Get over my straight best friend ... Not exactly.
No matter where I go or who I meet, I can't let Tanner go.
I'm back to tell him how I feel. To get the closure I need once and for all.
Only now I'm here and falling for him all over again, it's getting harder to say the words.  Because once I have my closure, I'll be gone.  And this time it will be for good.

## Tanner

When my best friend, Roo, left for Australia, it was the worst day of my life.
I thought we'd have each other always. But Roo needed the surgery so I let him go, thinking he'd come straight back.
Five years is a long time.
Now he's here, all I want is to hold on tight. I need to show him what he means to me. The problem is, I'm not exactly sure what that is.
My draw to him has always been confusing and different—everyone in town says so. But I struggle to understand it. All I know is I won't survive him leaving again. And I'll do anything to make him stay.

# More SAXON ...

## Austin

Dashwood Academy is a necessary evil. I learned that early on.
If I play their game and learn my role, when graduation comes around,
I'll be set for life. Exceeding all the dreams a guy like me ever had—even
if that means living a life that goes against everything I am.
But then Garrett Close enrolls at Dashwood and I can't stop thinking
about him. Wanting him. Watching him ...
And hating him for being the one person who can ruin everything.

## Garrett

I don't know what it is about Austin du Pont but he acts like king of the
academy. Too good for the rest of us and not ready to spare me a
second glance.
Not that I should be worrying about a pretty boy with dead eyes.
Dashwood is my ticket to a degree from an internationally-revered
college. To the kind of high-profile life my parents never got to lead.
So why can't I stop thinking about Austin?
And why does he keep popping up in the most random places?
All I know is the closer Austin and I get, the more I start to doubt
Dashwood Academy is the simple college it pretends to be.

# OTHER BOOKS BY SAXON JAMES

**THE WILDE MEN SERIES:**

Wilde's End

Ziggy's Voice

**ACCIDENTAL LOVE SERIES:**

The Husband Hoax

Not Dating Material

The Revenge Agenda

Just Romantically Invested

Not Catching Love

The Anti-Wingman (bonus prequel)

Friend for Hire (bonus novella)

**FRAT WARS SERIES:**

Frat Wars: King of Thieves

Frat Wars: Master of Mayhem

Frat Wars: Presidential Chaos

Royal Scoundrel (bonus novella)

**DIVORCED MEN'S CLUB SERIES:**

Roommate Arrangement

Platonic Rulebook

Budding Attraction

Employing Patience

System Overload

Forgotten Romance

Making Him Mine (bonus novella)

**NEVER JUST FRIENDS SERIES:**

Just Friends

Fake Friends

Getting Friendly

Friendly Fire

Bonus Short: Friends with Benefits

**RECKLESS LOVE SERIES:**

Denial

Risky

Tempting

**STAND ALONES:**

Himbo Hitman

**CU HOCKEY SERIES WITH EDEN FINLEY:**

Power Plays & Straight A's

Face Offs & Cheap Shots

Goal Lines & First Times

Line Mates & Study Dates

Puck Drills & Quick Thrills

See You in Boston (bonus novella)

**PUCKBOYS SERIES WITH EDEN FINLEY:**

Egotistical Puckboy

Irresponsible Puckboy

Shameless Puckboy

Foolish Puckboy

Clueless Puckboy

Bromantic Puckboy

Forbidden Puckboy

Possessive Puckboy

Stubborn Puckboy

**STAND ALONES WITH EDEN FINLEY:**

Up in Flames

The Bastard and The Heir

Money Shot

**FRANKLIN U SERIES (VARIOUS AUTHORS):**

The Dating Disaster

A Stealthy Situation

And if you're after something a little sweeter, don't forget my YA
pen name

S. M. James.

These books are chock full of adorable, flawed characters with big hearts.

https://geni.us/smjames

# WANT MORE FROM ME?

Follow Saxon James on any of the platforms below.
www.saxonjamesauthor.com
www.facebook.com/thesaxonjames/
www.amazon.com/Saxon-James/e/B082TP7BR7
www.bookbub.com/profile/saxon-james
www.instagram.com/saxonjameswrites/